THE FIFTH
CRYSTAL

Eric W. Day

To order additional copies of this book, contact:
Xlibris Corporation
1-888-795-4274
www.Xlibris.com
Orders@Xlibris.com
23066

THE FIFTH
CRYSTAL

PROLOGUE

The blood red sun, setting over the distant mountains, illuminated the carnage strewn over the Lenarian prairie. A woman of regal bearing was struggling to exit her overturned carriage as a stockily built, masked man mounted on a sweat-lathered, black horse cantered up to the broken and mangled carriage. One of the wheels was still spinning lazily. In the background, the ring of clashing swords reverberated in the stillness of the early evening air, but it was evident that the battle would soon be over.

"Can I help?" asked the rider. The woman was having difficulty finding handholds, so that she could pull herself through the broken and splintered door of the carriage. She glared up at the man with a wilting intensity. "I don't need help from such scurrilous reprobate as you. You vagabond! You murderer!" The masked man chuckled at the outburst. "You don't appear too be in any position to be hurling insults."

The woman was wearing a dark blue dress with white laced collar and cuffs. She had the skirt of the dress hiked up over her knees finally standing on top of the carriage, she turned to receive a tightly woven reed basket that had been handed up to her. A, soft, whimper escaped from underneath the blanket within the basket. She set the basket down beside the opening that she had just exited and offered her hand to someone still inside the carriage. With difficulty she managed to pull a distraught and sobbing woman through the dark opening. A capricious wind, blowing dust and dead grasses across the dry prairie, seemed to galvanize the wheel, as the momentum of its spin increased and the axle creaked, eerily.

The quietly sobbing woman crawled down from the destroyed carriage standing between the axles. She accepted the reed basket from the regal woman, still on top of the carriage. The regal woman, clutching the hem of her dress, jumped to the ground. She staggered when she landed, but she didn't fall.

She stepped away from the carriage, delicately stepping over a dead soldier. The other woman, clasping the reed basket to her bosom, followed but stumbled over the dead soldier lying at her feet, nearly dropping the reed basket entrusted to her. The regal woman caught her before she fell. "Be careful!" she said tartly.

The woman approached the masked man, on the magnificent warhorse, glaring up at him with her piercing green eyes. The corners of her mouth turned down. She stood tall, to show that she wasn't intimidated. She was of medium height and curvaceous, her auburn tresses cascaded over her squared but delicate shoulders. By this time the rest of the masked man's similarly disguised cohorts had rode up behind him and were watching the drama unfolding before them in silence.

"What are your intentions!" she spat out. The man dismounted with a surprising alacrity, considering he was of short stature and stockily built, landing within inches of the woman. The woman refused to budge forcing the masked man to step back. "The same old Cienya, arrogant and overbearing, has to always be in control. Prides herself on her self-control and power."

Cienya drew in a deep breath in shock and surprise. Her beautiful, green eyes grew wide. She recognized the cruel edge to the man's voice. "It's you!" she exclaimed.

"I knew you were a man of little moral fiber, but I never suspected that you might actually be evil," she chastised. The masked man chuckled and pulled his mask off. He had a small nose in a broad face with steely-blue eyes and thin lips. He ran his fingers through his disheveled, shoulder length blond hair.

He was dressed in a brown leather tunic and trousers. He wore lizard skin boots that reached above the calves. His belt and scabbard were black leather. Dangling at his side was a plain, bone-handled sword.

The blond haired man stuffed the mask in his belt. A determined expression framed Cienya's face and she asked. "What are your plans for us?" The man shrugged his shoulders and answered. "I suppose I'll have to kill you since you know who I am. My original plans were a little robbery and rape." He snarled at her. "My High Queen."

Cienya blanched at the blond haired man's candid remark, and took a step back. "Not so haughty now are you, Your Highness," he remarked sarcastically. The men behind him laughed, as they leered at the two helpless women.

"I wasn't good enough for you. I loved you but you wanted to be Queen, and you married that wretched old man," the blond haired man spat out angrily. He then grabbed Cienya by the arm. The strength of his grip sent burning pulses of excruciating pain up and down her arm. The pain brought tears to her eyes, but she refused to cry out.

Twisting her arm against his thumb, she broke free and with the other hand she slapped him as hard as she could, unleashing all her anger, fear, and frustration into the blow. The impact of the slap turned the man's head, leaving a red imprint of her hand on his face.

Her assault sparked a cruel and unchecked rage. He retaliated with a backhand across her face, the force of which sent her reeling backwards, slamming her into the broken carriage right below the now slowly turning wheel. Cienya's companion squealed in fear, and a wail erupted from beneath the covers in the reed basket.

The blond haired man, with long and determined strides, approached the fallen woman, as passing clouds cast their shadows across the ground. The blond haired man grabbed the woman and pulled her towards him violently. He shouted, "If I can't have you in love, I'll have you in hate!" He then began to rip her clothing off as more shadows moved across the ground.

His men cheered him on with enthusiasm. One of the onlookers dismounted and ran up to the woman holding the basket. He wrenched the basket from the woman's arms and tossed it to one of the mounted men. He ordered. "Dispose of this for me." Then, with closed eyes, he threw his head back in laughter.

The wind picked up in velocity, tormenting the broken wheel, causing it to spin more violently which created a loud ear splitting screech. Cienya, in the grips of the madman, now naked to the waist, pulled up her skirt to retrieve a small, jeweled dagger that she kept in a scabbard strapped to her upper leg. In one fluid move, she raked the dagger across the blond haired man's face, slicing a gaping furrow from cheek to the lower jaw.

The man screamed in pain. He released her and took a step backward. Blood flowed freely from the freshly opened wound. The injured man pulled the cloth mask from his belt and used it to cover the viciously pulsating gash.

The man that was assaulting the other woman released her and turned to the blond haired man in confusion. The blond haired man screamed at Cienya. "You bitch! You royal whore!" His eyes were like burning infernos. In his rage, he pulled his sword and drove it, up to the hilt, into Cienya.

Cienya gasped with surprise as the blade sliced through her body exiting her back, pinning her to the underside of the carriage. Her eyes agape, as if in wonderment, were sharp and clear. She looked down and watched as her life fluids drained from her body in a warm crimson river. Slumping, she gasped once more before her body gave up its Essence.

The other woman screamed in horror and tried to escape. As she ran away, the blond haired man grabbed a dagger from the other man's belt and threw it. The dagger unerringly whistled by its owner's ear and struck its mark with a thud. The woman gasped in an attempt to scream, but the dagger punctured her lung causing her to wheeze instead as she pitched forward, burrowing her face in the ground.

The man holding the reed basket had pulled back the blanket to reveal a small baby. He was preparing to kill it when, sharp pains erupted in his shoulders, as six razor sharp talons hooked him. Screaming, he was lifted from his mount.

Pandemonium erupted. The blond haired man turned in time to evade a dragon bearing down on him. The shadows that he had taken for passing clouds had, actually, been dragons circling overhead.

Grabbing the reigns of his mount with one hand and holding the bloody mask over the still free-flowing wound with his other hand, the blond haired man vaulted into the saddle. The other man was picked out of midair as he tried to mount and was crushed as he screamed in terror.

The blond haired man and his fellow brigands dispersed figuring every man for himself. The man that held the reed basket, now considerably high in the sky, released it, as he writhed in pain. This turned out to be a mistake because the dragon promptly released him and dove to delicately pluck the basket out of midair before it smashed into the ground.

Darkness captured the prairie and concealed the carnage of the day. As the stars twinkled in the heavens above, a peace settled over the killing field. The creatures of the night exited their boroughs and places of hiding as if nothing unusual had occurred, and the carriage wheel gently spun to a stop.

CHAPTER 1

It was early in the Harvest Season. The sun glittered like a precious jewel set in the firmament. The sky was the most perfect blue, mottled with wisps of fluffy white clouds.

Simentoo gazed upward as sweat saturated his forehead and invaded his eyes. He wiped his stinging eyes and forehead with a piece of cloth that he had torn from an old tunic. He thought to himself that this was an unusually warm day for the mountains, considering the time of the year.

He was traversing a well-worn but seldom used trail. The dusty, rock strewn trail was perilous and more of a backdoor to his destination. He could hear the roar of the Calowi river. He hoped that the bridge crossing the Calowi Gorge was still in good repair, or he would have to travel several days out of his way down river to find a crossing.

Simentoo was lean, muscular, of average height with broad shoulders. His hair, dirty brown, shaded his ears which was atypical for him. He normally kept it military style, close cropped. He had a small nose planted in a broad face. His eyes were alert and light green in color. Simentoo's body was covered from head to foot with sweat-streaked, dust.

He was dressed in his tan military tunic, belted at the waste, with the flaming crossed swords embossed on the shoulders, the insignia of the Lenarian Elite Corp of which Simentoo had been Captain. His trousers were made of the same tan leather as the tunic, and his boots were made of Desert Lizard hide.

He had a broadsword strapped across his back and a short sword and dagger at his side. There was a brace of throwing knives draped over his shoulder and chest. He also had throwing knives tucked inside of his boots.

He sat on a rock near the edge of the gorge overlooking the river below. The cool air that rose out of the river gorge was relaxing. He took a swig from his water skin. The water was warm, but it cut the gritty dust that coated his mouth and throat.

He watched the foaming, blue-green waters raging over the rocks of the river bed. The white foaming caps made Simentoo think of great white birds surfing the surface of the river, and the thunderous roar of the river was their song of elation. The spray that wafted above the river as it plunged over the falls reflected the colors of the rainbow. The multicolored rocks of the cliff face were spectacular. Even though Simentoo was raised in these mountains, he never tired of the river's beauty.

Simentoo was debating with himself about what he should do next, whether to return to his home village or go on down into the Caspar Valley and report to King Falef. He would be the next in the line of command after the High King of Lenar.

The Kingdom of Lenar was divided into Upper and Lower Lenar. Lower Lenar had just fallen to the Zealots of the Prophet of the Desert Nomads. The Lenarian army had been crushed. They had been betrayed. Someone had poisoned the army's provisions. By the time anyone in command had realized what had happened, half the army was either sick and dying or already dead.

The High King ordered a retreat, but the enemy had anticipated this possibility and set an ambush which held the Lenarian army long enough for the main force to arrive. Being outnumbered five-to-one, although they put up a good fight, they had little chance.

The Lenarian's were massacred to the last man, that is, except for him. He had been knocked unconscious during the battle. He would never be able to outlive the shame. He should have died that day protecting his King. He had been the Captain of the Lenarian Elite Guard. The protectors of the High King. It was his duty to die protecting the High King. He had failed and to make things worse, he had survived.

When he had regained consciousness, he had found himself under the High King's disemboweled body. In essence, the High

King had saved his life. The enemy, because Simentoo was covered in the High King's gore and blood, had missed him.

From that moment, until he had arrived at this spot, time had blurred. He could remember very little of how he had come to be here or what had happened in those days of confusion and guilt. The only thing he could remember was changing his uniform and washing up in a river. He scoured his body with the river sand until it was raw and bleeding.

Tears began to well up in his eyes as he sat there, shoulders slumped, chin cupped in his hands with elbows propped on his knees. His head began to nod as he struggled with fatigue.

The hairs on the back of his neck bristled as cold chills coursed down his spine. His senses were heightened. His instincts alerted him to danger but he continued to sit as if he were unaware of the threat. Simentoo didn't know what threatened him, but he also didn't want them, or it, too know that he was alerted to their presence.

Simentoo's heart began to beat a little faster as adrenalin began to course through his veins like liquid fire. He glimpsed movement on his periphery. The battle hardened soldier was mentally preparing himself to do battle. Elation and excitement was beginning to build, but it didn't manifest itself.

He began to run an inventory of possible foes through his head. Maybe it was mountain tribesman not loyal to Caspar or Lenar. There were a few that had refused to ally themselves with anyone, or possibly Cave Dwellers. Trolls were unlikely because they didn't bother anyone that didn't pose an overt threat.

Simentoo had taken the back trails in hopes of avoiding any hostile contacts. Evidently, he hadn't been as stealth in his movements as he had hoped. Of course, he should've known better.

With blood curdling screams, the unknown assailants launched their attack. Simentoo, with the speed and agility of a Mountain Cat, sprang to his feet. He freed his broadsword from its restraint. Pivoting on the balls of his feet, he turned to face his attackers in one fluid motion. Muscle and sinew strained against his skin as if trying to escape.

Simentoo took a step back so that he had the Calowi River Gorge protecting his back. The bridge would've been a more defensible position for one man, but it was to far away. He wouldn't be able to reach it before they cut him down from behind. Plus he was tired of running. If it was time for him to die, so be it.

Simentoo was surprised by the identity of his foes. There were both mountain tribesman and Cave Dwellers. Two unlikely allies, if there ever were any. Simentoo disemboweled the nearest attacker with a sweeping stroke of his broadsword.

A blood splattered Simentoo turned to face his next assailant, loping the attackers head off with a backstroke. Simentoo mentally assessed his situation. It appeared hopeless. There were way too many. But, he thought to himself, he would take a great many of them with him.

A mountain tribesman cautiously moved in on Simentoo's left while a brash Cave Dweller, wielding a club wildly, rushed in from the right. Simentoo parried the wildly swung club. Then Simentoo stepped to the side as the Cave Dweller madly rushed by into the river gorge to disappear below the rapidly flowing waters.

Simentoo staggered as loose gravels rolled under his foot. The mountain tribesman, sensing Simentoo's unsteadiness, attacked.

He thrust his sword at Simentoo, but Simentoo was able to twist his abdomen enough to avoid the deadly strike. The sword only grazed Simentoo, inflicting a flesh wound to his side.

Balance regained, Simentoo planted one foot while kicking out with the other, crushing the mountain tribesman's throat. The others rushed Simentoo. He fought valiantly, trying to hold his attackers off, but the numbers were too great. Simentoo slashed, parried and dodged, but he was tiring.

He knew the end was near, but he didn't fear death. In fact, he welcomed death. He looked forward to his demise. It would end his many years of guilt and suffering for his inability to protect the ones he loved.

Simentoo was surprised when he heard the song of an arrow as it streaked by him. The arrow hit with a thwack and the reverberation of the rapidly vibrating shaft echoed over the gorge. One of Simentoo's attackers screamed and clutched the offending missile protruding from the boney center of his chest where it had splintered the bone and pierced the heart. The stricken man staggered forward and pitched over the edge of the gorge.

Arrows then began to fall like rain. Simentoo, surprised by this unexpected intervention, lost his concentration. He didn't see the Cave Dweller that had designs on his head. Simentoo was unable to avoid the glancing blow that struck the side of his head. He stumbled backwards, falling into the gorge.

As he tumbled and rolled head over heels through the air, his life flashing before his eyes, he closed his eyes, and everything flashed white. When he reopened his eyes, the world around him seemed to be moving in slow motion, and the roar of the quickly approaching river was muted.

Just before he entered the biting cold of the snow fed mountain river, his perception returned to normal. The roar of the river returned in all its intensity. Simentoo, before he plunged into the river, faced his certain demise not with fear but with resolution. His head struck a submerged rock, knocking him unconscious, and the swiftly flowing current swept him away. If he didn't drown or wasn't slashed to pieces by the razor sharp rocks protruding from the river bed, then surely he would be dashed and broken when he was swept over the falls.

CHAPTER 2

Kanef had just awakened from a restless night's sleep. There were too many things on his mind. News from below the ice fields was disturbing. Lower Lenar had fallen and Upper Lenar, the Kingdom of Caspar, his homeland, was being threatened by an alliance between the Cave Dwellers and rogue mountain tribesman. Kanef now regretted his brash actions of a few seasons back when, in anger with his father, he had denied his role as the Prince of Caspar and exiled himself to the Ice Valleys.

Kanef's thoughts were interrupted by a knock at the door. Kanef sitting on the edge of his bed asked, "Who is it?" "Rollof, Your Majesty," came the answer from behind a doubled planked oak door, held together by iron rivets, hung on large iron hinges, bolted to a stone frame work, set in an ice packed wall. "Come in, and don't refer to me as Your Majesty. I find the title distasteful," Kanef scolded.

Kanef stood as the door opened, creaking eerily in protest, sending chills racing down his spine. He was slightly taller than medium height. He was clean shaven with a slightly off center nose, a disfigurement that had occurred in childhood. His hair was close cropped and a sandy brown in color. His body was lean and sinewy but not especially muscular. Most women considered him handsome. His eyes were a strange combination of brown and green, and at times his gaze was unsettling.

Kanef quickly threw on a black, fur lined shirt with pants to match and boots made from the same material. Rollof entered the room. "Good morning, Rollof." "Good morning, sir." Kanef shook his head at Rollof's formal address but knew there was no sense in complaining.

"What brings you to my door this morning?" Kanef queried. "You have a visitor from Caspar," stated Rollof with a hint of chagrin shading his voice. "A visitor? Who would trek all the way up here into these ice entombed valleys to visit me? I hope its not someone else with bad news. Show him in, don't leave him standing in the cold wind." Commanded Kanef. As if, in emphasis to Kanef's comment about cold winds, a brisk blast of snow clogged air followed the visitor into the dimly lit room.

The man entered the room with a flair, swirling his cape with a flick of the wrist. His tall slender body reminded Kanef of a sapling about four seasons old. The man's face was long and slim with a prominent chin. His upturned nose was a bit over proportioned for his face. His eyes were a deep black and slightly squinty. He wore his bright yellow hair in long foppish swirls that brushed his shoulders ever so lightly.

His dress consisted of heavy leather pants and a shirt lined with wool, suited for cold weather travel. The pants were dyed a bright red while the shirt was a dark blue in color. He wore black leather boots that reached above his calves. The cape was black, embroidered with intricate animal designs in silver and gold thread.

Kanef nearly burst out with laughter. The man looked like a giant bird, fluffing its feathers and strutting its stuff in some absurd mating ritual. He turned his head so that the man didn't see his amusement.

Rollof was not so easily amused. "Lord Asmoth of Caspar, Second Family to the Throne," he stated. He then turned his head and spit into the corner of the room as if he had taken a bite of Bitterroot Weed. "Lets not be rude," scolded Kanef light heartedly.

Asmoth tended not to notice Rollof's bad behavior. He was inspecting the room into which he had just entered in great detail. The ceiling was slightly higher than his height. It was a small cubicle with only enough room for a bed and a couple of wooden chairs. The walls were covered with tapestries painted in summer themes.

Asmoth stood a head taller than Rollof. Who was approximately the same heights as Kanef. Rollof was broader across the shoulders than Kanef and Asmoth. Rollof had a long back with short muscular legs and long muscular arms. Rollof had a broad face with a truncated pug nose set between dark brown eyes. His hair was straight and the purest black which reached just below the ears.

Kanef, sitting on the edge of his bed, gestured with an open palm to one of the gnarled wooden chairs. "Please sit." "I haven't come here to sit or have friendly conversation with you," Asmoth curtly stated. "I was sent by your father, the King. I don't know why he needs to see you, but I suppose it has something to do with the dire situation of the Kingdom. I'm just the lowly messenger," he spit out bitterly.

Asmoth stood quietly, glaring at Kanef with deep seated animosity. He was breathing deeply to help control his anger and hatred of Kanef.

Rollof's anger was building. He stood slightly to the side and behind Asmoth. He moved his feet to present a more aggressive stance which would open up his sword for a quicker retrieval.

Asmoth took this as a sign of eminent attack and with the celerity of swordsman, of which he was preeminent, he threw back his cape and drew his short sword. Rollof unsheathed his blade, nearly as quickly. Both men stood face-to-face ready to do mortal combat.

Kanef moved quickly across the room. He placed himself between the two men, grasping Rollof's wrist. With a low guttural voice, he said to Rollof, "Put the sword away." Rollof looked into Kanef's eyes. Kanef could see the deep seated rage and anger simmering within his friend's soul, but he continued to exert his will over Rollof. He knew his friend, even though he was good with the sword, was no match for the expertise of Asmoth.

Slowly the tension drained out of Rollof's arm, and his rage subsided. Rollof cautiously backed away from Asmoth and put his sword away. Asmoth, assured that he was safe, followed suit. Asmoth backed up to the door, his hand resting on the pommel of his sword. He unlatched the door, and with his usual flair and flamboyance he exited the room and asked, "What shall I tell your father?" "I'll come," answered Kanef.

Kanef shut the door after Asmoth and then turned to Rollof. He said. "We're going to Caspar City. Get our things ready for the trip, and when ready, let me know. We leave today."

CHAPTER 3

J arret wiped his brow with his shirt sleeve as he gazed up at the sun. His horse, a black mare, was sweating profusely and would need rest and a drink soon. The animal had done him well by out pacing his pursuers. He patted the horse on the neck affectionately.

The trail had begun to narrow as he neared the Calowi River Gorge and the footing had become quite treacherous. Jarret dismounted. It would be safer to lead his mount along this section of the trail.

The trail wound through the Caspar Mountains. On one side was a steep cliff face which lessened in acclivity higher up. Where the steepness lessened, small pine trees clutched tenaciously to the mountainside. Higher up the mountain, the slope leveled off even more allowing the growth of Large Leaf Oak trees. The other side of the trail was a chasm which hosted a forest of a variety of trees and bushes, but the rift was so deep one couldn't distinguish one species from another.

The roar of the Calowi was becoming the predominant sound, drowning out the cacophony created by a wide variety of creatures living in the mountain reaches. Finally, as he rounded a bend in the trail, he came upon the river gorge. There was a small trickle of water snaking down the side of the mountain which pooled before it crossed the trail.

Jarret allowed the horse to drink first. Then he removed his bow and quiver from his mount before he stooped down to quench his thirst at the crystal, clear pool. Jarret was dressed in green pants and shirt with a dagger belted to his side. The typical garb for a huntsman. Jarret seldom carried a sword. He found swords to be balky and cumbersome in the forests.

22

Jarret was drinking from his cupped hands. When he was startled by a piercing shriek and the clash of weapons. He, quickly raised into a defensive crouch, dagger in hand. His horse, frightened by the unexpected scream, reared and began to paw the air wildly. Jarret had to retreat up the trail to avoid the maddened beast's hooves. The animal lost its footing and teetered on the edge of the chasm before it disappeared over the side.

Jarret looked up and down the trail. Seeing no imminent danger he sheathed his dagger and retrieved his bow and quiver. He notched an arrow just to be on the safe side.

Then Jarret's attention was drawn to the battle scene unfolding across the river gorge. An outnumbered Lenarian soldier was fighting for his life against a small group of mountain tribesman and Cave Dwellers. The man didn't appear daunted by his predicament.

Jarret was impressed with the prowess of the man. His speed and agility were astounding, and he handled himself well, but Jarret knew that if he didn't help, the soldier was doomed. Taking aim he, let an arrow fly, and as soon as one was sailing across the gorge, he had another following.

Jarret was so involved in what he was doing that he failed to hear the horses rounding the bend on the trail below him until it was too late. Jarret turned when he became aware of the approaching threat, arrow notched. Out of the periphery of his eye he saw the soldier across the gorge fall into the angry river.

It was the Casparian Guard coming up the trail. He hadn't been as successful in losing them as he had thought. They had been pursuing him for days, and now they had him in their clutches.

Sargent Krylan, in the lead, spotted the archer as soon as he had turned the bend in the trail. He quickly assessed the situation. When the archer had become aware of him and his men, he charged, slamming his horse into the huntsman, knocking him off balance.

Jarret, unable to avoid the collision with the lead man's horse, was launched into the air with bow, quiver, and arrows. When Jarret reached the apex of his trajectory, he appeared to be suspended, in midair, over the river gorge, before he began the deadly plummet. But Jarret's luck hadn't run out as of yet. There was one lonely and scruffy Callenberry Bush, clinging tenaciously to the side of the gorge, its roots taking advantage of a small crevice in the cliff face. Jarret snagged the truncated bush with one hand as he passed.

Pain shot through his shoulder as muscle and tendons were strained to near breaking in protest at the sudden exertion. Pain framed Jarret's face as he reached up with the other hand to gain a better purchase. Dangling from the bush, Jarret heard a terrifying sound of tearing roots and breaking limbs.

With a final snap and a crack the bush gave way. Jarret figured he was finished, when a rope appeared beside him. He snagged the rope with one hand. He slid down the rope for a short distance before he was able grasp his life line with his other hand. The pain was excruciating where the rope had burned deeply into his hand. He wrapped the rope around the wrist of his uninjured hand and let go of the rope with the other.

Sergeant Krylan reigned his mount in. He hadn't meant to push the huntsman over the cliff. He had only meant to knock him off balance. Edging his mount up to the precipice, he peered into the gorge. To his surprise, he saw Jarret dangling precariously from a scrawny callenberry bush, speckled with withered and half ripe berries. The Sargent quickly unhooked his climbing rope and tossed one end over the cliff edge and wrapped the other end around his saddle horn. When the rope pulled taut, because there was no room to maneuver his mount, he ordered several of his men to pull Jarret up.

Krylan spotted Simentoo lying on the rock ledge below. Simentoo had an arm and leg hanging over the ledge. His fingers brushing the swiftly flowing water. Krylan ordered a few of his men to cross the bridge and repel down the cliff face to retrieve the man whether dead or alive.

Sergeant Krylan turned his attention back to the huntsman. They had been trailing him for several days. The huntsman had been sentenced to death by decapitation, but had managed to escape while being returned to the dungeons.

The Sergeant felt that the huntsman had been wrongly convicted. He had gone to the aide of a woman in the seedier side of the city. Then he was set upon by thieves. The huntsman had managed to kill one of the thieves, but the woman had accused Jarret of being the thief. It was obvious that she had been part of a plot to lure him into a trap, so that her partners could rob him, but they had picked the wrong victim.

Krylan shook his head in disgust. There didn't seem to be justice in Caspar any longer which made his job as Sergeant At Arms more difficult. He hated enforcing unfair convictions, and he was quite sure that the King knew the truth.

Krylan removed his plumed helmet and shook his head so that his full, wiry, red hair flowed naturally and came to rest on his shoulders. He ran his fingers through his hair too untangle the knots. It was unusual for a soldier too wear his hair long. Krylan liked his hair long because it added much needed padding to his helmet.

He put his helmet back on tucking his hair in. Krylan was short and stockily built with muscular and broad shoulders. His belly protruded a little bit, but Krylan was no longer a young man at forty-seven seasons. But he was as deadly with a sword as any man. He had a heavy brow line and droopy eyelids which left the appearance that he was half asleep all the time. His eyes were a steely blue, and he had a slightly receding chin.

He had the typical accouterments for a soldier: a broad sword across his back, short sword, and two daggers at his side. He had a flaxen shirt under chain mail leather pants, and heavy leather boots that covered his shins and calve muscles. He carried a shield and light lance which were held by specially designed straps, so they could be attached to the tack carried by his horse but easily accessible when needed.

The soldiers he had sent after the fallen soldier in the river gorge returned with the man strapped across a pack horse. Sergeant

Krylan was assured the man was still alive by the gentle and rhythmical heaving of the man's back. Jarret was in custody and firmly secured to another horse. Sergeant Krylan, quite pleased with himself, order his men back to Caspar City. The small troop urged their mounts back the way they had come.

CHAPTER 4

Talok entered the Casparian Valley by the main road which wound along the Caspar River. He had trouble persuading the sentries at the guard post to allow him entry but finally managed to convince them that he was of no threat. The main road, once through the river pass, deviated from the river for a short distance, skirting the mountain range before returning to the river.

The Caspar Valley was a large valley province nestled within the craggy, snow capped, peaks of the Caspar Mountain Range. The valley had large stretches of forests commingled with large cultivated fields.

The reds, golds, and browns of the harvest season were unusually spectacular this year and the aromatic scent of the falling leaves was tantalizing. Talok loved walking forest trails when the leaves were falling. Their soft caressing touches were soothing and relaxing.

The valley's main exports were timber, wheat, and Snow-Melons. The snow-melon grew on a low profile ground vine. The vines grew in a circular pattern, spreading out from the center. The melon produced had a sweet red pulpy center, an outer sour orange layer protected by smooth white outer skin. It was considered a delicacy and brought a high price on the open market.

Talok didn't linger. He had no time to bask in the beauty of the valley. His destination was Caspar City. There was an expedition of great significance about to be launched from the city. He had been dreaming about it for many nights and knew he had to be part it. This was his payment for the magic he had requested and been given. Talok had been satisfied with the results of the magic.

Talok set a surprisingly good pace considering his odd shape. He had abnormally short, thick, and muscular legs, similar to the legs of a dwarf. Talok's arms where of the same configuration. His torso was elongated, and his neck was short and muscular. He was broad across the shoulder and narrow at the hips. Talok's eyes resembled two dark deep pools of stagnant water. He had a large nose that appeared to be squashed against his face, a strong chin with a deep cleft down the center, a high forehead, and ears that protruded like fins. His kinky brown hair radiated, without discipline, from his head.

Talok was dressed in a bear skin tunic that draped to his knees. He had large feet which were covered by deer hide moccasins. The tunic was belted at the waist. He had throwing hammers, one on each side, hanging from his belt and a battle ax draped across his back.

Talok's odd and bedraggled appearance solicited looks and stares from the occasional traveler and the farmers working nearby fields. Talok ignored the rudeness of others most of the time. But once in awhile he would glare at someone gawking at him until they turned their gaze. This would give him a sense of deep pleasure.

Lieutenant Clanton was leading his troop on its daily patrol when he came across this, for lack of better words, large dwarf. Reigning in his mount, he set himself crossways in the road blocking Talok's path. His horse fidgeted nervously as it flicked its tail. It didn't much care for the stench of this creature.

The Lieutenant was stopping and questioning all suspicious looking persons, and this character fit that criteria to the finest point. With the fall of Lower Lenar and silence of the dwarves in Caspar's neighboring province of Kelat, the Lieutenant wasn't taking any chances. Most anyone could be a spy.

The Lieutenant asked, with a commanding inflection in his voice, "What is your name and what is your business in Caspar?" Talok, perturbed, answered irritably. "Talok is my name, and I'm a mercenary looking for work."

The Lieutenant sat back in his saddle, the reigns in one hand and rubbing his clean shaven chin with the other, as he sized up the oversize dwarf and let his mind digest what he had been told. The Lieutenant was a slender man, not very muscular. He even appeared a little frail for a soldier, but it was dangerous to underestimate him. He was a very capable soldier.

Lieutenant Clanton was dressed in the dark blue of the Casparian Patrol Corp. His accouterments consisted of plumed helmet that covered the ears with the typical nose guard extending down from the brow guard, chain mail hood with vest and shin guards. His weapons consisted of broad sword, daggers, light lance, and short sword.

The plume on his helmet waved friskily in the brisk breeze that had just began. The winds that blew across the valley this time of the year could be coquettish, brisk, or gale force, but they were always capricious.

The Lieutenant, still suspicious, said. "I'll let you pass, but you will have an escort. They will report back to me, once you've been presented to the Office of the Sergeant At Arms." Talok, vexed, agreed to the terms with a nod of the head. He figured, he didn't have much choice in the matter.

The Lieutenant moved his mount aside so that Talok could pass. With hand motions, he chose an escort for Talok, two of his most capable men. The other soldiers moved aside, forming a corridor, so that Talok and his escort could pass.

*   *   *

Zulnee lowered himself down a chimney shaped tunnel. He had to be very cautious because one misstep would cause him to plummet to his death. The lack of light made the decent even more precarious. There was light in the damper caverns and tunnels because light algae could grow in the more moist mediums afforded by water seepage.

He had been carefully and covertly pilfering dragon eggs from the deep recess of their mountain nests. Zulnee didn't think that his thefts had been noticed as of yet, because he had been carful not to steal to many eggs from a single nesting area.

But he knew, the odds were stacking up against him. Dragons were telepathic, and he had managed, so far, with his magic, to shield his thoughts, but he was tiring cognitively. He had eleven eggs and only wanted one more to complete his collection.

Finally reaching his destination, he dropped, the last short distance quietly into the chamber below. Although the blue-green light of the light algae was diffuse, the sudden change in brightness temporarily blinded him.

Therefore, he heard before he saw the dragon waiting, patiently for him. "Gotcha *elf!*" reverberated through Zulnee's mind as if the dragon was shouting at him. Dragons didn't speak. They roared a lot. They were unable to wrap their split tongues around words, so they used telepathy.

Zulnee's eyes finally adjusted to the dim light. He searched desperately for an avenue of escape but found himself surrounded by dragons twitching their tails back and forth and flicking their tongues in and out of their mouths nervously. The nearest dragon snapped his tail, striking the elf on the side of the head, knocking him unconscious.

CHAPTER 5

Crysillnia was sitting on a high ledge overlooking the Caspar Valley and the main road. She was concerned for the valley that was her home. The world she knew seemed to be crumbling around her. Caspar was isolated with the fall of the lower provinces.

Crysillnia's thoughts were disrupted by a soft but firm voice that seemed to waft along with the breeze. "What are you thinking about, my child?" She turned to face a decrepit looking old man in a brown robe, cowl pulled back. The brown robe indicated that the truncated old man was of the Order of Kelatan Monks. Seeing the old monk standing there reminded her of the first time she had met him as a child of twelve seasons.

He had saved her from her stepfather's predations. Her mother had died when Crysillnia was young. She had no known relatives, so her stepfather raised her. He was a cruel and hateful person and forced Crysillnia to help out at his tavern, nearly from the day her mother had died.

The particular day that she had met the old man, Calert, she was tending tables at the tavern and one of the patrons made a lascivious remark about what he would like to do to her. Crysillnia was, just, hinting at her beauty to come.

Her stepfather heard the comment and said, "Not without paying." "How much?" the man asked with excitement. Her stepfather looked her up and down and said, "I'm going to put her up for bids." He then grabbed her around the waist and popped her on the bar. She remembered being frightened and confused. He had pulled her dress up to exhibit her white and shapely legs. She had struggled futilely and frantically to cover herself.

"She's still a virgin. Therefore, I expect a high price or I'll have her first and then whore her out." Her stepfather had declared.

31

ERIC W. DAY

Crysillnia was brought back to the present temporarily as wind whipped grit and sand into her eyes. She rubbed her tearing eyes in an attempt to clean them. She wasn't sure whether the tears were from the irritation of the sand or from her remembrances.

After wiping her eyes, she drifted back to that fateful day. One of the patrons shouted. "How do we know you haven't already burst that flower?" Her stepfather, with a licentious glint in his eyes answered, "You'll just have to take my word on that."

Another patron spoke up. "Let us inspect her first." Her stepfather didn't comment immediately but then with a roaring laugh agreed. "But you must pay to see, and you may touch but no probing." The men formed an unruly line. Crysillnia remembered her uncontrollable sobbing as the first man in line began to rip her clothes off. The sound of tearing fabric, to this day, sends cold chills racing down her back.

Then someone in the back of the tavern said in a quiet but menacing tone, "Unhand the girl." But no one payed any attention, especially the man who was pawing the girl. He became more excited and began to rip and tear more quickly and violently. Crysillnia remembered screaming in pain when the man's filthy fingernails began to rip into her flesh. Her stepfather rapped the man across the knuckles with a club he kept sequestered behind the bar and said, "You're damaging the merchandise."

The man yelped in pain and backed away, and another man took his place. The man with the sore knuckles grabbed the man that had taken his place by the shoulders and said, "I'm not done!" He then spun the interloper around and shoved a massive fist into his face which ignited a brawl.

Crysillnia remembered this was the first time that she became aware of her magic powers. It started as a tingling feeling over her entire body. Every hair on her body began to prickle and tingle. It felt like there were bugs crawling on her skin.

Frightened by the sensation, she closed hers eyes, clinching them tightly. One of the men fighting over her, fell up against her, driving his elbow into her stomach. The air whooshed out of her and agonizing pain coursed through her abdomen. Anger began

32

to build within her and a prick of something she had never felt before, hatred.

She lashed out in her anger. There was a strange burning stench, and then she heard a scream. Startled by the wail, she opened her eyes. One of the men who had been fighting over her lay at her feet, eyes wide open, skin scorched. He was dead.

The repercussion of her magic drew the attention of everyone in the tavern. All eyes were on her, mouths hung agape, stunned expressions framed their faces, and a hush fell over the crowded tavern. There were broken tables, chairs, plates, and mugs scattered across the floor.

This was the first time she had seen the shadow which had, now over time, grown to be a friend. It supported and encouraged her, but it told her to never tell anyone of its existence. The shadow never told her why.

The old man, fearing the crowd might turn vigilante, invoked a spell to put everyone to sleep. He asked her if she wanted to go with him, and she agreed. From that moment on he became her tutor. He never told her how he had happened to be there.

"Child," came the voice, again, more firmly. "What are you ruminating about?" Crysillnia's thoughts, interrupted, came back to the present. "Oh, nothing," she answered.

She turned her gaze back to the undulating floor of the valley with its mix of forests and fields. The color mix of the changing foliage of the trees, ambers of ripe grains, browns of newly plowed fields, and greens of trees that didn't change colors with the change of the seasons, and the blue ribbon of the river flowing through the valley were spectacular. She saw the confrontation between a man and a patrol. Then the man being escorted towards the city.

"Grandfather," that's how she referred to Calert, "what's going to happen to the world?" "That I don't know but its time for us to go forth and see if we can help. The world is in a precarious flux." "What do you mean?" Crysillnia asked. "There are powerful forces trying to disrupt creation. That is the only answer I can give at the present time."

Crysillnia, tired of sitting, stood. She knew it would be a waste of time to query him any further. Crysillnia raised her arms over her head, then she bent forward and then backward to stretch her back, and last she stretched her legs.

Crysilinia was a beautiful woman now of about twenty-two seasons. She was slender of build and average height. Her breasts were well formed but not extremely large. She was narrow of hip, almost boyish, with long muscular legs. Her long firm arms ended with thin petite fingers. Her face was oval in shape with a petite nose set between dark brown eyes. Her hair was the deepest black and flowed over her shoulders to the middle of her back, and her skin was a deep golden-bronze from her extensive exposure to the sun.

Calert said. "Lets go pack. We must go to Caspar City." Crysillnia shrugged her shoulders in acceptance.

CHAPTER 6

As the sun set on Caspar City, taking its cheery and warmth-giving rays behind the mountains, an old decrepit beggar rose slowly from his chosen spot before the gates of the city. He had been watching with a curious eye the comings and goings of the city. He stretched slowly to loosen cramped muscles.

He attracted the attention of a nearby guard. The guard watched as the beggar emptied the few coins he had collected during his daylong sojourn at the gate, into a deep pocket sewn into his bedraggled garment. The guard felt sympathy for the beggar, because the coins that the beggar had collected were of little value.

The guard felt a cold chill course through his body when the beggar glanced in his direction. There was a cold piercing hatred in those eyes. The guard felt that, if the beggar could, he would just as soon kill him as to look at him. The coldness quickly left the beggars eyes as if pulling a shade down.

The beggar smiled at the guard and nodded at him in acknowledgment. Then the beggar shuffled through the gate which was slowly winched closed. The clank of the gears from the winch and the creak of the gate predominated the air. With a final thud, the portcullis dropped into place.

The guard pulled his cloak tighter around him. The encounter with the beggar had been unsettling. He felt he had just had a brush with the Death Maker.

Outside the gate, the beggar seemed to be invigorated. A man approached him leading two horses. The beggar took the reigns of one of the mounts and lithely mounted the steed. The beggar appeared to have shed many seasons with the new agility he displayed. Reigning their mounts around, the two men urged their horses into a slow canter. They headed away from the city towards the mountains.

"Tanof, where are we going?" the second man asked. The beggar pointed towards the mountains but said nothing. The second man looked at Tanof with an expression of incredulity. Then he said' "We're going to cross the mountains?" He turned his attention to the soaring snow capped peaks. "How?"

Tanof shook his head in disgust, then replied, "Crenshak! You are a dunderheaded fool. We are going through the mountains, not over them." Crenshak looked back at Tanof, perplexed, but said nothing.

Tanof was annoyed by the stupidity of his partner. He had agreed to bring him on this mission only because his employer had requested it. Tanof was in the business of collecting and selling information. Albeit some might call it spying, he considered himself a businessman with a commodity to sell.

Tanof was recalling and sorting what he had seen over the last week but not much happened until today. The highlights of his report consisted of: Prince Kanef returning, a suspicious looking monk with a beautiful young lady entering the city, a Casparian Patrol of the Sergeant at Arms returning with a murderer and a soldier of the Lenarian Elite Guard, of which the latter was unconscious, and a Casparian Patrol escorting a rather mean looking, large dwarf into the city.

The woman had unsettled him. She looked right at him and he felt as if she could sense his real identity and knew what he was doing. And at the same time she seemed familiar. He felt like he should have known her.

When Tanof and Crenshak reached the mountains, Tanof steered his mount towards an old mountain goat path just barely discernable. If you didn't know it was there, you probably wouldn't find it. They passed a dilapidated old shack which looked like a strong breeze could topple.

Tanof reigned in his mount and gazed at the ramshackle hovel as if reminiscing. Then, suddenly and violently, Tanof gouged the flanks of his mount unmercifully. The horse, startled, frightened, and angered by the cruel and unwarranted treatment, reared, nearly unseating its rider.

The horse streaked forward and raced precariously up the trail. Crenshak followed close behind shouting, "Tanof! Tanof! What are you crazy? Are you trying to get us killed?" Tanof reigned in his mount, as suddenly and violently as when he had urged it forward. The horse came to a sliding halt, shaking its head in protest.

Tanof turned in his saddle as Crenshak approached, nearly careening into the back of Tanof's horse. Tanof glared at his companion, and said, his voice low and dangerous, dripping with venom, "Never, but never, call me crazy or on my mother's grave, I'll open your belly and roast your entrails over an open fire." To put emphasis on his statement, he rested his hand on the hilt of his dagger. Crenshak threw his hands up obsequiously.

The two riders approached a cliff face. Tanof gave three distinct whistles of differing tones, and a rope snaked down from an aperture in the cliff. The riders dismounted and removed the horses reigns and saddles. They slapped the horses across their rumps which sent them racing back down the narrow trail.

Tanof and Crenshak tied the rope to their tack and had it pulled up into the narrow crevice. Once their equipment was secured, they quickly scrambled up the dangling rope and disappeared into the side of the mountain. After the men vanished into the mountainside, a dark and mysterious shadow detached itself from a nearby boulder and followed the frightened horses down the trail.

CHAPTER 7

Talok had been pacing back and forth in his room most of the morning. He was now standing by the arched window that over looked a private courtyard, taking in the brilliant colors of the changing leaves and late blooming flowers, when a spectacularly, beautiful woman with long flowing black hair entered the courtyard below.

Talok's heart began to beat quicker, and his stomach became a little queasy. Talok stood at the window watching, as the woman wandered through the brightly colored courtyard. He was caught up in her eloquent beauty, the way she seemed to glide across the pavement stones, and the intriguing way she flicked her head to clear the hair from her face.

He had never felt this way about anyone before. He believed that women would never be attracted to him because of his odd build, so he had protected himself from the pain of rejection by shutting down the emotion of love. But this woman had roused his deeply buried desire and need for love. He would do anything for this woman, no matter the consequence. He would die for her, no matter how she treated him.

She was bending over to smell one of the aromatic flowers when the door behind him began to shake and rattle violently in its frame. The woman, startled from her reverie, looked up. She acknowledge Talok with a nod of her head and smiled sweetly at him. Talok's heart nearly burst from his chest with joy.

A boyishly foolish grin framed his mouth as he waved awkwardly at her. Angered at his embarrassing and adolescent behavior, Talok turned towards the offending noise and shouted at the perpetrator on the other side of the door. "What are you trying to do? Knock the door off its hinges!"

The pounding ceased. "Sorry, Sir, but I've been knocking at your door for quite awhile. I thought you might be sleeping and needed waking," answered a muted voice. "Well, what do you want?" asked Talok more civilly with an edge of gruffness.

"The King, Sir, . . . um-ah . . ." "Go on man!" interjected Talok, his anger and impatience building. "The King would like you to join him for breakfast," continued the meek voice.

Talok glanced back into the garden. The woman was gone. "Yes," he answered more calmly. Striding to the door with purpose, he opened it. The hall servant was a small boy, probably no more than twelve to thirteen seasons. The boy bowed obsequiously and then turned, leading Talok down a long and narrow high-ceilinged hallway. Talok felt some remorse about his rude treatment of the boy as he fell in behind him.

*　　*　　*

The boy left Talok with a tall and thin ferret-faced man. The demeanor of the man was dark and somber. He said nothing to his charge. The ferret-faced man unlatched a huge double planked door and ushered Talok into the kitchen.

Talok entered a room that was twice as long as it was wide. A wooden table occupied the center of the room, just far enough away from the end walls to allow three men abreast to pass. The table appeared to be carved out of a single log. There were racks suspended from the ceiling above the table for the hanging of pots and pans.

One wall was dedicated to huge brick ovens for baking breads and cakes, and open fireplaces, complete with spits and huge kettles, for roasting and stewing meats and cooking vegetables. The opposite wall had openings built into it for the storage of fruits, vegetables, and grains.

There was an opening in the far wall. This led to a chute for the disposal of garbage. Talok didn't know whether this went to the outside or a dumping room in the lower recesses of the keep for later disposal. There were also hooks on the back and front walls, many of which were empty, for hanging kitchen utensils.

The clang and clabber was deafening, as the cooks and their helpers bustled around the kitchen, preparing meals for the day. The aromas of roasting meats and freshly baked breads were tantalizing. Suddenly Talok realized he was hungry.

There was a short rotund man marching up and down the table. He would taste the meats and breads, then bark out instructions. He reminded Talok of a drill sergeant. He guessed him to be the head cook. The man glanced up at the intruders with a frown on his face but said nothing.

Another man at the far end of the kitchen spotted Talok and his escort. He was short and stockily built with a barrel chest. He had a broad face with a large red nose set between sharply blue eyes. He wore his long, bright, yellow hair bunched together in a tail.

The man approached Talok quickly. From a distance the man appeared to be fat but that was a misconception. As he approached, it was quite apparent that he was solidly built. And another feature that couldn't be detected from a distance was a bright red scar on his cheek. It looked raw, as if it hadn't completely healed.

The man approached Talok, hand extended, with a warm and magnanimous smile and greeting. "Talok! Talok! Good to see you. I'm King Falef." Talok's hand engulfed the King's, but the King had an iron grip. "What is a soldier of your renown doing in Caspar?"

Talok, taken aback by the King's directness, quipped, "Looking for work, Your Majesty." "Work?" queried the King speculatively. "Yes, work," repeated Talok with less emphasis. The King said, with a sly smile and devious sparkle in his eyes, "I may have a place for you."

"I thought you might. I heard you were hiring mercenaries." King Falef, still gripping Talok's hand, pulled the dwarf closer. Then the King put a finger to his lips, demanding silence. Talok was surprised by the King's strength.

King Falef said, "Follow me." But before he turned to lead the way, he took the ferret-faced man aside. Talok was unable to hear what was said, but the servant left the room without a word. Talok followed the King across the kitchen to a small table in the back corner.

"Sit," said the King. "Bring us some breakfast!" he shouted cheerfully. The King sat across the table from Talok, still wearing a tight lipped grin. Talok recognized an insincere grin for what it was.

This was a dangerous and untrustworthy person sitting across from him, and he must be wary of any deals cut with this man, thought Talok to himself. The raw red scar on the King's face seemed to pulsate with agitation as the King spoke and laughed. The man would habitually massage the scar while talking.

The King said, "I like to eat in the kitchen, especially in the winter, because it is the warmest room in the castle, and I like the smell of the food being prepared." To emphasis his comment, the King raised his nose in the air and took a big whiff.

The cook's helpers soon produced two plates heaping with roasted meats and fried bread. Talok quickly finished his plate and another was provided. Talok took his time to savor this plate of food, since the edge was taken off his appetite. Finally satiated, Talok pushed himself away from the table and locked his hands behind his head.

The King was preparing to continue the earlier conversation when the ferret-faced man returned, escorting several other people. "Well, I think we'll continue our conversation later," the King said. "Follow me." Talok did as he was more ordered than asked.

The King opened a small door located in the back wall of the kitchen. The room was lit by oil lanterns hanging by chains from the ceiling. Detailed maps of Lenar and Caspar were painted on the walls, a map rack was standing in one corner of the small room, and a round marble table surrounded by wooden chairs was situated in the center of the room.

With open palm the King gestured with a sweep of his hand and he said, "This is my war and strategy room. Have a seat." Talok took a seat directly across from a high-backed chair that was slightly elevated above all of the other chairs in the room. That chair, he assumed, was the King's.

The others who were following the ferret-faced man entered
the war room. A Priest of the Crystals, dressed in his flowing white
robes, entered the room first, followed by Charranif the High
General of Caspar, and a tall man dressed in a black robe with his
cowl pulled so tight that one couldn't distinguish his facial features.
An old monk dressed in a brown robe, cowl pulled back, was the
fourth entrant.

After everyone had taken a seat, the King introduced them.
Talok, mistrustful of the man in the black robe, spoke. "I've heard
of everyone here but this man, Shasheek from the Island Nation of
Tarkitom, concealed in the black robe. Where is Tarkitom located?"
The darkly shrouded man responded, "Far beyond the Brosnian
Sea in the Endless Ocean."

Talok's suspicions not satiated, queried. "Why are you
concerned with what happens here?" The King, agitated at Talok's
presumption that he could take over his meeting and demand
answers, cut the dwarf short. "He is an expert in Demon Lore and
has been helping us develop a strategy to deal with the vile creatures.
Besides it's not your right to interrogate my guests." But deep
down the King was as mistrustful, of the man in the black robe as
Talok. Talok acquiesced but didn't apologize.

The door opened once again and the beautiful black haired
woman from the courtyard entered the room. Talok felt his heart
skip a beat and his face became flushed, but no one seemed too
notice. All eyes were on the woman. "This is my granddaughter,
Crysillnia," said the monk.

"Have a seat, dear," said the King as he perused her body with
a licentious eye. Crysillnia ignored the King's rude behavior. She
was becoming use to the way men behaved around her. In fact, she
sort of enjoyed it. She knew her beauty gave her a special power
over men.

After Crysillnia seated herself, the King opened the meeting
by asking the High General about the campaign against the
demons. "I sent the cavalry into the mountains in an attempt to
drive them back. But when the horses get a whiff of a demon they

go mad and can't be controlled." "Can we send the infantry in to drive them out?" asked the King.

The High Priest spoke. "I beg your Majesty's indulgence, but I believe the only way too combat the demons are with the Crystals." King Falef didn't appear to be pleased with the High Priest's suggestion.

The monk, Calert, entered the discussion on the side of the priest. "I think the High Priest could be right, but the Crystals are an unknown variable."

King Falef focusing on the High Priest asked, "Do you know where the Crystals are?" "Legend has it, that the Crystals are under the stewardship of the dragons." The King asked, voice dripping with sarcasm, "And how do you propose to get them then?"

The taciturn Talok, not trusting anything or anyone, especially anything to do with religion, asked the High Priest, truculently, "How do you know, priest, that the dragons have the Crystals?" The High Priest, a little anxious due to the King's interrogative manner, glared angrily at the impudent dwarf.

The King, chagrined by the dwarf's interruption of his interrogation of the High Priest, turned to the dwarf and said, "Please don't interrupt. Yes, how do you know the legend is true?" The High Priest sat there dumbfounded and said nothing.

Calert, feeling sorry for the High Priest, asked rhetorically, "How do you prove any legend?" No one said anything for a few moments as they mentally digested the question. Then Calert continued, "Unless you go in quest for them."

The room settled into a deep and uneasy quiet as the ramifications of what Calert was suggesting was being mulled over in their minds. The King broke the silence. "Whom do you propose to send on this quest of yours."

Calert responded, "First off. We need to send someone with magical powers, because only someone with magic can handle the Crystals and even that is risky." "Then you plan on going?" Asked the King. "No, I have other duties too tend to."

Another hush fell over the room. Then the King asked, "Who do we send on this quest," Calert shifted his attention to Crysillnia.

"She has magical powers, still raw but, I believe, she has sufficient control to handle the Crystals. As long as she refrains from utilizing the power of the Crystals."

Crysillnia was taken aback by Calert's volunteering her services. She still didn't feel comfortable with her powers. In fact, she felt at times they were in control of her and many times she felt as if there was evil deep in her soul. She didn't trust herself.

Shasheek finally broke his silence. "It's true. The dragons took stewardship of the Crystals as part of The Treaty of Baleek." "How do you know this to be a fact? The Treaty of Baleek has been missing for generations," asked the High General.

"I have read it." Gasps of surprise echoed around the table. King Falef asked, "Where and when?" "The treaty is in the Tarkitom Archives," Shasheek lied. He couldn't tell them the truth or his identity would be revealed and that would do no one any good at this point in time. "And you do need to send someone to retrieve the Crystals," continued Shasheek.

King Falef said, "Your not suggesting we send her alone." "We could send a small troop of soldiers as an escort," The High General argued. "We can't send armed troops because they have to pass through the Elf Woods, and the elves would consider that an act of aggression'" protested the King. "And we don't want to attract unnecessary attention; therefore an escort should be no more than five or six," added Calert. "I'll volunteer" said Talok.

The High Priest said, "I really think that she is the wrong choice. A priest of the Crystals should be the one retrieving the Crystals." Shasheek asked, "Do you have a priest with magic powers?" "Well, no," replied the High Priest. "Then a priest would be of little use," added Talok acerbically.

"Its decided then. Now I need to find some capable men willing to go with her. That is if she is willing to take on the task set before her. I haven't heard her accept," said the King.

The High Priest objected again fervently. "Your Majesty! You can't leave the safety of the Crystals in the hands of a woman, a novice witch." "Did you not say you had no wizards in the Priesthood?" the King asked, anger tinging his voice. The High

Priest averted his eyes to a ding in the tabletop and shook his head in affirmation. "Then it's up to her."

The King focused harsh eyes on Crysillnia. "What is your answer," he asked gruffly. Crysillnia reluctantly shook her head in agreement. The King threw his hands up in the air and said, "Then it's settled. I'll find her an escort. Starting with you Talok since you so conveniently volunteered. By all the gods if I wasn't King, I would follow such beauty to the end of time myself."

Talok, embarrassed by the transparency of his feelings, looked down at the table, to avoid eye contact with anyone else at the table, especially Crysillnia. Crysillnia blushed at the King's insinuation and felt sympathy for the dwarf. The King chuckled at his own joke.

"I have a couple of men in mind. This meeting is ended." "But . . ." the High Priest started to speak, but a blistering stare from the King cut him short. The King stood and without further word exited the room.

CHAPTER 8

Malik sat on a bench sharpening and preening over his ax. Malik was the Executioner of Caspar, and he took great pride in his title. The people loathed and feared him, even though he was a truncated and grizzled old man. This imbued him with an aura of power, he otherwise wouldn't have had.

Malik listened, lovingly, to the ring of the whetstone sliding across the ax's cutting edge. He looked in wonderment as the sun glinted off the freshly oiled mirror finish of the ax head. He delicately caressed the well-worn, slightly curved handle.

He was contemplating the excitement, he would experience when he separated the huntsmen's head from his shoulders. The thwack of the ax followed by the clunk of the head as it dropped into the bucket. Malik began to hum to the ringing rhythm emanating from the ax.

Malik was wrested from his reverie by the crash of thunder. There was a storm brewing and by the sounds of it, a brutal one at that. He was looking forward to the promised rain. It was an unusually hot and sultry day, but he hoped the rain would hold off until after the execution.

Malik turned his attention to the gathering crowd as they pushed and shoved to get closer to the executioner's platform. He chuckled to himself. They talk about me being sick and macabre. They've come to watch the show I provide and some hope to be splattered with the criminal's blood.

Malik returned his attention to the battle in the mountains as the thunderous crescendo increased. The sun had retreated behind the clouds, and the once clear blue sky had become a deep dark purple. The clouds roiled, like stew in a pot, menacingly, promising dire consequences for anything or anyone in their path.

The storm dropped out of the mountains like an avalanche. Malik turned to one of the guards and asked in a high pitched and squeaky voice, "Where is the condemned man?" The guard shrugged.

The execution platform was located in a small square near the dungeons. The main businesses occupying Dead Man's square were seedy taverns, brothels, and retail shops. The square was accessed through four narrow streets, and there were guards posted at each one.

Malik heard a commotion behind him. He turned to see a balding, well dressed, rotund man gesticulating wildly. He was shouting something, but Malik couldn't make it out at first over the cacophony of the fractious mob surrounding the platform as it swayed and shifted chaotically. The rotund man's words wafted towards Malik with a shift in the winds, "Stop him, he stole my purse! Thief! Thief!"

A young boy, probably no more than nine seasons, burst forth from the crowd running up the street. He frantically dodged the two guards blocking his exit from the square. With a few jukes, turns and pirouettes, he succeeded in avoiding capture. Once by the guards, he sprinted up the narrow street but the thieve's luck had run its course.

The guards delivering the condemned man were marching down the street blocking the boy's escape. The boy stopped in mid-stride. Looking from side to side, like a wild animal caught in a trap, he searched for a new escape route. One of the guards the boy had eluded was close on his heels with sword drawn. The angry man rapped the boy on the back of the head with the flat of his sword, driving the boy forward and downwards. The boy landed face first on the hard stone cobbled street, knocking him unconscious.

The guard grasped the scruff of the boy's neck and drug him out of the way of the dungeon guards. Malik, pleased that his victim was coming, grinned happily, a crooked broken tooth grin. And the restless crowd began to applaud with joy and excitement, like children with a new toy, at the sight of the condemned man. Their entertainment for the day.

There were four guards escorting the condemned man, two in front and two behind. The man's hands were tied behind his back with leather thongs. He was slightly under average height with rust colored hair of medium length, a slender frame but sinewy and muscular. He had a finely shaped nose set between piercing green eyes. His skin was darkly bronzed. He was dressed in tattered and soil smudged, waist length tunic, and loose fitting pants that came down to the ankles. His shoes were made of roughly sewn leather.

Jarret looked on with amusement, as he was paraded through the square, at the people taunting him and calling him rather risque names. His apparent lack of fear seemed to anger the crowd and made them more restless and unruly. They began to push and shove. This mood change alarmed his escort, and they hustled him up the stairs on to the platform.

While one of the guards blindfolded Jarret, Malik gave his ax a final wipe with his oil cloth. The crowd, by now, had begun throwing things at the prisoner. This was, for them, part of the fun of an execution, humiliating the condemned man.

The guard put his hand on the back of Jarret's head to indicate that he needed him to kneel and to guide the his head to the proper position on the cutting block. Malik stood. He took some practice swings. The crowd applauded wildly as the ax whistled through air. Malik's heart swelled in his chest. He loved his job. He basked in the feeling of power. The power of life and death.

A hush fell over the crowd in anticipation punctuated by the thunderous roar of the approaching storm as Malik stepped up to the cutting block. Spiderweb-like lightening streaked across the sky as the storm rolled across the valley bottom. Malik kissed the flat of his ax drawing cheers and applause from the crowd.

The maddened crowd began to chant. "Malik! Malik!" Malik raised the ax over his head, standing there as if posing for the crowd for a few short moments, adding drama. A resounding crash of thunder echoed off the walls in the square and a sizzling streak of lightening snapped like a whip over head. Malik could smell the burning air. This only excited him more.

The ax arced downward. Then all pandemonium broke loose. A fiery bolt of lighting licked out of the sky striking the head of the ax, shattering it. Then torrential rain and gale force winds struck the square.

Malik was thrown off the platform from the repercussions of the exploding ax head. Jarret felt himself flying through the air as the wind lifted the executioner's platform off the ground launching it through the air.

Jarret's fall was broken by the people in the crowd. He could hear the screams of fright from people that had been temporarily blinded by the white hot flash of the lightening. Then his ears were assaulted by screams of pain and agony, when the platform landed crushing many of the people in the crowd.

Although a bit banged up and singed, Jarret moved with alacrity. He tucked his knees into his chest and brought his hands around his feet so that they were in front of him. Then he pulled his blindfold off and stood.

He ran through the milling and disoriented crowd with little difficulty. A hand reached out of the crowd and grabbed Jarret's arm. Jarret, instinctively, jerked his arm free. Then a soft feminine voice said. "Let me help you. A knife appeared out of the crowd cutting the leather thongs that bound his hands together.

A spectacularly beautiful woman was holding the knife that had freed him. Jarret couldn't help himself as he gave her body the once over. She chastised him for his rudeness. "You men are all the same. There's only one thing on your mind, even when you're in dire danger."

Jarret, embarrassed and blushing, looked up at the woman's face apologetically. She had a quirky smile on her beautiful lips and her dark eyes. He was enchanted. He was mesmerized. He could have stood there and basked in her beauty until the end of time.

She grabbed his arm once more and said, "Snap out of it! Pull yourself together! We need to get out of here now before the guards find you." Still grasping the sleeve of his tunic, she led Jarret, winding their way through the crowd pushing and shoving when necessary.

They entered a low ceilinged, dirty and smokey tavern filled with loud drunken patrons. Bawdy and lascivious language was being bantered back and forth by the inebriated men. The squeals of prostitutes and barmaids bounced off the tavern walls in response to the men pinching their breasts and bottoms.

The woman had released Jarret when they entered the tavern. She threaded her way around tables and drunken men. She burst through the double kitchen doors knocking a barmaid, carrying a tray loaded down with food and drink on her backside. The offended woman let loose a line of expletives that would make the most crude and uncouth person blush.

The woman crossed the kitchen, ignoring the barmaid, to a door in the back. They entered a small corridor lined with sconces on either side. She took the only lit torch from the first sconce. The acrid smoke from the torch wafted towards the ceiling, where it collected and built downwards, creating a smoky haze which irritated the eyes causing them to water profusely. The corridor led to a stairwell.

They descended the stone stairwell which ended in a damp and musty cellar. The walls were lined with ale and wine barrels. There were the putrid remains of deceased rodents lying in the middle of the cellar floor. There were quarters of smoked meats hanging from hooks in the ceiling.

The woman began to tug on one of the barrels. She looked up the stairwell when she heard a commotion in the tavern above. The woman refocused her attention on the obstinate barrel. Then she said, "Must be the guards." Exasperated at the stubborn barrel and the huntsman's lack of help, she said, "Help me move this barrel! They'll be down here soon."

Jarret, embarrassed at his failure to help without being asked, latched on to the barrel. The two in unison managed to tip the full barrel of ale on end so that they could maneuver it away from the wall. The woman began to probe the wall where the barrel use to sit. Jarret heard a click and a massive stone in the wall, grinding and grating, swung inward.

"This used to be my stepfather's tavern. He used this secret passage to smuggle black-market goods in and out of the city. They caught him a while back and removed his head," she said nonchalantly.

The door in the above corridor banged loudly as the guards rushed in. "Hurry light one of those torches!" a guard commanded. The woman grabbed Jarret's sleeve and ushered him through the aperture in the wall. Then with a grinding and grating sound, the stone clicked back into place, concealing their escape route.

The passageway they had entered was narrow and low ceilinged. The ceiling was so low that they had to stoop to traverse the dark and dank corridor. They walked a narrow ledge to avoid the raw sewage that covered the drainage way's floor. The service walkway was slimy which made footing difficult.

The dark corridor spiraled downwards, and the stench was suffocating. The stink was so bad that the two fugitives had to cover their mouths with pieces of cloth torn from their clothing. The corridor leveled off at a juncture where it entered a larger corridor. They were now able to stand upright, but the stink had become almost over powering.

This corridor had a slighter acclivity and the gurgle of water was considerably louder. "We must hurry. With the way it was raining, these sluices with be filling up quickly," said the woman.

Jarret was totally confused as they threaded their way through the labyrinth of corridors. Sometimes they went up but their general direction was downward. Jarret had been waiting for the woman to introduce herself but it became apparent that she wasn't planning on volunteering this information. He finally asked, "What, may I ask, is your name?" "Yes, you may ask." But she went no further with the conversation. "Well! What is your name?" queried Jarret in exasperation. "Oh, sorry. Crysillnia," she replied in a preoccupied manner.

"Where are we going?" Jarret continued to question. "The sewers drain into the swamps," was Crysillnia's reply. Jarret noticed that the water level was nearly level with their walkway, and the roar of the rushing effluent was becoming deafening.

Crysillnia turned to face Jarret and shouted, "Can you swim?" Jarret nodded in the affirmative. He was surprised when Crysillnia jumped feet first into the rushing water. He hesitated momentarily before he followed her.

Like a great hungry beast, the wild and churning effluent gobbled the fugitives up. The two bobbed up and down in the maelstrom and were bounced off one wall then the other like so much flotsam. The fugitives struggled desperately to keep their heads above water.

The next moment the fugitives found themselves somersaulting through the air, arms flailing, like being spit from a great beast's mouth. With two loud splats followed by sucking sounds, Crysillnia and Jarret were deposited in the Mud Swamps below the city. Startled swamp birds took flight.

Like miscreants, Crysillnia and Jarret extracted themselves from the odorous and viscid mud. Tepid pools of water lay all around them and the biting insects buzzed madly about their heads, looking for places to feed. Crysillnia and Jarret began to swat wildly at these hungry and insatiable tormentors.

They moved away from the gushing sewer's outlet looking for a fresher pool of water so that they could wash off. The mud ran down their faces and body a little quicker as the rain mixed with the thick mud and made it more fluid. They looked like mud monsters.

Jarret looked over at Crysillnia. The corners of his mouth turned upwards and then he began to giggle which quickly erupted into a full blown and gut wrenching laughter. Crysillnia, incensed by this obvious mirth at her expense, glared at Jarret.

"I wouldn't laugh if I were you. You're no pretty sight yourself," she commented. Jarret, gasping for air, eyes watering, and trying to control his laughter, raised his hand apologetically and said, "No insult meant. I was really laughing at the both of us. I was imaging how the both of us would appear walking out of the swamp like this. I wonder what some superstitious farmer would think." As she began to think about it, she cracked a smile.

Crysillnia turned away from Jarret and began to march through the tepid pools of water. She said, "We need to be out of the swamp by nightfall. The swamp is fairly safe in the daylight but it's quite another story after dark." Jarret fell in behind her, still trying to stifle a few latent giggles.

CHAPTER 9

King Falef, sitting at the head of a long rectangular, oak table, glared at the man sitting across from him. "Kanef! I will not accept this insolence from you. Even though you are my son, I expect respect and will receive it." The King punctuated the last statement by slamming his open hand down on the tabletop.

Kanef stood and approached his father. He knelt, one knee on the floor, head bowed in an obsequious fashion. Kanef said, sarcastically, "Your Majesty. I am yours to command." He then stood and turned his back on his father, an unforgivable insult.

"Sit son, please," the King pleaded in resignation. "What has brought us to this sad state of affairs. We used to be close." Kanef turned and fixed his father with a cold stare. The hatred emanating from Kanef was almost tangible. "You dare play ignorant with me, father!" shouted Kanef, rattling the solid oak table when he struck it with a clinched fist. Kanef was visibly shaking with emotion.

The King retaliated in anger. He stood. "You still whining about that serving winch, that whore! What I did was for your own good. She was a lowly whore."

Kanef, blinking back tears as he battled his tempestuous emotions, turned away from his father's cold harsh glare before he was tempted to strike him. "Father, I can't bring myself to forgive you for what you had Asmoth do to Calina and me. I loved her no matter what . . . I wish not to discuss this matter any further. Father, all I desire at the moment is an explanation for your summons."

"Son, I had hoped for a reconciliation of our differences especially since the death of your brother." "Don't you dare try to use Zolef's death as a pawn to manipulate me into forgiving you," said Kanef, verbally lashing his father. "I didn't ask him to defend my honor. He chose to follow that road on his own." Then, fixing the King with a suspicious look, he asked warily, "Or did he, father?"

The King, unable to control his anger any longer, leapt from his chair. Holding his dagger to Kanef's throat, he said in a quivering voice,. "Now, son! It is quite evident to me that there is no salvaging our relationship. But I am your King and you will treat me with respect like any of my other subjects."

Kanef unperturbed by his father's threatening demeanor, noticed that the raw, red, scar on his father's face was throbbing violently like it always did when his father was angry. When he was a boy, he had asked his father where he had got the scar, but his father would never say. Kanef looked his father square in the eyes and said, "Yes, Your Majesty."

The King stepped back and with a flick of his wrist threw the dagger. The dagger struck the oak table with a splintering thud, penetrating the ancient table until it was stopped by an iron joint bolt, quivering. The reverberations of spent energy echoing throughout the room, Kanef then prostrated himself, mockingly, at his father's feet.

The King turned away from his son. He was trying to regain his composure and self-control. Returning to the high backed chair at the head of the table, he flopped down with a sigh of resignation.

Then he commanded. "Stand cur!" Kanef complied, facing his father. "Sit! I wish not to strain my neck." Kanef did so without protest.

"Our relationship may be damaged, but I know you love the Kingdom and would do anything to protect it and its subjects. Therefore what I'm about to ask you is for the good of Caspar and its people not just myself," continued the King. "There is a small group gathering in Groulan to quest for the Crystals, and I wish you to be part of the venture."

Kanef, sitting in the high backed chair at the opposite end of the table from his father, said nothing. He was observing his father closely, trying to ascertain his father's true motivesalert was suggesting was bein behind this quest, but the King was impossible to read. He knew his father too well to take his words at face value. His father did nothing for the good of others unless he had more to gain.

After several moments of silence, Kanef stood and began to pace. He realized that if his father was interested in these Crystals, they were valuable. Coming to a decision, Kanef turned and said, nodding his head in the affirmative, "Yes, I'll go."

The King's face brightened. Snapping his fingers, the King called out, "Cadoff!" The ferret faced servant appeared from behind one of the tapestries that lined the walls of the Great Hall. The tapestries served two purposes: that of decoration and also insulation against the winter cold. "Show my son out," commanded the King. The ferret faced man appeared to glide across the room.

Kanef crossed the room quickly. Cadoff opened the gigantic double doors to allow Kanef out. Kanef never much cared for Cadoff. Kanef was surprised to see one of the Elite Lenarian Guard standing in the hallway.

"Cadoff, show in the guardsman," ordered the King. Kanef stopped in the corridor and watched the guardsman enter the Great Hall. Kanef stood outside the door of the Great Hall for a few moments after the doors clicked shut. The King's Guards stood at attention staring at the opposite, ignoring Kanef. He finally turned and walked down the corridor, still wondering what his father was up to.

Simentoo stood at attention before the King. With a scrutinizing eye, the King looked the guardsman over, carefully sizing the man up. "A Captain of the Elite Guard still alive while his King and the rest of his men are dead," said the King.

The heat rushed to Simentoo's head as he battled with the conflicting emotions of anger and shame, but he said nothing. "You may stand at, ease, soldier" said the King. Simentoo moved his feet to shoulder width and cupped his hands behind his back.

The King queried, "How is it that you're still alive and everyone else is dead? And look at me when you answer." Simentoo reluctantly complied with the King's demand. He had never had contact with the King of Caspar before now even though he was raised in the mountains above the valley. He was surprised and even a little shocked at the cold, harsh reality of the King's personality as revealed by his cold cruel eyes.

Simentoo answered the King. "I was knocked unconscious during the battle and when I awoke, I found myself buried under the bodies of others." Simentoo stood there in silence for a few moments, then he continued. "If you wish Your Majesty, you may execute me for my failure."

The King slid his chair closer to the table, resting one arm on it, drumming his fingers nervously on the table top. A fleeting smile crossed his face before he replied, "Simentoo. Is that your name?" Simentoo shook his head in the affirmative. "I don't want your head, just your services. I have a quest I want you to participate in." The King went on to tell Simentoo about the quest for the Crystals.

CHAPTER 10

It was another unusually hot and sultry day in the valley. The white fluffy clouds were wandering haphazardly across a crystal blue backdrop. Simentoo entered the grimy little village of Groulan. The village was situated close to the mountains. Its sole purpose was to support the mining and timber industries.

Simentoo rode through the village searching for the rendevous point, the Red Flower Inn. The raucous little village consisted mostly of sleazy taverns, inns, brothels, and dilapidated hovels where the miners and lumberjack's families lived. The streets were dry and dusty in the summer and mud holes during the winter.

The King had introduced Simentoo to his son before they had set out together. He had traveled with Kanef and Rollof most of the way to Groulan, but outside the village, they separated. They thought it would be less noticeable if they arrived one at a time.

Kanef posed as a merchant and Rollof as his servant. Simentoo decided the disguise that fit him best was one that didn't stray far from his real vocation, that of a soldier of fortune and adventurer. That would go far to explain his many scars.

Simentoo passed the Red Flower Inn. He casually and nonchalantly reconnoitered the inn. He was not one to enter an unknown situation without familiarizing himself with the lay of the land. He was looking for suspicious characters which would probably be hard to delineate considering the clientele. He would have to rely on his instincts. He was also looking for defensible positions and escape routes.

The inn was a large two story, badly weathered, clapboard building. It set slightly back from the street with a large double door entryway. One side of the inn set snug against an, equally weathered clapboard building, and a narrow alleyway separated the inn from a clapboard building on the opposite flank. The narrow alley terminated in a stonewall about half the height of the surrounding buildings. There was a weathered plaque with a fading and flaking red rose hung over the entrance to the inn.

Simentoo rode farther down the village's main street keeping a critical eye open for anything he would deem suspicious. The buildings began to thin on the outskirts of the village. Simentoo spied a squalid little stable and smithy. He decided this would be a good place to stable his horse.

Simentoo was greeted by a troll as he approached the squalid affair. The troll stood a head taller than Simentoo. The troll had a rough and wrinkled complexion with a large nose flattened against its face. The troll had a massive mouth filled with broad flat teeth for grinding rock, their main food staple.

In a deep, rumbling, grating, and barely articulate voice, the troll asked Simentoo, "How can I help you?" "I would like to board my horse for the night," Simentoo replied. The troll approached rider and horse, cautiously, so as not to spook the animal.

"We mostly board oxen and repair wagons here. Plus the fact, that horses aren't very comfortable around trolls," stated the troll. Simentoo patted his mount on the neck and replied, "This horse is trained for combat. He fears very little."

The troll appeared reluctant. Then he asked, "Wouldn't you rather board your beast at human establishment?" "If I wished to have done so, I wouldn't be here," answered Simentoo, a tinge of annoyance coloring his voice.

The troll slowly walked up to the horse and, with a surprisingly gentle hand, stoked the animals mane. The horse showed a nonchalant indifference to the troll's presence. The troll gave Simentoo a big toothed grin which surprised Simentoo. He had never seen a troll smile before. Trolls were usually taciturn and never seemed to find anything amusing. It was even thought that troll's were anatomically unable too smile.

"What a remarkable beast you have sir," chortled the troll. "Imagine, a horse that has no fear of trolls. Who would have thought that possible," rambled the troll.

Simentoo, amused by the troll, said, "In my business, a skittish horse would be a dangerous liability." "May I inquire what your business is?" asked the troll. "I'm a adventurer and soldier of fortune," answered Simentoo. "Then you should be able to find plenty of adventure and soldiering in these unstable times, but I don't know about fortune," said the troll.

A silence fell over the two as they were at a loss for words. The troll broke the silence. "Well, back to business. I usually charge one copper piece for boarding an ox. But I'm not set up to stable horses. I'll have to send my stable hand out to fetch better feed." The troll brought his hand to his chin as he calculated the extra costs that he would entail. "Since this is a unique occurrence and will bring me much notoriety, I'll charge only three copper pieces." "Deal," said Simentoo.

Simentoo dismounted and handed the reigns of his mount to the troll. He reached into the purse attached to his belt and dug out the payment. He placed the three copper pieces into the open palm of the troll. The troll led Simentoo's mount into the stable, still bubbling with enthusiasm.

A smaller troll standing in the doorway of the stables watched in utter surprise. He was immediately galvanized into action by a commanding grating sound from the larger troll. With a long loping gate, the smaller troll headed down the street.

Troll language always sent chills down his back, Simentoo thought to himself. Feeling confident in the troll's abilities to care for his mount, he headed back towards the heart of Groulan and the Red Flower Inn.

Simentoo decided to take a back street that paralleled the main street. He wanted to stay as inconspicious as possible. The sun, high in the sky, battered the hard-baked street unmercifully.

The clamor and clatter of passing wagons, mounted men, pedestrians, and the shouts of hawkers trying to sell their wares was calamitous. Simentoo threaded his way through the crowded streets of the village. He skirted a brawl that had erupted from one of the taverns into the street.

The combatants appeared to be timber cutters. They were wielding long bladed knives. Blood was pouring profusely from the many cuts and lacerations that they had inflicted on one another.

Simentoo quickly left the fight behind him. But he had allowed himself to be distracted by the brawl enough that he didn't see the man and woman walking towards him. The three collided with such force that all three fell to the ground in a heap of flailing arms and legs.

The man and woman let fly long lines of expletives and insults at Simentoo for his clumsiness. Simentoo, red-faced, disentangled himself from the writhing heap. Apologizing profusely, Simentoo helped the woman to her feet. He offered a helping hand to the man and received a jolting cuff to the ear for his troubles. "I'll help myself up! You lout! You ought to watch where you are walking," said the irate man. The man stood and busily brushed the dirt from his clothes.

The man was dressed in black silk blouse and pants. The blouse was trimmed in white lace with his initials embroidered in silver thread over his right breast. Simentoo figured him to be of noble birth probably from Caspar City.

Simentoo ignored the tirade directed at him by the foppish nobleman. He was more interested in the woman or a truer description would be girl. She continued to tongue lash him and was in the middle of a long line of insults directed at his family and its lineage. Simentoo couldn't help but grin which angered the girl even more.

The girl was slightly plump but not fat. If she survived her childhood, which might be questionable considering her choice of vocation as a prostitute, she would probably become quite a voluptuous woman. Her beautiful yellow tresses, although they were in need of a good washing, accentuated her perfectly rounded face which she disguised with heavy coats of face paints. This girl had the potential of being a heartbreaker someday.

Apparently flabbergasted by Simentoo's amused expression, she turned in a huff and walked away with her dress swishing with every step she took. Her nose, high in the air she entered the next doorway with the foppish man in hot pursuit.

The girl's independent attitude reminded him of someone dear to him from his past. Simentoo continued down the street, his mind preoccupied with the young girl.

He turned a corner walking up the street that would lead him back to the main street when he spotted a surly group of men that appeared to be following him. Simentoo ducked into a tavern. The establishment was a dingy, little, one-room affair with few patrons. The floor was mud caked with garbage strewn about the floor and tables. The barkeep was as unappetizing looking as the barroom as he scratched various parts of his body and fished lice and fleas out of his long, filthy, black hair.

There was one bright spot in the dingy, smoke filled room. A buxom redheaded barmaid standing by the bar. She wore a white and brown pullover dress belted at the waist. The dress was low cut, revealing a considerable amount of cleavage. Simentoo caught himself staring at the woman's breasts. This apparently didn't bother the woman because she gave Simentoo a suggestive smile and winked at him.

Then she asked, "Can I help you Milord?" "Ya-Yes. I would like a table near the back door," He stuttered like a juvenile whom had had his first lurid proposition from a woman. She smiled coyly as she walked towards him, flaunting her considerable attributes and said, "That's not exactly what I had in mind." Simentoo found himself speechless as the blood rushed to his head as well as other places.

Pleased by his reaction, she burst forth with a titillating, harmonious, and rhythmic laugh. She turned erotically, her dress making a wide sweep. She gestured provocatively for him to come to her.

Simentoo followed the woman. He was mesmerized by her sexual aura. He mumbled to himself, "I wish, I had time to get to know her better."

She stopped at the table near the kitchen door and turned back to face Simentoo with a radiant smile. Sweeping her open hand down towards the table, palm up, she said, "Your table

Milord, and I didn't quite catch what you just said." She smiled impishly.

Simentoo was quite sure she had heard him or had a good idea of what he had said. He sat down clumsily facing the entryway and said, "Nothing important." The woman, now enjoying her control of the situation, continued to ply her seductive charms, smiling all the while. She reached from slightly behind him, over his shoulder, brushing his back with her breasts, to remove an empty mug. Simentoo moved away from her nervously.

She whispered into his ear and arched her eyebrows' "What would you like?" Simentoo asked, "What do you have?" The red-headed vixen raised her arms over her head and pirouetted, then replied, "Isn't it obvious? And I'll even give such a handsome gentleman as yourself a discount."

Simentoo, now blushing openly said, "No! No! That's not what I meant." Then he said, "I'll just take an ale, please." Disappointment tinged her voice. "Is that all?" Her curt question drew the attention of the other patrons, and one commented, "Maybe he likes boys." The woman turned in a huff and went to the bar to draw Simentoo's drink.

The buxom redhead plopped Simentoo's drink down in front of him, sloshing some of the contents on to the table, and said haughtily, "You're getting the worst of the deal." She then returned to the bar wagging her fanny at him.

Patrons came and left as he nursed his mug, but there were no signs of the men that he thought were following him. When he finished the last dregs of ale, he decided it was time to leave. So he quietly slipped past the redhead as she glared at him angrily and exited the tavern through the back door.

*   *   *

Crysillnia was sitting at a table in the Red Flower Inn with Talok, Jarret, and a new companion, Kanef, Prince of Caspar. They were seated on shaky stools placed around a well-worn wooden table perched precariously on wobbly legs. They were swigging on mugs of sweet beer, waiting for their final companion.

Crysillnia was facing Kanef with her back to the door. She was lost deep in her own thoughts. She was surprised that the King would send his only son on such a perilous mission.

Crysillnia's curiosity so consumed her that she began to probe his mind. The ability to enter the minds of others was one of her magical powers, but she had to be careful so that the one being mind read wasn't aware of the violation. Crysillnia met resistance. Kanef was a strong mind and willed person. She found herself having to probe and push a little harder than usual.

Finally, she began to detect a deep felt sadness and, as she probed deeper, a primal and raw anger directed towards his father. This anger was connected to the sadness. While the anger shocked, her the sadness weighed heavy on her heart. A long lost love. A mental image of a woman began to form, the woman looked familiar.

Crysillnia's intrusion was interrupted when Kanef's body stiffened, and he began too shuffle his feet. Her first reaction was that, she had pushed too hard, and he was now alerted to her spying. She glanced up at Kanef expecting to meet accusing and angry eyes. But he was looking over her shoulder toward the door and a spark of recognition flickered in his eyes.

Kanef said, "He's here." Then he turned his attention to Crysillnia. "I'm aware of what you were doing, witch. Please stay out of my mind. My thoughts are mine and mine alone." Crysillnia, embarrassed by the Prince's rebuke, blushed and apologized. "I'm sorry. It won't happen again." Kanef acknowledged her apology with a nod.

Simentoo went over to the bar. He wanted to make sure he hadn't been followed. He ordered an ale then turned his back to the bar. He thought to himself all these places looked the same. Small, dingy, smokey, rooms filled with drunks, prostitutes, and buxom barmaids.

With this thought, his mind slipped back to the redhead, but his daydream was short lived when a rowdy crew of teamsters entered the tavern and approached the bar. Simentoo heard the bartender place his mug on the bar. Simentoo turned and paid the man. He picked up the mug and took a sip, but he never took his wary eyes off of the loud and boisterous teamsters.

A big burly teamster slammed his fist down, rattling the mugs sitting on the bar, demanding in a loud voice, "Barkeep, I want service and now!" The bartender scurried up to the man and asked meekly, "What would you like sir?" The burly teamster chuckled at the obsequious bartender. "A round for all my friends here." His companions roared with enthusiasm at the generosity of their companion.

While waiting to be served, the burly man turned and leaned back against the bar. He was surveying the women in the tavern with approval. When his eyes lighted on Crysillnia, a big smile lighted his face. Self-assured, he swaggered over to her table. The unshaven and unkempt man stopped beside Crysillnia. She attempted to ignore him. Her companions placed their hands on their weapons preparing for the trouble sure to come.

"Hey wench, how much for a roll," Jarret began to stand, but Crysillnia, sitting beside him, grabbed his hand, impeding him, forcing him to sit back down. She whispered out of the side of her mouth, "We've a difficult enough road ahead. Ignore the oaf."

The burly teamster saw Crysillnia restrain Jarret and heard her whispering but not what she said. "Better listen to her, son. A common tramp isn't worth taking a beating over, especially one that lies with freaks." Directing his last comment at Talok.

There was a definite chill in the air as a pall of silence fell over the once noisy inn as tensions rose. Everyone was watching the drama unfolding in the rear of the inn. Talok sat quietly, his usual taciturn self, ignoring the insult.

Jarret's face turned a deep shade of red as his anger built. Kanef gripped the hilt of his short sword tightly knuckles turning white. The unruly teamster's companions walked up behind him in a show of solidarity.

The burly teamster latched onto Crysillnia's arm, squeezing it painfully bringing tears to her eyes. Jarret erupted into a flurry of action. He slammed his fist into the burly teamster's face. The burly man, caught off guard, released Crysillnia's arm and staggered backwards, blood flowing freely from the mashed pulpy blob in the middle of his face that use to be his nose.

The burly teamster raised his hand to his pulverized facial feature in shock as if trying to figure out what had happened to it. Then a dark and dangerous anger flashed in his eyes. The teamster ripped a piece of cloth from his tunic and put it to his nose in an attempt to staunch the red river. In a gurgled and muffled shout, he commanded his companions to attack.

His comrades had watched in disbelief, but, with the command, they sprang into action. They numbered about ten, and in unison, they headed towards the table. With the alacrity of the seasoned soldier, Simentoo acted. He pulled a throwing knife from his boot, and, with a flick of the wrist, he threw the knife across the room. The pommel of the flying instrument of death struck the burly teamster in the back of the head.

The force of the blow drove the now unconscious man forward, slamming him into the table which Crysillnia and her companions had previously occupied. The man slid across the table face first, smearing gobs of blood and flesh on the tabletop. The table upended, tossing the battered and unconscious man against the rear wall of the inn. The burly teamster slumped into an unconscious heap on the inn's floor.

Simentoo then grabbed the back of the tunic of the nearest teamster. He pulled the man back against him and pulled a dagger from his belt and laid it across the man's throat. He whispered with deadly intent into his captor's ear, "Tell them to stop." The frightened man yelled out as loud as he could, "Stop!"

The group of teamsters stopped and turned. It was quite clear the message Simentoo was sending as the sparse light in the room glinted off of his deadly persuader. "Okay, gentlemen, now that I have your attention," Simentoo said in a low guttural and deadly voice. "You will pick up your rude friend over there and leave quietly."

The teamsters hesitated. Simentoo sensing this hesitation applied pressure against his captor's throat, drawing blood. The frightened man, urine running down his leg, said in a high pitched and screechy voice, "Do as he says!"

The frightened man's companions, realizing how serious Simentoo was, complied. Simentoo released his captor once the teamster's had exited the inn, pushing the urine fouled man towards the door.

Jarret scrutinized the man who had just intervened on their behalf as he approached them. The stranger picked his knife off the floor and sheathed it. The adrenalin was still pumping wildly through Jarret's veins.

Kanef extended his hand in welcome and said, "Quite a display." Kanef then turned to his other companions and introduced Simentoo.

Kanef continued, "That was rather impressive, how you managed to end the confrontation so quickly and with out killing anyone." Jarret chimed in. "They should have died, especially the one that laid his hand on Crysillnia." Talok grumbled, "The brashness of youth."

Jarret turned on the dwarf like a viper, "I'm not a child and why shouldn't we have killed them. We were within our rights." Talok responded, "And if this had turned into a bloodbath, one of us or maybe all of us could've been killed.

Jarret didn't have a response to counter the dwarf's argument, so he said nothing. Simentoo looked into Jarret's eyes with understanding and said, "Here are a couple of maxims I adhere to, One only kill when there is no other option, because once a life is taken, you can't give it back. And two, those that are strong have an obligation to protect those that are weak."

"I think it's time we get down to business," said the dwarf brusquely. "Rather like a dwarf, crude and rude," snapped Kanef. This earned Kanef a dark look from Talok. "Lets not feud amongst ourselves," cut in Crysillnia.

The barkeep had righted their table and cleaned it the best that he could, but the tabletop was permanently stained with blood which gave it a dark splotchy appearance. They reseated themselves, but Crysillnia refused to rest her arms on the blood stained table.

Simentoo said, "We need to select a leader." At this point, Rollof approached the table. "Have a seat," invited Kanef. Rollof pulled up a chair. Kanef introduced Rollof around the table.

Simentoo repeated what he had just said for Rollof's benefit. Then he continued, "I think since Crysillnia is the one with the power to handle these Crystals that she should be the leader." Everyone sat quietly to mull the suggestion over.

But Crysillnia objected, "I don't have the experience to be a leader." Simentoo put forth his supporting argument for his idea. "The odds are that we all won't be there for the completion of the mission. And since none of the rest of us can handle the Crystals, we don't have the right to lead." The others agreed with Simentoo. So to her chagrin Crysillnia was chosen to be the leader.

After their meeting ended, Simentoo went to purchase the needed supplies: trail rations, pack animals, blankets, and the like. Simentoo had stepped out of the supply house when he noticed a commotion up the street.

Simentoo, curiosity getting the best of him, walked up to the near riotous crowd. There was a torn bag of feed lying at the edge of the crowd with its contents scattered around the street. People in the crowd cursed at Simentoo as he shoulder his way through the mob.

A man was wielding a cudgel vigorously. He was striking what appeared to be a quivering pile of rocks lying in the street. Simentoo recognized the young troll from the stables. The man wielding the cudgel had a badly smashed nose and many abrasions on his face. Simentoo thought to himself, maybe Jarret was right about killing this man.

Simentoo pulled his short sword and stepped into the circle that had formed around the battered troll. "Let the troll go," said Simentoo threateningly. The burly teamster was surprised to see this menacing man with drawn sword standing before him. Still gripping the cudgel, he dropped it to his side.

Then one of the men in the crowd said, "That's the guy that hit you in the back of the head, Creedok." Rage flashed across Creedok's face. The burly teamster took a swipe at Simentoo's head with the cudgel.

Simentoo easily danced beyond the cudgel's reach. The teamster took another swing. Simentoo sidestepped the blow, but it was close enough that he could fill the swish of disturbed air. Simentoo pirouetted bringing his sword into action. He struck Creedok on the back of the head with the flat of his sword, knocking the big man to the ground, driving his already, damaged face and nose into the dirt street.

The teamster pushed himself up onto his knees, shaking his head. Blood was once again flowing profusely from his nose, and with a roar, he stood. He turned to the crowd looking for help. "Get this troll lover!" he shouted.

The crowd surged forward, and Simentoo found himself buried under a pile of humanity. Simentoo thought to himself, "Well, my quest has ended." Then he heard screams of pain and what sounded like the cracking of tree branches in a high wind.

Simentoo's assailants got off of him and began to run. He now found himself lying on the ground looking up at a cloudless blue sky. Simentoo sat up and spotted Creedok running down the street.

Simentoo wasn't done with Creedok, so once again, he drew his knife and with a flick of his wrist, he hit the man on the back of the head with the pommel. A loud crack could be heard when the knife made contact with the teamsters head, sending the burly teamster face first into the dirt street again.

Then a rock-like arm was offered to Simentoo. Simentoo clasped the offered appendage and was easily lifted to his feet. Simentoo was face-to-face with the larger troll, whom still wore his blacksmith's apron, from the stables. "Thank you for saving my son," he said in a grating voice. Simentoo nodded his head in acknowledgment.

The burly teamster was just beginning to stand although rather shakily. Simentoo, nodding his head in the direction of the shaken teamster, said, "He's the one that was beating your son." "Was he now? Would you check on my son? I'll take care of the troublemaker," said the troll. Simentoo nodded his head.

While the troll went over to deal with the burly teamster, Simentoo knelt beside the smaller troll. There appeared to be no serious wounds. Trolls were hard to kill. Simentoo looked up when he heard a scream and a crushing sound. The troll had popped the teamster's head like a snow melon.

Simentoo now took the time to survey the street and was astounded at the carnage that the enraged troll had inflicted on the poor fools of the mob. What he had thought sounded like breaking tree branches were bones being popped like so much kindling. Dead and dying men were strewn about the dusty street. The groaning of men in misery and pain wafted over the street like ghostly wails.

The troll quickly returned to the side of his son. "How is he?" asked the troll with a worried inflection in his voice. The smaller troll rolled over and sat up. "I'm alright," he answered. Then he stood up and turned to Simentoo and said, "Thank you. I would have died if you hadn't intervened when you did." Then he showed Simentoo and his father the crack that had been opened up in his stony hide.

The troll wrapped his huge arms around Simentoo, picking Simentoo's feet off the ground, in gratitude. The troll squeezed Simentoo so hard that it pushed the air out of his lungs, and he found himself gasping for air.

The troll put Simentoo back down and then said, "Come with me. I have something for you." Simentoo raised his hand in objection and said, "I require no reward for doing what was right."

The troll gave Simentoo another one of those grimaces that passed for a smile and wrapped his coarse, stony arm around Simentoo shoulders in a camaraderie fashion, indicating that he wouldn't take no for an answer.

The smaller troll took the lead with a nearly imperceptible limp. The sun had just set, and the moon was casting an eerie blueish-white light over the street in front of the dark hulking stables which cast a sinister shadow. The smell of urine and feces wafted on the early evening breeze, and an occasional cloud temporarily blotted out the soft glow from the moon, casting larger and darker shadows over the nearly vacant street.

The smaller troll opened up the huge double doors of the smithy. A yellow-orange glow emanated from the forge. The stamping of hooves drifted out of the double doors as some of the animals inside displayed their displeasure at being disturbed.

Simentoo was surprised at how immaculate the troll kept his work area. Harnesses, straps, and various leather and hemp ropes hung from the rafters and on hooks along the walls of the smithy. Strips and blocks of iron in various shapes, sizes, and weights were stacked neatly on the floor along the walls.

Simentoo stood outside the livery while the trolls entered. The larger troll went to the back of the livery and rummaged around on a high shelf. With a grunt of satisfaction, the troll removed a small, well worn, rectangular box from the shelf. The hinges on the small wooden box screeched in protest from lack of use when the troll raised the lid.

The troll took a small round object out of the box and then snapped the lid shut. The troll approached Simentoo with hand open, palm up. There was a magnificently beautiful gem nestled in the troll's rough palm, beckoning to Simentoo.

The gem was perfectly spherical, nearly translucent with a light blue center radiating veins of red quartering the gem perfectly, and the surface was polished to a high sheen which reflected the diffusive light of the moon and appeared to magnify the moonlight. Simentoo exhaled, not realizing he had been holding his breath, before he spoke. "I can't accept this. The gem's value must be tremendous."

The trolled made a deep grating sound at Simentoo's comment. Simentoo took it as a chuckle. The troll then said, "You are correct but the stone's worth isn't calculated in monetary value. This is a Life Stone. This is a special gift, one that can't be refused without offending all trolls. Once offered it can't be refused or taken back. It can't be sold or stolen. The Life Stone will attune to you and no one else. It becomes a part of you."

"A Life Stone has never been offered to a human before. This is a great honor. This makes you a troll brother. The stone will keep record of your life and when you die, it will find its way back to the troll council where it will be read, and if your death was due to treachery or murder, then the Troll Nation is obligated to exact revenge on your behalf."

The troll reached out with the hand holding the Life Stone and grasped Simentoo's hand. The troll's hand completely enveloped Simentoo's. The troll deposited the Life Stone in Simentoo's hand. Simentoo could feel a warmth radiating from the stone course through his entire body. Troll and human stood in the quiet street gazing into each other's eyes, a bond between two different races coalesced and made them as one.

The troll released Simentoo's hand. Simentoo looked at the shining gem he held, then tucked it away in the purse on his belt. "All trolls will know you as Troll Brother and will come to your aid when needed, but you are also obligated to help the Troll Nation when called. If the stone is separated from you, as long as you have breath in your body, it will return to you.". The troll finished turned abruptly, leaving Simentoo standing silently in the street, stunned by what had just happened.

CHAPTER 11

They had left Groulan five days back and were in the foothills on the far side of the mountain from the Caspar Valley. They were about to enter the Ravaged Lands, a wild and dangerous place.

Jarret was turning a spit over an open fire. He was preparing their morning meal, a mountain viper. He had raided a den of the hibernating reptiles. Crysillnia approached the fire to warm up. It was a frigid morning. "The snake smells good, but I'm still not to happy with the cuisine," she commented.

Jarret had to shade his eyes from the rising sun when he looked up at her. "We need to save our supplies whenever possible, especially since we lost our pack horse with the bulk of our supplies. There will be times that game won't be available, and we'll have to rely on the meager rations we have left."

Simentoo hunkered down by the crackling warmth of the fire and rubbed his hands over the fire to warm them up. "Viper is delicious," said Simentoo in an attempt too reassure Crysillnia.

Crysillnia was embarrassed by her squeamishness, but, even with Simentoo's reassurances, she was dubious. Jarret handed her his dagger with a sliver of viper dangling from it. Crysillnia took it reluctantly. She nibbled at the morsel daintily and found the flavor spectacular. Her hunger piqued, she quickly devoured the offering and asked for more.

Crysillnia took her second helping from a smiling Jarret and sat cross-legged by the fire. She began to observe and evaluate her companions. They were, by now, all sitting around the fire, eating.

Talok was a taciturn and unfriendly type. Jarret was young, rash, and quite handsome. Kanef was quiet and anger seethed deep within his soul. Simentoo was well disciplined but carried a deep sadness within. Rollof was a burly ruffian, almost roughish, but very loyal to Kanef and seemed to be a lost soul. He reminded her of someone but didn't know who.

Simentoo glanced up at the sun nudging itself over the mountain peaks behind them and said, "It's going to be another hot day." Crysillnia, her back turned to the dying fire, was trying to peer through a thick fog hovering close to the ground. "The sun will burn the fog off in short order," he continued. Rollof was filling up their water flasks from a trickle of water seeping out of the mountainside while the others finished their meal.

Crysillnia, curiosity getting the best of her, asked, "What happened to the Ravished Land?" Kanef answered, "They say it has to do with the elves using magic that was not their own."

The fog dissipated quickly revealing a stark landscape of twisted and warped trees and bushes. A stink that reminded Crysillnia of rotten eggs, wafted up the mountainside to assault their senses. There were no green leaves or grasses. The land appeared shattered and broken.

"There are tales of horrendous and terrible creatures living in the Ravaged Lands. Mothers would threaten to send their children here if they didn't behave. One thing I do know for sure is that goblins live here," continued Kanef.

Simentoo said, "We're packed and ready to go." He took the lead, as they stumbled, slid, and floundered down the last few feet of the mountainside to be faced with a putrid and truncated forest. They began to follow a trail that skirted the sickly looking trees. The trees had black and mottled bark infested with pus, and oozing scabious lesions. The smell had changed from that of rotten egg to the putrid smell of rotting flesh. This smell was emanating from the greenish-yellow ooze leaking from the lesions on the trees. The smell was so bad that even the most hardened among them had a hard time holding their morning meal down.

The trail took a turn heading into the forest. Talok stopped, then said, "This is truly an accursed land." "Do we dare go into the forest? If you can call it that," Crysillnia spat out disgustedly. Simentoo said, "I don't think we have much choice."

They continued to follow the winding, loose-stoned trail. They detoured around a bushy tree that crowded the trail. Once around the tree, they were stopped in their tracks by another tree growing in the center of the trail as if it were planted there to block further transgression into the forest. It stood in stark contrast to the other trees surrounding it. This tree wasn't diseased.

The tree appeared to be healthy. It had a full compliment of lush green leaves decorated with bouquets of beautiful blossoms. The petals of the flowers were crimson trimmed in a deep blue which highlighted the golden-yellow center. The sweet smell emanating from the blossoms was intoxicating.

After admiring the beauty of this strange anomaly for a few moments, they approached the tree. Jarret plucked one of the flowers from the tree, and handed it to Crysillnia and said, "A beautiful flower for a beautiful lady." Crysillnia accepted the proffered gift with a smile, blushing. Talok looked at Jarret jealously, but no one noticed.

They began to circumvent the tree when a voice floated down from the branches above, halting them. "I wouldn't go in there if I were you." All pulled their weapons looking for the originator of the disembodied voice. Jarret placed himself protectively between Crysillnia and the tree, and Rollof exclaimed, "In the name of the Creators, a talking tree!"

"What foolishness is that! Trees can't talk not even in an accursed land such as this!" screeched the voice with exasperation.

Crysillnia searched the tree branches and finally spotted the speaker. Pointing, she said, "Up there, near the top." "Why, it's a bird!" exclaimed Talok incredulously.

"A bird!" squawked the chagrined fowl. "I'm here to help you, and you ply me with insults," continued the irate beast. "I'm no ordinary bird. I'm a parrot and a very fine and intelligent one at that dwarf," scolded the beast. The parrot fluffed its feathers in a further demonstration of its indignation.

"I'm sure Talok meant no insult right, Talok," said Crysillnia apologetically. Talok answered acerbically. "If the feather fits . . ." Then he mumbled something, more or less to himself.

Kanef, addressing the red feathered creature, asked, "Why shouldn't we enter the forest?" "Foolish human, is it not evident," answered the brilliantly feathered bird condescendingly. "The forest is diseased. Just one of the more obvious misfortunes of this poisoned and desolate land."

"I sense you have little credence for my warning. I do not know why I bother' but I will give you a demonstration." With its beautifully curved, black, beak, it snapped a very thick and sturdy branch from the healthy tree.

Flapping its blue-tipped, crimson wings, the parrot laboriously began to fly, gaining altitude slowly, the weight of the branch hindering its effort, the parrot began its dive toward the forest. The parrot, gliding along the forest's blackened tree tops, dropped the healthy branch.

The branch twisted and turned in the breeze as it plummeted towards the forest floor. The branch bounced and bumped its way chaotically through the twisted, truncated and grasping trees of the forest. The limb stuck upright in the forest floor.

The trees near their newly planted neighbor began to sway, gently and then began to shake violently as if in an isolated wind storm. At the height of the isolated maelstrom, a corrupt viscid fluid erupted from the scabious lesions that covered their mottled bark.

This viscous fluid coated the errant branch. The weight of the glutinous ichor toppled the haphazardly planted branch. Then cracks appeared in the bark of the branch as the fluid was absorbed. Bubbles began to form as if it were boiling. Then the too familiar lesions began to form on the trunk of the branch.

In shock, Crysillnia and her companions stepped back from the forest's edge. "Need I say more," squawked the parrot with an I told you so attitude. "In which direction do you suggest we go, bird?" asked Simentoo. "Do not call me bird!" squawked the parrot lividly.

"My sole purpose in being here is to warn travelers not to enter the forest, not to give directions. I suggest you return the way you have come. That is my suggestion to you human."

"That isn't a viable option, because there may be greater dangers behind us," answered Simentoo. The parrot now sitting on one of the lower branches, said nothing. It was thinking through what Simentoo had just said.

Finally, the parrot continued, "More dangerous than disease spreading trees, goblins, capricious storms and the many other strange maladies of this cursed land? Things must be really bad out there. If you insist on going forward, I must guide you through the labyrinth of dangers and evil that entwines this blighted land."

"Thank you very much for your selfless attitude. We greatly appreciate it," said a grateful Simentoo. "How do we know our feathered friend can be trusted?" asked Talok snidely.

The parrot, glaring at Talok, began to respond, "I will have you know . . ." when Jarret interrupted, "The parrot's recent intervention ought to count for something. Besides, we don't appear to have much choice." Talok grunted his acquiescence truculently, then countered, "If you betray us, I'll have roast parrot for supper."

The parrot was about to respond to Talok's threat when Crysillnia interceded with a harsh edge to her voice. "Enough of this bickering. We need to continue our quest. Now lead on, bird!" she commanded. The parrot, vexed by Crysillnia's use of the title bird, mumbled something to himself about birds, then said, "Follow me."

The parrot launched himself from his perch effortlessly. Soaring high into the air he began to do loops, swoops, and twists. Crysillnia figured he was trying to show off and Talok made a comment in the same line of thought.

The parrot flew along the edge of the forest and suddenly disappeared. Alarmed, the travelers began to call for the fowl. The parrot reappeared as quickly as it disappeared. It swooped over their heads and asked, "What is all the noise about? You have to be quiet or the goblins will hear you."

Jarret replied angrily, "How do you expect us to follow you, if we can't see you." "Oh, sorry, I have the magic of the chamaeleon. I blend in with my surroundings if I don't mentally concentrate to control the magic."

"Then I suggest you put that great mind of yours to work, bird!" snapped Talok sarcastically. "Don't call me, bird," protested the parrot. "Getting under your feathers, am I," said the dwarf as he chuckled cruelly. The parrot flew away in a huff.

The parrot disappeared in the distance. "Looks like you managed to chase off our guide," said Rollof. The Dwarf just shrugged his shoulders and continued to walk in the direction that the parrot had flown.

They stayed close to the forest edge but not close enough to have to worry about being splashed by the cancerous ichor of the forest. The day had begun cool, but as midday approached, the heat had become sultry and oppressive. Sweat was rolling off their brows in rivers.

The line of the forest was beginning to pull away from the foothills and head toward a group of small hills in the distance. Rollof was in the lead, followed by Simentoo, Crysillnia was directly behind Simentoo flanked by Kanef and Jarret, and Talok was the rear guard. The small troop trudged on arduously towards the low lying hills.

Crysillnia, sweaty, grimy and tired, sat down in the shade of a huge boulder, resting her back against it. An equally grimy Jarret, standing over her, said in a jesting manner, "Looks like you need a bath."

Crysillnia let her hair down and began to pick dirt and pieces of dried grass out of it. She looked up at Jarret not at all amused by his jest and snapped, "Don't you have anything better to do than poke fun at my wretched appearance."

Jarret a sinking feeling in his stomach, quickly apologized. "Sorry. No insult intended." Crysillnia was embarrassed by her snappy retort. She looked up at Jarret, shading her eyes with one hand while running her fingers through her hair with the other, and smiled.

She asked Jarret to sit by her. She wanted to get to know him better. It was obvious that he had more than a passing interest in her. A thought flitted across the back of her mind. This man's interest may prove to be useful at a later date.

Jarret pleased by the request of this disheveled, tantalizingly beautiful woman, plopped down beside her like a child with a new toy. They sat there, quietly, not knowing what to say. Crysillnia broke the silence. "Jarret where is your family from?"

Jarret looked down at the ground and unconsciously picked up a twig, using it to idly excavate small stones. His face flushed slightly. "You don't have to answer, if you don't wish to."

"No, I'll answer your question. I don't know who my family is. I was raised by elves that lived on the edge of the Elf Forest. The only thing the elves told me was that my mother had been murdered. They would tell me no more. They said, the time would come and the truth would be revealed or it wouldn't. Typical elf reasoning and arrogance. Where is your family from?" The tables turned, it was Crysillnia's turn to blush. She was hesitant to answer. "My mother was of Casparian peasant stock. My father unknown. It is rumored that he is of noble blood, but I doubt it."

A crash of thunder interrupted their conversation. A foreboding and dark roiling cloud appeared suddenly without warning. The cloud appeared to be burning within as lightening erupted violently from the cloud's center. The violent white bolts of energy lashed out at the surrounding landscape as if it were punishing the land for existing.

The storm appeared to have no definite direction, as it wandered erratically across the sky, but it appeared to be heading in their general direction. Simentoo shouted as a howling wind descended upon them and began to whip and blow violently around them. "We need to find shelter!"

The parrot appeared out of nowhere, squawking loudly. "Come! Come quickly! Follow me! This is a storm born of wild magic of which there is plenty in this accursed land."

The six of them followed the parrot without question, but there appeared to be nowhere to hide, and the storm was gaining on them. They were running wildly across the debris strewn ground. Crysillnia stumbled over an exposed tree root causing her to falter. Jarret, running behind her, was looking over his shoulder and bumped into her.

The two collapsed into a heap of flailing legs and arms as they rolled down a slight acclivity terminating in a small murky stream. They struggled clumsily to separate themselves while Jarret anxiously looked back at the approaching maelstrom.

The storm appeared to have singled out Crysillnia and Jarret. It bore down on them with a vengeance. A dread filled Jarret. A blue-white shaft of energy emanated from the dark and oppressive, churning cloud. The energy shaft ravaged the diseased forest unmercifully. Wild and untamed winds gusted from the clouds, to the ground, tossing and flinging loose debris.

The energy shaft coiled around a nearby boulder, and to Jarret's astonishment, the inert object began to swell. The energy shaft began to pulsate as it infused the boulder with its magical energy. The infused boulder swelled to twice its original size. Then it began to throb like the heart of a giant, before it exploded, sending projectiles of shattered rock in various sizes and shapes in all directions.

Jarret covered Crysillnia's body with his own to protect her. The projectiles whistled overhead, dangerously close, but lying in the insignificant furrow created by the dark, meandering stream protected them. Some of the least energized pieces of the victimized boulder precipitated on them. One of these pieces, a very sharp sliver, buried itself in Jarret's shoulder.

Crysillnia lying under Jarret's protective body heard a faint groan escape her protector's throat. Crysillnia worried, asked frantically, "Jarret, are you alright?" But before he could answer, their ears were assaulted by a shrill ear piercing whine, and then there was complete silence.

Jarret rolled onto his back and slowly sat up. Crysillnia pushed herself to her knees and looked out over the scarred and ravaged land. To her astonishment, the storm had dissipated as quickly as it had appeared.

Crysillnia turned her attention to Jarret. With a grimace, he had pulled a jagged piece of boulder from his shoulder. Soaking wet, Crysillnia went to the aid of her protector. The wound was bleeding but not profusely.

Crysillnia noticed that there was a blue-green moss hugging the water's edge. This particular moss had excellent healing properties and was good for stanching blood flow. She pulled up a handful and shook it vigorously to dislodge the loose dirt and rocks that clung to the roots. She then immersed the moss into the stream. After removing the moss from the stream, she wrung out the excess water, then applied the cool swatch to Jarret's wound.

Jarret sighed with relief as the moss began to do its work. Immediately on application, the painful throbbing began to abate and within a few moments the pain was completely gone. Then he could feel a deep tingling in his shoulder. It sort of itched. A sign that the miraculous healing powers of the moss were at work.

Simentoo and the others came over to see if Crysillnia and Jarret were okay. Simentoo knelt down beside Jarret and asked, "Are you seriously injured?" Jarret shook his head no. Simentoo removed the moss, so he could examine the wound. He replaced the moss and said, "The moss will do the job."

Kanef, perplexed, asked, "Why did the storm end so suddenly?" Rollof commented, "Maybe we should ask the parrot. He claims too have knowledge of this wild land."

At that moment, the parrot reappeared. "Where have you been, our brave protector and guide?" snipped the taciturn dwarf. The parrot turned on the dwarf to parry the sarcastic remark. Crysillnia, tired of this silly conflict between the dwarf and bird, shouted, "Enough! We've more important things to worry about! I've heard all I want to hear from the two of you and this silly feud!"

Silence reigned over the group for a few moments, finally broken by Kanef. "Parrot do you know what happened to the storm, why it ended so suddenly?"

"The only thing I know about the storm is that it is a reaction to the presence of other strong magic that has entered the land." The parrot looked at Crysillnia and Jarret, then commented rhetorically, "One of you possess magic?" You don't need to answer that question. I know because the storm had targeted the two of you."

The parrot continued. "I don't know why the storm ended so abruptly. It normally doesn't quit until it destroys the invading magic." Crysillnia was staring beyond the truncated tree stump on which the parrot was perched. She sensed something out of place in the disease and storm ravaged forest, something was moving amongst the trees. There it was a dark shadow threading its way through the forest. Then it disappeared.

Jarret, still sitting with his back to the parrot but facing Crysillnia, noticed the flicker of alarm cross her face. "Something wrong?" he asked. "No," she said with a tinge of uncertainty in her voice.

"Well, we better continue our trek then," said Simentoo. "Wait a minute. Please may I borrow your dagger," asked Crysillnia. Simentoo produced the weapon without question but curiosity did frame his face.

Crysillnia accepted the proffered dagger. She pulled her sopping wet, mud caked hair over her shoulder, and twisted it into a tight tail, and with one clean swipe of the dagger, cut it off. With no further fanfare she said, "I'm ready."

The parrot took flight and said. "Follow me. We ought to be able to reach the Sundered Hills by nightfall." Everyone fell back into their original formation as they followed the parrot towards the distant hills.

CHAPTER 12

The night was cold. Nights were usually cold on the Halhoren Plains even during the hottest times of the year. Calert was feeding his campfire with the dung of the kantra, a large herbivore that roamed the plains and one of the staple foods of the Halhoren Horsemen.

The Halhoren Horsemen were very dangerous and vicious nomads who roamed the plains. They would raid the border provinces of Lenar but not often. When rumors that the horsemen were on the prowl circulated, shivers of fear would course throughout the lower provinces.

The Halhoren Plains ran the full length of the lower border of Lenar, situated between Lenar and the Great Desert. Although the horsemen were dangerous and a nuisance to the Lenarian Alliance, they did serve a useful purpose. The horsemen, until recently, had always been a protective buffer against the desert nomads.

Calert was waiting for Kroll, a subchief of the Halhoren Horsemen. Rumors had it that he and his warriors had gone renegade and were disrupting the hierarchical order of the Halhoren Tribal Council. Calert was hoping to convince Kroll and his followers to ally themselves in the war against the enemies of Lenar.

Calert was mesmerized by the fire's blazing embers and the gambit of colors they displayed: orange, yellow, green and blue. Calert was nudged from his thoughts by a deep and gravelly voice. "Sorcerer you should be more aware of your surroundings. If I had been an assassin you would now be dead." Then the man chuckled cruelly. Calert realized that he had made a mistake. This man wasn't an ally. He was more likely an enemy.

Calert, vexed by his misjudgement of this man and the man's attitude, said, "You need not worry about me. Please approach."

Kroll did as requested but did so cautiously. When he was within striking distance of Calert, he was thrown back violently by the invisible repelling shield that Calert had erected around himself.

"Need I say more." "Point well taken," replied Kroll darkly. Kroll motioned to someone beyond the light of the campfire and said, "By the way, I found this elf skulking in the dark."

Two men escorted Shasheek out of the darkness and threw him to the ground at Calert's feet. "What do you suppose, he was doing out there?" asked Kroll, suspiciously. Calert shrugged his shoulders indicating that he had no idea.

Kroll, nodding his head toward Shasheek said, "Kill him." Calert pointed a finger at the elf and uttered an unintelligible word. When Kroll's men tried to carry out their orders, they found Shasheek to be protected by the same spell as Calert.

"I'm not going to allow you to kill him. We need to know what he is doing out here, and we can't get that information if he is dead. Bind his hands so that he can't conjure magic." Kroll begrudgingly agreed and ordered his men to bind the elves hands behind his back.

"Sit, Kroll. We need to talk." Kroll approached the fire, but before he sat, he ordered his warriors to pitch camp. Kroll was typical of the Halhoren breed: tall, muscular, flaring nostrils, dark eyes, shaved head, and deep rich ebony skin.

"What do you want, sorcerer?" asked Kroll truculently. Calert didn't respond immediately. His original purpose here had changed. He knew that Kroll was unreliable at least and at worst could be an agent of the enemy.

"I need someone to keep an eye on the plains and report any unusual occurrences to me," Calert finally said. Kroll contemplated the request, then asked, "If I agree to do this, how do I communicate with you?"

Calert rummaged through his pack a few moments and grunted with approval when he found what he was searching for. He pulled a gold necklace with a red orb attached from the pack. He dangled the prize before Kroll. The faint light offered by the fire glinted off the chain and orb.

The Halhoren warrior appeared to be mesmerized by the beautiful piece of jewelry. Kroll snatched the necklace from Calert's hand and placed it around his neck adoringly. Kroll said curtly, "I'll do it."

Then Kroll asked, "How does it work?" "When you have something to report, all you need to do is grip it and think of me and what you want to say. I will hear your thoughts," said Calert.

Suspicion reflected in Kroll's eyes. "Hear my thoughts?" He questioned leerily. "I can only hear the thoughts you wish me to know. No others," Calert lied.

The necklace would let him know whatever Calert wanted to know. He was giving this necklace to Kroll so that he could keep tabs on Kroll whenever he wished. In fact, the moment Kroll had put the necklace on, it had revealed what Calert suspected the moment Kroll walked into the camp. He was an agent for the enemy.

Kroll's greed and a little bit of magical help offered by the talisman hanging around his neck convinced him to agree to the arrangement. The two talked late into the night. Just before daylight, they broke off their negotiations.

*   *   *

Crysillnia was awakened by the early morning bustle of the others preparing to continue their travels. "I see you've finally awakened, sleepy head," said Jarret fondly as he handed her a piece of jerked meat. The early morning light was sneaking over the distant Caspar Mountains.

Crysillnia accepted the enticing morsel gratefully but stayed wrapped up in her blanket, to keep the chill of the morning air at bay. Hunger partially satiated Crysillnia got up and quickly donned her cloak. She rubbed her hands briskly to warm them, since there was no fire. They had decided not to light a fire because it could attract unwanted attention.

They were on the road by the time the sun had peeked its head over the mountain tops. They entered the Sundered Hills just before the sun hit its height on its trek through the firmament. Crysillnia was amazed by the devastation these hills had suffered. She couldn't imagine what catastrophic event could have caused such destruction.

They had to pick their way carefully through the winding maze like trails. Loose footing, hidden chasms, and falling rocks hindered their travels. It made one think that they were under assault from the hills themselves. Gases and vapors seeped from cracks in the ground, and tunnels bored into the hillsides. At times it felt as if the ground was a living writhing entity as it rose and fell.

The parrot informed his wards that the tunnels were dug by goblins and that they should all be very quiet so as not to attract the goblins. But the bird wasn't inclined to follow its own advise. It had been prattling nonstop from the moment they had entered the dark and foreboding hills and gullies. The brooding and truncated hills appeared to hover over the travelers, oppressing their moods and making them very nervous.

Kanef finally fed up with the parrot's nonstop prattle, snapped irritably, "Parrot, practice what you preach and be quiet!" The parrot,who had changed its color to a bright yellow so that it could be seen easier by his companions, raised his head haughtily and with indignation, flew on quietly.

The gorge through which they were traveling narrowed significantly, and the walls on both sides were so sheer and high that direct sunlight couldn't reach the trail they were following. Although it was still the middle of the day, it appeared to be late dusk at the chasm's bottom.

Talok, still bringing up the rear, began to glance over his shoulder repeatedly. "I don't like this," he said. "A perfect spot for an ambush." Ominously, as if in response to Talok's misgivings, the ground rumbled, creaked, and groaned as it lurched spasmodically under their feet.

Everyone was knocked off their feet by the minor quake as rocks and soil dislodged from above began to pelt them unmercifully. They quickly regained their feet and began to run in hopes of avoiding the bruising shrapnel.

The parrot began to behave erratically. He flew high above the chasm's floor turning his head sideways to get a better view of the trail below. The parrot then dove, buzzing the six companions, squawking loudly. "Turn! Go back! The goblins are ahead. They know we are here! Hurry! Quickly! Run!" The companions needed no coaxing. They turned in their tracks making a hasty retreat.

As they ran back through the narrow confines of the gorge, the parrot continued to fly overhead, frantically urging them to run faster. Talok, now in the lead, ran rather ponderously. Dwarves were not known to be the most fleet of foot, and Talok was no exception.

Talok rounded a sharp bend in the trail and came to a complete stop nearly causing the others to collide with the person to their immediate fore. The parrot bringing up the rear began to screech. "Stupid dwarf . . ." But the parrot stopped in mid-insult when it realized that the dwarf had no choice but to stop.

The trail was blocked. One side of the narrow chasm had collapsed. The pile of debris was loose and dangerous to attempt to scale. They were trapped.

They would have to fight. The trail here was wide enough for two to stand side by side. Rollof and Simentoo took up a defensive position. The goblins in hot pursuit rounded the bend in the trail unaware of what was waiting for them. The lead goblins ran into the bristling and unforgiving weapons of Simentoo and Rollof.

The goblins following their unfortunate companions were able to halt their forward motion with some colliding, bumping, and a lot of confusion. Simentoo and Rollof took advantage of the confusion and went on the offensive. They drove the goblins back. But their advantage was short lived. The goblins, quickly regrouped, and there were many more goblins than humans. The goblins counter attacked, driving Rollof and Simentoo back.

Goblins were grotesque creatures. They were about half the height of the average human. Their foreheads sloped backwards, making one wonder if they even had a brain. Their noses were flat against their faces with huge nostrils which drained continuously and they were always sniffing the air. They had wide mouths filled with razor sharp teeth and were able to dislocate their jaws, so they could open their mouths wider if necessary. Their limbs were long and ungainly. Their toes and fingers were long and supple tipped with suckers and retractable claws.

Goblins were sunken chested and looked emaciated which gave the false impression that they were a weak creature. They were covered with a dark, coarse, and fur-like hair. Although goblins were stupid, they were also wily and always ran in packs of twenty to thirty.

The goblins broke off their attack because they were taking heavy casualties. Simentoo and Rollof were formidable opponents. The goblins began to make more probing attacks, searching for weaknesses in the humans' defenses.

Talok and Kanef were the second line of defense, and Jarret stood behind them as Crysillnia's final defender. Although they were trapped, Simentoo thought that they had a good defensible position. The numerical advantage of the goblins was of little use in the narrow confines of the gorge.

But he soon realized his underestimation of the goblin's determination, when some of them began to climb the sheer sides of the gorge. The companions watched helpless as the enemy surrounded them. Jarret reached instinctively for the bow he no longer carried. Once the goblins were in place, the goblin leader ordered the attack with a high pitched squeal.

The battle was violent and ended quickly. Rollof was dead and the others had wounds of various severity but none fatal. But the casualties suffered by the goblins were far greater. The now five companions were marched out of the gorge where they were then trussed up to long poles.

The lead goblin picked out ten of the goblins to carry the prisoners. This brought disgruntled howls of displeasure from those chosen. Crysillnia thought as she lie on the ground that the goblins were complaining about the heavy work they were required to do. But she quickly saw the light, when those not called into labor began to roast the dead that they had drug out of the gorge. Their complaints were because they couldn't participate in the feast.

Crysillnia, horrified and sickened by this barbarism, turned her head. A scuffle broke out over Rollof's corpse. Evidently the goblins preferred human flesh over the flesh of their own.

Like beasts being carried to the slaughter, Crysillnia and her companions were hefted off the ground, their backs nearly touching the ground. The companions now prisoners began a new trek. This trek, Crysillnia thought, would probably end over a roasting pit. Some of the tales Crysillnia had heard as a child about goblins came back to haunt her. She hoped it wasn't true that goblins preferred to eat living flesh.

Talok was the most difficult to carry. The goblins had to stop several times to change carriers. As the day waned there appeared to be a dispute brewing. The disagreement came to a head in a narrow grassy valley. The goblins dropped their burdens unceremoniously and without warning, extracting painful groans from the trussed up prisoners.

The leader became quite irate with the rebellious goblins and harangued them until a brawl ensued. The companions couldn't determine who was fighting whom, but the battle was short lived. There were several dead goblins, including the leader. A huge and extremely grotesque goblin stepped forward.

This huge and grotesque goblin began to beat his chest and growl ferociously in challenge. None of the other goblins accepted the challenge, therefore, the large and grotesque goblin began to issue orders which were followed promptly and without complaint.

The goblins set up camp. The prisoners were cut from their poles. Then their hands were bound behind their backs and they were tethered to stakes driven in the ground. Two goblins were posted as guards.

The prisoners moved close together as the night wore on for warmth. The day had been hot, but the night was becoming frosty. It was cold enough for them to see every breath they took.

Crysillnia enviously watched the goblins sitting around a huge fire. Talok commented. "When do you suppose they plan on roasting us?" Crysillnia glanced over at the dwarf with a shocked expression framing her face.

But before anyone could answer, one of the goblins let out a squeal of pain. He had been searching Simentoo's pouch but not very astutely. Simentoo lashed out. The ball of his foot connected with the unfortunate miscreant's throat, crushing it.

The goblin clutched its throat as it gasped for air. The goblin fell to the ground convulsing and writhing violently. The creature finally ceased moving as it lost its fight for life.

The new leader heard the commotion and came over to see what was happening. When he saw his dead companion, he uttered something in the high pitched goblin language, and two other goblins came running. They picked up the recently deceased goblin and drug it over to the fire. Crysillnia watched in horror as they gutted the dead goblin and spit it for roasting.

The huge goblin approached Simentoo with a grotesque and crooked smile that looked more like a grimace. Then he spoke. "We not sure who to eat first. You solved that for us. We eat comrade first and you second."

The huge goblin began to laugh and pointed at Simentoo. Several goblins rushed Simentoo. Simentoo struggled valiantly with his captors but was subdued. Even being tied and tethered, Simentoo exacted some retribution. He managed to kill one more goblin and break the leg of another.

The goblins dragged their dead and wounded comrades to the fire and gutted them. The wounded goblin was gutted alive. Its screams of pain shattered the silence of the cold night air. Crysillnia, cringing in fear and disgust, turned her head.

Simentoo continued to struggle violently as the goblins dragged him towards the fire. One attempted to grab him around the waist but Simentoo twisted free of the goblins grip. The goblin lost its balance and fell, ripping open the pouch draped around Simentoo's waist.

The Life Stone, freed from the confines of the pouch, bounced along the ground towards the fire. The light from the fire ignited the inner brilliance of the stone. A thin, fiery-red, beam of light leapt into the night sky like a beacon.

The goblins dropped the struggling human. When Simentoo hit the ground, the wind was driven out of his lungs leaving him gasping for air. The goblins backed away from Simentoo and the pulsating Life Stone in awe and fear. The goblin leader looked at the stone and then at the breathless Simentoo.

The goblin leader pointed a quivering finger at Simentoo, and then with an accusatory tone said, "Troll brother!" Then he pulled a double edged dagger from behind his back. Simentoo figured he had finally met his end. The goblin continued to speak, fear palpable in his voice. "We want no troll enemies."

The goblin stepped forward cutting Simentoo's bindings. The goblin pointing toward Simentoo's companions said. "Take friends and go." Then with a gesture he ordered the others freed. The goblin bowed before Simentoo and asked for his forgiveness, and then the goblins faded away into the darkness.

The five companions standing in the darkness against the background of a dying fire were astonished. Jarret, looking at Simentoo, curiosity painted across his face, asked, "What was that all about?" Simentoo retrieved the Life Stone. He held it in the palm of his hand so that everyone could see the stone which radiated a warm and comforting light before he tucked it back into the pouch.

Talok, impressed, asked, "When did you come by that and what did you do to earn one of those? Trolls don't give those out lightly." Simentoo explained how he had come into possession of the stone.

Dawn was beginning to break. Kanef said, "We best be moving before our former hosts have a change of heart." "That won't happen," said Talok. "Like they said, they don't want any problems with the trolls."

Crysillnia asked, "The stone is so beautiful. Why do the goblins fear it so much?" "They don't fear the stone. They fear the fact that since he is in possession of the stone, he is considered a troll brother and anyone whom kills a troll brother will have to face the wrath of the trolls," replied Talok.

The goblins had left them their gear and weapons. So they quickly gathered their possessions and moved out nibbling on jerked meat. The parrot returned squawking shrilly, setting everyone's nerves on edge.

Talok picked up a stone and chucked it at the noise box. "Watch it dwarf," quipped the parrot. "You almost hit me." "That was my intention," snapped the surly dwarf. "You scare me like that again, and I'll have your gizzard for supper." To illustrate his last statement, the dwarf licked his lips.

The ground under their feet began to quake ominously. "So parrot, which way do we go?" asked Kanef, irritably. "Follow me," said the parrot. There numbers shrunk by one, they continued their arduous journey.

CHAPTER 13

Tanof pushed his plate away, and leaned back in his chair, hands behind his head. He watched the patrons in the smoky little tavern frolic. Many were drinking, some were singing bawdy songs, others were passed out slouching over tables or in their chairs, and a fight broke out across the room.

A woman caught Tanof's eye. She was moving from table to table engaging the tavern's patrons in conversation. Most just waved her off but some pushed her away violently. Tanof guessed she was a prostitute trying to hock her wares for which she couldn't find any buyers.

The woman approached Tanof with a magnanimous but twisted smile. She had a voluptuous body. Her bodice was cut low, barely able to contain her firm round breasts, but her face was badly scarred.

She asked Tanof in a whiny, nearly begging tone, "Would you like a roll?" "Not interested," said Tanof with a hard and callous edge. Kneeling beside Tanof, the woman ran her hand sensuously up his leg to his groin. She was trying desperately to seduce Tanof. Tanof, with an iron grip, grasped the woman's hand, squeezing hard enough to bring tears to her eyes, and pushed it away.

The woman stood up cursing Tanof and making snide remarks. "Like boys, huh!" Then she giggled loudly. Tanof, angry, stood up and back-handed the woman. The power of the blow sent the woman reeling backwards against another table. The table capsized sending the woman and the drunken occupants tumbling to the floor in heap of flailing arms and fluttering petticoats. "Leave me alone, whore," he said.

One of the men that had been knocked to the floor stood up rather unsteadily and shouted, "That's no way to treat a lady!" He then looked down at the woman and continued, "No matter how ugly she is." The man stood a head taller than Tanof and was twice as wide across the shoulders. His scarred face was covered with a unkempt, drool streaked, black beard.

Bawling, like an angry bull, he charged. Tanof wasn't intimidated by the large man. He coolly sidestepped the charge. Then he slipped his dagger from its sheath and drove into the man's back as he passed, up to the hilt. The dagger penetrated the man's lung, preventing him from screaming.

The combined force of the skewered man's momentum and Tanof's blow drove the man into the wall. The dying man tried futilely to take air into his blood filled lungs. Blood flowed from his mouth as he slid down the wall into a writhing heap of flesh on the tavern floor.

Tanof walked up to the dying miscreant and pulled his dagger from the man's back just as he took his last breath. Tanof wiped his bloody dagger on the dead man's shoulder to clean its blade. A hush had fallen over the tavern. Tanof gave everyone in the tavern a challenging glance. No one took up the challenge.

The woman still lying on the floor looked up at Tanof, fear etched on her face. When Tanof gave her a hard look, she turned her head. Tanof picked a mug of ale off of a nearby table and swilled it. He slammed the empty mug on the rough hewn table. He wiped his mouth with the back of his sleeve and said, "Killing makes me thirsty." Then he abruptly left the tavern.

Tanof merged with the street traffic. Daylight was waning. He needed to find a place to spend the night. He had conducted his business with Canshious and would leave town in the early morning. The man he had just killed would probably have friends looking to avenge his death.

Tanof was in a small, one street town called Thieves Den in the Elata Mountains. The dwellings were carved into the multicolored, folded sandstone, canyon walls. The long narrow and winding canyon was nearly siege proof and impossible to assault with an army of any size.

This made it a perfect hideout for criminals of all sorts and that was the sole purpose for this town's existence. The town was run by Canshious. He offered safe haven to anyone trying to escape the law for a price. If you didn't have money, he would ask for services in lieu of payment.

Tanof's purpose for coming to this hole in the mountains was to sell Canshious the intelligence he had collected while in Caspar. Tanof had no idea why Canshious wanted this information and didn't care. He had been paid well and that's all that mattered. Smiling, he rattled the cold hard coins in his purse.

Tanof began to shiver. There was a cold icy wind funneling through the canyon. Snow had begun to fall. Tanof had forgotten his cloak in the tavern and thought it better he not go back for it. So he went to the stables on the out skirts of town to fetch his spare.

By the time he reached the stables it was dark, but there was a full moon that peeked through the occasional snow burst. Tanof decided not to stay the night in Thieves Den. He saddled his mount and headed down the narrow, rocky, and treacherous trail leading out of the canyon.

CHAPTER 14

The parrot was explaining the dangers of the Elf Woods to his temporary wards. The sun was rising on the crisp and frosty morning. Crysillnia was rubbing her arms in an attempt to coax the blood closer to the surface.

It had taken the travelers two more days, after their captors had freed them, to reach the Elf Woods. They had spent a cold and haunting night at the edge of the forest. They still dared not light a fire. They not only feared the goblins but didn't want to draw some horrible magic creature from the Elf Woods.

Crysillnia's nerves were beginning to fray from the constant and shrill chatter of the parrot. She couldn't wait until the annoying creature left them. Then she began to have feelings of guilt for her unkind thoughts. The parrot was only trying to help.

"Be sure you don't stray from the trail," said the parrot. "There are many dangers lurking within the dark recesses of the Elf Woods. They are not necessarily evil, but the danger they pose is inherent in their nature. These magical creatures are attracted to the living and are unaware of the harm they may inflict in their curiosity."

"Is this path the wisest choice?" questioned Simentoo skeptically. "Considering our present situation this is the safest and shortest path. The trail is enchanted and, as long, as we stay on it, we are safe" answered the bird.

A chill trailed down Crysillnia's spine as she peered deep into the forest. She could feel the pulsating power of the woods. She shivered involuntarily. The woods emanated a low rhythmic humming sound. If one listened close enough, it sounded like a chorus of voices singing in an unintelligible language.

The parrot led the five companions into the woods. The parrot cautioned, "Stay together and don't lose sight of the person in front of you."

Simentoo balked at this statement. "Wait! I thought the trail was suppose to be safe." "There is nothing in this world without risk and this place is more dangerous than most," answered the parrot tartly. Simentoo, with an incredulous demeanor, said, "That is a rather ambiguous statement." "That is the only answer I have for you," said the parrot truculently.

Crysillnia, tiring of this discussion, said, "Let's move on before we lose more daylight and maybe we can get through this haunted place quickly." Simentoo reluctantly acquiesced and led them into the woods. As they entered the forest, Crysillnia glimpsed a brightly shimmering object embedded in a boulder.

Curiosity piqued, she was drawn toward the light. It was a plaque, engraved with intricate runes, embedded in the stone. Crysillnia was mesmerized by the beautiful artwork that had gone into this plaque.

She was so taken by the plaque that she reached out to rub her fingers over the wonderfully enchanting runes. Crysillnia was jolted out of her revere by a rough hand grabbing her shoulder. She could hear someone speaking but the voice was unintelligible.

She was angered by this interruption and the buzzing in her head the voice created. The buzzing finally stopped, and she could now make out the words. "No! No, Crysillnia! Don't touch that! It's an Elf Magic Rune Plaque! It will kill you!" shouted the voice emphatically. Comprehension began to infiltrate her consciousness and dissipate the magical lure of the plaque.

Crysillnia finally recognized the tormenting voice that pulled her back from the brink of disaster. It had been Jarret's voice and hand that had broken the spell cast by the rune plaque. She was staggered by the mental repercussions of the broken spell.

Instinctively, she knew why she had been subjected to the spell of the rune plaque. It was her inherent magic that had drawn the attack. It was a defensive attack on an alien magic that trespassed and didn't belong in the realm of elf magic.

Crysillnia leaned on Jarret's shoulder for support. She was exhausted by the struggle between the two differing magic energies. The human magic rooted in the spirit and elf magic rooted in the power of the land.

Crysillnia sat down to rest and Jarret went on to explain the purpose of the plaque, "The plaque was set here to keep the trails open and safe, and to protect the elf lands. There are plaques throughout the elf woods which keep the magic in balance. These plaques are what creates the low humming sound which is a sign that all is in balance."

Everyone listened intently to Jarret's explanation. Finally, Crysillnia felt a resurgence of energy. She stood, and taking the lead said, "Lets move on." The others followed without protest.

*   *   *

Deep within the Elf Woods a dark and sinister being roused itself from a long slumber, casting a deep chill over the immediate vicinity. The manacling entity took flight, casting a dark and dangerous shadow across the forest floor. The shadow inhibited all light and warmth from caressing the fauna and flora below. The forest life, plant or animal, magical or mundane, fierce or timid, quaked with fear, when touched by the shadow.

Once the shadow passed' the fortunate ones were dead, for the ones still alive went mad. The creature was flying in an ever widening spiral so as not to miss a single inch of the forest below.

The creatures in the forest were running confused and frightened. The trees and ground cover plants wilted as their life energy was drained for this dark creature from the abyss of despair fed on the life forces of others.

A small winged creature watched in anguish at the destruction. The small creature stayed out of reach of the darkness. Then, like a blink, the creature disappeared as the destruction of the Elf Woods was methodically carried out.

*   *   *

They were deep within the Elf Woods when the sun set. The darkness of the night seemed almost hostile and under the canopy of the forest the daylight was squelched quickly. Crysillnia thought to herself that she felt like a captive to the darkness of the night. She watched as the men bustled to set up camp. She felt strangely attuned to this haunting place. Her senses were heightened to the magic of the forest. Crysillnia felt her magic stirring within her as if in response to the magic of the forest. She didn't know if this feeling was good or bad. Crysillnia was struck by an agonizing pain and fear. Something wasn't right in the forest. It was in pain. She didn't know from what or even how she knew but there was something definitely wrong. The disorienting emotion that had swept through her soul had gone as quickly as it had come.

Her attention was drawn back to her companions by a strange conversation that Kanef and Jarret were having. "Did you say not to light a fire?" asked Kanef. "Yes," replied Jarret. "And why not?" quizzed Kanef. "Because the trees wouldn't like it," answered Jarret nonchalantly.

Crysillnia couldn't see Kanef's face but could imagine the expression of incredulity framing it. "The trees wouldn't like it," repeated Kanef dubiously. Jarret chuckled before he continued his explanation.

"The trees are more aware in the Elf Woods. They are sentient, and they fear fire for obvious reasons. The trees will protect themselves if they feel threatened."

"Sentient!" exclaimed Kanef dubiously. "Yes," chimed in Talok. "There are some very dangerous trees in this forest if their ire is roused." "OK! OK! I believe you!" said Kanef as he raised his hands in a gesture of surrender.

"Another cold supper and night," commented Crysillnia in disappointment. Everyone dug out a piece of jerked meat and sat in silence. They chewed methodically and with little enthusiasm on the tough and tasteless meal.

*　　*　　*

A small gray rabbit sat near the Rune Plaque. It nibbled timidly at the sweet green scions at the base of the boulder. The rabbit stood up on its hind legs, eyes wide, nose twitching nervously, ears pricked, as it sniffed the air. Something had disturbed it, but the rabbit wasn't quite sure what.

The rabbit's keen eyesight was able to discern a darker shadow against the backdrop of the dark night. It was heading in his direction. The rabbit's curiosity over came its instinctive urge to flee.

Then a flash of blue light erupted from the shadow. The small and timid creature was taken by surprise and was unable to move quickly enough. The burst of energy hit the plaque dead center causing the plaque to disintegrate. The small gray creature was caught in the residual backlash from the bolt of energy, frying it on the spot.

*   *   *

Crysillnia awoke with a start. She wasn't sure why but there was a feeling of imbalance. The low and near inaudible rhythmic hum of the forest had changed. It had become a jumble of disconcerting and undisciplined noise.

Her magical instincts were setting off alarms in her head. She knew what was wrong. One or more of the rune plaques had been destroyed. Her stomach began to knot with fear. The rune plaques were what kept the magical creatures of the forest at bay and made the trail safe to traverse. "Awake! Awake!" she cried.

Simentoo was standing watch. He sensed something dire had just, happened. He couldn't put his finger on it but something was wrong. He began to search the darkness and could sense nothing approaching but something was definitely wrong.

Simentoo was startled by Crysillnia's cries. He turned back towards the camp searching for an evidently very cunning foe but could see nothing.

The others awoke in various states of awareness. They reached for weapons preparing to defend themselves. A deep screeching wail emanated from the forest sending waves of cold chills down the backs and raising the hair on the arms of the five companions.

Jarret, attuned to the pulse of the magical forest having lived in its shadow all of his life, knew what must have happened, and reacted. "Quickly, into the forest! We're in great danger here! Keep together!"

A loud roaring sound erupted in the distance and increased in crescendo as it came nearer. "Hurry! Hurry!" coaxed Jarret urgently. "Chaos is rapidly approaching." No one needed any further warning. They quickly entered the dangerous and enchanted environ of the forest. The once protective trail, now behind them, erupted into a conflagration of confusion and chaos. The repercussion from the eruption of broken magic knocked everyone violently to the ground as it raced along the trail, destroying everything in its path.

CHAPTER 15

Alaquin was sitting by the Peaceful Lake communing with the environment. Her revere was broken by a twinkle of light. A small winged creature appeared before her. She opened her hand palm up. The small winged creature landed on the proffered hand.

The beautiful and delicate creature was a ganlion, the magical, forest messengers of the elves. The ganlion looked like a miniature lion with wings. The male was adorned with an extravagant golden mane which encircled its neck, flowed down its back terminating in a tuft of fur at the end of its tail. The female had no striking features but was covered in dark tan fur.

The small creature displayed no fear of Alaquin. Alaquin was alarmed by the ganlion's exhaustion. Alaquin waited patiently for the ganlion to regain its composure. The ganlion's tiny but sharp claws pricked her palm.

The ganlion was an amazing creature. They appeared to disappear in a twinkle of light but that was a trick of lighting. The ganlion's gossamer wings were covered with a shiny film. When a ganlion takes flight it moves so fast, it projects the illusion of disappearance.

Alaquin pulled a flask from her belt and deposited a drop of greenish liquid on the palm of her hand. The ganlion consumed the liquid voraciously. Appetite satiated, the small creature began to preen its wings which indicated that it was rested and would soon be ready to communicate. Finally finished with its grooming, the small creature began to relate its message to Alaquin.

Alaquin had to listen intently because the high pitched tone of the ganlion was hard to understand. To human ears, it sounded like the buzzing of an insect. Elves were the only ones that could hear the spoken word of the ganlion.

Alaquin was alarmed by what the ganlion had witnessed but didn't know what it meant. She decided to hurry back to her village and relate the ganlion's message to the Council of Elders. Alaquin was a young elf and wasn't well versed in elf lore. She lifted her hand above her head and gave the ganlion a light toss. The creature took off and quickly disappeared in a twinkle of light.

Alaquin didn't possess the typical physical attributes of an elf. Elves were a tall slender people with narrow faces and silver hair. They appeared to be a delicate creature which was far from the truth. Elves were a strong and durable people.

Alaquin was shorter and more stocky than other elves. She had a rounder face framed by bright yellow hair which she wore shoulder length. Her eyes were a strange shade of green while all other elves eyes were black. Her nose was petite and slightly upturned at the tip. Where elves ears ended in sharp points, Alaquin's were more rounded. They were still pointed but not as well defined as a normal elf ear. Alaquin was more rounded and voluptuous than the normal elf female.

According to the elf's image of beauty, Alaquin was ugly and revolting, but in human terms, she would be considered quite beautiful and desirable. If not for her slightly upward curving and pointed ears, she could be taken for human.

Alaquin was of marriageable age but she had no suitors because rumor had it that her mother had had a human lover and that Alaquin was the cursed progeny of this unacceptable relationship. Therefore, if any boy showed an interest in Alaquin, the boy's parents would put a stop to it.

Alaquin's mother died giving birth to her which was rare among elves and considered a bad omen. She didn't know who her father was, and had no way of finding out, and her mother's family refused to accept her which left Alaquin without a family lineage. This lack of lineage labeled her an outcast.

Shasinook, the Chief Elder of the Council of Elders, took her in to provide for her needs and to be sure she was properly educated in The Way of the Elves. To him, etiquette was all important for maintaining discipline and harmony in the Elf Nation. Many elves considered him overzealous in his attitude towards proper elf behavior. She received no love from the elder and his family, but she had been well taken care of and educated.

Alaquin ran recklessly between the randomly placed hovels, creating havoc and drawing curses from irate elves that she happened to blunder into nearly knocking a few off their feet. Alaquin slowed down and approached Shasinook's small but well kept hovel quietly and with proper respect. For Shasinook was known for setting magical reminders for rude and disrespectful elves.

She stood quietly and erect, her arms crossed her chest in respect. "Ah, Alaquin my dear. How may I help you? Please come in," came a shallow and wavering voice from inside the hovel.

Alaquin, no longer able to contain her excitement, rushed headlong into the small hovel, nearly knocking the elderly occupant down, which she regretted, because a large bucket of water appeared out of nowhere, drenching the impudent elf girl.

Sopping wet, vexation quite visible in her demeanor, Alaquin stood quietly and waited for a sign from the elder elf. Shasinook, anger fading from his wrinkled face, asked, "Where is my apology?" Alaquin knelt before the elder elf, one knee touching the ground and said, "Please forgive this impetuous elf girl."

Shasinook looked down on the prostrate elf girl. The corners of his mouth down turned down in displeasure. "That is a rather weak apology, but I will accept it. You may stand." The elder elf continued to scrutinize Alaquin with an admonishing demeanor before asking, "Okay, young lady, what is so important that you nearly maim a decrepit old elf?"

Finally, the stone faced, old elf grinned at Alaquin. She sighed with relief and then, albeit incoherently, blurted out her encounter with the ganlion. "Girl!" exclaimed Shasinook. "Slow down, and quit your blubbering. I can't understand a thing you're saying."

Alaquin did as the old elf commanded. After finishing her story, Shasinook asked her several poignant questions. Shasinook collapsed into a large high-backed wooden chair. The color blanched from his face with fear mirrored in his eyes.

He mumbled more to himself than speaking to Alaquin. "The Chaos Demon." Then without further comment or explanation, he left the hovel. Alaquin, confused by the elder elf's rude behavior, followed him.

Alaquin welcomed the warm and comforting rays of the sun. She didn't much care for closed in places. Alaquin wandered between the elf huts. The sun was beginning to settle over the horizon.

She rounded the corner of one of the huts and spotted a close friend. "Chandok!" she hollered, waving her hands, frantically, in an attempt to draw his attention. He ignored her. A chill raced down her back. Chandok appeared to be in a trance.

Her heart weighed heavy. Chandok must have joined the cult of the Shadow Elves. She lowered her head and began to weep, feeling sorry for herself and Chandok. Chandok was one of the few elves that was attracted to her and had accepted her for who she was. He had promised her, no matter what others thought, that he would marry her someday.

Even though she knew that talk of marriage was all bravado on Chandok's part, she felt a great loss, because once an elf joined the cult, they no longer associated with non-cult members. She had lost her only friend.

The cult had a crucial effect on elf society. It was draining useful elf skills from the populace. Once an elf became a Dark Elf, they withdrew from elf society.

Alaquin, not wanting anyone to see her cry, fled the village. She wildly raced through the forest, sobbing uncontrollably. Finally exhausted by her maddened dash, she collapsed to the ground. She lay in a heap on the forest floor and cried herself to sleep. A shadowy creature approached the prone elf girl and briefly placed his hand on the top of her head and then slipped back into the forest.

Alaquin began to dream of darkness, a deep darkness. She didn't know where she was. She began to wander through the darkness. She felt that she was on a quest. She was searching for something but was unaware of what or why. The darkness closed in around her. Alaquin was cold, so cold. The cold ate away at her Essence. The darkness was trying to steal her very being.

She awoke emanating a piercing scream. It was well after sunset. Alaquin sensed something was wrong. There was a palpable and deep dark foreboding welling up from deep inside of her. The darkness and air of the forest were oppressive. She couldn't catch her breath. Then the cacophony began.

Elves have excellent night vision and once Alaquin's eyes adjusted to the darkness, she was shocked at the madness she was witnessing. Small animals were attacking much larger creatures, and the larger beasts refused to defend themselves. Some of them would even cower down and allow themselves too be torn to shreds. Alaquin, fearing for her safety, searched frantically for a place to hide. As she scuttled along the ground, so as not to draw attention to herself, she happened across a small, unoccupied cave under a huge rock. She wiggled and squirmed through the small and restrictive aperture.

She was sure this was a fox's den. The acrid scent of urine was sickening but she had no choice. She curled up into a ball and closed her eyes. There she huddled for the remainder of the night in abject terror, shivering with fear, as the outside world whorled in madness.

She dozed off occasionally into fitful bouts of sleep only to be awakened by maddened screams of fear and pain. Finally, fatigue won out, and she fell into a deep sleep. Alaquin awoke with a start, flailing her arms violently as if defending herself. She looked around her small refuge searching for an assailant, but there was none.

She laughed nervously and then yelled, "It was the light!" Then she repeated to herself, speaking more meekly. "It was the light that startled me." To assure herself, she reached for the thin beam of light that penetrated the dark recesses of her refuge.

Alaquin waved her hand back and forth through the narrow beam of sunlight. She watched the light dance across the back of her hand, then she cupped them as if trying to capture the ethereal beam. "Alaquin, what are you doing! You're acting as mad as the forest creatures last night," she scolded herself out loud.

She moved towards the opening of the cave apprehensively. She slowly stuck her head out of the aperture. She looked around and listened for any signs of danger. The forest was quiet except for a high pitched and disconcerting whining sound.

Alaquin extracted herself with some difficulty from the cave. Her first attempt to stand ended with her collapsing to the ground. Her legs had gone to sleep and were cramping badly. Before trying to stand again, she massaged them vigorously. Once the blood returned to her oxygen starved muscles and the painful tingling ceased, she ventured to stand again. This time she was successful, albeit rather unsteadily.

Fussily, she brushed at the smelly bits of dirt and grass that had clung stubbornly to her clothing, with little success. She smelled of urine. Realizing the futility of her efforts, she gave up. "I'll just have to find a place to wash," she said determinedly. Although a bit wobbly, she headed out through the ravaged forest. She wandered aimlessly, not going in any particular direction. Alaquin was finally brought to her senses by cries, groans and curses from an ensuing battle. Silently, she glided towards the commotion. She couldn't possibly imagine anyone daring to enter the Elf Woods.

Then the memories from last night resurfaced. Maybe the elves were engaging the Chaos Demon Elder Shasinook mentioned last night. Alaquin burst forth into a small meadow and was taken aback by what she saw.

CHAPTER 16

Crysillnia rushed into the forest but found it difficult to stay close to the others. The magic of the place confounded her senses. She crashed through low standing bushes which punished her severely by tearing at her legs, leaving brush burns and lacerations.

Fear took root as she fled wildly through the forest. She thought she sensed something pursuing her. All Crysillnia could think of was flight and escape. She screamed and collapsed when a hand reached out of the darkness and grabbed her shoulder. She began to sob. Then she said, "Don't, father! Please, don't." Her stepfather materialized before her eyes, out of the darkness, hand raised to strike and pummel her into submission.

"It's only me," said Jarret with concern. Jarret stooped enveloping the frightened and sobbing woman in his arms to comfort her. He rocked her back and forth, gently caressing her shortened and dirt matted hair.

Crysillnia quickly regained her composure and pushed Jarret away, embarrassment mirrored in her face. "I'm sorry for my moment of weakness," she apologized. "There is nothing to apologize for," Jarret reassured her.

Jarret abruptly changed focus. "We must find the others and quickly. We are all in great danger." Fortunately the others were nearby. Once they were back together, Jarret, with apprehension etched on his young face and distaste coloring his voice, said, "We need to leave the forest immediately. The magical creatures within the confines of this accursed place will be attracted to our Essence."

Simentoo, while listening to Jarret, was keeping a vigilant eye. Simentoo spoke, "Where did that pesky bird disappear to this time?" The dwarf answered, his voice reflecting sarcasm and contempt' "Flew off with his tail feathers tucked."

A shrill screech penetrated the darkness cast by the canopy of the forest, and the parrot flew out of a nearby treetop. He lighted on a gnarled and scraggy limb near the huddled group. "I am still here, you big oaf!" snapped the indignant fowl.

The dwarf, no longer able to contain his anger, freed one of the hammers hanging on his belt. He threw the heavy maul with alacrity and unerring precision. The huge missile struck the limb that the bird was perched on, near the trunk of the tree, severing it. Limb and bird fell to the ground in an unceremonious heap.

The bird was spared injury by the plush moss that covered the forest floor. Everyone's attention was focused on the unfortunate fowl. The parrot picked himself up and staggered around in a circle as he regained his equilibrium. It was all they could do to keep from laughing.

The parrot ruffled its feathers in indignation. The bird raised his head and glared at the amused spectators. The petulant bird emitted the shrillest screech yet and in its anger, it temporarily change. It took the form of a small putrid-green, scaley, webbed-wing reptile.

Simentoo's warrior instincts began to tingle as the parrot or scaley creature squawked a warning a split-second before the attack. Simentoo unsheathed his broadsword and turned to face the threat. The creatures were long, snake like, sinuous creatures, with hundreds of legs on their underbelly. Jarret and the others fell in beside Simentoo, weapons drawn, forming a defensive line between Crysillnia and the snake-like creatures.

The creatures, their surprise attack foiled, approached the defenders captiously, flicking forked tongues in agitation. The creatures opened their mouths wide baring razor sharp teeth in hopes of rattling their intended prey, panicking them into fleeing so that they could pick them off one at a time. There were better than six of the horrible creatures.

One of them approached close and Simentoo lopped off the careless creature's tongue. A bone chilling shriek of pain emanated from the serpent like monster as it retreated. The others keened in empathy for their comrade's injury which nearly unnerved the companions. Even the usually undauntable Simentoo was slightly shaken.

The creatures, facing their wounded compatriot, formed a circle around it. They began to dance in a strange gyrating manner, heads low to the ground. Then they began to sway in unison to the rhythm of their keening. Then, abruptly, they fell silent. Except for the low vibrating hum, an ominous silence fell over the forest.

Simentoo motioned for the others to back off slowly, but as quickly as the attack had halted, the creatures resumed the assault. Crysillnia's defenders formed a circle around her.

The strange sinuous creatures began to circle their victims moving faster and faster. They tightened the circle with each revolution. Then as if orchestrated, they lunged at the group of five which left each of the companions no choice but to fend for themselves.

Crysillnia, armed only with a dagger, dove to the right as one of the creatures attacked her. Head tucked, she rolled away from the assault. She ended her roll in a standing position, dagger drawn at the ready.

Alaquin, distressed by the plight of the five unfortunate travelers, reacted instinctively. Alaquin began to chant and form rune signs in the air before her. The serpent creatures, startled by the elf girl, ceased their attack and focused their attention on the new adversary.

Realizing that the elf girl was calling on elf magic, they attacked. She pushed her hands forward, palms open. The, multicolored rune letters, suspended in the air, floated in the direction of the snake like monsters.

The tingling feel of magic in the air was palpable as the runes circled the companions protectively and them moved out from them. The runes encircled each of the horrible snake-like creatures, entrapping them in an envelope of magic. The sinuous creatures began to pulsate with the multicolored glow of the runes. Then a burst of cascading energy pulses radiated from the creatures.

The flashes were so intense that the companions had to shield their eyes. When they looked back on their former attackers, they were taken aback. The many legged creatures were now wriggling on the ground, legs gone, wailing in agony and fear. The creatures slithered away into the protective embrace of the forest.

CHAPTER 17

The bedraggled group emerged from the enchanted forest onto The Plains of the Dragons. Crysillnia gasped with exhilaration at the unexpected beauty. The wildflowers were in full bloom. A spectacular carpet of red, blue, yellow and many variations on each of these colors were arrayed at her feet.

Crysillnia commented, "I almost feel ashamed to trample such beauty underfoot." Crysillnia was surprised when Talok grunted in agreement. She glanced over at Talok and grinned. The dwarf appeared to be mesmerized by the resplendent beauty of the plains.

Alaquin broke the ambiance of the moment. "I must be leaving. I have to warn the elders about the chaos reigning over the far forest, but before I leave, I have a question." "What is your question?" asked Kanef.

Alaquin looked over at the parrot, contemptuously. "Why are you traveling with a demon?" "A demon!" blurted out Talok. "I knew it! I knew there was something strange about that changeling." Everyone but Alaquin and Crysillnia reached for their weapons.

"Hold on, wait! Please hear me out! I mean you no harm!" Squawked the parrot. Realizing the charade was over, the demon shed its disguise. The creature was oozing a putrid black slime. It sort of looked like an oversized bat. "I truly am here too assist you. There is a small faction of demons that wish to break free from the Horde and we feel that we can be valuable allies. I was dispatched to help you navigate the forest and warn you. The Horde knows what you are up to."

The demon, finished with his explanation and fearing reprisals from the humans, began to flap its wings erratically and a bit comically. The breeze that gently caressed the plains caught the demon's wings and lifted the grotesque creature into the air. The creature, once in flight, appeared more graceful.

The demon caught a more vigorous updraft which sent it soaring into the azure sky. The misshapen creature, silhouetted against the setting sun, yelled back, "My mission is complete. I will leave you now."

All stood in silence, confused, not sure what to make of the demon's last revelation. Alaquin broke the mood by reiterating her need to depart. Crysillnia responded, "Thank you, Alaquin, for your timely rescue and for warning us about the demon." The elf girl turned and faded back into the forest, leaving the five companions alone as the cloying night mists began to form hauntingly at the forest's edge. A chill of foreboding raced down Crysillnia's back.

The others began to set up camp for the night, and Crysillnia climbed to the top of a huge, strangely out-of-place boulder to sit and think. The Mountain of the Dragons was a hulking, dark blue silhouette on the far side of the plains. What dark mysteries do those mountains hold she thought.

The sun dropped over the horizon taking the heat of the day with it. It was going to be a damp and chilly night, so she pulled her cloak tight. Heat emanating from the rock helped cut the night air chill. She pulled her knees tight against her chest and wrapped her arms around them. Exhausted, caution lulled, Crysillnia fell into a fitful sleep.

Crysillnia was awakened by the aroma of roasting meat. Her hunger piqued, she scuttled off the rock, nearly landing on top of Talok, who was standing guard over her, concealed within the dark shadow cast by the boulder.

Seeing Talok standing guard made her feel warm inside. She knew, at that moment that no matter the circumstance, he would follow her. Guided by the pale light of the moon and the glow from the dancing campfire, she approached the camp with Talok in close tow.

Jarret was turning a spit over the fire, which held several small carcasses. Simentoo was sitting near the fire tending to his array of weapons, the consummate warrior. And Kanef sat further away from the fire, back against a tree. He appeared to be deep in thought.

Crysillnia sat on the ground next to Jarret. Her mouth was watering with anticipation. Jarret, smiling, handed Crysillnia his dagger with a steaming hunk of meat on the tip.

Crysillnia nibbled at the tasty morsel. She turned her attention to Kanef. He was the quiet brooding type. She believed he carried a great tragedy on his shoulders. She often caught Kanef watching her as if she reminded him of someone. This made her feel uncomfortable.

Crysillnia quickly turned her attention to Simentoo when he dropped one of his weapons. He was dedicated, brave, and unyielding. Crysillnia sensed a sadness about him. Although he was an elite soldier, she sensed that he was also a bit of a scholar. Her deduction was based on the way he expressed himself and his tendency to observe things around him and note them in his journal.

Talok approached the fire. He sliced a big chunk of meat from one of the roasting carcasses. Crysillnia's attention, now on Talok, sensed a deep seated anger in the taciturn dwarf, from what she could only guess.

Jarret was a hunter and a jester. He always appeared to be in good spirits. Jarret was attracted to her as she was to him. He was fun to be around. She sensed no sadness or regrets, just an acceptance of circumstances as they were. She didn't know whether this was innate or a manner cultivated by the elves that had raised him.

Crysillnia's thoughts were broken by the night's chill. The dew was heavy, and the grasses bowed their seed-crowned heads obsequiously. The grasses were so moisture laden that one got the impression that it had been raining. A fog was rising and insinuating itself between the companions. Shivering, she pulled her cloak tighter about her and sidled closer to the coals of the dying fire.

Crysillnia awoke again to the smell of roasting meat. She had fallen asleep sitting by the fire. She stretched her cold, cramped, and stiff muscles. She stood slowly, her stiff muscles protesting painfully and shucked her cloak, basking in the warmth of the morning sun. The others were doing various chores preparing for their departure.

They ate their morning meal quickly, with little conversation. They picked up their packs and headed toward the mountains. The mountains were a misty blue shadow against the back-drop of a azure sky dotted with fluffy white clouds. About midmorning, they came a cross a deeply rutted and obviously seldom used wagon road. Jarret commented, "Not much traffic on this part of the plains." Crysillnia, basking in the warmth of the shining jewel in the sky and absorbing the sweet aromas wafting in the gentle breeze, caressing the plains, asked, "Why not?" Jarret answered, "The soil is poor and the farmers are afraid of the forest. See those small groves of trees scattered across the plains? They're called Quignut trees. They are about the only thing, other than the wild grasses, that flourish on this part of the plains. These wagon tracks are made by Quignut Gathers. The nuts bring a good price on the open market."

They followed the road since it headed in the general direction of the mountains. They had only been on the road for a short time when Crysillnia spotted two people leaving a Quignut grove, heading in their direction. After close scrutiny, Crysillnia was able to discern that it was a man and woman.

Simentoo had also noticed the approaching couple. The woman was worn and truncated from years of hard work, and the man was tall and muscular with leathery, and sun cracked-skin, but it was evident that he had also lived a hard life. The woman was yoked to a two wheeled cart. She was struggling arduously to pull the cart across the grassy plain.

The woman slipped and fell to her knees. Crysillnia was now close enough to hear the woman whimper and groan in agony. The woman struggled to her feet with extreme difficulty and continued her arduous task.

The wretched couple entered the road a short distance ahead of Crysillnia and her companions. They trudged by the small troop, heads down, in fear that they might provoke an unwanted attack. Crysillnia turned when she heard the poor woman drop to her knees once again, obviously exhausted. The cart was loaded to the top with nuts.

The man cursed at the woman and slapped her across the back of the head. The woman began to weep as she desperately tried to rise. It appeared to be an effort in futility. Crysillnia noticed Simentoo's muscles tense. He retraced his steps and approached the man.

The man didn't notice Simentoo until he was almost upon him. The man faced Simentoo, his face twisted into a cruel scowl which quickly changed to a broad smile. The man scooped a handful of nuts from the cart. He was hoping that Simentoo was interested in purchasing some nuts.

The man's face blanched and he dropped the nuts when the soft but deadly whisper of sword and sheath parting company echoed across the lonely expanse of the plain. Simentoo struck the man's upper shoulder with the flat of the sword. The man staggered backwards in pain and shock from the impact of the blow.

The woman let out a small yelp and cringed in fear. The man dropped to his knees obsequiously before Simentoo and cried in fear for his life, "You can have what ever you want. My wagon, my wife or both, if you wish! Just spare my life!"

The woman collapsed where she sat, fear overcoming her completely. Simentoo leaned over the man and whispered something into his ear. The man's eyes opened wider, and he became even more pale. Simentoo then approached the woman. She looked up at him, completely incapacitated by fear.

Simentoo offered her his hand. The woman looked fearfully at the proffered hand. Simentoo emphasized his offer by opening his hand wider and dropping into a crouch so as not to be intimidating. The woman slowly and reluctantly placed her hand into Simentoo's.

Simentoo gently but firmly gripped the woman's hand. He stood up and pulled the woman to her feet. He bowed politely to the woman and said, "Have a good day, Milady." The woman, not sure how to respond to such unexpected kindness, wiped the tears from her eyes, smearing more dirt on her, already dirt encrusted face, gave Simentoo a weak smile and curtsied awkwardly.

Simentoo sheathed his weapon and gave the still prostrate man a withering glare. The man looked down at the ground fearing further retribution. Simentoo returned to the group with a quite contented expression. He said nothing, and they asked nothing.

The sun was waning when Jarret exclaimed, "Look. See the fields of grain! We are nearing the inhabited parts of the plain. There is another grove of Quignut trees, probably the last we'll see for awhile. The nuts are delicious. Lets go pick a few."

Standing under one of the trees, Talok was looking up at the brown oval-shaped nuts. "How in the name of the Gods are we going to pick them?" Crysillnia had the same thought as she peered up into the tree with the grayish-brown bark. The tree was very tall and slender with large, dark-green, tear-drop shaped leaves.

Jarret searched the ground diligently. He stooped and picked up a rock. With a sly smile, he hefted the rock, tossing it into the air as if he was gauging its weight. He said,

"Watch." Peering into the tree tops, he put two fingers to his lips and let out a shrill whistle.

Suddenly, as if out of nowhere, small creatures appeared. The creatures were covered with a light gray fur with red stripes running the length of their flanks. They had long, furry, red, prehensile tails. Their front legs were shorter than their larger more powerful back legs, but their feet resembled human hands.

Some of the creatures were hanging by their long tails while others perched precariously on the rounded surfaces of the tree limbs. They chattered and whistled incessantly, creating a deafening cacophony. Jarret shouted over the bedlam, "Better run!" Then he tossed the rock at one of the creatures in the tree.

The rock rattled around in the tree before it fell to the ground. Jarret turned, grinning from ear to ear, and began to run with the others close behind. The creatures, in retaliation for the unprovoked attack, pulled nuts from the tree and began to pelt the fleeing companions.

Kanef cursed when a nut bounced off his head with a resounding thud. Talok said, "This is a rather painful way to pick nuts." Jarret laughed and replied tauntingly, "Would you have climbed one of those trees?"

Out of throwing range of the irate creatures, Jarret stopped. He was laughing uproariously. Wiping tears from his eyes, he said, "Quigrats are quite vengeful creatures." Kanef, a stern look on his face, rubbed the back of his head and said, "And they have a very good aim."

The Quigrats soon lost interest in their antagonists and faded back into the grove of trees. The companions gathered as many nuts as they could carry. It was nearing sunset so they set up camp for the night a short distance from the Quignut grove.

Crysillnia noticed Kanef sitting by himself. He had been silent since the death of his friend, Rollof. She cracked open one of the nuts with ease. All one had to do was squeeze the nuts along their seam and they popped open and revealed their fleshy white meat. The flavor of the nut was tantalizing. She had never eaten anything so tasty.

She greedily gulped down a few more nuts before she returned her attention to Kanef. He quickly averted his eyes when she looked over at him. He had been observing her again. This wasn't the first time she had caught him watching her. She sensed he was trying to reconcile something in his mind about her. What, she didn't know. Satisfied with their evening meal of nuts, everyone except the person whom had guard duty, curled up by the fire to sleep.

CHAPTER 18

It was slightly after midday when they came across a small but bustling farming community. Hordes of refugees from the provinces ravaged by the war were funneling through the village, creating chaos. "Where are all those people going?" asked, a perplexed Crysillnia. "Dragon's Pass," answered Simentoo.

"Where's Dragon's Pass, and why are they going there?" Crysillnia continued. "It's the road that passes between the Elf Forest and Dragon's Mountain," continued Simentoo. "It leads to the Xlantan Plains beyond the mountains," chimed in Jarret.

Talok headed toward the village. "Let's wet our throats." Jarret mirthfully said, "I agree," as they shouldered their way through the throngs of people. Crysillnia had to shout to be heard over the cacophony of the crowded streets. "What's the name of this place?" Jarret, following behind her, answered, "Dragon's Peek. And before you ask. I'll explain where the name comes from. At one time, the dragons would fly over the village on a daily basis. They would harm nothing and no one. So the villagers figured the dragons were just curious and wanted a peek at the lowly humans. Thus Dragon's Peek."

*   *   *

Tanof was seated at a small but sturdy oak table in the back, near the kitchen, of a small, smoked-filled and poorly lit tavern. He liked to sit out of the way and near the rear door in case he needed to make a hasty exit. He was sipping on a mug of ale. He kept a sharp eye out for possible trouble.

The tavern was the main attraction in Dragon's Peek. The village was situated in the center of the Dragon's Plains and was the life's blood for the surrounding farmsteads. The village was usually a quiet, dusty, and insignificant farm village, but with the collapse of the Lenarian Kingdom and the death of the High King, that had ended.

The Provincial Kings had to use their forces to combat the invaders, so there were no troops available to combat crime which was running rampant. There was no safe place left in Lenar except for maybe Caspar, and King Falef wasn't allowing anyone to enter his province. That was the reason for the present exodus to the Xlantan Kingdom.

Tanof's attention was drawn to an escalating dispute on the other side of the barroom. The disagreement was over a barmaid. Tanof shook his head in disgust and mumbled to no one in particular, "Women, nothing but trouble, that's all they're good for."

The ring of weapons being drawn echoed across the tavern, and the room fell silent. Tanof scooted his chair away from the table, but no one noticed. Everyone's attention was focused on the two combatants, as they began to circle and feint.

Tanof stood, sipping from his mug, so that he could get a better view of the deadly entertainment. He stood in the shadows but had an excellent view of the combatants and the entryway. He was surprised when the door opened, and the black haired woman that he had spied in Caspar walked through entered the tavern. She had cut her hair but there was no mistaking that beautifully, chiseled face.

She projected an aura that caught everyone's attention. The circling and feinting men stopped. They no longer seemed to be concerned about their disagreement as they turned to watch the woman. Tanof couldn't shake the feeling that he should know this woman. She reminded him of someone from his past, but he didn't know whom.

The tavern remained silent, except for the noise from the street, as the tavern's patrons drank in the woman's beauty. The seemingly magical spell cast by the woman was broken when an odd looking dwarf entered behind her followed by three others. The tavern owner scurried over obsequiously to greet his new customers, as everyone else went back to what they were doing before the altercation. In fact, the combatants seemed to have forgotten their grievances.

"How may I help you?" "We would like a room, a bath and a meal," answered Crysillnia. "The meal and bath are possible but I have no vacancies," replied the tavern owner regretfully, as he wrung his hands nervously. Jarret began to protest but Crysillnia cut him short, "That will be fine."

The hostilities between the two men heated up again when one pushed the other, propelling him towards Tanof's table. The man, arms flailing as he tried regain his balance, capsized a table as he fell to the floor, sending plates, mugs, and patrons flying. The man rose from the floor, glaring dangerously at the man who had pushed him.

The first man, weapon in hand and screaming horrific curses, attacked. The fight that ensued was violent and bloody. When the final blows were struck, there were no winners. Both men lie gasping on the floor, dying.

Crysillnia, shaken by the violence, stood up, appetite gone. "Lets leave," she said. The others agreed, and they left the tavern. They left the village behind as they continued their trek to the mountains.

CHAPTER 19

Alaquin remained at the forest's edge until the strangers continued their journey next morning. She wanted to be sure nothing from the forest slipped out during the night to harass the travelers. Alaquin knew the mischievous nature of the magical creatures that made the forest their home. Some could be dangerous, but most were just annoying. She did have to turn some of the creatures back, but nothing dangerous ventured out. Alaquin headed back to her village in the central part of the forest. She needed to inform the Counsel of Elders about the strange happenings in the forest. She flitted through the forest like a wraith. During her travels, she passed through ravished sections of the forest. She was astonished and saddened at the absolute desolation.

Alaquin entered the village just before dusk. She became alarmed when she entered the deserted streets of the village. This was usually the most active part of the elf day. There should be elves bustling around haphazardly placed hovels, performing their end-of-day chores.

Alaquin quickly threaded her way between the humble elf homes. She assumed there was a Council Meeting. That would explain the empty streets. She was correct in her assumption. There was definite activity within The House of Elders.

Although the elves homes were unpretentious, the House of Elders was a large and extravagant, rectangular-shaped structure. It was large enough for all elves to be seated. The walls consisted of Elder Grape vines which had been trained on a lattice frame work and the roof was constructed of wooden shakes.

The Elder Grape was a food staple of the elves, plus it made a fine wine. The vines grew thick and luxuriant and never shed their leaves in the fall and winter. The fruit was a deep red bordering on purple with a shiny gloss when ripe, and the vines produced several crops throughout the year.

Alaquin approached the hidden entryway and whispered the magical password. The grapevines parted allowing her entrance. Elf magic sound-proofed the building, so that what was discussed in the building wouldn't escape and be absorbed by unintended ears. Alaquin silently and meekly entered the council house. She sat in the last row so as not to draw attention. Alaquin listened quietly.

It was unusual to have a council meeting in the middle of a cycle. All the Elders weren't present. Some were still in the forest attending to their duties.

The Elders were sitting on a circular stage in the center of the room, and the stage was surrounded by the rest of the elf populace from the village. Elves were very politically minded. The Elders were the legislative body, but for major decisions all elves had a vote.

The elves, sitting on pillow boughs, were listening intently to the heated discussion on the stage. The pillow bough was harvested from a special type of pine tree. The needles of the Pillow Pine were soft, fluffy, and aromatic. If not for the heated discussion, the scent from the pillow bough would have put her to sleep.

"That was decided yesterday," stated Kraarnok. "Natas is the humans problem. We have enough of our own with the Shadow Cult corrupting our youth and with the forest's magic being out of balance. We must deal with these problems first." "No!" Shouted someone near the stage. "You have another problem," continued the unknown voice. This rude and unprecedented interruption caused a low rumble of whispering. Elves were gawking and looking around them, trying to see who spoke out of turn.

Kraarnok pointed down at the crowd of agitated elves, and said, "You! Soothsayer! Why do you so rudely interrupt? And what problem are you speaking of?"

"I have seen in my dreams, the Chaos Demon, and he is abroad," answered the Soothsayer. Shocked gasps reverberated around the Council House which developed in to a low rumble of frightened whispers. The low rumble burst into a roar as frightened elves jumped to their feet, nervously looking around as if they expected the Chaos Demon to appear before them.

Kraarnok, taken aback by the Soothsayer's revelation, cried out with incredulity etched on his face, "I don't believe you!" This denial seemed to soothe the elves somewhat and helped quiet them.

"The Chaos Demon hasn't been awake for generations, if it even exists," argued Kraarnok. "There is someone in this room who has been in the presence of the Chaos demon and has witnessed its devastation," replied the Soothsayer.

The Soothsayer then pointed in Alaquin's direction. Alaquin tried to duck down, as the attention of everyone in the Council House focused on her, to little avail. She could hear some of the elves from across the room asking who the Soothsayer was pointing at.

Kraarnok's angry eyes focused on her. She felt as if those eyes would burn holes right through her. "Is this true?" Alaquin, unsure of herself and unsure of what the Soothsayer was talking about, cringing under Kraarnok's angry glare, said nothing.

"Go on child," encouraged the Soothsayer. "Tell us what you have witnessed in the forest." Alaquin sat up straight, and under the watchful and supportive eye of the Soothsayer, she told her story.

As she told her story, gasps and cries escaped the throats of the gathered elves. Kraarnok admonished the unruly elves. "Quiet! Allow her to tell her story." But it was quite evident that he too was shaken by her tale.

When she finished telling what she had witnessed, the room burst into bedlam as astonished and frightened elves began to discuss what they had heard with those around them. Angry, Kraarnok raised his arms over his head, trying to quiet the unruly elves. Finally, his appeal for order was heard, and the elves sat back down and silence reigned over the room. He turned to the Soothsayer and asked, "Did your dream reveal a solution?"

"Yes, or should I say, in a manner," replied the Soothsayer. Kraarnok, with an expression of exasperation at the Soothsayer's ambagious answer, queried, "By all that is Elf! What kind of answer is that!"

The Soothsayer, not at all intimidated by the Head Elder's truculent attitude, answered the nearly distraught Kraarnok. Pointing at Alaquin, he continued, "She must enter the Realm of the Void and all will be revealed." This brought further startled gasps from the seated elves.

Alaquin jumped to her feet in protest shouting. "Why me? I'm no more special or different than anyone else." "Ah, child, but there is more to you than you know," answered the wizened old Soothsayer cryptically. Alaquin caught a glint of deep darkness in the old man's eyes which quickly faded.

Alaquin, frustrated by her predicament which was not of her creation, became irate with the Soothsayer. She screamed at him nearly in tears, "Why are you doing this to me?" "What do you mean?" asked the Soothsayer, exuding innocence. "Put me in such danger!" snapped Alaquin, seething with anger.

She felt a burning rage. It began to pulsate, creating a sense of strength and power that she had never felt before. The air around her began to glow and spark with energy. The Soothsayer, alarmed, stepped back.

Kraarnok, appalled and shocked by Alaquin's unprecedented display of magical energy, especially when she wasn't trained in the Arts, shouted, "Alaquin cease and desist before you destroy us all!" But Kraarnok's reprimand appeared to enrage her even more.

First, pointing her finger at Kraarnok, and then waving it at everyone else in the Council House, in an emotion filled voice, she said, "Why should I listen to anyone here? None of you have accepted me. You all treat me like an outcast. I've heard the sly comments made behind my back. You refer to me as the ill omen, a bad seed. Why is that? Is it because my ears are more round than other elves?" Her voice began to tremble and tears began to flow "or the fact that no one knows who sired me and you suspect my father may be human, which makes me even more of a monster. A dreaded half-breed."

Years of subduing her frustrations and anger at being rejected by the others, erupted. The pulsating blue-green energy that had enveloped her began to expand. Then, with a resounding crackle, it exploded.

The force of the explosion pinned everyone but Alaquin to the ground and decimated the Council House. Alaquin, in tears, ran blindly, from the devastation, into the forest, she had just caused. How long she ran through the forest, heedless to direction, she was unaware. Finally, in exhaustion, she collapsed, back against a giant nut tree, still sobbing. Alaquin drifted off into a deep, undisturbed sleep.

Back in the elf village, stunned elves picked themselves out of the wreckage of splintered trellises and twisted grape vines. A dark shadow separated itself from the prone soothsayer, unseen, and flitted off into the forest in the direction Alaquin had taken. Kraarnok, wide-eyed with shock, stuttered some curses as he walked around the remnants of the Council House.

CHAPTER 20

Carric complaining, talking out loud to himself, said. "With all our technology, how did I end up in this accursed desert?" His black, Galactic Security uniform had changed to match the surrounding sand.

The uniform's cooling system had failed. He was looking forward to the coolness of the coming night. Carric continued to fret out loud. "What is it about this planet that frazzles our technological wonders?"

The terrain around him was beginning to change from desert dunes to a semiarid land of rolling hills and tough, dark green, narrow-leafed grasses. Carric was preparing to set up camp when he heard the distinct clang of metal striking metal, but he couldn't distinguish from which direction it was coming.

Carric continued up a slight acclivity that led to the top of a knoll from which he could see the surrounding countryside. He quickly spotted where the clamor was originating from. A group of dark-skinned men on horseback were attacking a single dark-skinned woman on foot.

The woman had a magnificent physique and her skin glistened with sweat. She was wielding her broadsword superbly and deftly. Three of the men were bleeding profusely from gaping wounds, while the others had minor cuts. The woman appeared to be untouched and was enjoying the battle. She was a human fighting machine.

One of the seriously wounded men fell from his mount. The way he was lying, with his head cocked at an awkward angle, indicated he was dead. Carric was so fascinated by the spectacle that he stood there and did nothing to help. And Carric didn't know who was in the right. He had learned in his many years of service with Galactic Security that often things weren't always what they appeared.

Two more of the men slumped over with runnels of blood flowing off their mount's sides, most likely dead. The remaining three men had lined up side-by-side and were charging the hell woman. When the charging horses reached her, the woman turned her side to the charge making herself a smaller target. She then struck the middle horse a crushing blow between the eyes with the pommel of her sword. The poor creature first stumbled and then collapsed, throwing its rider.

She ducked, avoiding a sword swipe by the horsemen closest to her. The two remaining violently reigned their mounts around. The woman pulled two daggers from her boots and with a flick of her wrists, sent them into flight, skewering the two mounted men.

The man who had his mount cut out from under him had finally untangled himself from his fallen horse and faced the woman defiantly. Words passed between them, but Carric couldn't make them out.

The man approached the woman cautiously. He feinted. The woman moved to counter the attack. The man then pivoted on the balls of his feet. He swung his broadsword in an attempt to decapitate her. The woman parried his blow with little effort. The man, unable to control his deflected sword, had to follow it through which cost him his life. The woman spun the other direction and loped the man's head from his shoulders.

The woman kicked the decapitated head to the side and cleaned her bloody sword on the headless corpse's tunic. She then spat on her victim and said something to the headless body. She then raised her sword to the sky and began to laugh insanely.

"Bravo! Bravo!" shouted Carric, from the knoll, clapping his hands. Carric then walked down the hill. The dark-skinned woman, whose back was to Carric, turned deftly on the balls of her feet and moved into a defensive crouch to face this new challenge.

Carric stopped dead in his tracks and raised his hands in submission. This appeared to relax the swarthy-skinned woman. She raised from her defensive crouch, but she still watched Carric suspiciously.

"May I continue?" Carric asked. The woman nodded her head in the affirmative. Carric continued his descent. Carric extended his hand in friendship. The woman backed away, warning Carric, "Don't come any closer." A dangerous edge to her voice, Carric stopped immediately retracting his hand, sensing the danger he was courting.

Nonplused Carric spoke, "My name is Carric Soutland and yours?" "None of your business pale one," retorted the truculent woman with obvious disdain shading her voice.

The woman was muscular and towered over Carric. She had long legs, long arms, and broad shoulders. She had a broad forehead, narrow nose, and wide mouth. When she had spoken, Carric had noticed some of her front teeth were missing.

Without warning, she let out a shrill whistle, startling Carric. Carric reached for the sword which hung at his side. Carrying a sword felt strange. This wasn't typical weaponry for the Galactic Security Force but power cell weapons failed on this planet after a few uses. So he had equipped himself with a weapon that would work. Fortunately, the Guard required training in many types of weapons, and he was quite good with the sword.

The woman reacted to Carric's move by launching an attack. Carric managed to fend off the woman's assault, but the power behind her blows drove Carric backwards. Carric realized this woman's skill was far beyond his. He had to do something, or he was going to end up like the other men lying nearby.

The woman knocked the blade out of Carric's hand. He pulled a black box from his belt and pointed it at the woman. He fingered a button on its side. A red energy bolt surged forth striking the woman full in the chest, knocking her off her feet.

At first, an expression of shock framed her face which quickly turned to anger. With a menacing and accusative edge in her deep gravelly voice, she exclaimed, "Astarian wizard! You may work your magic on me, but I will never submit to slavery!" In a blink of an eye, she retrieved a dagger from her boot sheath. "I'll take my life first." She raised the dagger in a double hand grip preparing to impale herself.

Carric shot a bolt of energy at the dagger, knocking it free of her grasp. She dove for the weapon as it slid away from her, across the ground. Carric shouted, "Stop! I'm not here to enslave you or even hurt you!" But the woman continued to crawl after her fleeing weapon. Carric adjusted his energy weapon, took aim and hit the dagger with a blue bolt of energy which incinerated it.

The woman, still lying on the ground, stopped and turned to face Carric, hatred painting across her face. Carric continued, "I've no idea what you were referring to when you called me an Astarian Wizard, and I'm definitely not interested in enslaving you."

The woman, voice dripping with ire, accused, "You can't fool me. Your clothing betrays you." Carric became excited. "You've seen others dressed similar to me?" "Isn't that what I just said," snapped the woman sarcastically.

"Am I allowed to stand?" she asked. Carric nodded his head in the direction of the sword and said, "As long, as you stay away from that. At least until we straighten out this misunderstanding."

Carric heard the sound of hooves racing in their direction. He asked the woman, "More friends?" She chuckled before answering, "No, that is only my horse. It's answering my call."

A dark brown, shaggy-haired horse galloped up to the woman. She offered her hand to the horse, and it nuzzled her hand lovingly. The woman cooed to it affectionately.

"You mentioned others dressed like me. Do you know where I can find them?" quizzed Carric. The woman returned her attention to Carric, a coy glint in her eyes. "I may for a price," she answered.

"What is your price?" asked Carric. A sly grin stretched across her face. "I want your magic box." Carric looked down at his weapon and then looked back up at the woman. He was reluctant to give primitives advanced technologies, but he knew the weapon, which usually recharged itself, was incapable of recharging on this world. In short order it would be useless.

"Before I agree, I've two other conditions. One tell me your name, and two, you must guide me not just tell me where they are. The woman looked at the weapon greedily, and then shook her head in agreement and said, "My name is Schwellen."

Before Carric handed over the weapon, he switched the safety on. The woman grabbed the weapon and pointed it at Carric. "You're foolish pale one." "Go ahead. Shoot me," said Carric. The woman pushed the trigger mechanism to no avail.

Accusatory anger flashed in Schwellen's eyes. "It doesn't work," she said. "Oh, it'll work, but I'll have to activate it," replied a grim faced Carric.

"Now can we get serious. I need your help. Will you help me?" Schwellen looked over at the dead men and then back at Carric. "I suppose I've nothing to lose. I can't return to my people, especially after what happened here today," replied a melancholy Schwellen.

"Give me the weapon," said Carric. Schwellen reluctantly handed Carric the weapon. While setting the weapon to active, he asked, "What was this all about?"

Schwellen walked over to the dead men's horses and began rummaging through their packs. "I'm not your typical Halhoren female. The women in our society are subservient to the men. We are suppose to prepare meals, bear and raise children, and take care of the men. I refuse this serfdom. I consider myself their equal and am as good a warrior as any man and better than most." To emphasize her last statement, she made a sweeping motion in the direction of the dead men and said, "The evidence."

Carric nodded his head in agreement. "Here," she said, "Put these on." Then she handed him a shirt, a pair of britches, and boots from one of the packs, all made from the hide of some furry creature, similar to what she was wearing. "You're to conspicuous in that outfit."

While Carric was changing, Schwellen continued her story. "I was given an ultimatum, conform or die. I slipped away and these were the men sent to hunt me down."

Carric was running his hand over his new outfit in admiration. He was surprised at the comfort of the primitive clothing. Schwellen gathered up her weapons and those of the dead men. She packed the weapons that weren't hers on the dead men's horses. She then released the beasts. She turned to Carric and asked, "Can you ride?" Carric answered, "Yes I'm not an expert, but I can handle a mount."

"That's good. We need to get out of this area before nightfall. This is the land of the changelings." "Changelings?" repeated Carric. "That's what I said. No one is sure whether they're people that turn into animals or animals that turn into people but whatever they are, they're dangerous," answered Schwellen.

They mounted. Schwellen reached into to her saddle pack and produced two slices of jerked meat. She handed one to Carric. Carric bit off a piece and was surprised at the extraordinary flavor. The two then rode off leaving the dead men behind.

*　　*　　*

Alaquin roused slowly. She shook her head groggily. Finally, fully awake, she looked around. She was confused and frightened and unsure of where she was and how she came to be here. She was curled up on a thick, lush, green carpet of grasses and moss.

Alaquin didn't get up. She rolled onto her back. She searched the canopy of leaves that swayed languidly in the gentle morning breeze. Her clothes were wet from the heavy dew that had blanketed the forest floor.

Alaquin was soaking in the forest sounds. The birds were flagrantly voicing their songs of territorially claims and warning off any possible usurpers as they sat high on their thrones in the treetops. She could hear the babbling of a nearby brook. Also, there was a loud plopping sound she didn't recognize, as if something were falling into the brook.

Curious, Alaquin sat up, searching for the source of the noise. She stood up and walked over to the brook. She cautiously approached the point from which the sound emanated. She heard a cracking sound and then saw a nutshell plop into the water which was quickly carried away by the current.

"Hello, elf girl." Alaquin, startled by the disembodied voice, cried out, "Who's there?" "Just me, a lowly demon," answered the voice. "Where are you?" asked Alaquin. "In the tree above you," came the reply. Alaquin looked up but still had trouble discerning the speaker from the foliage mottled by the sunlight that filtered through the forest canopy.

Alaquin finally spotted the speaker when she saw a shimmer and a black ichor dripping from a limb hanging directly over the brook. "You!" she shouted. "Me, yes me." replied the demon, surprised by the elf girl's accusative tone. The demon opened and closed its leathery wings nervously.

"What are you doing in the forest?" asked a chagrined Alaquin. "My purpose?" reiterated the grotesque creature. "Here to help you." "Help me?" questioned Alaquin incredulously.

The demon sat back on his haunches and scrutinized the elf girl. Alaquin still irate at the demon's unwanted intrusion into the forest and at the creature's impetuous insinuation, that she would need or even accept help from a vile creature such as him, glared at the demon. The silent tension between the two of them was almost tangible.

Finally, the demon broke the silence, a little angry himself. The demon snapped, "I'm here to protect you from your own ignorance!"

Alaquin's anger began to simmer. The demon, sensing the danger, flexed his wings again. Opening them, he leapt from the limb, squawking loudly, diving at the elf girl.

He struck Alaquin on the shoulder. The elf girl's squeal of fright quickly became one of pain. She was sent sprawling on her backside into a Thorn Berry bush loaded with vermillion colored berries.

A berry speckled Alaquin forgot her anger as she concentrated on extricating herself from the thorny and painful predicament in which she found herself. She delicately worked herself free from the cloying and grasping thorn covered limbs of the bush. Finally, back on her feet, she began to wipe away the crushed berries clinging to her clothing. She even popped a few of the sweet juicy fruits into her mouth.

"I hated to do that," chortled the demon, "but you gave me no choice." "You appear to be quite pleased with yourself," challenged

Alaquin, as she gave the demon an angry glance from the corner of her eyes. The demon moved his wings in an upwards motion as if he were trying too imitate a shrug.

"Now will you listen," pleaded the demon. "No! You listen to me. You shouldn't even be in the forest. How did you manage to circumvent the forbidding?" snapped the elf girl.

The demon began to rock back and forth on his new perch, clearly becoming vexed with Alaquin. "I have had enough of your hostility, elf girl! The forbidding is no longer effective. In fact, if you have not noticed, elf magic is failing all over the forest. A combination of the Chaos Demon being on the loose and the general weakening of the rune magic is leaving the forest open to a variety of undesirables." Stunned by the demon's vehemence, Alaquin looked up, mouth open.

The demon, seeing the effect that his tirade had on the elf girl, began to calm down and feel pity for her. "What do you mean that the rune magic is weakening?" asked Alaquin.

"The times are changing. I do not know why Rune Magic is losing its potency but part has to do with the arrival of the Chaos demon," replied the demon.

"The Chaos Demon, is it one of your kind?" queried Alaquin. "No. The Chaos Demon is an elf curse, I believe. Let's get back to the subject at hand. The reason I am here. You need help, whether you realize it or not. I am here to advise you and to be sure you do not fall into the hands of Natas' minions."

"Advise? What kind of advice can a demon give an elf?" Alaquin asked with incredulity. "For one thing, you need to control your magical outbursts when you become angry," snipped the demon. "So much energy being released uncontrolled creates vibrations in the firmament. In fact, all magic creates some magical ripples. But the waves you have been creating are detectable by all who are attuned to magic. All demons are able to detect the waves you have been creating. How do you think I found you? The only reason I found you first is because I was closer than the others. Natas will also be able to detect your magic, which will draw him to you." "Why should I fear Natas?" asked Alaquin. "Because he would like to corrupt you and use your magic to further his evil designs. If you proved to be incorruptible, he would consider you a threat and destroy you," answered the demon.

Alaquin no longer felt threatened by the demon, but she felt he wasn't being completely truthful and that he had purposes of his own for helping her. She didn't trust the demon but decided to accept the demon's help for the time being. "Ok, I'll accept your help."

With no special destination in mind, the two odd companions followed the brook upstream, deeper into the forest, the demon flying and the elf girl walking. The demon continued to talk about magic, in particular, Alaquin's.

"You are unique elf girl." "In what way?" asked Alaquin "Your magic is a mixture of Rune Magic and Spiritual Magic. You have dominion over both elf and human magic. Don't you find that odd?" Alaquin glanced up at the demon. She wondered what he was insinuating.

She started to reply when, with an ear-splitting squawk, the demon flapped his wings wildly and then dove towards the ground in front of her. The grotesque creature plopped itself down in Alaquin's path, nearly tripping her.

"What are you trying to do! Kill me!" shouted Alaquin. But the demon didn't answer her right away. He began to look at her closely as if he didn't recognize her.

"Your ears aren't as pointed as most elves and your body build is heavier. One could speculate that you have some human blood coursing through your veins," stated the demon nonchalantly.

Alaquin, angered by the demon's comment, gave the creature a stone-faced look and then stormed off. Heading deeper into the forest, Alaquin ignored all efforts made by the demon to apologize. "I meant no insult," apologized the demon pleadingly. Alaquin replied, "I"m not really angry with you, but I've had to deal with that accusation all my life."

The elf girl stopped suddenly, looking around her nervously. "I've never been in this part of th forest before." The trees loomed over the two threateningly. A thick mist wafted eerily between the trees, cloying tenaciously to the two intruders as if trying to seduce them.

"I believe we may be in grave danger," said the demon nervously. "But I am not sure from what." "What was that?" Asked Alaquin, pointing into the thick gray mist. "I did not see anything," answered the demon.

"Can't you see it! Movement over there," Alaquin pointed. The demon then spotted what Alaquin was pointing at. The demon finally understood their danger, and knowing he would be of little help, abandoned the elf girl. As he flew away he warned, "Do not use your magic, unless your life depends on it for Natas is searching for you and he is far more dangerous than what you are about to face now."

Exasperated, Alaquin cried out, "Where are you going. I thought you were here to protect me, not abandon me in my greatest need." But the demon didn't answer. "Coward!" she shouted, emphasizing her anger by shaking her fist at the retreating demon.

Suddenly, out of the mist, appeared several creatures. They approached the elf girl warily and began to circle her. They tightened the circle with each completed revolution. Alaquin was completely stunned by what she saw, mouth agape.

Alaquin rubbed her eyes to make sure she wasn't hallucinating. Standing before her were creatures of legend. Terrible stories were told of these creatures to keep elf children in line. The creatures were half horse and half man.

Half horse and half man was not an accurate description. They were more horse than man. They had a head, long neck, shoulders, and arms similar to humans, set on the body of a horse. The bodies of the creatures were covered with a dirty-brown hair. They had four muscular legs which ended in cloven hooves.

Their faces were broad with eyes set wide apart. Their heads were covered with mane like hair which started at the top of their rounded heads truncating where the shoulders and neck met. Their faces were a stark white with large irregular brown splotches covering the human parts of their bodies. The creatures had wide mouths filled with sharp fang-like teeth, which suggested they dined on flesh and not grasses. Their long muscular arms ended with huge hands and talon like fingernails.

Alaquin felt the sickening sensation of fear in her belly as panic began to take control of her emotions. She searched desperately for an avenue of escape. "Fear not' Alaquin. We are here to assist you in your quest," said the largest of the grotesque creatures. Alaquin, although frightened and taken aback at the mention of her name ceased her desperate search for an escape route. Curiosity piqued, Alaquin focused on the creature that had spoken her name. "How do you know my name?" "The listening bush informed us," answered the creature. "I Shouldn't be so rude. My name is Clodtrip and the leader of what is left of my kind. We are not so numerous as we once were," the creature said as his eyes glazed over as if in deep thought. Tears began to form in the corners of his dark brooding eyes.

Alaquin found herself feeling empathy for Clodtrip and his followers and found that she felt at ease with these poor misshapen creatures. She asked, "What quest do you speak of? I am on no quest." "Why, your quest for the Wisdom Tree," answered Clodtrip.

"I've no intention of searching for the Wisdom Tree," quipped Alaquin, her anger growing with the feeling that she was being manipulated by others for their own gain. "I don't believe you are aware then, that although you may appear to be roaming aimlessly, you are heading towards the deep valley, the place where the tree supposedly exists." Abashed, Alaquin had no reply.

"Beware!" came a shout from high in the trees. Alaquin began to feel a queasiness in her stomach. She became dizzy and began to shake and quiver. The forest around her began to pulsate and waver. Then a black hole, beginning as a minute speck, grew and expanded in front of her.

"What's happening!" she screamed in sheer terror. "I don't know," shouted Clodtrip in panic. "Run! Run!" shouted the demon from the canopy above. "Someone is opening a doorway into the void." Alaquin's senses were overwhelmed by the loud roar of escaping air.

CHAPTER 21

Crysillnia felt oppressed by the cavern walls of the Dragon's lair. Their trip from Dragon's Peek to the mountains had been uneventful. They had been met in the foothills by an ominous looking creature.

She had never seen a real dragon before now, but she had seen drawings and paintings of the ghastly beasts. The paintings and drawings didn't convey the true terror that one of these creatures emanated. But yet, in their own way, there was a beauty and gracefulness not projected in any rendition. Crysillnia and her companions were led deep into the bowls of the mountain. They were assailed by what seemed like multitudes of smaller dragons in the confines of the narrow, low vaulted, caverns. The larger dragon that was leading the way roared its displeasure, and the smaller creatures dissipated.

The cavern walls were rough and uneven, and Crysillnia was not sure whether they were naturally created or hewn. The walls and ceiling were coated with a luminous lichen which cast a haunting but steady light. They were led into a huge cavern.

The centerpiece of the cavern was a huge circular hole. Crysillnia stood on a ledge overlooking the abyss. It appeared to be bottomless. Crysillnia felt a bit queasy as she peered into the darkness below.

"Climb onto my back," commanded the dragon. We need to cross the pit and since I'm the only one that has wings, I will have to be your steed although the thought repulses me. You humans and dwarfs alike are useless and annoying creatures."

Crysillnia was amazed at the way dragon communicated with them. The dragon didn't verbalize but communicated with them telepathically. Crysillnia and her companions boarded the creature grudgingly and with some apprehension. The dragon spread its huge, web like, leathery wings and hopped off the ledge.

The dragon slowly descended into the depths of the pit using the updraft from the abyss to keep it from plummeting into the dark depths below. Talok asked, as he hung on to one of the bony protrusions on the dragon's back, "What is that noise?" "It sounds like a battle," replied Kanef. "I wonder who the dragons would be battling?" queried Jarret. Crysillnia asked with amazement, "Who would dare battle such formidable creatures?" Simentoo, with an unusual inflection of mirth in his voice said, "You'd be surprised at who would dares such foolishness."

The dragon was more graceful in flight than Crysillnia would have thought considering its size. Air whistled around her ears and through her truncated hair. It was a comforting sensation.

The dragon landed on a narrow ledge before another lichen illuminated tunnel. The dragon pulled its wings back into place, high on its shoulders and running the length of its flanks. The creature trundled into the lit corridor rather awkwardly. Once inside the corridor, it crouched low so that its passengers could dismount. Once everyone was off, the dragon shook itself like an animal trying to shake itself dry or remove something disgusting.

Their guide led them downwards, deeper into the bowels of the mountain. It led them into a huge cavern, basically circular in dimension. The walls disappeared into the darkness above. Their guide took flight, vanishing into darkness of the cavern.

Crysillnia and her companions looked at each other in bewilderment. "Now what," stated Kanef, a touch of ire in his voice. "I am here," echoed a voice in their minds. Then a much larger dragon soared out of the darkness.

The dragon landed near Crysillnia and her companions. Its talons, scratching the stone floor of the cavern, sent chills down Crysillnia's spine. "I am the Dragon Queen," she continued.

She scrutinized the four humans and dwarf with a critical eye. "It's hard to believe that so much of the future rests with the likes of you." The dragon emphasized her disbelief with a shake of her ponderous head.

She continued to ramble on through the minds of the companions, "But only you Crysillnia. A child of the throne of Caspar." "What do you mean?" asked a confused and stunned Crysillnia as she took a step backwards.

Kanef, angered by the Dragon Queen's comment stepped forward and said, "What foolishness is this? This girl has nothing to do with the throne of Caspar. I'm the heir to the throne." "Do not harangue me, human." The dragon's eyes began to glow red as her anger grew. "But I should have realized. Just another failing of you humans. You lack the innate ability to sense your own progeny. Believe me. She is an heir to the throne of Caspar. She is your daughter.

But to more important matters." Then the dragon queen raised her massive head towards the chamber's ceiling. A dragon descended out of the darkness. Crysillnia watched in amazement as the creature flapped its massive wings before it landed.

The two beasts appeared to be in disagreement. What ever they were saying appeared to agitate the larger, queen dragon. The two dragons began to growl ominously. The smaller dragon turned briskly taking a swipe at Crysillnia but Jarret's quick reaction saved her, when he pulled her out of the path of the sweeping tail.

The Queen dragon trumpeted her displeasure at the attack. Her roar resonated off the surrounding walls of the cavern. The offending dragon lowered its head and slunk away. The Queen turned to Crysillnia. "Sorry. As you see, we dragons disagree at what is the best approach to this situation. But enough with apologies. There are more important things to discuss and very little time to do so. Time is running out. The demon hordes are already within the mountain and there are far more of them than us." The queen swished her tail nervously.

"Time is running out for us. The demon spawn are overrunning the lower levels. We may have to abandon our home soon." The Dragon Queen lowered her head in sadness.

Then raising her head proudly, she continued, "But they will remember us for eternity." She shook her head defiantly, and the red glow of her eyes brightened.

"Back to your situation. We, the dragons, are the Keepers of the Crystals. They were given to us long ago. The lands at the time were in great turmoil, and there was fear that the power of the Crystals would fall into the wrong hands. Also the elves were threatening a war of their own if the Crystals were not secured. Albeit reluctantly we accepted the responsibility, because we realized what havoc humans could cause with these talismans of power or, even worse, if Natas should get his hands on the Crystals.

We now possess only four of the Crystals. The fifth was spirited away by one of our own in the throes of madness. We have tried to retrieve it but the dragon has hidden it in tunnels to narrow for us to enter."

Talok, skeptical of the Queen Dragon's explanation, asked. "How is this thief able to enter tunnels so narrow that other dragon's can't follow?" The Dragon Queen growled at the disrespectful title of thief that Talok had attached to her fellow dragon.

"This dragon you so callously refer to as a thief is my mother. She is ancient, even by dragon standards. The reason she was able to travel in tunnels too narrow for the rest of us is because she shed her wings which allows her to enter the narrow passages. Once a dragon enters the latter stages of their existence, they lose their wings. This shedding of the wings is unique to each of us. My mother's longevity of life must have delayed her shedding. But she must have been aware that her time was upon her, when she stole the Crystal.

I ask only that when you retrieve the Crystal that you put her to the sword so that what dignity she still has is spared." The Dragon Queen's wings slumped noticeable, she lowered her head, and the fiery red glow of her eyes dimmed considerably. A pall of melancholy blanketed the cavern.

The mood was broken when another dragon, small in comparison to the Queen Dragon, entered the room. The new arrival's scales were lighter green in color, the knobby protrusions that ran down its spine were smaller and more rounded. Its wings had more tapper and were much shorter compared to its body length than the other dragons in the cavern. Jarret, standing behind

Crysillnia, leaned forward and whispered into her ear, "He's a male." Crysillnia shook her head in acknowledgment of Jarret's explanation for the dragon's diminutive appearance.

While the two dragons held a silent conversation, Simentoo took the time to study their surroundings. He didn't trust the dragons and there was something about this new arrival, clutching an insignificant leather pouch in one of its long-taloned forepaw, that set off instinctual alarms. He was searching for a possible route of escape but he, quickly, realized that they were at the mercy of the dragons.

Their hostess, the Dragon Queen, was becoming more agitated. Indicated by the nervous twitch in her long serpentine tail and an increased intensity of the red glow in her eyes, the other dragon moved into a more aggressive posture, squatting on its haunches as if it were either preparing to pounce or take flight.

Without warning and emitting a reverberating roar, the Dragon Queen pounced, striking the other dragon with her powerful tail. There was a loud sickening crack as the smaller dragon's wing broke. Using her weight and momentum, she drove the offending dragon against the cavern wall.

The battered creature slid to the cavern floor. She then used her huge, needle sharp talons to rip huge chunks of scaly hide from the smaller dragon, killing the unfortunate creature outright.

Still angry, she reached down and picked up a large boulder and crushed it into fine powder and small pebbles. Kanef, Jarret, Talok and Simentoo stood protectively in front of Crysillnia, weapons drawn.

The Queen looked over at the humans, disdain etched in her, hard, craggy face. "Don't worry. You're not in danger from me. But even if you were, your puny attempts at defense would be useless."

She looked back over her shoulder at the twitching corpse. "He was my mate, but he betrayed us. In fear for his life, he had allied himself with the demons. He was foolish to think he could hide his betrayal from me."

She returned her attention to Crysillnia and her companions. "Time is short. Our defenses below have been overrun. My soldiers are running a delaying action, to give us time to escape. Follow me and quickly. Wait! What a fool am I!"

The dragon queen lowered her long serpentine tail. "Climb on to my back." The companions climbed up the dragon's tail. Crysillnia was surprise at how supple the dragon's hide was. The scales were rough but warm to the touch. When they were all settled, the dragon queen opened her leathery wings.

Slowly she began to flap her wings so that, she wouldn't unseat her passengers. Her powerful shoulders, where the wings attached flexed, and her back began to undulate. This motion flowed down the dragon's back to her tail. It gave Crysillnia the sensation that she was riding a lazy ocean wave.

The dragon queen increased the motion of her wings as she climbed towards the ceiling of the cavern. She landed gently on a ledge that protruded from the cavern wall. She gripped the edge of the ledge with her talons and took a step forward to secure her position. She lowered her tail so that her passenger could disembark which they did gladly.

The dragon led the companions down a dark and narrow passageway. There was just enough glow lichen growing on the ceiling to cast a wan, eerie light. The Dragon Queen's wings scrubbed the passageway's sides which explained the lack of glow lichen on the walls.

There was a slight downward acclivity to the passageway. Even with the meager light, Crysillnia felt like the darkness was closing in around her. The feeling scared her but yet was exciting.

After what seemed to be hours but was probably a much shorter time, the weary companions entered another cavern. This cavern was much smaller than the dragon's Council Chamber. There were sparkling crystals embedded in the cavern walls which amplified the light cast by the glow lichen. A spring welled out of the center of the cavern which flowed to one side of the small room and exited through a crack in the wall.

The dragon slurped water from the spring. When finished, she moved away from the spring. She hunkered down resting her huge head on her forepaw, talons retracted and tail curled around her. She reminded Crysillnia of a cat at rest. "You must take sustenance and drink while I finish my story." The Dragon Queen, with her large, red, slitted eyes watched the humans eat and drink. Her tail twitched, like that of a cat's watching its prey, as she continued her tale.

"The Crystals are not of this world." With that statement she produced the small leather pouch that her mate had been carrying. "Come, Crysillnia, these belong to you." The dragon then placed the Crystals on the ground.

Crysillnia approached the dragon warily. The dragon's demeanor and size were intimidating. Keeping a wary eye on the dragon, she leaned over and snatched the pouch containing the Crystals off the cavern floor and quickly backed away.

A deep coughing sound came from deep within the dragon's chest and a glint of mirth was reflected in the creature's piercing red eyes. Crysillnia guessed that the dragon was laughing. The pouch was made of a soft leather, like none she had ever seen before, closed with an iridescent but translucent drawstring. The pouch was the size of two closed fists. She sensed it was ancient but it wasn't worn or dirty like one would expect from something from long gone days.

She was mesmerized by it. The pouch was warm to the touch and she sensed a calling from the contents within. She delicately pulled on the mouth of the pouch, and an unexpected desire for power washed over her. She felt exhilarated, invincible, and all powerful.

But there was something else, deep within in her Essence, stirring. She felt a darkness, an evil, and she revered in it. This darkness of being was invigorating, stimulating, and all encompassing. Alarm came with the realization of what she was thinking. Blinking her eyes and shaking her head, she broke the uncanny spell that the contents of the pouch had cast.

"Very good," said the Dragon Queen. "I feared we may have lost you. The Crystals are powerful magic and must be handled cautiously and with reverence. One without the strength of will and magic of her own would have been consumed by the power of the Crystals. You've just passed a critical test for, if the Crystals had possessed you, I would've been obligated to destroy you."

Jarret, whom had been seated, jumped up and cried in anger, "Why didn't you warn her of the danger!" The dragon caught Jarret with a baleful eye and said, "You wouldn't understand, human, but it was a necessary test to be sure that she was worthy of the Crystals. This is just one of many challenges that she will face as long as she possesses the Crystals. I hope she will fare as well then. The Crystals are the key to all creation. If they fall into the wrong hands, it would bring an end to this world and many others. It would mean the end of all creation." Crysillnia, somewhat enthralled by the energy emanating from the intriguing pouch, was paying little attention to the Dragon Queen's explanation. She reached into the pouch and found too her surprise, that each Crystal was nestled into a separate pocket within the pouch.

Crysillnia retrieved one of the Crystals. She held it in the palm of her hand. The Crystal was the deepest black she had ever seen. She felt as if the Essence of her being was being drawn into the Crystal. She felt foreboding, despair, and fear, but she also felt excitement and exhilaration.

Crysillnia also felt exposed. She felt like the Crystal was a mirror to her inner-self, reflecting her emotions, deepest secrets, and darkest thoughts.

The Dark Crystal, as she thought of it, was half-moon in shape, flat on one side with three circular recesses, and rounded on the other side. Crysillnia became weak at the knees. Her hand, in which she cradled the Crystal, felt warm. Crysillnia suspected that the Crystal was trying to rob her of her Essence. She quickly placed the offending object on the cavern floor.

One by one she pulled the other Crystals from the pouch, each was cylindrical in shape, and placed them on the floor before her. Each Crystal had its own color. These colors were the deepest hues imaginable of red, blue, and green. Crysillnia felt like each of the Crystals were trying to devour her Essence. They tugged at her and called for her. She felt it would be wonderful to succumb to their seductive lure.

Crysillnia felt a gentle nudge. She flailed out with her arms in an attempt to discourage the annoying attempt to distract her, but the offender persisted. Then she realized that the perpetrator was in her mind. She attempted to close off her mind by concentrating more intensely on the alluring call of the Crystals.

Then a searing jolt of pain raced through her head. The trespasser in her mind was not to be put off or ignored. Crysillnia's spellbound mind was freed. She felt the familiar sensation of the Dragon Queen's thoughts. "You need to be very careful with the Crystals for they will steal your Essence. It is in their nature too take back what was once theirs. They are a little less dangerous if you have the White Crystal to help control them but only slightly. No one is sure what the purpose of the Crystals are or their domain of power. Legend has it that the domains of the Crystals are: Green for life; Red for land and fire; Blue for the firmament, winds, and water; Black is the element of corruption; and White is the purifier of the magic."

The deafening din of battle began to reverberate from the tunnels leading down into the bowels of the mountains and echo off the cavern walls. "The battle is coming closer. My soldiers won't be able to hold out much longer, our lines of defense have been breached, but they will die to the last dragon." Despair emanated from the giant beast nearly overwhelming Crysillnia and her companions with sadness. Even the acerbic and taciturn dwarf was affected, apparent by his watery eyes, as he fought back tears.

The Dragon Queen turned her attention to a corridor that entered the cavern from behind the companions. They all turned to see what had drawn her attention away from them. They were surprised to see an elf enter the cavern, escorted by a dragon nearly as large as the queen dragon. The elf appeared to be a reluctant guest.

The elf was disheveled but defiance burned in his eyes as he approached the Queen dragon and her other guests. The elf was tall and slender of build. His skin was very pale and his hair was a pale-blond, nearly white. His eyes were a piercing gray, his face was narrow with a strong chin, and his ears were sharply upturned and pointed. He was dressed in dark clothing which created a stark contrast against his complexion. Crysillnia thought to herself that elves reminded her of the walking dead. The thought sent shivers down her spine.

"We caught this elf stealing eggs from the brood room. I tried to probe his mind in an effort to find out where he was hiding the eggs but I couldn't penetrate deep enough. I have decided not to kill him but will send him with you."

Kanef stepped forward radiating anger. "It's bad enough that I have to travel with a deformed dwarf, but I absolutely refuse to take on a dirt sucking elf as a companion." The elf turned angry eyes on Kanef.

The elf began to rune write in the air and chant. He was creating a spell. Kanef quickly unsheathed the short sword at his side and stepped towards the elf. Brightly colored runes of red and blue began to dance in the air around the elf.

The Dragon Queen roared which shook the solid rock walls of the cavern sprinkling the companions with bits of dirt and pebbles. Her roar commanded the attention of everyone in the cavern. "Stop this foolishness! We have enough problems to worry about without creating more. Put your prejudices and hatreds aside. We all have a common enemy. One which will destroy us all, if we fail to stick together."

Everyone was stunned by the mental barrage the Dragon Queen had unleashed on them. Crysillnia began to massage her temples in an attempt to soothe the headache caused by the Dragon Queen's reprimand. The Dragon Queen continued, "First off! Your trek with the others is over Kanef." "Says who!" challenged Kanef. "Says I," snapped the Dragon Queen with such emphasis that it sent more acute pains through Crysillnia's head. She noticed from the others' expressions that they were experiencing similar pains.

Kanef, still being obstinate, replied, "I'll go where I want, when I want. No one orders me around." "Do not try my patience, human," snapped the Dragon Queen, as she raised up on her haunches, towering over Kanef menacingly, forcing Kanef back several steps.

Weapon at the ready, Kanef prepared to defend himself. Realizing the ignominy of their situation, the Dragon Queen began that deep coughing sound that Crysillnia took for laughter. The Dragon Queen sat back on her haunches using her tail for stabilization.

"Kanef, you need to return home and take command of your father's forces. He has been building a new form of cavalry, in secret, for many years. It is a heavy armored cavalry. I believe your father's intentions were to use this force to usurp the High King of Lenar. This force could be vital in the upcoming battles."

Kanef, still seething from the Dragon Queen's attempt to intimidate him, replied tartly, "First you have the audacity to order me around and now you insult my father's honor and integrity. And, as far as this armored cavalry goes, I have no idea what you're talking about."

Roaring, the Dragon Queen extended her wings in agitation and anger. Glowering at Kanef, she said, "You know as well as I, that your father is not an honorable man. He cares only for himself and no one else. Rest," she commanded, you will have to leave soon."

The Queen dragon then turned abruptly and exited the cavern followed by the dragon that had brought the elf. Tensions were running high, especially between Kanef and the elf. Crysillnia spoke in hopes of relieving the tension. "We should rest. We've an arduous task ahead." This appeared to lighten the tension, as everyone settled in for a rest.

*　　*　　*

Crysillnia was sleeping restlessly when the Dragon Queen, rushed into the cavern, screaming in her mind, "Awake! Awake!.

The lair has fallen!" Crysillnia awoke with a start, her back against the cavern wall, the din of battle echoing around the room.

Crysillnia was shocked by the Dragon Queen's appearance. The once proud, indomitable, and impregnable queen was disheveled with many cuts and lacerations. She was bleeding profusely from many of her wounds.

"Many brave dragons have died here today and gone to their eternal sleep on this infamous day!" said the Dragon Queen. "Quickly, follow me," the dragon urged.

The abrupt appearance, declaration, and exit of the dragon, left the companions in confusion. They scurried around, like rats cornered by a hungry cat, gathering their gear. The Dragon Queen mentally nudged them to hurry. They needed no further coaxing, as they entered the narrow passageway. The intimidating echos of many clawed feet behind them spurred them to greater speed.

Their downward sloping escape route was even narrower and darker than the previous tunnel, but there was still enough light to see where they were going. The hulking darkness of their guide led them steadily downwards. The Dragon Queen's wings scraped the walls and ceiling of the tunnel sending chills down Crysillnia's back.

After many twists and turns, the tunnel finally leveled out and abruptly ended in a shaft that rose perpendicular to the tunnel. There was enough room at the bottom of the shaft to allow the Dragon Queen to maneuver without crushing her followers. There was a gentle light seeping through a breech high in the shaft.

The shaft was cylindrical in shape and the walls were smooth. They appeared to be polished, because the dim light from above reflected off of the walls. There were well worn hand and footholds leading up to the narrow breech.

The dragon urged the companions on. "Quickly, climb. They are coming. I will hold them off while you make your escape." Snuffling, squeals, and scratching was heard in the tunnel they had just traversed.

"No! I am a Captain of the Lenarian Elite Guard. I'll not abandon you. It would irreparably impinge my honor," exclaimed

Simentoo, unsheathing his broadsword. The Dragon Queen replied, "Foolish human. Do you have a death wish?" "No, but I don't fear death. It's been a fate I have accepted as part of my duty," he replied brusquely.

Their antagonists were quickly upon them. The demons poured out of the tunnel like sewage from a storm drain. The unclean creatures were grotesquely malformed versions of more familiar life forms. They ranged from the reptilian to twisted facsimiles of humans, and some were beyond imagination. They ranged is sizes from small to gigantic. Their stench was nearly overwhelming.

They slobbered, squealed, and grunted as they attacked. Simentoo commanded the others to escape as he wielded his broadsword. The dragon was swatting, slashing, and pulverizing the attackers with her massive claws and razor sharp teeth. The dwarf was using his war hammers, the elf was casting spells while Jarret and Kanef were using short swords and daggers. Crysillnia was standing with her back to the wall, dagger in one hand and the pouch with the Crystals in the other.

CHAPTER 22

The attack ended suddenly and without reason. The demons retreated back the way they had come. The beleaguered and exhausted defenders were surrounded by heaping piles of dead and dying demons. Jarret, gasping, said in jest as he grimaced a smile, "I think that went well enough."

The dragon responded," "These were only the seekers and scouts. They are the most fleet and the least dangerous."

Simentoo sprang into action. "We must get out of here before they return with reenforcements," he said. Everyone except Crysillnia had a minor wound of one sort or another. These wounds were inflamed and burned insufferably.

With Simentoo's direction, the companions, using the foot and hand holes, climbed the wall. The climb was a slow process because the depressions in the walls were so worn that securing a firm purchase was difficult. "You must hurry!" implored the dragon emphatically. "They are returning. I hear them."

The companions needed no further urging. They threw caution to the wind, as they recklessly scaled the wall. Talok had taken the lead and was the first on the wide ledge that lead to the aperture.

Crysillnia was behind Talok. She was having a modicum of difficulty. She was tired and her muscles burned in protest at the abuse. The muscles in her arms began to spasm. "Come on, Crysillnia," she thought to herself. "You don't have much further to go."

She reached for the next handhold and pushed herself upward with the opposite leg, but the leg cramped. She found herself suspended in midair, as she began to fall away from the wall. In desperation and fear, she reached upwards and screamed.

Talok's large and calloused hand caught her's. Crysillnia found herself momentarily swinging in midair like a falling leaf caught in a mountain breeze before Talok, deftly and without difficulty, pulled her to safety. She hugged the large dwarf with relief, as she trembled uncontrollably, and her heart palpitated wildly.

While the others scaled the wall, Simentoo stayed at the bottom of the shaft as rear guard with the dragon. When everyone else had scaled the wall, he turned to the Dragon Queen ans asked, "How do you plan on escaping?" He then looked up at the narrow aperture. "I don't believe you can fit through that hole." "Don't worry about me, human. I can take care of myself, but thank you for your concern. Now, you must go," replied the dragon.

Simentoo scaled the wall with the alacrity of a mountain climber. He had climbed many, more dangerous escarpments as a child. Being raised in the mountains, climbing was something taught to the children of his people at a young age.

Once on the ledge, he looked back down the shaft and watched the dragon begin her climb. Then he turned to follow the others. They had already exited through a short, narrow, and low-ceilinged passageway. He had to bend over slightly to avoid bumping his head. He still wondered how the dragon expected to get out.

The Dragon Queen looked up the narrow shaft and watched the human scale the wall. She grunted with admiration at the ease in which Simentoo climbed the sheer walls of the shaft.

Realizing that there wasn't enough room in the shaft for her to spread her wings so that she could fly to the top of the shaft, she dug her talons into the smooth rock walls and began her arduous climb, grinding, crushing, and pulverizing the rock face as she moved up the shaft.

Simentoo covered his eyes as he stepped from the darkness of the tunnel into the bright sunlight. The difference in temperature and humidity between the bowels of the mountain and the outside struck Simentoo like a hammer hitting an anvil.

Simentoo slowly lowered his hand as his eyes adjusted to the bright sunlight. He was overwhelmed by the panoramic view that unfolded before him. There was a lush tropical forest in the valley below. The canopy that obscured the jungle floor was mottled with a wide range of green from slightly subtle shades to the boldly sublime.

Dark and ominous thunderheads hovered on the far side of the valley, illuminated by jagged shards of lightening. The rumble of thunder could be heard, and waves of the assaulted and tortured atmosphere washed over them.

Simentoo's revere was broken by a fervent but truncated warning to flee. Simentoo, without thought, followed the others as they ran down a rock strewn, foliage-choked, and winding trail. The ground began to tremble and shake causing further trepidation. Simentoo feared a quake was about to open the ground and swallow them or bring the mountainside down on them.

Then the Dragon Queen burst forth from the small opening that the companions had just exited, raining rock and dirt debris down on the companions and leaving a ragged and gaping hole in the mountainside.

The dragon shot like an arrow from a bow, upward into the sky. She faded to a speck, looped around, and plummeted back towards the ground. Leveling off, she flew low, her shadow flitting over the ground, and with a resounding crash, back legs extended and talons protracted, she collided with the mountainside directly above the rent that she had created.

The results were calamitous as she tore and rend the mountainside. It began to slide, albeit reluctantly, in one fluid motion covering the gaping hole. In alarm everyone continued to run, down the winding trail, slipping and sliding.

Although lithe and well coordinated, Crysillnia stumbled as the trail broke and dropped from under her. Simentoo, close on her heels, reached for her but was swallowed up by the same slide.

Hand in hand, the two tumbled along with the migrating mountainside. They both figured they would be crushed under the tons of rubble moving around and along side them. Crysillnia closed her eyes tightly. She figured if she were to die, she didn't want to see it.

She began to pray, one hand clasping Simentoo's hand and the other grasping the pouch containing the Crystals. Amidst her prayers, a stray thought crossed her mind. She wished that Simentoo and she were safely at the bottom of the trail.

The thunderous crashing sound of the slide abruptly faded as if it were in the distance. She thought that she must have died. When she opened her eyes, she gasped. She was disoriented and filled with confusion. They were sitting at the edge of the jungle, the mountain trail rising behind them. Judging from Simentoo's expression, he was no less astonished.

As her surprise diminished, Crysillnia felt a tingling warmth in the hand that held the pouch. This is when she realized that she was grasping the pouch. She didn't remember taking the pouch from around her neck where she had placed it when she had begun to scale the shaft wall. With a startled cry, she reflexively opened her hand. The pouch fell from her hand, landing with a thud, spilling the Crystals.

Simentoo nonchalantly picked himself up and began to dust the dirt from his clothing. The heat and humidity were oppressive. Rivulets of sweat ran like rivers over his brows and into his eyes, causing them too burn painfully.

Simentoo rubbed his eyes with the back of his grimy hands which created more painful problems and elicited a long line of expletives. Crysillnia cried out. Simentoo unsheathed his weapon. He looked around, blinking his eyes trying to clear his blurred vision, searching for the reason of Crysillnia's distress.

Simentoo was finally able to focus on Crysillnia as his vision cleared. She was bedraggled and filthy. An expression of concern, amazement and fear painted her face.

She was staring at the Crystals lying on the ground at her side and clasping one of her hands to her body. Her expression quickly turned to one of pain as tears began to streak her face. The Crystals were glowing ominously.

Crysillnia turned to Simentoo perplexed and asked, "How did I do that?" Simentoo shrugged and answered, "I don't know, Lady Crysillnia."

Simentoo offered Crysillnia his hand to help her stand. She accepted the proffered hand but delicately. The hand she had been clasping to her body was red as if it had been burned. Once on her feet, she dusted herself off.

Crysillnia turned once again toward Simentoo and asked, "Why did you call me Lady Crysillnia?" He answered, "According to the dragon, you're a Princess. Therefore, you are due the respect of your station."

"Please don't refer to me in that way," she said, as she warily reached for the offending Crystals. Simentoo said, "What ever you wish, Mi-um . . . Crysillnia." Crysillnia quickly but delicately placed the no longer glowing Crystals back in the pouch. "Thank you," she said as she smiled brightly.

She examined the drawstring of the pouch closely to see if it were broken but found it to be sound. She pulled the drawstring over her head so that the pouch was once again nestled into the cleavage of her breasts.

"What do we do next?" she asked. "Set up camp and wait for the others to catch up," replied Simentoo. "There's a brook below. We can set up camp there," he continued. Simentoo gathered long dead wood to build a fire that would create little smoke.

When the others stumbled into the camp bedraggled and exhausted, expressions of astonishment and incredulity framed their faces. Then, completely out of character for the usually taciturn dwarf, Talok smiled and said, "Praise be to the great God of the Cold Winds. I didn't expect to see the two of you again on this side of the Veil." Then the dwarf let out a raspy chuckle.

Jarret rushed down to embrace Crysillnia. "Let me go, you son of a desert lizard. You're hurting me," she scolded. Jarret released her and stepped back with a goofy grin framing his mouth.

The elf scrutinized Crysillnia a with a look of mistrust. Crysillnia noticed that Kanef wasn't with them. "Where's Kanef?" She asked with concern.

*   *   *

Kanef had finally sort of, begun to understand and master the dynamics of riding on the back of a dragon. Dragons, like birds, took advantage of the air currents. Their huge webbed wings rotated slightly upwards to catch the updrafts, and they flapped them languidly when their were no upward flowing air currents to assist in keeping them aloft. But one always had to be prepared for a sudden loss of altitude when a dragon entered a stagnant pocket of air.

Kanef pulled his cloak closer as the dragon soared through the mountain valleys and peaks. Kanef was taken aback by the breathtaking beauty of the contrasting colors of the flowing landscape. He had never seen anything so magnificent. He envied the dragons their gift of flight.

The sun had settled high in the sky when they exited the mountains. Kanef relaxed his grip as his confidence in his abilities to ride the back of the dragon increased. This complacency nearly cost him his life. When the dragon banked and dove towards the ground suddenly, Kanef desperately grasped two of the horn spikes that girded the beast's neck. It felt like his heart was in his throat, and Kanef fought back the demand of the acid contents of his stomach for release.

Kanef projected a mental image of his anger at the dragon for the unexpected maneuver. "Look behind you," answered the dragon. Kanef did as the dragon instructed.

There were two huge, grotesque, flying demons following them. Their wing spans were twice that of the dragon's. The creatures' bodies were covered with sickly green scales tipped with prickly spines. They had large heads with eyes situated on the side and huge nostrils that flared rhythmically and spewed black slime as they labored to catch the dragon. Curved, razor-sharp horns adorned their long protruding snouts. The miscreant creatures had long muscular tails equipped with very long, sharp spikes.

"We have problems," said the dragon. "You're not overstating the obvious," replied Kanef. "They will soon overtake us, and I am no match for them physically. I must put you down, so that I may battle them. I will hover above the ground and you jump off. I would be at a great disadvantage if they caught me on the ground," said the dragon.

The dragon dove towards the ground, with the adversaries in close pursuit, at such speed that Kanef could hear the wind whistle in his ears. The dragon leveled off just above the ground which allowed Kanef to dismount. When the dragon rose back into the sky, she startled two riders, a man and a woman. The man lost his balance and fell.

As the dragon banked to face her attackers, she stated to Kanef, "You know what you need to accomplish." Kanef felt a sadness as he watched the dragon engage her foes. At first the dragon's intelligence and better maneuverability appeared to give her the advantage she needed to win. But one of the misshapen creatures delivered a powerful blow with its tail. The blow tore the webbing on one of the Dragon Queen's wings. She spiraled to the ground.

Kanef watched helplessly as the dragon plummeted from the sky. The dragon hit the ground in the distance with a resounding crash. Kanef began to run in the direction of the fallen dragon, but he pulled-up short when the vile and putrid creatures focused their attention on him. The rasping sound of steel being run across wood and metal echoed across the plains as Kanef drew his broad sword from its scabbard. He realized he was doomed, but he wouldn't go down without a fight.

The largest of the creatures swooped down from the direction of the setting sun. All Kanef could see was a dark, shapeless silhouette, but he could smell the corruption. The stench was so bad he actually believed that he could taste it.

Kanef struck the creature, but his broadsword bounced off the creature's hide as if it was made of stone. Pain coursed through Kanef's hand and arms as the vibrations caused by the strike flowed down the steel blade and through the bone handle. He dropped his weapon.

Kanef dove to the ground to avoid the attack of the second creature which had followed the first. He grabbed his sword, as he rolled across the ground. The creature screamed in frustration at missing its intended victim.

He came to his feet in a low crouch searching the skies for the next attack. Before he could spot his attackers, he heard an agonizing cry. He turned in the direction of the cry and was surprised to see a blue beam of energy open up the larger of the two creatures, spilling its entrails over the ground. The creature made a feeble attempt to escape but fell to the ground not far from its stunned would-be victim. Kanef watched in astonishment as the creature writhed in agony before it died.

"Down you fool! Here comes the other one!" Kanef dove to the ground, face first, at the prompting, but this time he didn't roll. He hit the ground flat and didn't move. He heard a sound like meat sizzling over an open fire. Kanef rolled on to his back so he could see what was occurring. He watched as the second creature met the same fate as the first.

Kanef stood and deftly sheathed his broadsword. Kanef scrutinized his rescuers as they approached. One, a Halhoren woman on horseback, and the other, a man on foot. There was horse following the man closely. The man was covered with dirt from head to toe, and he didn't appear to be in a very pleasant mood. Kanef rested the palm of his hand lightly on the hilt of his sheathed short sword.

The dirt covered man smiled at Kanef and said, "Hello, my name is Carric." Kanef didn't reply. Carric, discomforted by Kanef's silence, absentmindedly did a visual inspection of himself. He chuckled and then looked back at Kanef and said, "I must be a sight. It appears, my horsemanship needs some polishing." Kanef stood silently.

The woman, with a bit of snip in her voice, spoke up, "Are you mute or just rude?" Kanef, realizing how rude his caution appeared, responded, "Thank you for your help, Wizard." "Isn't that like a man. He automatically assumes that the man is the warrior and not the woman," echoed the woman with disgust. "I'm the one that saved your pale hide," she needled.

Kanef, taken aback and a little irritated by the woman's vehemence, countered, "Are you not Halhoren?" "Yes, is it not evident," she retorted. Kanef ignored the sarcastic remark and continued, "Then, if I recall properly, your people abhor magic." "Yes!" the woman answered.

"That took mighty powerful magic to bring down those beasts. So I assumed, albeit incorrectly, that he was the one that had the magic." The woman, flustered by Kanef's logical assumption, didn't know what to say.

She held up a black box cupped in her hands and said, "Magic had nothing to do with it. This is a great weapon from Carric's homeland." The man appeared to be aggravated at the woman's revelation. Kanef looked from one to the other, his curiosity piqued. He noticed how perturbed the man became with the petulant woman. Such an odd couple, Kanef thought to himself.

"Where is your home?" asked Kanef imperiously. The woman quipped in response to Kanef's attitude, "You're acting rather highhanded. You're not our leader." The man put up his hand to stop the woman's tirade which she did with a huff.

"I'm from across a far sea," answered the man with a wave of his hand in no particular direction. Kanef knew it would do no good to question the mysterious man any further on where he was from.

"What is your destination?" queried Kanef. "To Astaria," blurted out the woman, annoyed by the fact that she was no longer the center of attention. "Why?" asked Kanef. "Let's set up camp, and I'll tell you," said Carric.

CHAPTER 23

Alaquin was frightened. According to her demon guardian, they were in the void. Here the darkness was absolute, completely devoid of light. So much so that she was unable to distinguish the form of her hand, even when she brought it to within inches of her face.

"Where shall we go?" asked Alaquin. "Nowhere," answered the demon. "What do you mean? Nowhere!" asked Clodtrip with a truculent edge to his voice. "We are in the void. There is nowhere to go," answered the demon, in a matter of fact manner. "We just can't stand here until we cease to exist," countered Alaquin in a slightly quivering voice.

"Well, we could wander around and maybe with some luck find a doorway back," replied the demon. "But I don't expect such luck." "We need to try something, demon," replied Clodtrip poignantly. "I suppose," replied the demon dubiously.

"How shall we keep from being separated?" questioned Alaquin. Then Alaquin heard a faint voice, almost like the whispering of a gentle midsummer nights breeze, rustling the leaves in a forest. "Did you hear that?" asked Alaquin, of no one in particular. "Hear what?" queried Clodtrip with an edge in his voice. "I hear nothing," replied the demon.

"I thought I heard someone call my name," answered Alaquin. "The void does strange things to one's imagination," said the demon. "No!" cried Alaquin sharply. "There it is again, even louder." "I hear nothing," reiterated Clodtrip. "And neither do I," echoed the demon.

"Someone is calling me. From that direction," Alaquin pointed foolishly. "Or something," grumbled Clodtrip, in a barely audible voice. Alaquin, ignoring her disgruntled companion, said, "Grab the tail of my tunic, and I'll follow the voice and we'll see where it leads."

"How will our protector follow?" asked Clodtrip sarcastically. The demon ignored Clodtrip's insult and replied, "I can follow your scent." "Oh! You telling me I need a bath?" jibed Alaquin.

"No, insult meant, elf girl," replied the embarrassed demon. "But I can smell all creatures. Even our illustrious companion, Clodtrip," answered the demon in retaliation for Clodtrip's earlier comment.

"I see you're not content with insulting just one of us," said Clodtrip mirthfully sticking with the spirit of the moment set by the elf girl. The demon, not knowing how to reply, said nothing. Alaquin, feeling sorry for the now silent demon, replied. "None taken."

Alaquin could no longer resist the alluring voice echoing in her head. Evidently, she was the only one able to hear it. Following the faint call, Alaquin took the lead but found it very difficult to walk. "It feels like I'm walking through a stagnant pool of water," said Alaquin. "That is typical for a first timer," replied the demon. "A first timer?" repeated Alaquin in a questioning tone. "This is your first time in the void. You will eventually become accustomed to difference in density between your world and the void," answered the demon.

"I hope I'm not here that long!" replied Alaquin. The demon fluttered his wings as if in answer but said nothing. Alaquin took that as a sign that the demon considered their situation hopeless but didn't want to discourage her by stating the possibility.

Alaquin's attention was drawn back to the alluring and sensuous voice within her head. As she struggled arduously through the syrupy void, the voice became louder and more pronounced. Pointing again, Alaquin asked excitedly, "Do you see the light!" "Where!" asked Clodtrip, standing behind the elf girl. "Ahead of us! Can't you see it? Ooh, it's gone," she said, tears welling up in her eyes, the disappointment apparent in her voice, as she lowered her head.

"No! No! It is not gone. I see it, too!" shouted the demon excitedly. Clodtrip strained his eyes and finally spotted a dim light in the distance. In his excitement, he nearly trampled the elf girl, as he started towards the faint glow of hope.

"Could it be a hole in the void?" asked Alaquin hopefully. "No, it couldn't be a hole," replied the demon, worry apparent in its voice. "How would you know?" snipped Alaquin, upset at having her hopes dashed. "Because if it was a hole, we would be in the midst of chaos as the two dimensions tried to achieve an equilibrium," answered the demon.

"Then what is it," asked Clodtrip. He stopped in apprehension. Alaquin was jerked to an unceremonious stop because Clodtrip still gripped the tail of her tunic. The demon flew into the back of Clodtrip's head.

Clodtrip swatted at the demon, brushing its wing. The disoriented and out of control demon flew into the elf girl's back. The demon's momentum knocked Alaquin flat on her face. She squealed in fright and pain.

Confused and still highly agitated, Clodtrip asked, "What happened?" Alaquin, beginning to realize what had just occurred, explained to the best of her abilities. The horseman, still anxious from the remnants of adrenalin still coursing through his veins, snipped, "You should be more careful elf girl!" Alaquin picked herself up. She retorted angrily. "Me! I'm not the one who stopped without warning!"

She could feel her anger building and the magic begin to surface. "No," Alaquin heard, but this time the others could also hear the voice. "Control that temper, young lady," the mysterious voice said. "Who's their?" Asked the horseman, as he pivoted, looking for the source of the mysterious voice and expecting an attack at any moment.

"Come to the light. I am there," was the mysterious voice's reply. "Why don't you come to us?" badgered Clodtrip. "I am unable to. Please come! We have little time, and I need to talk with Alaquin," continued the voice with urgency. Clodtrip was about to make another challenge when Alaquin spoke, "It's alright, she's no threat." Alaquin made the gender assessment of the deep raspy voice, because their was a definite feminine quality of the voice.

"How can you be so sure?" questioned Clodtrip. "Instinct," answered Alaquin. When they approached the light, images began to clarify. What they saw resembled a tree or maybe a web. It radiated a blue-green light. "Oh, isn't she beautiful." reflected Alaquin verbally. Clodtrip looked around, searching for someone else. Perplexed, he asked, "Who are you talking about? I see only the three of us, and I'm quite sure you're not referring to our demon friend when you speak of beauty." "I would appreciate it if you would keep your opinions of beauty to yourself. Where I come from, I am considered quite attractive," said the demon with a slight hiss.

Alaquin, brought back to reality by the disgruntled hissing of the demon, said, "Her, the tree." "I've never heard of a tree being referred to by gender," replied Clodtrip. "The elf girl is correct in her own mind." Clodtrip, startled by the voice, began to walk around in a circle, prepared for an attack. "Where are you? Show yourself!" said the nervous horseman. "I am right in front of you."

Alaquin, mesmerized once again, began to soak in the beauty and well being that was being exuded. There was more of an ethereal, rather than a corporeal, presence. The tree, web, or fabric of time was more akin to a luminous outline rather than a solid entity. It penetrated the infinite darkness of the void.

A bright yellow rounded object with a dash of crimson appeared to be suspended in the vastness of the void. Alaquin, fascinated by the object, reached for it. In her mind, the closest thing she could relate it to was some sort of wild and exotic fruit. It was like nothing she had ever seen before.

The voice said, "That is, for the lack of a better description, the fruit of knowledge." Alaquin, wary and a slight bit afraid, took a step back.

"Then if I hadn't stumbled on to the hole, there would have been no way for me to have completed my quest. No one told me that my destination existed in the void." Alaquin stated vexation apparent in her voice.

"This is your destiny. You didn't enter the hole by accident. I opened it for you. You were chosen by those who oppose chaos and disorder. Once you partake of the orb, or as you think of it, the fruit, everything will become clear."

"Then you're The Tree of Knowledge?" questioned Alaquin. I'll have to answer that with a yes and no," said the presence. "Yes and no. That is a rather contradictory statement. That's like saying something is true and false," snapped Clodtrip truculently.

"I will explain my cryptic answer the best way I can. Please be patient with me, Clodtrip," replied the voice. "I am called Eden, The Tree of Knowledge, The One and All, and many other names from many different cultures. To answer the yes and no question. I need to explain the nature of the void. The void is what holds all creation together. The best way to explain this concept would be to use an analogy. We'll use a piece of cloth. The cloth is created when fibers are woven together. Without the fibers and the weaver, the cloth couldn't exist."

"I am the fiber and weaver. All of creation is the cloth. I was created by those who lived in a place where nothing but magic existed. But there is a serious problem. The cloth is beginning to unravel. My magic is beginning to weaken and a war over magic between the creators hasn't helped."

"Magic comes in many forms. Your world is blessed with natural magic but, on other worlds where magic doesn't exist, the inhabitants have created false magic. This magic is referred to as technology. One of these technological worlds has created something that unravels my creation."

"This object is now on your world. The concentrated use of magic is also tearing holes in the cloth, such as the temper tantrum you threw at the Council of Elders. You, Alaquin, created a small tear, one that I was able to mend without to much difficulty, this time. What frightens me most about the incident is that was only a fraction of the power you are capable of utilizing. I don't have the energy to combat both problems. You and your niece have to control your use of magic more carefully." Alaquin interrupted the dissertation. "My niece?"

"Ah, yes, you are unaware of your linage," continued The Tree of Knowledge. "My mother died birthing me, and no one knew who fathered me," confirmed Alaquin. "The person I am referring to is Crysillnia," replied the presence.

"The woman I helped in the forest?" questioned an incredulous Alaquin. "Yes, and Kanef is your brother." Stunned by these revelations, the elf girl took a step backwards. Shaking with excitement, mouth agape, tears welled up in her eyes. Alaquin found that her legs would no longer support her so she plopped down on the ground. Her legs folded under her.

"How did it happen?" the elf girl asked. "I take it you mean, how your mother came to be impregnated by the King of Caspar?" questioned the presence. "Yes," answered Alaquin. "Ah, my dear, that is a hard story to tell but, I suppose, it must be told, continued the voice.

"Your mother was a wonderful elf. She harbored no ill feeling or prejudices towards anyone. On the other hand, your father is an evil, greedy, and self-serving person. Your mother was adventuresome and free-spirited. She would venture out of her homelands and mix with the humans, although this went against the accepted mores of elf behavior."

"She was censured by the Council of Elders many times. Finally, the council banished her from the forest for because she refused to abide by the rules. Although she was sad at being forced to leave her home, she took it as a new and exhilarating adventure. But her grand adventure became a disappointment. She found that most human's prejudices and hatred for elves were unconquerable."

"So she moved back to the edge of the forest, where she found an old farmer and his wife trying to eke a living from the poor soils near the forest. Your mother befriended the old couple and used the rune magic to increase the crop yields. One afternoon, in late spring, she was seeding a field for the farmer while he went to Dragon's Peek for supplies."

"Your father was out on a pillaging spree, something he did every spring since his adolescence, until he became King of Caspar. He told his father he was going hunting, but he would gather a few of his outlaw friends and raid the poor farmers of the neighboring provinces. Sometimes he would rob coaches along the roads if, by chance, he encountered any, killing all the passengers to insure their were no witnesses. Although they wore hoods, he feared someone might recognize a voice or see something that would identify the bandits."

"On this fine afternoon, your father was returning to Caspar.

This would be his last criminal excursion for your grandfather was gravely ill, and your father was to be coronated the next day. He came across your mother while she was setting her final spell for the day. She was unaware of his presence; therefore, he was able to surprise her, and she was unable to use her magic to protect herself. He raped and brutalized your mother. She lay in the field all night unable to move or even cry for help."

The old farmer, fearing for her when she hadn't returned by the next morning, found her near death and brought her back to his home and nursed her back to partial health. The injuries your mother had suffered were to severe to be totally healed."

"Your mother was broken emotionally, so the old farmer returned your mother to the elves near the time of your birth. He realized that your mother would have no chance of surviving your birth if she stayed with him and his wife. He set up camp and waited until the elves came for your mother. The wait lasted for two weeks but finally the elves, considering your mother's delicate state, realized they wouldn't be able to assuage their consciences if they allowed her and the child to die."

Alaquin pulled her knees up to her chest, encircled them with her arms and bowed her head, resting it on her knees and began to weep. Clodtrip walked over to stand by the grief stricken elf girl and gently laid his hand on her shoulder in an attempt to comfort her. The demon settled down beside her and nestled up to her side in an attempt to console Alaquin.

After a few minutes the voice continued, "Your father is not only evil but has a terrible temper, where your mother was kind, gentle, and loving. You need to harness that anger and control it because you have both spiritual magic inherited from your human side and the land magic heritage from the elves. Alaquin, you could be a great force of destruction or a great builder of good." Alaquin looked up, eyes bloodshot, with tears streaming down her cheeks. "Why me? Why me?" she repeated defiantly, but softly. "Fate, my dear," replied the voice.

"I feel a disturbance in the fabric of creation. I fear your niece, Crysillnia, is drawing on the powers of the Crystals." Then the voice emitted a trilling noise. The fabric of the universe began to quake. Alaquin, startled, leapt to her feet, while Clodtrip pawed the air with his front hooves, and the demon took to flight.

"Oh, oh! The pain!" screamed the voice. "Quickly, eat the fruit, Alaquin. You are the only one that has the power to repair the rend but you need the knowledge. The fruit will supply that knowledge along with much more that will be useful."

Alaquin reached for the fruit but the spasms in the void made it difficult to reach the glowing orb of knowledge. "Such power . . . I didn't realize she possessed so much of the spiritual energy," said the voice. "Hurry, child." "Hold still. I can't reach the fruit with you jerking it around like that," yelled Alaquin. "Sorry, my dear," apologized the voice as she took control of her pain. The spasms ceased so Alaquin could easily reach the orb.

Alaquin gently tugged on the brightly glowing object until it pulled free in her hand. She examined the now pulsating object closely. It was so beautifully colored and perfectly round. Its texture was smooth. It reminded Alaquin of a divining crystal.

"Eat, child, eat. Don't stand there and look at it. Once picked it will quickly lose the knowledge stored within and it will take many years for me to fruit another." Alaquin, shaken from her reverie by the voice's adamant scolding, quickly put the fruit to her lips but was still reluctant to mar the fruit's beauty by taking a bite.

Closing her eyes, Alaquin took a small tentative nibble. The sensation was indescribable. At first the fruit seem extremely sweet, then a bitter taste inundated her mouth, nearly causing her to spit the offending bite on the ground. Then she had a distinct hint of salt which quickly changed to a sour sensation, causing Alaquin to pucker up, sending cold chills pulsating through her entire body.

Then she felt the blood rush to her head, and then she became sick to her stomach and disoriented. She nearly fainted and would have collapsed if not for Clodtrip reaching over to steady her. He asked if she was alright. Then a feeling of euphoria, sexual excitement, and a sense of well being engulfed Alaquin.

Alaquin shook her head. It had ended as quickly as it had begun which nearly brought her to tears. Looking down at her open hand she was surprised to see that all she held was a seed of the fruit. She didn't remember eating the whole fruit. With anger, she turned on her companions. "Who ate the rest of the fruit! It was my due!"

Taken aback by the accusation, Alaquin's companions didn't know what to make of her behavior. Finally, Clodtrip replied, "Only you ate the fruit, elf girl." Holding her hand out, showing the seed to Clodtrip, Alaquin said with an angry and dangerous edge to her voice, "I recall taking only one bite, and this is all I have left. Clodtrip replied, a bit perturbed at Alaquin's behavior, "When you bit into the fruit, It exploded with a bright blue flash of light, and once the light faded, the seed was all that remained." Alaquin was dubious of Clodtrip's explanation and was prepared to refute it when the voice intervened.

"Yes, my dear. The Fruit of Knowledge is nothing more than pure energy. Once you broke the seal that entrapped the Energy of Knowledge, you were inundated with the knowledge of the universe. What is useful to you and what your mind can comprehend was absorbed by you. The rest was scattered to infinity, where eventually it will be reabsorbed and fruited for future generations."

Alaquin felt a puff of air tickle the hairs on her arm. At first she thought that something was crawling on her arm. This was the first noticeable movement of air that she had felt in the void. The puff of air became a breeze. Then the breeze increased in velocity, becoming a full blown gale. "Crysillnia has ruptured the Fabric of Existence. You must go to her and repair the tear, Alaquin." "How! How do I repair it!" cried Alaquin desperately. "You have partaken of the orb or fruit or what ever you wish to call it. You'll know what to do when you get there," answered the voice.

The wind by now was tearing at Alaquin's clothing as if it were trying to undress her. Her long soft hair was flying in the wind, wrapping around her head, and covering her face. She had to pull her hair out of her mouth before she gagged on it. Then Alaquin felt like she was airborne as the force of the gale began to push her ahead of it. It was as if it was an intelligent entity trying to hurry the elf girl along. As the wind carried Alaquin away, she heard the voice say, "Don't forget to plant the seed."

Then Alaquin was blinded by bright light as she was tossed from the void, along with her companions and other dark and vile creatures. Tumbling across the ground and rolling into a heap with her companions, Alaquin struggled to untangle herself from legs, arms, hooves, and wings.

CHAPTER 24

"Kanef went with the dragon. She was going to take him home. He wasn't pleased, but she convinced him he had no choice," Jarret answered Crysillnia. Crysillnia was hungrily devouring the last morsel of rabbit that Simentoo had snared for their evening meal. She hadn't realized how tired she was of cold rations.

Simentoo suggested, being this close to the dark and forbidding jungle, that it would be safer to have a fire. It would discourage any of the wild beasts that lived in the foliage clogged jungle from entering their camp. The first moon had risen and the second was just making its appearance over the horizon. The second moon was the harbinger of winter. The Double Cast Moon only occurred once a year.

Crysillnia complained. "You wouldn't know that winter was just around the corner in this furnace." Even though the sun had set, it was still sultry. No one dared to sit near the fire. The sweat poured off them in runnels. The two moons cast an eerie, bluish luminesce over the landscape. The light shed by the two celestial bodies almost gave one the impression that it was a heavily overcast day and not night.

A cry of consternation escaped from Jarret's lips. He was inspecting and cleaning his weapons. His dagger, the first weapon he had inspected, was pitted and corroded, and the scabbard that held it was nearly eaten away. In his hurry to escape the mountain after their battle with the demons, he had sheathed his weapons without wiping them clean.

The others quickly inspected their weapons. Those not made with Keltian steel had similar damage. With great difficulty, they cleaned and put new edges on their damaged weapons.

Simentoo said, "We should rest now. I'll take first watch." Jarret volunteered to take second watch, and Talok accepted the third by default. The elf didn't volunteer and wasn't expected to. No one in the group trusted the mysterious, egg stealing elf.

The elf faded into the darkness. He sat quietly listening to the life and death struggles of the nocturnal creatures of the jungle. He had his own plans to complete. He didn't have the option to help his new companions. As soon as was feasible, he would slip away.

Crysillnia, exhausted from the day's events, tossed and turned through the night. She was unable to sleep. The grunts, screams, and cries of death and triumph from the jungle permeated the air.

She finally fell in to a restless sleep. Crysillnia began to dream. She dreamed that her ethereal-self had separated from her corporeal-self and was floating and wafting freely in the darkness of night. Then a lilting breeze began to caress and seduce her with its gentle promise of peace.

The euphoria of the moment engulfed her. Crysillnia's ethereal-self began to drift away from her body, but she was not aware of this subtle occurrence.

The strength of the breeze increased which finally caught Crysillnia's attention. She struggled against the breeze and tried to return to her body, but the harder she struggled the stronger the wind became. She found to her chagrin that she was unable to prevent the separation.

Crysillnia ceased her struggle and accepted the segregation. She rose higher into the night sky. She realized that she was flying and was able to control her flight. She soared over the canopy of the jungle and found she was part of the jungle. Then she rose into the heavens and danced with the stars and became one with them.

Crysillnia felt a tug at her spiritual-self, but she ignored it. She wanted to stay amongst the beauty of the stars, but the pull became more persistent. She began to plummet from the heavens. Her fall was sudden and quick. She began to fear for her life.

Then, just as suddenly as her fall began, it ceased. It was now daylight, and she was hovering over a desert. The air shimmered from the heat radiating up from the desert floor, but she didn't feel the heat.

She hovered over the desert floor of sparkling white sands, sprinkled with rocks and boulders of various sizes and shapes. There were patches of shrubs, grasses, and trees trying to eke out an existence in the harsh, hostile, and barren environment. She floated and wafted, without a care in the world, through a narrow and jagged ravine. She was jolted out of her reverie when she picked up a mental image from a desert creature.

She searched the desert floor in hopes of spotting the creature. She finally located it. It was a Desert Dragon a far distant cousin of the Mountain Dragon. It resembled a lizard more than a dragon. Desert dragons didn't grow wings. They were sentient but stupid.

Crysillnia picked up a stray thought from the dragon sunning itself. It was hoping dinner would come along soon. She realized that she was reading its thoughts. She seemed to be drawn into the dragons thoughts. It referred to itself as Gurlag. She was encompassed by his thoughts, and then she was Gurlag.

She could feel the soothing warmth of the sun on her scaly hide. She felt the strong twinge of hunger. She flicked her long forked tongue. She was testing the air for possible prey.

Crysillnia felt Gurlag's annoyance and fear. He felt her presence in his mind. In an attempt to soothe the desert dragon's trepidation and fear, she joined with his Essence. She became one with him.

Gurlag felt strange. He felt like he had been two but now he felt normal once again. His hunger was growing. He flicked his long slender tail, nervously.

Gurlag raised his head. There was something moving across the desert. Gurlag's vision was weak but he was sure there was something moving towards him through the shimmering veil of heat.

Gurlag, the persistent hunter that he was, waited patiently. But, to his chagrin, he realized it was a human. This human was strange. It appeared to wink in and out of existence.

Gurlag thought to himself this is too much, it's time to move on. Gurlag sidled off the rock. Humans were dangerous enough with their pointy tails but humans with magic were even worse. Gurlag scuttled into the nearest hole he could find.

Crysillnia felt the urge to return to her corporeal body. She separated from Gurlag, but before she returned, she took note of the stranger. He was dressed in tight fitting attire that was unfamiliar to her. It was a one piece suit with no buttons or hooks and appeared to change colors depending on what surroundings he passed through. Hie boots appeared to be made of the same material. He was armed with a long and narrow sword.

The man was tall and lanky. His feet were too big and his arms short. He had a large nose and small mouth. His hair was dark and unkempt.

"Crysillnia! Crysillnia! Wake up!" said Simentoo with concern in his voice. Simentoo was worried. When he awoke, he found Crysillnia wan and sickly looking. She was taking short, shallow and ragged breaths. Simentoo's overt agitation brought the other's to Crysillnia's side.

Crysillnia's ethereal spirit, with reluctance, returned to her body. Someone or something was shaking her. She lashed out blindly at her tormentor. When she finally regained control of her addled mental faculties, she opened her eyes.

Talok and Jarret were standing by her side uncertainty and concern mirrored in their eyes. There was a crumpled heap lying beside her. Crysillnia felt a warm pulsating sensation in her hands. She sat up with some difficulty and opened her them. She found that she was clasping the pouch containing the Crystals. A multicolor light leaked out of the slightly opened pouch.

She looked up once again at the two men standing over her. Then she glanced over at the crumpled heap beside her and discovered, to her alarm, it was Simentoo. She dropped the pouch and raised her hands to her mouth, emitting a weak cry and gasp.

"What happened to him?" she asked. "Well, Milady, he was attempting to arouse you when a pulse of light from the pouch struck him in the chest," replied Jarret.

The elf approached Simentoo and said, "We must lay him on his back." He did so with help from Jarret and Talok. The elf then

173

sat cross-legged beside the stricken soldier and placed his hand on Simentoo's chest. "What are you doing, elf?" asked Talok suspiciously. "Searching for his spirit, and my name is Zulnee. Please refer to me by my name," snapped the elf.

"I wish not to be here anymore than you," continued the elf vehemently which was followed by a deep hollow silence. Then Zulnee began to chant in a very low monotone voice. Zulnee fell silent once again. His body stiffened, and he became pale as if all the blood had been drained from his body.

A short time later Zulnee's color returned, and he stood. The elf turned to Crysillnia. "Lady, you have greater powers than I suspected. Simentoo's spirit is lost in a dimension that I can't reach. You are the only one, with aid of the Crystals, that might be able to find his spirit and guide it back. This needs to be done soon, before his body dies. It may take a while for her to accomplish her task. We must find a place protected from the weather." Talok asked sarcastically. "Where do you expect to find a place like that in the middle of the wilderness?" Jarret answered, "There are probably caves this near the mountains." While Crysillnia stayed by Simentoo's side, the others went in search of shelter as a rumble of thunder from distant storm washed over them.

CHAPTER 25

Simentoo had awakened with the sun. It was going the to be another hot and humid day. He could feel the moisture in the air. In fact, the night hadn't cooled the air much from yesterday's heat. He began to perspire the minute he had began to move.

He checked the camp's perimeter and spoke briefly with Talok. He noticed that the elf was awake also. He wondered if the elf had slept at all. He was headed back to the fire to prepare breakfast, when he noticed how wan and pale Crysillnia appeared.

He stooped down beside her. He tried to awaken her but she didn't respond to his voice. Deeply concerned, he grabbed her by the shoulder and began to shake her. A pulsating flash of light exited the pouch. Simentoo felt a warm, tingling surge of energy course through his body which was followed quickly by excruciating pain. His body convulsed violently, and he crumpled to the ground.

Awareness gradually returned to Simentoo. He felt strange and disoriented. His body felt like it had no substance. He sat up. He was confused and bewildered. He didn't know where he was. The jungle was gone. He was in the middle of a expansive plain bordered by mountains. The mountains appeared to be a long way off but they also seemed to be nearby.

Simentoo began to examine himself for wounds, a soldier's habit. He ran his finger through his hair searching for lumps or abrasions. Finally, he was satisfied he had no injuries.

But where was he and how did he come to be here. He realized, with some trepidation, that he wasn't fully armed. His broad sword was missing. In desperation, he searched the ground around him for the missing weapon, hut it was nowhere in evidence.

Simentoo was confused. He didn't know what to do or where to go. He had never been in this sort of situation before. He searched the surrounding horizons, and they appeared to be identical. Nothing in any direction set itself off from the other.

A deadening pall of silence blanketed the plain. The only sound was the ringing in his ears. There wasn't even a breeze stirring. The plain was carpeted with wild flowers reflecting strange colors and hues, a surreal landscape.

There were clouds suspended in the skies above but they didn't appear to move. The sky was a dark blue, and there was no sun but there was light. Enough light to give one the impression that it was daytime. The light seemed to have no source. It was just there.

Simentoo started to trek across this strange and eerie plain. Maybe he could find a town, a farmhouse, or at least someone who could tell him where or what this place is. He noticed that his foot wasn't making contact with the ground. It appeared to fade or become less substantial.

His attention was drawn away from this peculiarity when a shadow passed over him. Instinctively, he reached for the short sword at his side. When he freed it from the scabbarded. It took on an insubstantial form. It appeared to be more of shadow than a weapon of hardened steel.

Simentoo sheathed his sword when the shadow failed to materialize and continued to move across the strange plain. Simentoo began to look more closely at the lush vegetation through which he walked. There were not only flowers but a variety of multicolored grasses, crowned with halos of seeds, in various stages of ripeness.

The shadow returned, but he didn't draw his weapon this time. He felt a familiarity in the shadow. He sensed no danger or malice from the it. The shadow followed him and at times took the lead.

The light of the day began to fade. Simentoo spotted a silhouette of something or someone in the distance. It was moving in his general direction. Simentoo stopped as he tried to assess the situation. He didn't know whether it was foe or friend.

Simentoo's shadow companion, as he came to think of it, hovered overhead. He sensed a nervousness about it. The silhouette was now coming directly towards him. His shadow companion became quite agitated. Simentoo pulled his sword once again and looked for a place to hide, but to his consternation, there was nowhere to conceal himself.

The silhouette finally took form and now was charging him. Simentoo recognized with what he was about to do battle. It was a Mountain Bear. One of the most dangerous beasts of the mountains.

The creature was twice the height of Simentoo and probably four times his weight. It had a long snout filled with teeth, as sharp as a freshly whetted dagger. Its paws were twice the size of a human's hand tipped with claws longer than human fingers. The bear was covered with a thick black fur that was difficult to penetrate with a broadsword let alone the short sword and dagger Simentoo possessed at the moment.

Simentoo knew that the only chance he had against the mountain bear was his superior agility and speed. The bear charged Simentoo. He sidestepped at the last moment. The bear took a wild swipe, grazing Simentoo's arm, drawing rivulets of blood.

The smell of fresh blood sent the bear into a frenzy. It pivoted, quicker than Simentoo expected, catching him off guard. Rising on its two hind legs, the bear embraced Simentoo and began to squeeze the life out of him. Simentoo drove his short sword into the creatures belly and his dagger into the beast's shoulder in hopes that the bear would release its grip. The bear roared in pain and released him.

Simentoo fell backwards gasping for breath. He was dizzy and disoriented. He felt a wrenching pain in his gut like he was being turned inside out, and he closed his eyes in agony.

When he opened them he found himself looking up at a high-vaulted ceiling decorated with paintings and carvings of strange beasts and people. There was a musty smell in the room. He slowly raised himself to a sitting position. A dizzy feeling engulfed him, and he felt sick to his stomach. He looked around the room in wonderment.

The walls were covered from floor to ceiling with books. The floor was pure white marble with an intricate forest design carved into it. The trees and animals were so finely detailed and painted that one felt that one was in the forest. There was a huge, finely finished, wooden double door in one wall flanked by stacks of scrolls.

Simentoo stood and began to walk around the room. The room was bigger than what it appeared, and there were smaller arched doorways which gave access to other larger rooms. These rooms were stacked from floor to ceiling with books.

In the center of one of the rooms was a table loaded with opened scrolls and books. He had an urgent need to enter this room. He followed this need. There were isles of bookshelves in the room. Simentoo paced up and down the isles searching for a tome. He didn't know exactly which one but he knew he would recognize it when he saw it.

Towards the back of the room, his attention was drawn to a large tome squeezed in between a host of smaller books. He grabbed the spine of the tome, and it began to pulsate. He tugged on the tome, but it resisted. It was held tight by the flanking tomes. He tugged harder, and the massive tome broke loose from the others' tenacious grip.

Simentoo found himself backpedaling and trying to regain his balance. The only thing that kept him on his feet was stumbling into a reading table. After steading himself, Simentoo turned and placed the book on the slightly inclined table. A lip along the bottom edge of the table kept the book from sliding off.

Simentoo laid his hand on the worn leather cover. The tome felt warm to the touch. He opened it and a flood of light burst forth. The pesky shadow that had been hovering above him and following him around the library retreated beyond the reach of the light.

When Simentoo's eyes adjusted to the light, he was amazed at what he saw. The book didn't contain words. It contained pictures and not just ordinary pictures. The pictures were moving. He was viewing a mountain scene. A small plateau overlooking a narrow sharp-cut valley. The pungent smell of damp soil and wild flowers wafted from the tome. The plateau looked familiar.

There was a young man sitting with his back resting against the trunk of small oak tree. The leaves were rustling in the breeze that blew up from the valley below. The young man was perusing a book. He was dressed in the white cloak of the scholar tied at the waist with a red sash.

Suddenly it dawned on Simentoo. The young man he was watching was himself. It was the day that had changed his life forever. The day he lost Renira. Tears flooded his eyes.

The sun was shining brightly. A youthful Simentoo closed his book and quickly tucked it into the pack by his side. He could hear Renira returning from the brook below. She had gone down to get some water.

He knew she would skin him alive if she suspected he was studying. They were here to picnic today. This was suppose to be their time together, and he loved her with all his being. A young Simentoo watched Renira as she approached him. She was smiling effusively. She was following a line of trees that were the outer edge of a small grove of pine trees.

Renira was petite and voluptuous. Her red hair flowed over her shoulders to the middle of her back ending in long rippling curls. Renira had a button nose, a perfect mouth, and flashing white teeth. Her eyes were a striking green and when she focused them on you in anger, you felt like you would dissolve right on the spot.

Many of the other young men in the village had shown an interest in Renira, to the chagrin of the other young women nearing their pairing years, but she chose Simentoo. He had been born into the warrior class, but chose to follow the path of the scholar and had decided to become the village historian and scribe.

Simentoo and Renira had started meeting in this hard to reach and secluded meadow to avoid the disapproval of their elders, when they were thirteen seasons. They would both soon be sixteen seasons. The age of pairing.

Young Simentoo watched in horror as a mountain bear crashed out of the pine grove where it had been sleeping and attacked the girl. He was paralyzed with indecision as he watched the bear maul his beloved. Her screams of fear and pain ripped through the air. Her eyes focused on Simentoo, pleading for help.

The young man finally jumped to his feet and ran towards the mayhem. He didn't know what he would do when he got there, because he didn't have any weapons. But that turned out not to be a problem.

The bear finished his attack and ambled nonchalantly back into the trees. The young Simentoo kneeled beside the dying girl. He cradled Renira's head in his arms. She opened her eyes and smiled at him. Love emanated from her eyes and she began to speak but she started gasping like a fish out of water. Blood began to trickle over her lips and with one last sigh, her head rolled back and her eyes glazed over.

Simentoo slammed the book shut and stepped away from the table. His eyes were brimming with tears. Simentoo swatted at the pesky shadow as it circled his head. Saddened and irate Simentoo shouted at the shadow, "Leave me alone! Who or what are you? Why do you pester me so?"

"Simentoo! Simentoo!" echoed a haunting voice. "Renira is that you?" he asked. "Yes and no," replied the disembodied voice, chagrin shading his voice. Simentoo queried, "What is that suppose to mean? Are you the shadow?" "No, but the shadow is a friend. You must follow it. I am the book, the bear, and Renira. I am your guilt. You must forgive yourself. There was nothing you could have done to save Renira."

"But if I had had my weapon . . ." Simentoo began to argue. "Even with a weapon, if you had been able to reach her in time, you would have died and you are needed now more than ever," the voice answered.

Then the bloody apparition of Renira appeared, hovering over the tome. "I thought you loved me" said the apparition. "I did, and I still do," said Simentoo, hurt cracking in his voice. "Then why have you entrapped me in torment? I can't cross the veil until you conquer your guilt. What happened wasn't your fault. It was my time to go," said the voice soothingly. The apparition of Renira faded back into the book, then pleaded, "Free yourself and free my spirit. Kill your mountain bear."

Simentoo found himself back on the plain, lying on the ground before the mountain bear. The beast, with the dagger protruding from its throat and sword in its gut, lumbered towards Simentoo. He jumped to his feet and grabbed the hilt of the sword with both hands and heaved upwards and in, opening the bear's belly. The bear grabbed feebly for Simentoo as its entrails spilled out of its body. The gory scene faded away, and Simentoo heard a low whisper. "Thank you. I'll always love you."

"Simentoo, Simentoo wake-up," a soft voice coaxed. Groggily, Simentoo awoke to unadulterated darkness. His eyes adjusted to the dark, and he rolled his head to the side. He spotted the simmering coals of a campfire wich cast very little light. Then he noticed a dark silhouette next to him. Instinctively he shied away.

"It's me. Crysillnia." Simentoo said, with tears rolling down his cheek. "I know, and thank you." Crysillnia said," "You're welcome." Simentoo then fell into a deep, restful sleep.

CHAPTER 26

Simentoo and the others entered the jungle about midday. The heat and humidity were stifling. They felt as if the jungle was closing in around them. There was a varied assortment of biting and stinging insects which made it miserable for all. Crysillnia swatted and cursed the relentless assault by the insects. The others appeared nearly as uncomfortable as Crysillnia.

The only one not affected was Simentoo. Although the insects were as harsh on him as the others, he wouldn't give into the misery as a good soldier should, he ignored the intolerable.

The trail meandered through the jungle aimlessly as if there was no special destination. The trees reached hundreds of feet into the sky as if striving to soar amongst the stars. Very little sunlight penetrated the jungle canopy. Moss hung from the trees with their roots and tendrils trailing along the jungle floor. Spider webs crisscrossed the well worn trail which was compacted like rock.

Simentoo was in the lead followed by Jarret, Crysillnia, Talok, and the elf. Crysillnia was alarmed by the creatures of the jungle. She could hear large creatures, crashing through the thick jungle under brush, startled by the travelers.

Crysillnia shivered at the screams of pain and fear that echoed throughout the jungle. The everyday drama of life and death played itself out, evidence of the dangers that lurked within the jungle's stifling embrace. Her companions, although alert, seemed undaunted by the living, writhing jungle. Suddenly, the jungle erupted around Crysillnia and her companions. They were under assault by a bizarre collection of humans.

Their bodies were painted with bright colors and strange characterizations of animals performing human deeds, chores, and dances. There were huge earrings dangling from their earlobes a which stretched and tore them. The battle was quick but brutal. Many of the attackers were felled by the defenders, but sheer numbers decided the final outcome. They were subdued and bound.

Crysillnia watched a tightly bound and gagged elf being carried into the jungle. She wondered what horrible fate awaited the unfortunate elf. Crysillnia and the remainder of her companions, badly battered, were tied together in a line on a stringer. One of the captors inspected the prisoners closely making sure that they were secure and had no hidden weapons.

When he reached Crysillnia, he began to fondled her breasts, leering at her licentiously while running his hands between her breasts. He accidently brushed the pouch containing the crystals. The man reached inside her tunic, grasped the pouch, tearing it away violently, but not before she sent a pulse of energy into the crystals. The man screamed with pure agony as the burst of energy disintegrated his hand and forearm to the elbow. The man lie writhing on the ground but received no sympathy from his companions. In a matter of fact manner, one of them ran him through with a spear.

The pouch containing the Crystals rolled into the jungle and none of the other warriors bothered to search for it. The painted warriors marched their captives down the trail. When the last man disappeared into the jungle, a dark, hairy arm thrust itself from the dense jungle foliage and gingerly picked the pouch up by the string. The Crystals disappeared into the jungle.

The beaten and bruised prisoners were cruelly marched along the meandering trail, goaded on by sharp spear points when they stumbled, fell, or slowed down for any reason. If they fell, they would be beaten and kicked ruthlessly until they regained their feet.

Crysillnia, tired and haggard from the relentless pace set by her captors, had become oblivious to her surroundings. She didn't notice the forest becoming thicker and more ominous. Even the painted warriors were nervous and more wary, as they searched the trees above them as if expecting an attack by a hidden and elusive enemy.

Simentoo was the first of the captives on the stringer with Jarret directly behind him. Two of the captors flanked the stringer directly behind Jarret, their short spears at the ready, prepared for any eventuality.

Simentoo could sense the tension of his captors. In an attempt to inform Jarret to be ready for most anything, he pretended to stumble which caused Jarret to collide with him. Simentoo grabbed Jarret by the leg, tripping and bringing the woodsman down on top of him.

"Beware of a chance to escape," Simentoo whispered. The guards following the two clumsy prisoners, angered by the tumbling duo, began to jab them with their sharp spears. Then, as if by magic and without warning, chaos broke out as large, black, hairy creatures spewed forth from the jungle canopy. These creatures had long arms and tails. They swung from the trees using their tails, hands, and feet.

The creatures attacked the warriors. Simentoo and Jarret took advantage of their startled tormentors and disarmed them. Using the spears, they cut their bindings. Both men, now armed, joined the ensuing battle. They were attempting to cut their way through to Talok and Crysillnia when two of the large hairy beasts, swinging on vines, swooped down on Jarret and Simentoo, carrying the two struggling men up into the tree tops.

But the creatures didn't stop there. They continued carrying the two away from the battle, swinging from tree to tree. All Jarret and Simentoo could do was hope their new captors didn't lose their grip and drop them to the jungle floor below. The sound of the battle quickly diminished.

Simentoo was quite uncomfortable. The hairy creature that held him reeked, and its hold was so intense, he could barely catch his breath. Finally, Simentoo forgot his discomfort as he watched the jungle floor flow below him like a green river. Simentoo was quite impressed by the agility and gracefulness these huge creatures displayed in their travel through the treetops.

Simentoo was being held around the mid-section, his arms pinned to his side, facing outward. He looked around in wonderment and noticed that there were several other of these creatures besides the ones carrying Jarret and himself. They were moving so quickly through the treetops that their long hair flowed behind them.

Suddenly and without ceremony, Jarret and Simentoo were plopped into what appeared to be a nest near the top of the canopy. Looking at each other apprehensively, Jarret and Simentoo remained silent not sure what to make of their situation. Jarret spoke first. "Do you suppose we're someone's meal?" "Such as?" Simentoo queried. "Maybe their young?" answered Jarret. With a laugh, a voice came out of a huge cluster of leaves above the nest. "Nonsense, nonsense, we aren't eaters of meat. What a grotesque idea" continued the mysterious voice.

Then abruptly a rather decrepit and truncated creature dropped in to the nest beside the two men. It had tattered long hair that ran in splotches on its wrinkled and leathery hide. The creature had a flat face with heavy brows, a flattened nose with large nostrils which appeared to twitch perpetually, and a wide mouth filled with enormous yellowed and gnarled teeth.

"Don't approve of my appearance, I take it, but no matter. I'm Grolian," said the creature. "I'm a priest and a Truth Teller." "Truth Teller. What is a Truth Teller?" asked Jarret. "One that divans possible futures," answered Grolian. "What do you mean possible futures," asked Simentoo with a truculent edge to his voice.

"Before we go on with this discussion, I think you should be fed," said Grolian. The mention of a meal reminded Simentoo and Jarret of their hunger. They hadn't eaten since morning and now it was near dark. Grolian clapped his hands twice and an obsequious servant brought a basket containing fruits and tubers. "Sorry," Grolian apologized, "but this is all I have to offer. We might be able to find you some grubs, if you wish." "No. This will do just fine," said Simentoo. Simentoo looked up at Jarret and continued, "I've eaten grubs before, and they're not to my liking."

Jarret retrieved a large, round, red fruit from the basket and shook his head in agreement with Simentoo's opinion on grubs. Simentoo took a long yellow tuber from the offering but hesitated.

He began to examine the root carefully. "Fear not," laughed Grolian. "If we had wanted you dead, we could have accomplished that without such an elaborate scheme as poisoning." Simentoo, seeing that Jarret hadn't died from his fruit that he was munching voraciously, began to eat the yellow elongated tuber. The fruits and tubers were quite succulent and sweet. The two enjoyed their meal immensely while Grolian looked on.

When they finished, Grolian spoke, "We were unable to rescue your fellow companions, but we do have this," and Grolian clapped his hands once again. A smaller, and most probably, a younger creature, similar in appearance to Grolian but with whiter teeth, dropped into the nest.

It had in its possession the pouch containing the Crystals. It held the pouch by the drawstring. The creature held the pouch away from itself as if it were afraid. "How did you manage to be in possession of these?" asked Jarret. "This youngster picked them up after the rather rude lout lost his arm," Grolian answered with a chuckle.

"Hand them to the King," Grolian told the smaller creature. The smaller creature hesitated as it first looked at Simentoo and then Jarret, unsure of which of the humans that Grolian was referring too. Grolian pointed at Jarret and grunted.

Jarret, with an expression of incredulity, asked Grolian, "What kind of deception is this, referring to me as King? I'm no King. I don't even know who my parents were. I was raised by an aged elf couple." "There is no deception," answered Grolian. Simentoo listened quietly to the verbal exchange between Grolian and Jarret.

"The medallion that you carry is the proof of your heritage and destiny," continued Grolian. Reflexively, Jarret gripped the collar on his tunic and the small round object sewn into it. He had been told since he was a small boy to keep the medallion hidden and to tell no one of its existence. "How did you know?" asked Jarret in astonishment.

Simentoo rested his back against the high wall of the nest, hands clasped behind his head, mulling over Grolian's revelation. The tension between Grolian and Jarret became almost tangible.

"I am a Truth Teller," Grolian replied with a shrug and a slightly sideways grin. Simentoo, taking on a more serious demeanor sat more erect, leaning forwards slightly, as Grolian continued. "King Jarret, please produce the medallion."

Jarret tore the seam of his collar and removed a small, round, golden medallion. The color was so rich that it reflected the near dusk light brilliantly. "Hand the medallion to your companion," commanded Grolian. Jarrett, without hesitation, presented the medallion to Simentoo and placed it in his open palm.

Simentoo was taken aback. The medallion was embossed with a tiara decorated with Callenberry blossoms and a flaming sword passing through it. It was a replica of the Queen's Seal. Although, he had never seen the actual seal, he recognized it from a tapestry which hung in the throne room behind the former Queen's seat.

"This appears to be the Queen's seal," said Simentoo, in a matter of fact manner. When he regained his composure, he asked, "How did you happen upon this? It would have been on the Queen's person when she was murdered by bandits many years ago. It was thought that the rogues had taken it."

"I was told this was my mother's," Jarret replied. Simentoo calmly met Jarret's eyes, trying to analyze the woodsman to see if he could detect a lie. He could detect no insincerity in the young woodsman, and Simentoo prided himself on his ability to judge the character of others.

Then, to Jarret's surprise and chagrin, Simentoo knelt before him, head bowed, and swore his fidelity to the new King of Lenar. Jarrett, embarrassed by his friend's obsequious behavior, fidgeted nervously, not knowing what to say or do.

"Get up!" said Jarret more shrilly than he had intended. "I'm no King," he protested loudly. "I'm just a lowly woodsman swept up into an impossible situation, not of my making." Jarret glanced, pleadingly at Grolian hoping the grotesque creature would reveal this to be a grand farce.

Grolian, raising his eyebrows, slipped Jarrett a beguiling smile, then said, "This is your destiny, Your Highness. No one but you can decide whether you are willing to accept the responsibility. It is a great responsibility that has been dropped unexpectedly into your lap. There are many lives at risk, and only someone of strong morals, humane character, and great tenacity should accept such a responsibility. But I have faith that you will make the right choice."

"What brought that sermon on?" asked an irritated Jarrett, as he threw up his hands in frustration, his agitation quite evident by the way he brushed his fingers through the unkempt and tangled knots that used to be silky soft hair. "Are you trying to manipulate me into accepting this Kingship deal?" asked Jarret accusatively.

"Who? Me!" replied Grolian with a sly smile and a slight coughing noise, that Jarret took as a chuckle.

"Yes, you!" Snapped Jarrett, again waving his arms emphatically.

Simentoo, now standing off to the side, began to smile at the comedic sparring between Grolian and Jarrett, although he was quite sure that Jarrett wouldn't find it funny.

"You have the medallion and you, yourself, said it belonged to your mother. I'm manipulating nothing. It's your heritage and not of my bestowing," answered Grolian, still smiling. Jarrett, sensing defeat, acquiesced reluctantly.

Jarret still quite agitated, turned to Simentoo. "What are you grinning about?"

"Nothing, My Lord," answered Simentoo as he tried to cover his mouth with his hand and, stifle a chuckle.

Jarret, in exasperation, threw up his hands once again and said, "I give up. This is hopeless. And don't call me My Lord!"

"Yes, My ahh—Jarret," replied Simentoo, "still grinning broadly.

"Back to the matters at hand," stated Jarret. "We need to rescue Crysillnia and Talok."

"That is impossible," said Grolian.

Simentoo wiped the grin from his face and fixed the Truth Teller with an dangerous gaze. "Impossible! And may I ask why?" Grolian didn't appear intimidated my Simentoo's change of mood. "There are several reasons: First, the stretch ears are in their village with their captives and second, you two are needed elsewhere.

What will happen to your campions, will happen despite your efforts. Your destiny lies elsewhere."

"Jarret's presence and leadership are needed to pull the remnants of the Lenarian Army back into a cohesive fighting force and you, Simentoo, will give legitimacy to his claim as King. You are well known and respected by the soldiers and their leaders."

"Also, Caspar has a strong and viable army but they have holed up in their valley, and King Falef refuses to even make an attempt to break the siege. The King's failure to act is threatening the whole land. The major part of the demon army is free to march on Xlanta."

"Xlanta can not be allowed to fall or there will be no hope of stopping Natas' minions and the Evil One's objective of enslaving the lands of Greater Laorisha and eventually the cataclysmic destruction of the Fabric of Existence. You must gather an army of significant enough strength to free up Caspar's army and convince the King of Caspar to join forces with you.

*   *   *

Crysillnia lay stunned, flat on her back, with one of the wildly painted warriors on top of her. She wasn't sure what had happened. All she could remember was loud shrieking noises and large shaggy creatures swinging on vines out of the trees above. Then Talok and Crysillnia were tackled by their guards.

Finally Crysillnia's guard lifted himself off of her, smirking at her in a provocative manner. Evidently this exercise had done more for him than her. There was a continuing commotion going on beside her.

Although Talok was securely bound, he was able to toss his tackler off with ease, creating several very intense moments. Many of the agitated warriors converged on the rebelling dwarf, spears at the ready. They appeared to be looking for a reason to skewer the truculent prisoner.

As Crysillnia surveyed her surroundings, she spotted the two guards who had been in charge of Simentoo and Jarret lying in growing puddles of their own blood, victims of their own weapons. Still looking at the dead guards, Crysillnia reached over and grabbed Talok's massive arm.

Talok, unaware that it was Crysillnia, reacted violently to her touch. "Talok! Talok! Look!" Talok, regaining control of his temper, looked in the direction that Crysillnia was now pointing with her bound hands. "Talok they're gone! Where did they go?" asked Crysillnia.

"I don't know," answered Talok, puzzlement shading his voice. A grin crossed his face, and then he said, "But they left a fine mess."

When the nearest warrior saw Talok's smile, he angrily struck Talok in the mouth with the butt end of his spear. The blow rocked Talok backwards, cutting his upper lip, causing it to bleed profusely. Talok shook his head and shot a burning glare at his attacker, a promise of future reprisals. The warrior, unsettled by the glare, took a step back.

"I hope they're safe and can escape from this accursed jungle," said Crysillnia. Talok shook his head in agreement. Their captors began jabbing them with the sharp pointed spears and speaking to them in their unintelligible language. They attempted to coax the two beleaguered and irate captives to continue their arduous trek. Angry, exhausted, and dirty, Crysillnia begrudgingly complied. Talok balked by lashing out at his captors, knocking two off their feet and snapping the neck of the warrior that had struck him earlier.

The angry jungle warriors mobbed Talok. They covered him in a flood of human flesh. Talok struggled valiantly but was finally subdued. A bruised and bloody Talok, with further persuasion from the jungle warriors' sharp spear points, stood up and continued the trek through the now insufferably steamy jungle. Crysillnia's anger with Talok's treatment by their captors began to burn and seethe in her gut but there was nothing she could do to reap revenge.

Their captors drove them relentlessly. The trail narrowed at times to a barely discernable footpath nearly choked closed by the insidious creep of the jungle. Crysillnia was tiring. She could barely lift her feet which caused her to stumble over the least unevenness in the trail. There were no rest breaks, and the prisoners were offered no water to replenish the fluids wrung out of them by the oppressive heat.

The trail widened when it intersected a trail that followed a river. They took the downriver trail. The river meandered aimlessly through the vastness of the choked and crowded jungle. The trees finally began to retreat from the river bank and more sunlight was allowed to penetrate the thick jungle canopy, as the river widened.

In fact, the light was so bright that it nearly blinded Crysillnia. Using her hand, she shielded her eyes from the irritating assault by the sun. She was surprised, when her eyes adjusted to the light, to see that they were approaching a sprawling village, scurrying with life.

The village consisted of a number of thatched roofed huts of varying sizes, lining both sides of the river as far as the eye could see. All the huts were basically rectangular in shape and were lined up in rows making perfectly aligned thoroughfares. The huts were exactly the same width but few were the same length.

As they were marched down the streets, people of all ages came out to watch the spectacle. Although she was exhausted and dirty, Crysillnia squared her shoulders and stood more erect. She wasn't going to let these people take her dignity. She was proud of who she was, and she would show it.

Crysillnia was intrigued by the demeanor of the spectators. They watched in rapt silence, and once the captors passed the villagers went back to what they were about as if nothing had occurred.

Whispering to Talok now walking beside her, she asked, "Have you ever seen a place with so many people this quiet? I feel like, I'm in a monastery."

Talok replied. "No."

Their whispering exacted a rather pointed reaction from their captors as they were pricked by this now very annoying method of reprisal, the hated short spear.

The village appeared to be divided up into neat blocks of ten as streets intersected at every tenth hut. Crysillnia was astounded by the meticulous engineering of what appeared to be a rather simple culture. There were huge dirt mounds constructed on both sides of the river. On these mounds, buildings were constructed which spanned the river and were flanked by swinging walkways. The guards led Crysillnia and Talok towards a small opening in the stone and dirt mound on this side of the river.

The opening was barely wide enough for Crysillnia to slip through, and she balked. Her guard struck her on the back of the head with the butt of his spear. Crysillnia, seeing lights flash before her eyes, cried out in pain as she stumbled through the opening.

She would have fallen flat on her face if not for Talok. He snapped his bindings and caught her before she hit the ground. Crysillnia looked back at Talok with gratitude. Talok, angered by the mistreatment of his ward, struck out at their tormentors.

There was a loud cracking sound as one of the unfortunate warrior's neck broke. The dead warrior's comrades attacked Talok, swarming over him like bees defending a violated hive. Talok fought back valiantly, but the numbers were too great. He collapsed under the onslaught of the vicious and vengeful painted warriors as they kicked and pummeled him with the hafts of their spears.

Crysillnia, fearing for Talok's life, launched herself out of the narrow doorway, screaming wildly in an attempt to help the beleaguered dwarf. Some of the painted warriors turned on her and began to strike her without mercy. One blow propelled her backwards against the dirt and stone mound resulting in a resounding thud. The wind, with a whooshing sound, exited her lungs. She gasped desperately for the taste of sweet and delicious air so that she could ward off the insidious clutches of unconsciousness which sought to drag her down into the abyss of darkness.

Her struggle kindled a fire deep within her soul. Whether this was good or evil, Crysillnia was unable to distinguish it at the moment. Her rage was in control. She felt a power growing within her, a feeling of omnipotence, all and everything was hers, to do with as she wished.

*   *   *

Jarret and Simentoo were traversing the lower plains silently but quickly. They were attempting to avoid the roaming bands of demons which were devastating the lower plains, killing anyone they encountered and destroying homes and villages. The wanton murder and destruction by these callous and vile creatures angered Jarret, especially now that he was aware of his responsibility.

They spotted a plume of smoke wafting skyward. They went to investigate and found what once had been a small and sleepy village which had been inhabited by poor, unfortunate, subsistence farmers. The disemboweled bodies of humans and animals alike torn limb from limb, were strewn about the narrow dirt streets between the burned out hulks of what had once been homes and businesses. Some were even partially eaten.

Jarret gasped in pain as he grasped the pouch hanging from his neck, nestled against his chest. Simentoo, in the forefront, hearing Jarret's gasp of pain, pivoted on the balls of his feet, sword at the ready looking for the silent attacker but was taken aback at what he was witnessing.

Jarret was grasping the pouch containing the crystals, trying desperately but futilely to pull them away from his chest. The pouch was glowing and pulsating. With each rhythmic pulse, the glow of the Crystals grew in intensity. The glow emanating from the Crystals engulfed Jarret completely. Before Simentoo could react, the glow expanded, also encompassing him.

Simentoo's first sensation was a searing and brutal heat. Then it felt like a bath of warm water, not dissimilar to the hot springs of the Fire Mountains. Then there was total darkness. He felt despair and total hopelessness, a hopelessness so deep that death seemed to be a welcome savior.

Then a many colored light like a rainbow burst forth carrying Simentoo before it. It was a light of hope and ecstacy. Simentoo felt the greatest joy and excitement imaginable. He wished for this feeling to never end.

Simentoo, riding the light of joy, began to distinguish images forming around him. The first he was able to recognize was that of Jarret. Then a large mound began to form with Crysillnia standing before it, her arms raised to the heavens. An omnipotent glow was cascading and dancing around her. She resembled a living Goddess from the past. She appeared to have grown in stature. Simentoo was struck with awe at her magnificence.

Then she began gesturing and pointing at what appeared to be a large, wriggling, alien mass with many heads and feet. At first Simentoo thought it was one of those strange and unholy demons. Then he heard Crysillnia, not so much with his ears but in his head, as if she were in his skull, "help Talok. They're killing him."

Simentoo was finally able to clearly distinguish what the wriggling mass was. It was a mass of warriors attacking Talok. He waded into the melee swinging his broadsword without discretion, nearly taking off Jarret's head who was beside him. An odd thought ran through his mind. How did he come by the broadsword he was using? The warriors had stripped him of it, and Grolian and his people hadn't been able to retrieve his weapons.

Then he became enthralled by the heat of battle. The two of them, Jarret and Simentoo, attacked viciously, bathing themselves in warm blood. Heads and limbs separated from bodies. Simentoo began to rejoice in the excitement of death and carnage that he was meting out.

A darkness began to grow within him. A feeling of omnipotence as he slashed, hacked, kicked, and stabbed. He heard himself yell at the top of his voice, "I am the reaper! I am carnage incarnate! I am the destroyer! I am the God of death! I, and I alone, decide who lives or dies! Worship me or die!" Simentoo couldn't believe that he was mouthing such words, such thoughts, but was still overjoyed at singing them, because they made him feel great, like a hero from childhood tales.

Talok burst forth from the pile, a madness glowing in his eyes. All of Talok's attackers were either maimed or dead. Simentoo, Jarret, and Talok stood amongst the carnage, oblivious to it. They were staring at each other, a madness upon them all. They began to circle, preparing to battle each other. There could only be one God of Death.

"Stop!" a shrill voice rang in their heads. "I am the all-powerful one. You are my minions! You are at my command! Watch!" she said with a deep low growl. Raising her hands once again, she began to gather the energy that flowed and pulsated around her.

The energy pulsated and writhed between her hands like a living entity. She caressed it lovingly. There was a look of euphoria on her face. Then she grinned evilly, an expression that made Simentoo tremble. Crysillnia released the energy. Projecting it in all directions. There was a rending sound as the firmament shuttered from the release of so much energy at one time.

The fabric of the universe began to tear and rend. The village disintegrated around them and disappeared into the void. Evil and vile creatures tried to enter through the rip. Crysillnia realizing what she had done, still in her euphoric state, fought the creatures. She knew, she couldn't win. That eventually she would lose. She was confused. She didn't know how to mend the fabric of time or space.

She began to tire. She watched in horror as demons began to enter the world. Then, amazingly, the elf girl with a man horse and the parrot slipped through the tear. The elf girl began to chant, weaving a spell to close the torn fabric of time and space.

Simentoo, exhausted and weak, awoke. He was lying in the high grass of the plains. Did he dream all of that? He looked over at an unconscious Jarret, lying beside him, then looked at himself. He knew it had really occurred because they were both covered in blood. Losing consciousness once again, he plunged into a deep but restless sleep.

CHAPTER 27

When Alaquin finally managed to pick herself up, she was shocked at the scene unfolding before her. Crysillnia, her niece, a fact, she was having a hard time reconciling, was standing by a heap of bloody and mangled bodies. The dwarf was standing in the middle of this heap. Blood matted his hair, drenching his clothes, running down his face into his beard and dripping from his saturated beard to the ground.

There was debris from trees, bushes, grass, and man-made objects swirling in the air around Crysillnia as if she were the center of a cyclone. The look on Crysillnia and the dwarf's faces were frightening. They looked like evil incarnate.

Wasting no more time, Alaquin sprang into action. Intuitively, she knew the spells to mend the tear in the Fabric of Existence. She began to chant in a strange and ancient language. She chanted melodically, and she began to move her body rhythmically, raising her hands overhead. She began to move her fingers as if weaving.

Crysillnia finally took control of her emotions which proved to be a very difficult task, because, somewhere deep down, there was a part of her that didn't want her to take control. There was a part of her that thrived on this uncontrolled release of power. The exhilaration, the excitement made her feel invincible, but she knew that if she didn't stop now, she would destroy the world. In fact, she could feel the ground begin to quake and heave under her feet.

But was it her fault, or was it the nature of her innate power and its interaction with the Crystals? Then she realized that she was clasping something in her hands. The object was warm and pulsating, sending tremors of energy throughout her body. Unclasping her hands, Crysillnia realized she held the pouch containing the Crystals.

How did she come in possession of them? They were lost along the trail. The warriors hadn't retrieved them when they were dropped. Then she began to remember what had happened. She had summoned Simentoo and Jarret. Jarrett had the Crystals. She remembered instinctively opening her hand and calling for the Crystals. The pouch responded to her call and jerked free from Jarret's neck.

Continuing to contemplate what had happened, Crysillnia feared that maybe Jarret and Simentoo were dead, and somehow she had summoned their ghosts. The thought brought tears to her eyes, and she felt sick inside.

Crysillnia refocused her attention on the elf girl. The gale force winds were beginning to diminish, but what was she seeing. She couldn't be sure. When she looked directly at the damaged spot, she could see nothing. But when she turned her head slightly so her peripheral vision came into play, she thought she detected dark creatures exiting the void through the tear.

Crysillnia realized that she may have done more harm than good. Finally there was quiet. The hole was closed. The elf girl turned around with a large grin and approached Crysillnia. "Hello, Crysillnia," said Alaquin. "We meet again and in another precarious situation."

"That appears to be the nature of our relationship. Me in distress and you coming to my rescue," quipped Crysillnia.

"Danger must be one of the things we have in common, among others," replied Alaquin.

Crysillnia suspected that there was more meaning to that ambiguous statement than was apparent, but she didn't question the elf girl.

"How did you happen to appear at this most opportune moment?" asked Crysillnia.

"Well, I happened to be in the void conversing with the Tree of Knowledge and partaking of the fruit when you so rudely interrupted," Alaquin replied capriciously.

Crysillnia couldn't restrain the grin that enveloped her whole face. This was the first time she had a reason to grin in a long time, and it felt good.

"You look haggard. You must have had a rough journey," continued Alaquin.

"If you consider fighting demons, having out of body experiences, being captured by wildly painted barbarians and tearing holes in the void rough, then yes I've had it rough," answered Crysillnia, allowing a sly grin to slide across her face.

"You have done considerable damage," said Alaquin as she surveyed the devastation.

"Yes, I have," answered Crysillnia, and her mood turned dark. "I wish, I had better control of the power I possess, but when I become angry, all reservation slips away. I think the Crystals are partially to blame," continued Crysillnia.

"You may have a good point. You need to retrieve the Fifth Crystal as soon as possible. It is the purifier of the magic contained within the Crystals," said Alaquin.

While the two had been talking, Talok and Alaquin's two companions had joined them.

"Where do I go from here?" asked Crysillnia. The demon, ensconced in it's parrot guise, flew up and perched itself on Alaquin's right shoulder.

Alaquin glanced at the parrot and continued her discussion with Crysillnia. "You need to cross the river and follow the jungle trail to the land of Xlanta and cross the Dead Desert. You might do well to go to Altonea, the city that lies on the northern border of the desert and hire you a guide."

"We don't have gold to purchase supplies let alone hire a guide," replied Crysillnia sharply.

"You'll find the necessary funds in the mound," answered Alaquin.

"Will you come with us?" asked Crysillnia.

"No. I have other duties lined up," answered the elf girl. "It is nearing dark and, I think, we should make camp for the night," Alaquin continued.

"And I agree. It's been a hard day," said the parrot.

"No one asked you," snapped Talok.

Crysillnia and Alaquin looked at one another and grinned.

CHAPTER 28

T anof had decided that it would be better to travel through the foothills, as opposed to following the heavily traveled roads. He didn't wish to attract any unwanted attention, plus with the chaos that reigned at present, the roads would be too dangerous to travel.

There were no well blazed trails through the foothills because of their peculiar nature. Rocky ridges extended from the mountains like the roots of a tree. Closer to the mountains, the rock ridges were more prominent with sharp jagged edges. The ridges became less obtrusive as they blended into the plains. This created, between the mountains and the plains, an undulating terrain.

This was Tanof's chosen route. The grasses that grew here were plush but hardy. This was Xlanta's best range land for grazing horses and sheep. Tanof expected to see either horses or sheep roaming the foothills, but there were none in evidence. The acclivities in this section of the foothills were difficult but not impassable.

Tanof was headed to Altonea on the edge of the desert. It was a raucous and nearly lawless city. Altonea was the Xlanta's haven for the licentious and most unsavory miscreants of the empire, an excellent place for someone to disappear.

Tanof had traveled this way many times and knew he was cresting the last ridge before he reached the seldom traveled road between Altonea and the jungle. In the last day he had passed from lush grasslands into a more arid land. What mostly grew here were scrub grasses, twisted and gnarled bushes, and blue-green lichens.

The footing was treacherous at times from loose rocks and gravel. Tanof's mount was skittish because of the unfirm footing, but the horse arduously puffed it's way up the steep hill. Tanof's thoughts had wandered off on a tangent. He was brought back to reality when he heard the clash of weapons from the other side of the ridge. He wanted to avoid any possible involvement, so he reigned in his horse which pleased the beast greatly. Tanof looked up and down the valley, but this was the only place to cross the ridge without adding arduous hours to his trek.

There was a huge outcropping which extended down into the plains. In fact, this rock crossed the plains and traveled all the way to the sea. There were only two ways through this escarpment. This one and the main road which lead to Altonea, and the Xlantan Army had an outpost there. Tanof doubted the outpost would be unmanned in these chaotic times.

Tanof had witnessed many strange things in the last few days. He had seen mountain animals in the foothills that never wandered this far from their usual range, wolves running scared and other creatures he couldn't describe. In fact, he had to do battle with one of those strange creatures a couple of days back. He heard a pack of wolves worrying with something, and his horse refused to go any further. His curiosity piqued, he decided to have a look. He dismounted and slung his broad sword over his back and crept stealthily up the side of the ridge.

When he topped the ridge, he was flabbergasted. There was a creature standing upright on two insect like legs which ended in three hooked talons. The creature had a torso similar to a gorilla and a huge bulbous head with six eyes on long stalks which enabled the creature to view all directions. The creature had a huge mouth with razor-sharp teeth and ears similar to a wolf. It had huge muscular arms that were similar to a human's but ended in five sharp talons.

The mountain wolves that were doing battle with the creature were large muscular creatures with black and gray fur, typical of their kind. On all fours, the wolves stood about chest high to an average man. The wolves towered over the strange creature but the creature was wreaking carnage among the half dozen or so wolves.

After the demon had slew about half of their number, the pack scattered and disappeared into the surrounding landscape.

As luck would have it, one of the wolves fled in Tanof's direction with the demon like creature in hot pursuit. The wolf streaked by Tanof, tongue lolling, with fear in it's eyes. The demon creature spotted the curious human and changed it's objective. With an ear piercing cry and a hopping, shambling gate, it moved in Tanof's direction. The creature closed in on Tanof in a remarkably short time.

Reacting from instinct, Tanof threw two of the knives that hung from his belt, which had little effect. The knives bounced off the hard chitinous shell that covered the creature's chest. Unsheathing his broad sword and crouching into a battle stance Tanof prepared to do battle. The creature, heedless of Tanof's weapon, attacked.

Tanof sidestepped, bringing his sword down on the creatures back. The loud clang of metal striking the creature's chitinous hide was deafening and traveled like a wave across the plain. Although the sword had cracked the monster's shell, it didn't penetrate. Tanof's hands, numbed by the impact, nearly dropped his weapon.

Fear twisted Tanof's gut into a knot. It occurred to him that he may not be able to win this battle. The creature wailed in pain and turned on Tanof and approached the human with more caution gnashing its teeth and swinging its great sickle like talons. All Tanof could do was retreat along the ridge avoiding the long sweeps of the creature's arms. Tanof stumbled on loose gravel and fell backwards. The demon, confident of a kill, felt no further threat and focused it's multifaceted eyes on the prostrate human. The creature's overconfidence was a fatal mistake.

The monnster loomed over Tanof, poised too kill. Its total attention on its hapless victim, it was unaware of the wolf's return. The wolf sprang on the creature's back. The wolf's momentum knocked the monster off balance, and it fell forward.

Tanof, seizing the opportunity, braced his sword on the rock strewn ground, point up. The combination of the creature's momentum and the weight of the wolf drove the sword completely through the doomed creature. The crunching and squishing sound of the sword skewering the grotesque beast was sickening. The whole backside of the shell popped off which saved the wolf from being skewered. The wolf rolled head over tail down the side of the ridge ending up a disheveled heap at the bottom.

Tanof cried out in pain as the corrosive fluid of the creature soaked him. The creature was still poised over Tanof, propped up by the broadsword. Using both legs and heaving mightily, he toppled the corpse. The monster, too, would have rolled to the bottom of the ridge. If not for the sword protruding from its chest, stopping it after one revolution.

Causing the creature to slide, as far, as it, had rolled.

Tanof ripped his blood soaked clothing off as rapidly as was possible and used any part of his clothing that didn't have demon blood on it to wipe the remnants of demon blood off his naked body. He now stood on top of the ridge, totally naked. He surveyed his surroundings. The wolf had quietly slipped away, and his horse, although battled trained, had run off. It took Tanof nearly half a day to track his mount down.

That was the reason he wished to avoid getting involved in business that was not his own. But, as fate would have it, he may not have a choice. He needed to cross here. He figured if he was quiet, he may be able to slip along the ridge unnoticed. Tanof topped the ridge and stopped.

A few weeks ago he might have been surprised by the unexpected, but now he would be worried if the unusual and unexpected didn't occur. There was a vicious battle below involving that magnificent looking, black haired, woman and her strange looking dwarf friend. They were battling a collection of miscreant, disgusting and vile demons. In hopes of not being spotted, he gently reigned his horse along and just below the top of the ridge and away from the battle.

Gently coaxing his mount into a canter with his heels he rode away from the beleaguered couple. Their problems were none of his business, or that's what he tried to convince himself of, but his conscience began to get the better of him. This was totally unexpected. He thought he had left guilt behind long ago with the death of his father. Tanof yanked hard on the reigns. His horse protested with a deep throated grunt and pawed the air with his front hooves at the rude treatment but quickly responded. He didn't know why, but Tanof felt a connection with the woman. He felt they had a shared destiny. Besides, he didn't care much for demons anyway.

Digging his heels deep into his mounts flanks, he charged down the ridge. He unsheathed his short sword and began to yell as loud as he could. He thought, to himself, how foolish he must appear, rushing to his death for strangers, dressed only in a loin cloth. Tanof chuckled to himself. He must've gone mad.

Tanof caught a glimpse of something on his periphery and was surprise to see the wolf streak past him. He thought it strange, but with this new ally, he felt invincible. As adrenalin coursed through his veins, he felt good about what he was doing and himself. Deep down, he knew he was doing something right and good. It had been along time since he had felt this way, and the feeling brought tears to his eyes.

He crashed headlong into the melee and chills of excitement ran up and down his spine. The battle was a blur. All Tanof could remember was hacking and stabbing viciously, over and over. He could remember seeing the wolf ripping and tearing with its deadly fangs, the dwarf crushing heads, and the woman slashing demons with her dagger. He remembered thinking to himself that she was very adept with the dagger.

*   *   *

Kanef gave the Halhoren horse a pat on the hind quarters. It would eventually find its way home. He would have to enter his homeland through a back door. The demons had Caspar under siege and the pass along the river was blocked.

Kanef had to be covert, even here, in the less traveled foothills of The Casparian Mountains. Enemy activity was in abundance.

Kanef, as a child, had explored the mountains surrounding his home thoroughly, so he knew all the narrow crevices, scalable walls and caves that would give him access to Caspar Valley.

He stealthily crept through the heavily forested terrain. He was reminded of one of his adventuresome excursions into the mountains. It was during his cadet training in the Casparian Home Guard. Each cadet had an objective of his on choosing to accomplish for graduation. The cadets had to choose a procurement objective or the mountain survival test. Most chose the procurement objective.

Kanef decided on the mountain survival test. He surprised and displeased all of his instructors when he chose the hatchet as his lone weapon, not a very effective weapon in battle. The mountains were dangerous for more reasons than the terrain. The Mountain Tribesmen and Cave Dwellers made their homes in the higher elevations and were quite hostile.

No amount of persuasion would deter Kanef from his reckless choice. If they had realized his real objective, the theft of a Cave Dweller Ceremonial Mask, they might have refused to allow him to go at all, because he was the next in line to sit on the throne of Caspar. It was early spring, and it was still cold in the high mountains. A small detachment of the Home Guard escorted Kanef into the mountains. The journey took two days on horseback. The night they reached their destination, a cold wind howled and whipped through the peaks, dropping the temperature well below freezing.

The next morning everyone was up at the crack of dawn. Breakfast consisted of jerked meat and a hard biscuit washed down with a harsh ale. The ale burned on the way down which helped warm the body. There was no fire because they didn't want to broadcast their presence. This was the last meal that would be provided to Kanef. Any meals from here on out, until he completed his task, he would have to procure for himself.

Kanef remembered watching, feeling self-satisfied and excited. When the detachment left, they took his horse and would post soldiers on the trail. He was required, as part of the test, to travel cross country to successfully complete his coming of age. His self-confidence and thrill quickly dissipated when he stood there all alone. The mountain peaks loomed over him ominously as if promising unforgettable and dangerous adventures.

The wind had lulled in the early morning hours but began to pick up with an unbridled intensity, and by the afternoon had brought snow with it. Kanef pulled up the hood of his overcoat in an attempt to ward off the gripping cold and driving snow. Somberly, he trudged deeper into the mountain vastness.

Late on the first day, he found what he was looking for in a shear rock face: a series of apertures which showed signs of cave dweller habitation. He hunkered down on a rock shelf across from the occupied caves and observed the traffic in and out of the caves. The Cave Dwellers were completely oblivious to his presence. Kanef watched throughout the night.

The new day dawned, gloomy, cold and blustery, spitting snow sporadically leaving no significant accumulation. He began too conceptualize what he was doing. This a was foolish and reckless attempt to impress his father. He wasn't very close to his father, and his mother had died when he was two or three. His father had ignored him after the death of the Queen, and he had felt lonely and abandoned. What was worse, was the fact that his father showed preference for his younger brother, attention that Kanef had envied and craved.

So he thought if he could do something grand, like bring back a big trophy, his father would see him in a different light. That's why he chose such a risky task, a choice he would regret for the rest of his life.

Kanef pulled his overcoat tighter. The wind had increased in ferocity, and the snow had turned from an occasional flurry into a full blown blizzard. The crystalline flakes felt hot against his skin. He thought that odd. Shouldn't snow feel cold and not hot?

No longer able to clearly see the activities on the other side of the canyon, Kanef tucked his face under his cloak. He was startled when he heard a stone roll down the path and across the ledge he was sitting on. Something or someone was coming down the path.

Furtively he searched the ledge for a way to escape. How foolish of him. He had failed to plan for such an eventuality. There was no way off the ledge. He was trapped. He had forgotten one of the most basic rules of a covert operation. Always have a plan for escape.

He had only one choice left and that was to fight. He pulled the hatchet from his belt and waited. Now he was aware of the feebleness of his choice of weapons. Maybe he should have listened to his advisors and chosen a sword. When the cave dweller appeared around the curve on the ledge, Kanef struck with all the force he could muster. Striking his adversary full in the chest, he heard the sickening crunch of breaking and shattering cartilage, bone, and the squishing of emulsified flesh. Kanef remembered the cave dweller's shocked expression, quickly turn to surprise and pain, before she collapsed into his arms. She was only a child. She couldn't have been more than six seasons.

He had killed a child. Something to this day he could never forgive himself for. He remembered cradling the child in his arms and seeing the fear, the pain, and the accusation in her eyes. He had watched helplessly as the light in her eyes faded away in a coughing and gasping fit. She breathed her last, spewing her life's fluid over Kanef's face and cloak. He didn't know how long he had sat there rocking the dead child, but he had finally come to his senses and hurried away from the accursed ledge before someone missed the child and came looking. Kanef no longer cared if he pleased his father. He had decided on that day that he would no longer attempt to impress anyone again, especially not his father. He returned home and resigned from the Home Guard. Kanef's father never forgave him for the embarrassment. This was the true beginning of their alienation.

Kanef was jolted back to reality when he tripped over a rock, nearly hurdling him head first into a very deep crevice. Kanef, regaining his balance, examined the obstacle carefully. The crevice was symmetrical. One would think that a great giant had cleaved it with a sword and then thrust his blade into the heart of the mountain. The sides were cleanly cut, and the crevice ran straight through the bowels of the mountain and exited on the other side.

Kanef had discovered the passageway during one of his solitary hunting excursions when he was a about fifteen seasons old. He had been fleeing an angry bear on the other side of the mountain when he came across this rent in the land. It had been well camouflaged by shrubs and trees. Too afraid to wait and see what the bear would do, he followed the crevice into the dark heart of the mountain. He had never told anyone of his discovery. So as far, as he knew, he is the only one aware of the passageway.

Kanef lowered himself over the edge of the crevice and dropped to the bottom. Bending his knees on impact helped cushion his landing. He cautiously entered the dark tunnel. There could be most anything lying in wait for unwary travelers. There was a steady draft wafting through the passage chilling Kanef to the bone. He shivered until his body adjusted to the cold breeze.

He moved through the dark passageway silently, like a wraith. He stopped suddenly, deep within the bowels of the mountain, to listen. The whisper of his short sword leaving its sheath, echoed through the darkness. He wasn't sure, but he thought he had heard voices. He waited patiently in the darkness. He heard them again. It sounded like the voices were coming from his right which led him to the conclusion that there must be other passageways branching off of this one. He stood silently, waiting.

The volume of the voices didn't change, so he determined that they were stationery and no threat to him. He started down the passageway leaving the voices behind, but then he stopped. His curiosity piqued, Kanef decided he had to know who else was down here and what they were up to.

He backtracked and then followed the voices. Although it was dark in the tunnel, the black rock of the mountain cast a darker image which made it possible, with the help of the draft, to traverse the tunnel without a torch. He thought to himself, it would be nice to have, at least, a glow stone. He ran his hand along the coarse and grainy sidewall of the tunnel for guidance. He quickly retracted his hand when he encountered a soft, slimy substance at the edge of an aperture in the wall. The spot where he had encountered the foreign substance began to glow with a soft, light-blue radiance. Kanef was taken aback by this unexpected phenomenon.

It was a rare lichen that grew in dark places and lit up when stimulated. He had heard of its existence but had never encountered it. He had heard that the Cave Dwellers cultivated the lichen for lighting but didn't realize it grew wild or was this a Cave Dweller's garden. His touch had started a chain reaction. All the lichens, as if in response to the first, started to glow.

In a way, he was glad for the light, but he also feared that the glow might alert those he wanted to spy on. Kanef continued, down the eerily lit side tunnel, cautiously. This passageway didn't run true like the main passageway. It had a lot of twists and turns, and then came to an abrupt end.

The light from the lichens began to fade. He noticed a crack in the wall. The voices were emanating from that crack. He put his eye up to the crack so that he could peer through to the other side. He could see the harsh yellow glow of flickering torches, their pungent and acrid smoke wafted through the crack. The only thing that Kanef could discern were shadows, but this was definitely where the voices were coming from. He put his ear to the crack, but the voices were too muffled to make out. One of the voices sounded familiar, but he couldn't make out what was being said or who was speaking.

Kanef could hear a hard guttural and hissing voice say, "We have an uninvited guest." Then the mountain began to vibrate and shake. Kanef, fearing a quake had struck the mountain, began to flee. The wall between him and the voices broke apart, sending rocky shrapnel flying in all directions, ricocheting and bouncing behind and all around him. The last thing Kanef remembered was a sharp pain in the back of his head and sprawling face first into the choking dust of the passageway. Then he spiraled into the dark abyss of unconsciousness.

CHAPTER 29

Carric and his female companion were lying on their bellies peaking over a grassy knoll.

"The road below is quite busy," said Carric.

His companion shook her head in agreement then she said, "Doesn't look good for the Xlantan's."

I've been witness too a lot of strange sights in my travels but nothing like those creatures," said Carric.

"Demons!" was the woman's reply.

"If we wait until dark. Maybe we can cross the road unnoticed into the forest and slip through the pass using the forest as cover," said Carric.

"Not a good idea," replied a voice from behind them.

Carric and the Halhoren warrior, galvanized by the unexpected voice, leapt to their feet. Fumbling for their weapons, they turned to face whomever had manage to creep up on them unheard. Carric was astounded once again, for standing before him was a rather attractive blond haired woman with a bird of some sort sitting on her shoulder and a creature that appeared to be half horse and half man.

A brisk breeze blew the blond woman's hair from around her face revealing slightly pointed ears. Carric was mesmerized by the beauty of this exotic looking woman. He had never felt this way before. There was a queasiness in his belly and a weakness in his knees. He had heard some of his friends talk about these feelings. When they became infatuated with a woman, they would loosely refer to it as love. The woman gave him a tender, sweet, and caressing smile, and he felt red in the face.

He wondered to himself if the way he felt was obvious. How foolish could he be. He didn't know this woman. How could she have such an affect on him? He thought himself above such base emotions but here he was, in love.

Schwellen, with a truculent edge to her voice, asked, "Who are you and what do you want?"

"My name is Alaquin, and this is my guardian." She then pointed at the parrot on her shoulder, "And this is Clodtrip," gesturing to her other companion with a bow of her head. "We've a common goal. Carric and I."

Carric was taken aback. He hadn't mentioned his name and yet she knew it.

Schwellen, becoming more intransigent, asked, "How do you know the Outworlder's name?"

Alaquin replied ambiguously, "I know much. I even know your name, Schwellen."

Alaquin's reply seemed to exacerbate the dark skinned woman's anger even more, indicated by her sour scowl.

Carric intervened with a question of his own. "Lovely lady, what common goal do you speak of?"

A smile crossed Alaquin's face. She felt slightly giddy around this man, and she didn't know why. He was an ungainly sort and not particularly handsome, but his affects on her were unsettling. Schwellen shot a look of disgust at Carric.

"I need to take you to the place where those from your world have parted the Fabric of Existence, so that you can disable the device," Alaquin answered.

Schwellen, suspecting she was about to lose her job, lashed out vehemently, "I'm his guide. I'm taking him to Astaria."

Alaquin, looked deep into the eyes of the irate warrior woman, showing no emotion, and said, "I can get us to Astaria quicker, and time is of the essence."

"How can you get there quicker?" Questioned Schwellen dubiously.

"Through the void," answered Alaquin.

Schwellen stepped back. "I don't believe you. No one can travel through the Void," argued Schwellen.

"I can," assured Alaquin.

"How do we enter the Void?" demanded Schwellen.

"There is a doorway in the forest," answered the elf girl.

"Ha! The forest!" exclaimed Schwellen incredulously. "The elves don't allow humans to trespass in their domain."

"I'll be with you," assured Alaquin in an effort to assuage the warrior woman's fears and doubts.

Schwellen didn't reply but just shook her head in disbelief. "You don't have to go. Carric and I are the only ones that need to go. You, Schwellen, may go home if you wish." Then, speaking to the parrot riding on her shoulder, she said, "That goes for you, too."

The parrot replied, "I am with you to the end."

Schwellen, her pride wounded, snapped back, "I back down from nothing. I will also accompany you. I promised this outlander that I would help him and my honor will allow me to do no less."

Carric spoke up. "That brings us back to the original problem. How do we get across the road? There are demons on it constantly."

"I will cloak us in an illusion. They will think we are part of their army," said Alaquin. Then she began to chant in a unintelligible tongue and outline ancient runes in the air which glowed a bright red and floated to encircle the group before fading away.

Alaquin warned, "Stay close to me or you'll fall outside the protective circle."

Slowly they ambled down the hill and crossed the road with no incidents. It was midday as Alaquin and her followers entered the dark and haunting forest. A dark shadow within the forest watched them enter.

*　　*　　*

Simentoo awoke with a start. He heard horses approaching. Quickly, he rolled towards Jarret whom was still either sleeping or unconscious. Simentoo wasn't sure which. Gently shaking Jarret, and called in a low voice so as not to alert the approaching horsemen, "my King, awake."

Simentoo noticed a hole burned in Jarret's tunic where the Crystals had hung, and there was a faint mark on the his chest. A low moan escaped Jarret's throat as he awakened. Simentoo clamped his blood caked, grimy hand over Jarret's mouth. Jarret began to struggle. He opened his eyes, a touch of paranoia reflected in them. It was obvious to Simentoo that Jarret was totally disoriented. Finally, Simentoo discerned the fire of recognition and comprehension in Jarret's eyes. Slowly and cautiously, Simentoo removed his hand but was still prepared to stifle him again if necessary.

Putting his finger to his lips for silence, Simentoo retrieved the weapon he had dropped when he had slipped into his, near unconscious state after his return from his surreal experience. If it wasn't for the blood that covered him and Jarret, he would have questioned his sanity or if the event had even occurred.

They were concealed in a concave, circular depression choked with high, heavy stemmed grasses. Weapon in hand, Simentoo stealthily crawled to the rim of the depression. The rumble of cantering horses had stopped. He poked his head above the rim of the of the depression and came face to hoof with several horses. His heart sank into his belly.

Simentoo was facing a dozen or so Halhoren horse soldiers with bows notched and directed at him and Jarret. Realizing the futility of fighting, Simentoo dropped his weapon. Without a word, about a half-dozen of the warriors dismounted and trussed up the two hapless companions then tossed them like baggage on the backs of their spare horses. Simentoo and Jarret found themselves staring at the underbellies of the horses. Their captors then looped a rope under the horses bellies and tied their feet and hands together. Simentoo knew he was in for an uncomfortable ride.

There were no words spoken during the entire incident. The party of horsemen, digging their heels into the flanks of their mounts, continued their travels.

Jarret shouted over the thunder of the horses' hooves to Simentoo, "You know, I'm tired of being a prisoner! It's beginning to wear on my ego!"

Simentoo shouted back, "I agree! We'll have to rectify this as soon as possible!"

*   *   *

Crysillnia was sitting on a ridge overlooking Altonea. Tanof had suggested, since night was approaching, that they should camp outside the city. He thought that it would be too dangerous to enter the city after dark. Talok didn't trust the newcomer even though, at extreme risk to his own life, he had come too their rescue, the dwarf had to agreed with his logic.

Crysillnia was soaking in the last warming rays of the setting sun. Even though the city was located in a hot and arid climate, the evenings were extremely cool. She enjoyed sitting off by herself. It gave her a chance to collect her thoughts and reflect.

She and Talok had been harassed by a montage of demons since they parted company with Alaquin and her companions at the decimated jungle village. Crysillnia suspected that many of those demons were here because of her behavior back in the jungle. She figured they had escaped the void when she had created the tear by her excessive use of magic.

Crysillnia was mulling over some of the things the elf girl had said. The most curious statement was the one about having things in common. Crysillnia thought that was rather cryptic and was wondering what the elf girl had been insinuating. Also, Alaquin had told her once she had attained the Fifth Crystal that she must go to the desert of blue sands so that she could be instructed on the use of the Crystals.

Crysillnia asked how to find this desert, and Alaquin had said that she would be given instructions when she was in possession of all the Crystals. Crysillnia had tried grilling the elf girl further, but Alaquin would say no more about it.

Alaquin had done another strange thing at their parting. She gave her a tender hug and a kiss on the cheek. The last person that had given her such a comforting gesture was her mother the day before she died. The thought brought tears to her eyes. She pulled her knees up to her chest and encircled them with her arms. This gave her a place to rest her chin. A deep and sad sigh escaped.

The sun had surrendered its domain to the rising moon which was full and bright. The gentle luminescent glow cast the city below in a ghostly bluish light, creating a rather haunting beauty for the ramshackle and dilapidated city. But it also brought out the more unsavory characters of the city.

Crysillnia turned her head in alarm when she heard the rattle of dislodged stones behind her. A ghostly figure was climbing the ridge and coming in her direction. She reached for her dagger. She was preparing to flee or defend herself but was relived to see that it was only Tanof. The knot in her stomach relaxed.

Tanof, as he approached, sensed Crysillnia's panic. "Sorry. I didn't intend to frighten you. I thought you might need your cloak." He raised her cloak to show her.

"That's alright and thank you," she said. She gladly took the proffered cloak.

"May I sit with you?" he asked.

"Sure," she answered.

They sat side by side for a few minutes, letting silence reign supreme except for the occasional rustling of a bush, disturbed by a variable and erratic gust of wind wafting across the rolling plains, creating isolated up drafts which resulted in small funnel like, whirlwinds. These eddies created small dust storms at the base of the ridges. Creatures large and small scurried through the darkness in their never ending struggle for survival.

Finally, Crysillnia broke the silence. "Why did you come to our aid today?"

The silence returned, as Tanof sat there contemplating her question. Crysillnia, tired of waiting, was about to reiterate her question when Tanof replied, "I don't rightly know. It just felt right." Tanof paused and Crysillnia was about too ask him for more detail, when he continued. "It's been along time, since I've done something right and good."

Crysillnia fixed the dark haired man with a scrutinizing eye. He was staring straight ahead in what appeared to be a trance like state of contemplation. She thought she may have spotted a tear slipping down his cheek. She glanced away not wanting to embarrass this strong and proud man and refocused her attention on the city below.

They returned to their silent vigilance.

Then Tanof asked, "Do I know you or your family from somewhere?"

Crysillnia, surprised by the question, replied, "Not that I'm aware of. Why do you ask?"

"You look vaguely familiar," he answered.

"Have you been to Caspar?" Crysillnia asked. "Wait! I remember you," she continued. "You were in that tavern at Dragon's Peek."

"Yes," he answered. Then he sat quietly for a short period before he continued. "We've been crossing paths quite often of late but I feel there is a closer connection between us."

Crysillnia looked over at Tanof and then said, "My mother has been dead for a long time, and I do resemble her. My father, I'd rather not talk about."

"What's your mother's name?" Tanof asked.

"Sholena," she answered.

Tanof supplanted his gaze from the far horizon and focused on her. There was a bit of fire in his eyes. Crysillnia felt somewhat unnerved by his sudden change in mood. "And your father's name?" he asked, clinching his hands.

Almost in a whisper, she replied, "Prince Kanef or so I've been told."

Tanof began to chuckle. Then he burst into full blown laugh. Crysillnia began to fear that he had gone mad. She began to inch upwards, preparing to flee.

"Sit down," he said. "I won't hurt you. I may appear to be a little mad, but I won't harm you."

Crysillnia sat back down but she kept a close eye on him, looking for any unexpected moves. "Relax, relax. You look like a scared rabbit," he said, more to himself than her. He continued, shaking his head. "So I have a Princess for a half sister."

Abashed by the comment, Crysillnia's mouth dropped open. She didn't immediately respond to Tanof's statement, as she mentally digested it and waited for clarification. But when it appeared that Tanof had no intentions of clarifying the statement, Crysillnia impetuously asked. "What are you talking about." She could feel the Crystals begin to pulsate with her growing agitation.

Sarcastically, and with a sneer, Tanof remarked, "Isn't it obvious? Sholena is your mother, and she is also my mother."

Crysillnia, a chill running down her spine, jumped up, hands on her hips.

"Mother never told me that I had a brother."

"Actually you have two brothers or more correctly, two half brothers."

Flabbergasted Crysillnia didn't know what to say. Her knees began to quiver with shock and excitement, nearly causing her to collapse. She sat back down. More to herself than to Tanof, she said, "I never knew. She never said anything."

"Your father. I mean, what happened?" Crysillnia queried.

"Your father took my, our mother, away from my father," answered Tanof, inflections of malice evident in his voice.

"How?" Crysillnia questioned.

"Ok! I'll tell you the story," said Tanof, as he stared at Crysillnia as if trying to burn a hole through her heart. After a few more moments of silence, he began to tell his story. He turned his gaze away from Crysillnia and looked out across the beautifully moonlit landscape. He adjusted his feet which dislodged a few rocks, causing them to roll down the hillside which dislodged more stones and small pebbles, creating a miniature landslide.

"Our mother was from peasant stock. She married my father at fifteen. He was about twenty seasons older and also very poor. I was born in their first season of marriage and Rollof came three seasons later."

"Rollof?" exclaimed Crysillnia. She was shocked at hearing the name of one of her late companions or maybe this was a different person.

"What happened to Rollof?" she asked.

"He joined the Castle Guards and became a close personal friend of your father's," Tanof answered with apparent disgust. "I've never have and never will forgive him for betraying our father's memory. I haven't spoken to him since."

Crysillnia said, with tears in her eyes, "You won't have to worry about speaking to him ever again. He was killed by goblins early in my journey."

Tanof turned to look at Crysillnia, regret and sadness reflected in his dark eyes. The look reminded her of the sadness she had seen in her mother's eyes. There was no doubt remaining in her mind that this man sitting by her side was her brother which pleased her immensely. She was excited that she had siblings even though one was dead. A great feeling of sadness nearly overwhelmed her at the thought of Rollof's death. The extreme changes in her mood agitated the Crystals igniting a cursory pulse. Crysillnia realized that the Crystals were becoming more attuned to her emotions.

Turning his attention to the ground in front of him, head down, Tanof continued with his narrative, the anger now gone from his voice. "When my mother met Kanef. She was taken by his good looks and the finery he wore."

"As you know, Mother had an exquisite recipe for bread which attracted the affluent, when the Royal Family tasted her bread, they hired her in the castle bakery. This is where they met. It wasn't long after she began to work in the bakery that she began to come home late. She always claimed she was asked to work late to prepare baked goods for some special occasion or another."

"Father suspected she wasn't telling the truth, and they would argue incessantly. Rollof and I would hide under our blankets and cover our ears, in a futile attempt to block out the frightening arguments between our parents."

"The night mother left, I listened more closely to the fight because I intuitively knew there was something different that night. She told father, that she was pregnant, and he wasn't the father. Father hit her and continued to do so until I came to him crying and grabbed his arm, begging him to stop."

"There was a madness in his eyes. He threw me to the side and raised his hand to hit her again but stopped. He turned to look at me lying in a crumpled heap by the dinner table. I had hit my head on the corner of the table and was bleeding profusely. He came to my aid and mother slipped out the front door. That night, she disappeared from our lives, never to return."

Crysillnia reached over and took one of Tanof's clinched hands and held it in her own, stroking it in an attempt to comfort him. Tanof clasped her hand with a strong but tender grip and looking in the deep dark pools that were her eyes. He began to tear up.

He said, "I regret what happened to Rollof. I really loved him deeply. It's a shame I allowed my hatred to taint that love. Now I'll never be able to let him know how I really felt. And I'm pleased to have you for a sister."

Crysillnia, no longer able to control her mix of tragedy and joy, threw her arms around Tanof's neck, hugging him as she sobbed uncontrollably. He wrapped his strong arms around her. Pulling her close, returning the affection, he sobbed deep within, not allowing himself to loose the raging turmoil of his grief and joy. The Crystals pulsed softly.

CHAPTER 30

Alaquin and her company of five silently and quickly moved through the dark forest. Alaquin had used her magic to hide their presence from the ethereal fairy creatures that made their home in the deep vastness of the forest. They had come across many places in the forest where the Chaos Demon had left its signature. Alaquin knew she was running out of time. She had to conclude her business and quickly.

Carric was astounded by this haunting forest and all of its frightening and dangerous inhabitants. The elf girl had done a strange dance and cloaked them with a mysterious enchantment. Even though the strange and macabre creatures couldn't see them, he had the distinct feeling that they were aware of their presence. But Alaquin's magic seemed to confound their senses and keep the creatures from finding the trespassers.

They entered a small meadow which was carpeted in a beautiful array of many colored wild flowers. Not one flower was a solid color, and many flowers had three or more colors. The meadow created a spectacular visual display. Carric compared the meadow to an artist gone mad and wildly splashed paint onto his canvas with no rhyme or reason.

Night was fast approaching, so Alaquin decided this would be a good place to stop and rest for the night. They hungrily devoured a cold meal, for they dared not light a fire.

Carric asked Alaquin, "Where are we going?"

She answered, "There is a natural doorway into the Void near here."

"Are you sure you can protect us?" queried Schwellen, dubiously.

"There are no absolutes," was Alaquin's answer.

Schwellen, irritated by Alaquin's ambiguity, lashed out verbally. "What is that suppose to mean? Either you can or you can't, elf!" She then turned to Carric. "You can't trust an elf."

Alaquin shrugged her shoulders and said nothing further.

"Where are we going and why?" asked Clodtrip.

"Astaria." answered the elf girl. "There is an outworlder talisman there. It's destroying the Fabric of the Firmament."

Carric interrupted, "I may be better able to explain the machine. "The science of our world is highly advanced and our technology requires a vast amount of energy. To fill this insatiable hunger we created a power plant that appeared to create energy out of nothing, but it wasn't long before we discovered that it created dead areas, areas where nothing would grow, because it was tapping the energy of space and time."

"We didn't know why and our science was unable to solve the problem, so we outlawed the use of the power plant but all the power plants weren't recovered and apparently one of them is here." Carric stopped for a moment, then said, "I evidently have two problems to solve. The other one is to put a stop to the illegal and immoral business of body part harvesting. This is only one of many worlds where this is happening."

Clodtrip scratched his head and then asked, "What is this thing called science?"

"Well, that's hard to explain." Carric paused to collect his thoughts. "The closest thing that science can be compared to is Elf Magic. We, that is our culture, have studied the nature of how and why things work, the physics of nature and then used this knowledge to manipulate these natural laws to our own purposes," explained Carric.

"Oh," said Clodtrip, appearing more perplexed.

Schwellen, disgusted with Carric's feeble explanation, said, "Now that we're more confused about this magic called science, I've another question. What do you mean by body parts harvesting?"

Carric didn't really want to get into a major discussion about medicine, so he decided to put it bluntly. "There are people who kill others for their body parts so they can sell them to people in need of these body parts."

Schwellen and Clodtrip were shocked hy Carric's revelation.

Finally, Schwellen said, "We might as well get some rest, so we can move on at first light."

Carric shrugged in resignation and offered to take the first watch. He was glad that he didn't have to explain anymore.

*   *   *

Kanef, floating through the dark and mysterious realms of unconsciousness, began to have vivid remembrances from his past. It was a fine, warm, early spring day in Caspar City. The sun shone brightly against the brilliant blue backdrop of the sky. Despite the wonder of the day, Kanef was in a dark and depressed mood.

He shouldered his way through the calamitous and crowded streets of the city. He heard his name being called above the cacophony which reverberated from the close walls of the buildings that lined the streets of the city. Kanef looked around expectantly, searching for the source of that beautiful lilting voice.

"Over here!"

Kanef turned his head in the direction from which the call came. He spotted her across the street and slightly to his right. Kanef's heart lifted at the sight of her. The woman he loved, Sholena. Her beauty was superlative in his eyes. She was nearly as tall as he, slender and curvaceous with long black hair.

It felt as if his heart would drop into his stomach whenever he was around her. Kanef watched her run, careless and without heed, across the street. She was nearly run over by a farm wagon loaded with grain, headed for the market. The wagon master reigned in his horses with great difficulty, just barely missing the woman. Cursing the careless woman, the burly wagon master shook his fist at Sholena.

Apparently oblivious to her near catastrophe, she threw herself into Kanef's strong and capable arms. She wrapped her long, slender arms around his neck and began to kiss him relentlessly. Kanef's felt his heart palpitate at her closeness. The love that he felt for her took his breath away. He enveloped her with his arms, sweeping her off her feet, as he returned her passionate kisses.

Then sadness returned to his heart. He had come here to tell her something. He gently pushed her away which she allowed reluctantly.

Frowning, she asked, "What's wrong darling?"

Dropping his gaze to the ground, he said, "I've something to tell you."

Sholena's frown melted away and her face brightened with expectation. "And I have something to tell you, too," she said. Her face glowed with excitement.

He gently took her hands into his. He admired her exquisite beauty. The red dress she wore, embroidered with gold color thread around the neckline and sleeves, cut low in the front which revealed a scandalous amount of cleavage, was his favorite. Red was her color. It highlighted her obsidian hair which cascaded over her shoulders, contrasting with her milky white skin.

Kanef's heart sank as he looked into bright but strangely dark eyes and said, "You first,"

"No, No silly! You first," Sholena urged.

Kanef looked deep into her eyes. He sensed a warmth and glow he had never noticed before. He mentally shook the feeling off. He continued looking down at his feet again.

"Silly, why have you all of a sudden become so fond of your feet?" chastised Sholena lovingly.

He began to choke up. He cleared his throat and then continued, "I love you with all of my heart. You know that don't you?"

Sholena, sensing that something bad was coming, took a step back as she answered, "Yes and I love you with all my being." Tears began to well up in her eyes.

She pulled her hands away. He reached for them but she jerked them away and took another step backwards.

"I can't see you anymore!" he blurted.

"Why?" she asked, exasperated, as tears began to roll down her cheeks. "What was I to you, just a dalliance? A cheap roll in the sack?" Her cheeks became flushed with anger. Then with a scream, she turned and ran back across the street.

"Sholena, darling, come back!" he shouted. Kanef tried to follow but lost her in the confusion of the busy street.

His last sight of her was the tail of her red dress as she turned a corner into a narrow, dark, and garbage strewn alleyway. When he had managed to reach the alley, she was gone. He had searched the rest of the day for her with no luck. He had sent men searching for her and finally one returned with devastating news. Sholena had taken her own life.

The traumatic remembrance nudged Kanef towards consciousness. He struggled through the soupy morass of unconsciousness and, with great determination and strength of will, he broke free of the insidious web woven by his mind.

At that, moment realization struck. He became cognizant of what she had wanted to tell him that fateful day. She had wanted to tell him that she was pregnant. And another realization surfaced. The men he had sent to find her that day had lied to him. Probably further machinations of his father. Grief for his true love overwhelmed him, and he began to weep silently for his loss but he also wept for being blessed with a daughter. A sweet reminder of his one and only love.

He lied on his back in the dark, unable to see. Kanef was surprised to find that he wasn't bound. Surely he was being held captive, he thought to himself, by the demons. He lied there on the hard, cold, and jagged cavern floor, deep within the bowels of the Caspar Mountains. He listened closely to every sound. He could hear water running in the distance and the scratching and scurrying sounds of the small creatures that claimed this dark domain as their home.

He heard the scuffling of feet. Someone was coming. The predicament of his situation came crashing down on him. He was in total darkness. Using his arms, he levered himself upwards, into a sitting position which initiated a spell of vertigo and nausea. He had a horrendous headache.

Carefully, he inspected the back of his head with his hand to find there was a fist-sized knot and a thick mass of blood-matted hair. The nausea was driving him back into unconsciousness. Kanef decided to lie back down in an attempt to control his rebelling stomach and the paralyzing darkness of the unconscious mind.

Who or whatever was approaching quickly. He lied on the cold unyielding cavern floor. The approaching footfalls were heavy and shuffling. Kanef decided the wise choice would be to fake unconsciousness. The footsteps stopped at his side.

"Get up, human," a gruff and nearly unintelligible voice commanded. Kanef didn't move.

Kanef grunted with pain as the owner of the voice kicked him in the side.

"The One knows you are conscious. The One felt your mind when you awoke."

Kanef, fearing another rude prod from the cruel and indifferent creature might break his ribs, sat up, a bit to quickly, causing him to empty the contents of his stomach, all over the feet of his tormentor.

In a rage the creature began to pummel and kick Kanef, yelling, "Don't spit up on me, filthy human!"

Kanef pulled his knees into his chest, rolling himself into a ball, covering his head with his arms.

When his assailant ceased its assault he heard it say something in its primitive guttural language. Two pairs of slimy and scale-covered hands hoisted Kanef to his feet. This didn't help his nausea much but he controlled the need to vomit. He feared, he might not survive another beating. Kanef between two of the creatures was forced too walk.

Kanef tried to oblige them but was unable keep up with the quick pace the demons set, so demons on both sides of him took an arm and drug him along. Kanef could smell the acrid stench of burning pitch from the torches before he was able to see their feeble light. The darkness was so absorbing that torch light was almost useless.

Kanef's escorts stopped near the torches and dropped him on the floor. Kanef pulled himself up to a sitting position and looked around. The torches were embedded in the wall above his head. The light emitted by the sputtering torches didn't illuminate much of his surroundings, so he wasn't able to tell whether he was in an underground chamber or just a passageway.

He could just, barely make out the hulking shapes of the two demons that had escorted him here. They were standing at the outer edges of the torches' illumination.

Kanef focused his attention on the sound of footsteps approaching in the dark. Kanef tried to focus on the new arrival but couldn't see beyond the arc of the torch light. The two hulking forms moved, one to each side, to allow for something or someone to pass between them.

What appeared frightened Kanef. He instinctively began to push himself backwards, scooting across the floor on the seat of his pants until his back came up against the cold stone wall behind him. The creature stood about twice his height. It sprouted three long and half-curled horns from a low forehead. The eyes of the creature were positioned at the sides of its head. The demon had a large snout with two nasal openings near the base and large pointed teeth.

The neck which was long and spindly blended into a massive chest. The demon's arms and hands were massive, and each of the three digits on the hands was capped with long, razor-sharp talons that nearly dragged on the ground. The creature shambled on its long and powerful legs into the torch light.

"I am called, The One of He" said the demon in its deep, guttural, and poorly articulated speech. The long snout made it hard for it to form human syllables.

Kanef, confused by the demon's odd name, asked, "Who is He?"

"Natas! Foolish human," replied the demon and then it began to laugh. A deep grating noise that raised the hairs on the back of

Kanef's neck. The other demons began to laugh, enjoying the joke, at Kanef's expense.

"Enough!" shouted The One of He. "You still live because an ally asked us to spare your life for the moment. He wishes to speak with you."

The demon then gestured for someone to approach, and to Kanef's incredulity, his father stepped into the weak, flickering torch light wearing a jackal like grin.

"Son. Fancy meeting you here," his father said.

Kanef, still in shock, stood there, mouth agape, not knowing what to say or even how to act, his emotions in turmoil. He knew his father was an evil person but he never suspected his father would ally himself with demons.

"Kanef, my son, you appeared stunned by my new associates," continued his father.

"Why, father?" asked Kanef.

"Why?" repeated his father. "Because they are the power to be and you know how I like to back a winner," Kanef's father answered.

Using the wall for support, Kanef stood. He began to chastise his father, his anger building as he spoke. "I knew, you had little moral backbone but to help these wretched and licentious creatures is even low for you."

Kanef's father, unperturbed by his son's critique, replied, with a sly smile. "I'll use any methods at my disposal to gain and keep power."

"How are you aiding these dastardly villains?" asked Kanef, sharply.

"Simple. I'm not moving my armies against them which will allow them to strengthen their forces against the Xlantan army."

Kanef, shaking his head, turned his back on his father and said, "I'm ashamed to be your son."

"Makes no difference to me. You're weak like your mother, too righteous for your own good. I'm ashamed to have you for a son."

The One of He chuckled.

"Do with him what you want. I've no use for the weak-hearted," said King Falef. Then taking one of the torches. He turned and walked away, knowing he had condemned his son to death.

The torch faded into the darkness. The One of He chuckled again and said, "And you call us evil . . . Your father just sealed you to a cruel and agonizing death."

Kanef, resigned to his destiny, sighed and collapsed, no longer able to combat the vertigo and resulting nausea. At this point in his life, he cared little whether he lived or died.

The One of He, looking down on the pathetic human, said, "I'm feeling generous today." He commanded his cohorts to dispatch him quickly. Then turning and laughing, the head demon disappeared into the forbidding darkness.

Kanef, slumped over, was listening to the demons discussing something between them. He was unable to decipher their conversation because they were talking in their deep guttural language of grunts and clicks. It was obvious they were having some sort of disagreement. The argument heated up quickly, and then the demons began to grapple.

Kanef sat up to watch the brawl. Chuckling, Kanef admonished himself, silently. Even the order to kill you creates a minor catastrophe. Typical Kanef luck.

Then someone dove out of the darkness, tackling the combatants. Kanef was unable to distinguish who or what it was. He didn't know whether it was friend or foe.

The scuffle, cloaked by the impenetrable darkness, reached a crescendo and then there was an absolute and overwhelming silence. Then Kanef heard heavy footsteps slowly approach him. To his shock and wonderment. The hulking form of a troll loomed out of the darkness.

The troll asked, or rather, stated, "You are the friend of our troll brother, Simentoo."

Kanef confounded by these new circumstances, stuttered a response. "Ye-es." "We will help you," continued the troll.

Kanef peered into the darkness beyond the sputtering torches. He could just barely discern the dark outlines of other ponderous masses behind the lead troll.

The troll swept Kanef up into his massive and unyielding arms. Kanef began to protest this treatment, but the troll said, "It is to dark for you to safely and quickly travel through the mountain." With that comment, Kanef discontinued his protest of indignation.

Kanef, usually not squeamish, shuttered slightly when he heard a squishing sound. One of the trolls, evidently, trampled on the remains of Kanef's former would-be executioners. The trolls moved swiftly through the lightless passageways. His head, although throbbing, wasn't bothering him as much, and his nausea had subsided somewhat.

They finally reached their destination, a warren of large cubicles which were carved into the stone walls of the passageway. The passageway and cubicles were well lit by many sputtering and crackling torches. The burning pitch wafting throughout the warren was quite acrid, causing Kanef's eyes to sting and water excessively.

The troll put Kanef down on a stone ledge carved out of the rear wall in one of the cubicles. Kanef wiped his eyes with the back of his hand, in a feeble attempt to clear his vision.

Kanef's headache had returned. Even with the headache, he was beginning to feel more like himself.

"Do you need a healer?" asked the troll.

"No, but I could use some water," answered Kanef.

The troll left and returned quickly, carrying a huge stone tub filled with water. Tagging along behind the large troll was a smaller version of the troll. It was carrying a stone bowl and cup. There was also a dull brown cloth in the bowl.

The smaller troll took the cup and tattered cloth out of the bowl. Laying the cloth on the stone bench beside Kanef, it filled the bowl and cup with water, also placing them beside Kanef. Once these tasks were completed, the smaller troll left.

The larger troll explained to Kanef, "The water in the bowl and cup are for consumption and what is left in the tub is for washing up. I know how obsessed humans are about this strange ritual of bathing."

"Thank you," said Kanef.

The large troll exiting the cubicle, said, "My son will bring you some nourishment."

Kanef nodded in affirmation.

After the troll left, Kanef rummaged through his carrying pouch, that was strapped around his waist. He sighed with relief, when he found the small cloth pouch which contained some powdered Callenberry Root. The Callenberry bush was a superb, all-around, medicinal herb which cures wounds to relieving headaches.

Kanef loosened the draw strings of the small bag. He put three pinches of the powdered herb in the cup of water. Finding nothing in the room to stir the concoction, he used his finger. Greedily, Kanef drank the medicinal concoction, then he lied down on the stone bench. He wiped the remnants of the concoction from his mouth with the back of a dirty sleeve before he slipped into a deep and healing sleep induced by the herb.

*   *   *

Simentoo was sitting by the center post which supported most of the tent's weight, hands behind his back and feet stretched out in front of him, bound with leather thongs. Simentoo rolled his shoulders in attempt to relieve an excruciatingly painful muscle spasm caused by his awkward position. He surveyed his surroundings. There were two others in the tent. Jarret was directly to his right and an elf directly across from him.

The elf was wearing a black robe with the cowl pulled back. Simentoo scrutinized the elf closely, wondering what an elf was doing here of all places.

The elf spoke to him. "I've sparked your curiosity." "Yes," replied Simentoo.

"In what way? Asked the elf.

"Well, I was wondering how you came to be in the hands of the Halhoren, considering you're so far from the elf homeland," queried Simentoo.

Jarret, sitting in silence, was taking in the conversation.

He was wondering what Shasheek, leader of the sect of Dark Elves, was doing here.

The elf turned his attention to Jarret before answering Simentoo. "Been a long time Jarret,"

"Yes, but not long enough," replied Jarret, venomously.

Simentoo weighed the exchange between Jarret and the elf carefully but said nothing.

Shifting his attention back to Simentoo, a slight grin crossing his lips, the elf answered Simentoo's query. "I was following someone and overestimated the power of my spell of concealment."

"What quarry were you stalking?" asked Jarret, his dislike of the elf still coloring his voice.

With a slight edge in his voice and without addressing Jarret directly, the elf answered. "I'm unwilling to divulge that information."

"Just like you, Shasheek!" snapped Jarret.

"Considering our circumstances," said Simentoo, "We need to get along, if we're going to successfully attain freedom. If not, we'll probably all die. And death at the hands of the Halhoren isn't very pleasant."

Looking from one to the other, Simentoo tried to gage the affect his speech had on the two antagonists. The elf's countenance was impossible to discern, but he could see that Jarret still seethed with rage.

"Agreed?" asked Simentoo.

"Agreed," confirmed Shasheek. Jarrett shook his head in acquiescence.

Simentoo had been busy rubbing the bindings that bound his hands against the center post. The thongs were frayed enough, that Simentoo, with a great amount of straining and groaning, was able to snap his bindings.

He quickly untied his feet. Rubbing his swollen and bleeding wrists, Simentoo stood. He then untied Jarrett and Shasheek. Simentoo slipped over to the entrance of the tent, so that he could appraise their situation.

There were two guards standing outside of the tent, one on each side of the entrance. Returning to the center of the tent, he crouched down and asked in a low whisper, if anyone had any suggestions on how to escape.

Shasheek said, "Now that my hands are free, I can use my magic."

Jarrett protested. "Isn't that what got you captured in the first place?"

Shasheek scowled at Jarrett and ignored the comment. Shasheek began to chant in a low monotone and to draw ancient elf runes in the dirt-floor of the tent. Simentoo wasn't sure but thought, he felt a slight tremor in the ground.

Shasheek stood up when he had completed casting his spell. There was a sheepish grin on Shasheek's face.

"What did you do?" asked Simentoo.

Shasheek held up a finger, indicating that he wished them to wait a moment. To Simentoo's surprise small animals, insects, and a menagerie of other creatures living in the ground, scrambled from their homes and places of hiding and began to dash to-and-fro in a state of complete and total confusion.

Simentoo and Jarrett looked at each other, shrugging their shoulders in bewilderment, wondering how this was going to abet in their escape. Shasheek motioned for Jarret and Simentoo to take up position on each side of the tent's entranceway which they did promptly. Suddenly, bedlam broke out in the camp. The horses began to scream and shriek. Men began yelling and running without direction or reason.

The guards entered the tent one at a time to check on their prisoners. Simentoo took the first guard, and Jarrett handled the second. They quickly and silently killed the guards by snapping their necks. Shasheek pushed the flap hanging over entranceway aside just enough so he could see the calamity outside.

Simentoo knew the horses had broken free of their tethers when he heard the drumming of their hooves as they ran past the tent. Shasheek frantically motioned for Jarrett and Simentoo to follow as he exited the tent, which they did without question. Simentoo was astonished and pleased with the total chaos of the camp caused by the elf's magic.

Each of the escaping captives singled out a horse from the stampeding herd. Grasping the maddened animals' wildly flying manes, they mounted and were off into the dark before the Halhoren could foil the escape.

CHAPTER 31

Crysillnia and Talok sat on the ridge overlooking the city of Altonea. Crysillnia sat with her legs outstretched while Talok's knees were pulled towards his chest so he would have a prop for his arms. Talok had a handful of pebbles which he meaninglessly flicked out in front of him. Crysillnia was twirling the stem of a weed that she had plucked from the hard and unyielding ground on which she sat between her fingers.

The sky was cloudless and the sun was near its zenith. The sun battered the two without forgiveness. Talok broke the monotonous silence when he slapped an annoying black fly that had landed on his cheek with a cracking wallop.

"Damn!" he said. "These abominable, flying insects."

Crysillnia looked over at Talok, not seeing him. Her thoughts were elsewhere.

A small lizard skittered by Crysillnia's feet, catching her attention. She was amazed at how fast such a small creature could move. It's legs appeared to windmill. The small and harmless creature passed below Talok, and he flicked a stone at it, striking the unoffending creature. The lizard tumbled down the slope haphazardly. Once it quit rolling, the small creature righted itself and continued on its way, disappearing into the hillside rubble of rocks, shrubs, and sand.

"Do you trust him?" Talok asked.

"Who?" answered Crysillnia.

"Tanof. Who else would I be asking about?" snapped a truculent Talok giving Crysillnia an annoying glance.

Finally drawn out of her hypnotic reverie of boredom, she looked into Talok's dark and simmering eyes. A disarming smile playing across her lips, she answered, "Yes, to a point."

Talok grunted in response to her answer. Then he returned his attention to the city below.

"I take it you don't trust him," she stated rhetorically.

Talok grunted in the affirmative. Neither continued the conversation and silence settled over them like a blanket. A weak breeze caressed the two silent partners, as they watched people and wagons entering and exiting the bustling city below.

Every so often, the breeze would carry a curse, the creaking of wagon wheels, or the sound of a horse's hoof hitting the hard packed dirt road below to Crysillnia and Talok as they sat, patiently waiting for Tanof to return from the city below. Tanof had gone into the city to see if it was safe.

Crysillnia was beginning to wonder if some misfortune had befallen their new ally. He had left for the city at dawn, and it was now midday and there was still no sign of him. She was about to give up on Tanof when she spotted someone heading in their direction.

Standing up and pointing Crysillnia said, "I believe I see him breaking away from the road."

Talok stood, dropping the handful of pebbles that he held, at his feet so that he could shade his eyes.

The man walking in their direction, leading his mount, was of medium height and build with medium length pitch black hair, similar in color to Crysillnia's.

"I think your right," said Talok.

The man below stopped when he saw the two standing on the ridge, watching him. He motioned for them to come down. The two retrieved their mounts from the other side of the ridge and traversed the rubble-strewn ridge, picking their path carefully Although the acclivity of the ridge wasn't dangerous, the loose rocks and pebbles made for precarious footing, causing their horses to be skittish and hard to handle.

Tanof watched his new companions approach. The unusually large dwarf was rather unkempt. His long black beard highlighted with gray and shoulder length hair framed his squarish face. The woman, even though grimy and disheveled from her harrowing adventures, was very beautiful. A very dangerous commodity in such a place as Altonea. They would have to keep as low a profile as possible.

Crysillnia and Talok finally reached Kanef.

"How does it look?" asked Crysillnia.

"It appears to be safe, but there is no guarantee in a place like Altonea. This is a city founded by criminals and run by criminals with their own sense of right and wrong," answered Tanof.

"Are you sure you want to enter the city?" asked Talok.

"Yes! I'm tired of sleeping on the ground, eating cold rations, and I would like a bath. Besides, we need to replenish our supplies," answered Crysillnia acerbically. Without further discussion on the matter, Tanof lead them into the city.

Even though she had watched the traffic in and out of the city, Crysillnia was still surprised at how busy and crowded the city streets were, considering its isolation and inhospitable setting on the edge of the desert.

She found the hustle and bustle of the dry and dusty streets exciting. There were merchants, trying to hock all kinds of wares, lining the streets. Dirty and wild children ran up and down the streets with mad abandon.

Crysillnia was mesmerized by the cacophony of sounds and the flurry of activity in this squalid little city on the edge of nowhere. She wandered down the main street heedlessly immersed in the experience to the point of being unawares of what was happening around her. This was nothing like Caspar City. Excitement coursed through her veins. Altonea wasn't a beautiful city, but it was vibrant and alive.

Suddenly and unexpectedly, she was jerked back into reality, as excruciating pain coursed down her arm. Someone had grabbed it, just above the elbow, and yanked her to the side.

Pulling her arm away from her offender, she exclaimed with an acidulous tone, "Ouch! Let go! Your hurting me." She turned on her offender in anger, prepared to strike out. She came face to face with Talok and then she saw the water wagon, splashing water over the sides of the huge barrels it carried as it rumbled by. Crysillnia realized that her careless behavior had nearly got her run over by the wildly careening vehicle. The driver of the wagon cackled derisively at his would-be victim.

"Sorry, I didn't mean to hurt you, but considering the alternative, I didn't have much choice," apologized the dwarf.

Crysillnia, embarrassed by her lack of attentiveness, said, "That's alright. It was my fault for not watching where I was going. I should apologize to you. Thank you, Talok. Thank you for being there when I needed you, once again." She turned her attention back to the wagon and watched it as it rumbled down the street eliciting curses and jeers from other pedestrians.

Astonished, Crysillnia commented, "I think he's trying to run people down."

And, as if in answer, the driver whipped his beasts into a frenzy and let out a bellicose laugh.

Turning to Tanof, embarrassed and attempting to cover up her acerbic reaction, Crysillnia asked with levity, "Is there a place to eat in this city? I'm starving."

Tanof said. "Follow me."

*　　*　　*

Darith was in hiding as he peeked around the corner from the regulators. Altonea didn't have laws in the normal sense of the concept, but the city did have ruling bodies which were referred to as Guilds. Each professional group within the city was organized in a specific hierarchy pertaining to its particular field, whether they were carpenters or thieves. The heads of the Guilds appointed regulators to rid the city of what was considered, by the Guilds, bad influences on the order of things. The regulators were given free-reign to solve these problems.

One of these supposed threats on Altonea"s society was orphaned and abandoned children roaming the streets, stealing to survive in the harsh reality of Altonea. The regulators would capture these unfortunate children and sell them into slavery. The Astarians were the main purchasers of these unfortunate children, but there were well to do businessmen from Altonea and other places who would purchase the children for their own perverted pleasures.

Darith had been spotted by a regulator patrol and had escaped capture, but he knew they were hot on his trail. He was being especially cautious, but he was hungry and needed to steal something to fill his protesting belly. He crept out of his hiding place. He hadn't seen any of the black and red uniforms of the regulators for awhile, so he assumed it was safe. The streets were crowded at this time of the day. Women were doing their shopping for the evening meal. Darith threaded between the jostling and shoving shoppers and had to, at times, scurry out of the way of men on horseback and wagons.

Darith was daydreaming as he searched for a likely victim to ply his pickpocketing skills on. He was thinking about his mother. She had been a prostitute and had died of a disease contracted as a result of her profession. She had died when he was six, that was five seasons ago. He missed her loving kisses and caresses at bedtime. She would tell him stories about wonderful places and people. He had promised himself, and still did, that he would visit those places and people one day.

"Gotcha boy! Thought-ya get away from me did-ya." Then the regulator laughed. A deep grating laugh. The man, easily, lifted the thin and spindly legged boy off the ground. Darith wildly kicked his feet in an attempt to break free of the regulators iron grip. The man just laughed at the boy's feeble attempt to break free.

"To the slave market you go boy and money in my pocket." said the regulator.

"Hey you! Let loose of the boy!" came a voice from behind the regulator.

The regulator turned his head to face the boy's advocate. "This boy falls under my . . ." And that was all the regulator was able to say before a huge fist struck him square in the face. Staggering, the regulator dropped the boy as blood burst from his nose like water from a broken dike.

Darith landed on his feet like a mountain cat and began to run. He couldn't believe his good fortune. Darith stopped abruptly when it struck him. Someone had actually helped him. That didn't happen often in Altonea, especially to an unwanted.

Darith's curiosity overcame his trepidations about returning to the scene of the altercation. He was astonished at the sight. An unconscious regulator was lying in the street, with blood flowing from his nose profusely, as a beautiful woman kneeled over him, a rag in her hand. The woman was trying, futilely, to staunch the flow of blood. All the while, she was admonishing a giant dwarf, hulking over her and the injured man.

"Talok, what am I going to do with you?" she asked. "All I wanted you to do was help the boy, not beat the man half-to-death," she continued, shaking her head disapprovingly.

The normally taciturn dwarf smiled at the gentle berating, and said, "Anyone that would sell children into slavery deserves worse, but I knew you wouldn't approve."

The woman, at first with a look of chagrin on her face, tossed her head, as if trying to clear hair from her face, then turned her head upwards and looked the giant dwarf in the eyes. After a moment of silence, she grinned and said, "You make a good point." She extended her hand to the giant dwarf which he took into his rough and calloused hand. Then he gently but with command pulled her to her feet.

Darith, eyes brimming with tears, watched the woman and dwarf join another man standing amongst the increasing crowd of spectators. The man motioned for them to follow him. Darith shadowed the three. There was something about the woman that had reminded him of his mother. It wasn't so much that she resembled his mother in appearance, but it was the gentleness that the woman radiated that was so familiar. No longer able to hold back the dammed up tears, they streaked down his cheek leaving dirty runnels on his face as he followed the quickly retreating trio. Leading the way, Tanof took them through a maze of streets and back alleys to a small dingy tavern. Crysillnia couldn't make out the name on the placard hanging above the entrance because the lettering was badly weathered and sun bleached.

Crysillnia followed Tanof, reluctantly and with some doubt, into the tavern. Talok brought up the rear, but before entering, he looked up and down the street. He finally entered the tavern with a frown framing his face.

Tanof said. "Do you have the same feeling as I, that we were being followed?" Talok shook his head and grunted in the affirmative.

Tanof scrutinized the dinghy, low ceilinged, and smoke- filled tavern. Without asking and ignoring the protests of the tavern owner, he went into the kitchen through a set of double doors situated in the rear of the small, crowded room. When he returned, he said, "There's a door in the rear of the kitchen that leads to a back alley, in case we need an escape route."

Tanof surveyed the tavern room. Small but sturdy wooden tables surrounded by just as sturdy chairs were arranged haphazardly across the litter strewn floor. The bar extended across the rear of the tavern but didn't impede access to the kitchen.

He chose a table in the back corner near the kitchen entrance. He asked Talok to sit at one end of the table, so that Talok was able to observe the kitchen doors, and Tanof sat at the other end, so he could clearly see the front door. Tanof had Crysillnia sit behind the table with her back to the wall.

A serving wench approached them with a smile. "What would you like?" she asked in a honey sweet and syrupy voice.

Crysillnia decided, she didn't like this woman. The woman was rather plain looking, not exceptionally attractive but still pleasing to look at. She was tall and had more of a athletic build than one would expect of a woman. She had luxuriously long, brown hair that swept down to the middle of her back, reminding Crysillnia of the long tresses she use to have.

Instinctively, Crysillnia ran her fingers through her short-cropped hair.

Crysillnia felt the Crystals pulsate. She supposed, they were reacting to her feelings of dislike for this woman. She really couldn't understand why she felt such animosity towards the woman. She had done nothing to her and didn't deserve her dislike, but still Crysillnia harbored a deep and irrational dislike for her.

Crysillnia lost interest in the woman when she noticed Tanof was closely watching a table across the room.

Tanof asked the woman, without looking at her, "What's on the menu?" she replied. "Meat and vegetable stew, bread-cheese and ale." Tanof ordered for the three of them. "We'll take three bowls of stew, three loaves of bread cheese and a pitcher of ale."

The serving wench stood there fidgeting, not moving.

Tanof looked up at the woman, and with a growl in his voice, he asked, "What are you waiting for woman?"

Even though Crysillnia didn't like the woman, she disliked the inflection of contempt evident in Tanof's voice. She surmised, he held women in low regard.

Nervously playing with her low cut and long hemmed dress, she said, "Gillich, the tavern owner, expects pay up front.

A tone of impatience in his voice, Tanof asked, "How much?"

The nervous woman, nearly in tears, said, "Five copper pieces. Please."

Tanof, nearly staring a hole through the now frightened woman, said, "That's a rather, stiff price, don't you think?"

The woman, now looking wan and feint, wrung her hands with anxiety said, "You'll have to discuss that with Master Gillich."

Tanof, with a cruel smile, pulled five copper pieces from one of his pockets and plopped them with a loud thump on the table. The woman snatched the copper pieces off the table as if she was afraid that her tormentor might drive a dagger through her hand. Crysillnia didn't think she liked her half-brother very much. Talok didn't appear to approve of Tanof's treatment of the serving woman either.

While they waited for their meal, Tanof motioned with his head and said, "Talok, I don't like the looks of those four at the far table."

"I know what you mean. They appear to be unusually interested in us. I've caught them glancing in our direction too often. They bear watching."

Crysillnia could still feel the pulsing warmth of the Crystals, hanging between her breasts. Strange, she thought to herself.

The tavern owner, with a scowl on his face, brought their meal to the table. When he put the bowls of stew, bread-cheese, and ale on the table, Crysillnia gasped and clutched the Crystals. They were so hot she could hardly bear it. The tavern owner, startled by her actions, nearly toppled the pitcher of ale, causing some of the golden brew to slosh out of the pitcher, splashing the table copiously.

Backing away, the frightened tavern owner was mumbling something about a witch.

Talok asked with concern, "Milady! What is wrong? Are you sick?"

Gasping with pain she answered, "The Crystals. They've activated, and I don't know why."

Reaching under her tunic, she clutched the pouch and tried to pull it away from her skin but was unable to do so. In desperation, she began to concentrate on the Crystals in an attempt to control the insidious jewels. After several minutes, she noticed a slackening in the heat. Shortly thereafter, the Crystals cooled. They didn't completely stop their rhythmic pulsations, but they were bearable.

Sweat beading her brow and with tears meandering down her cheeks, she said, "I'm alright." With a weak smile shadowing her face, she said, "Let's eat."

All three were famished and began to eat ravenously, although Crysillnia did eat a bit more mannerly than her companions. When she shoveled the first spoonful of stew into her mouth, the Crystals pulsed again before she slipped into unconsciousness.

The men at the far table came over to the unconscious trio and tied them up. The two men who took hold of Talok, cursed their misfortune of inheriting the job of hauling the dwarf to the wagon waiting in the back alley.

Darith was sitting and waiting for the woman and the dwarf who had rescued him from the regulator. He didn't know why, but he had a strange premonition that she would need his help. He noticed a small two wheeled wagon pulled by a scrawny, shaghaired pony, exiting the alley that ran directly behind the tavern. The pony was being led by a rather unsavory-looking character, and shortly thereafter three licentious miscreants furtively poked their heads out of the alley. When they were sure no one had noticed them, they unobtrusively slipped out of the alley and quickly blended into the crowded street.

Darith recognized the three men. They belonged to the Thieves Guild. Their speciality was abduction, and they were quite adept in their field. Two of the men followed the wagon and then crowded onto the narrow seat when they felt it was safe to do so. The other man went in the opposite direction. Darith decided to follow the wagon.

The wagon made slow progress through the crowded streets of the city. Darith crept up behind the wagon unnoticed. The wagon was covered with a cloth tarp. When the wagon halted at an intersection of streets to wait for a chance to merge, he slipped under the tarp to inspect the cargo and found the trio that had saved his life. They were tightly bound, gagged and unconscious.

*   *   *

Simentoo had left Jarret a few days after they had escaped their captors. Simentoo, Jarrett, and Shasheek had encountered another band of the Halhoren Horsemen. Fearing capture, they had tried to escape to no avail. Simentoo explained to the Halhoren Tribal Chief why they were in possession of Halhoren horses, and their mission of collecting an army to deal with the small contingent of demons that kept the Casparian Army bottled up in Caspar Valley.

Fortunately for Simentoo and his companions, the Tribal Chief that they were dealing with was Kenchon, the Head Chief of the Halhoren Nation. Kenchon had swiftly dispatched a force to deal with the renegade tribesmen and also sent a contingent of horsemen, to escort Simentoo, Jarrett, and Shasheek over the plains to help raise the siege of Caspar Valley.

During their journey they had managed to collect stray soldiers who either had been separated from their units during battle or they were the only survivors left of a decimated troop. When they had neared the pass leading into the valley, Simentoo scouted the demon force and decided there should be a coordinated effort with the Casparian forces.

That was why Simentoo was now skulking through the back roads and mountain trails of the Caspar Mountains. He realized, his caution was warranted when he discovered signs of activity along many of the usually seldom traveled trails, and some of the tracks were made by something other than human. It was cold in the high mountains, and there were intermittent snow flurries.

The ground was blanketed by several inches of snow, therefore, Simentoo stuck to the trails that showed signs of activity so that his tracks would mix in with the others on the trail. Of course, this was inherently dangerous because he might accidentally blunder into those traveling the back-ways.

The wind began to increase in velocity as he moved higher into the mountains. The intensity of the flurries matched the wind velocity making Simentoo's trek more uncomfortable and difficult as he fought the blinding and stinging, wind driven, snow. The trail had narrowed. To his right there was a canyon several hundred feet deep, and to his left was a cliff face of equal immensity.

Simentoo felt very uncomfortable with his present location. There was no escape route, except back the way he came, if he were to run into trouble. The trail was only wide enough for two men walking side-by-side. To make matters worse, the wind was howling and whistling so loud between the canyon walls that Simentoo wouldn't be able to hear anyone approaching.

Simentoo had to cling to the cliff face as he traveled higher into the mountains so that he wouldn't lose his footing on the ice and snow covered trail and plummet over the canyon wall to his death. He made note of a crevice in the cliff face. The crevice was wide enough for one man to pass through.

Shortly after he passed the crevice, the wind subsided and then things began to happen. A large creature came loping around a bend in the trail ahead of him. The creature reminded Simentoo of a mountain cat at first glance, but it was grotesquely deformed so Simentoo assumed it was more likely a demon.

The creature, spotting Simentoo at the same instant, broke into a full-fledged sprint. The creature became airborne when it sprang. Simentoo, taken by surprise, didn't have time to pull his weapon. Grabbing one of the talon-girded paws, he rolled onto his back. Taking advantage of the creature's momentum, he used his feet to catapult the creature over his head and off the ledge into the canyon. The creature let out a nerve-shattering wail as it plummeted to its death.

Simentoo completed the roll, ending with a crouching stance, facing his original direction of travel. Simentoo stood and was confronted with a bigger problem as a montage of creatures and mountain tribesmen rounded the bend. Simentoo pulled his short sword and dagger. He prepared to do battle but realized he was hopelessly outnumbered.

He decided, at this point, the better part of valor would be to retreat and do so swiftly. Simentoo began to sprint back the way he had come, but to his chagrin, he found there were more demons and mountains tribesmen coming up the trail. He was trapped. Then he remembered the crevice. He just hoped he could reach it before he was cut off.

Simentoo nearly ran by the narrow opening. Slipping and sliding on the ice covered trail, Simentoo entered the narrow passageway. He stumbled in the sudden dark on the uneven footing offered by the jagged wound suffered by the mountain in its long forgotten past. Sheathing his weapons, Simentoo struggled with the darkness, groping along until his eyes adjusted.

The acclivity of the crevice became increasingly difficult the deeper he penetrated it. To Simentoo's trepidation, the crevice appeared to dead end. He faced a solid wall of rock, but on closer inspection, he spotted grooves and cracks in the wall, giving him hand and footholds.

He climbed the stone face. When he topped the rock wall, he saw a brightness ahead, indicating that he may be near the end of the narrow and confining crevice. The crevice had leveled off and wasn't quite as rough, making it possible for Simentoo to travel more quickly. Simentoo had to stop when he exited the crevice, so that his eyes could to adjust to the abrupt change in illumination.

Simentoo found himself in a small, bowl-shaped depression. The rim of the depression was lined by strange appearing, rock formations. One would almost think that the rocks were set there purposely, sort of like sentries.

Simentoo was reminded of his dangerous situation by the increasing clamor of his pursuers. He struck out across the snow covered field towards a small aperture in the far wall of the depression. The going was slow and difficult as he trudged arduously through snow reaching nearly to the middle of his calves.

Disaster struck quickly and without warning as he neared the middle of the depression. He heard and felt the cracking of ice under his feet. With a resounding crack and in a fog of fluffy white snow, Simentoo sunk up to his chest, and he could feel the grip of ice cold water soaking him up to his ankles.

Simentoo heard the first of the demons entering the depression. It quickly advanced on him, but it didn't immediately close on its helpless victim. The creature was, in appearance, similar to the one that Simentoo had tossed off the ledge. The creature grinned ghoulishly. It was enjoying itself. The creature circled the helpless human as it waited for its companions to join the party.

Simentoo was temporarily distracted from his predicament. He could have sworn, that one of those rocks along the rim of the depression had moved, but that was impossible. Simentoo's view of the rock was blocked the montage of demons and mountain tribesmen crowded around him. Simentoo figured his life was forfeit. He was prepared to die. In a strong voice, he said, "My darling, Renira, I now come to you."

Simentoo was jolted out of his revere by a loud roar accompanied by an equally loud shriek. Then a melee broke out around him. He felt like he was in a slow motion dream and was witnessing a mad macabre dance of death as he watched, helplessly, the battle ensuing. His tormentors were being decimated by a half-dozen or so trolls. Simentoo realized that those rocks that had encompassed the depression had been troll guards.

The reverberations of the ensuing battle finished the breaking of the ice that disguised a swiftly flowing underground stream, toppling Simentoo, demons, mountain tribesmen, and trolls into the bone-chilling water. Simentoo gasped from the shock of cold water as he plunged beneath its surface.

He could feel himself being carried away by the unrelenting current. He struggled to regain the surface. Before he crossed the barrier of unconsciousness, he felt hard, unyielding hands grasp him.

*   *   *

Calert was entering a ravished section of the Elf Forest. The awakening of the Chaos Demon was upsetting the delicate balance of the already unstable magic. Having to deal with this problem was also interfering with his plans of meeting Crysillnia in Altonea.

Calert stopped at the edge of the devastated area. He wove a protection spell, so that the Chaos Demon's magic wouldn't harm him. When he finished his spell, he sat down cross-legged and began to meditate. He was calling for the Chaos Demon. He slipped deeper into a trance-like state.

A dark shadow entered Calert's mind.

It asked, "Who's calling me? Who dares to summon me? I am all that is unstable. I am destruction incarnate. I am all that is evil and all that his good. I am the darkness, and I am the light. I ask once again. Who summons me?"

"It is I, Calert of the Kelatan Monks," answered Calert.

There was a few moments of silence as the Chaos Demon considered Calert's reply. Then it replied, "You do not fool me. I know who you are. Natas!"

"Who I am is none of your concern!" retorted Calert. "I've come to put you back to sleep. You are creating unnecessary problems."

A deep and unsettling laughter resounded through the deep recesses of Calert's mind. "You think quite highly of your meager powers," said the Chaos Demon, as his laughter faded, leaving only a faint echo reverberating in Calert's mind.

Calert, realizing he may have underestimated the power ana energy this vile creature was capable of generating, decided to be more tactful and diplomatic because he wasn't sure that he would be victorious in an all out test of wills and power.

"What would it take to return you to your slumber?" asked Calert.

"I may not wish to return to my slumber," replied the demon.

Not willing to give up easily Calert continued his interrogation. "What disturbed your slumber?"

"Discord and disharmony in the elf heart," was the curt reply from the Chaos Demon.

Calert, confused and unsure where to go from here, sat in silence.

"I sense ignorance and lack of understanding in your meager mind," continued the Chaos Demon disdainfully.

Calert refused to be bated into a useless tirade of insults. He sat there and waited. Calert sensed that the arrogance of this phenomena or disturbance in the fabric of space and time, the Chaos Demon, would cause it to reveal more on its own than if he questioned the creature directly.

The creature broke the quiet state of Calert's mind when it continued its present tangent of thought.

"The collective soul of the elves is in disharmony with the magic of the land. This disharmony has awakened me, as you so blithely put it. The elves have abandoned the true path, the path of correctness and are following the path of destruction. Their failure to assist the humans in the struggle against evil will lead to the destruction of elf magic. I am their conscience and their salvation, if they heed me."

"The elves are unaware of this," replied Calert.

"Not my problem," snipped the Chaos Demon. "I've a possible solution. I'll bring the life force of the Head Elder to meet with you and you can show him the truth."

Not waiting for a reply Calert began to weave a spell, a very powerful spell, a spell that could upset the delicate balance of the universe. A bright flash of light erupted around Calert and the spirit of the Head Elder appeared before Calert. Calert stood and walked away leaving the bewildered spirit of the Head Elder of The Counsel of Elves to the Chaos Demon. There was nothing more he could do.

CHAPTER 32

Alaquin and Carric emerged from the void into a fog shrouded land. They could barely see their hands through the thick and cloying mist that wrapped around them like a living writhing creature.

"I thought visibility in the void was bad but this is almost as comparable," said Carric.

Alaquin, apparently giving Carric's statement little thought, said, "We must be on the island of Astaria."

"Why do you think that?" asked Carric.

"Can't you hear the surf and taste the salt in the mist as it plays across your lips?"

Carric listened more astutely and could hear a the low rumble of rolling waves lashing out violently at the land that impeded its progress. He ran his tongue across his lips, allowing the acrid taste of salt tainted seawater play havoc with his taste buds.

"I agree we're near a coast, but what makes you think where on the isle of Astaria?" asked a cynical Carric.

"Trust me! I know!" answered Alaquin tartly, a frown crossing her lips indicating that she didn't appreciate Carric's doubts.

Carric quipped blithely, "The last time someone told me to trust them, I ended up being stranded on this dreary world." Alaquin struggled heroically to avoid allowing a giggle to escape but failed dismally at first with a slight chirp which evolved into an uproarious outburst.

Carric found this most beautiful, wonderful, and, seemingly ethereal creature's laughter infectious and couldn't help but to join in. Alaquin, without thought, wrapped her arms, affectionately around her ungainly companion. Carric returned the embrace enthusiastically. Alaquin thought to herself, I love this man with

all my being. The two were brought out of their joyous reverie by
a cascading of stones somewhere in the blinding mist which was
followed by a chorus of curses.

Carric and Alaquin quickly crouched behind a copse of
truncated and twisted bushes as the authors of the voices
approached. Their hearts seemed to thunder loudly as they waited
apprehensively. Carric reached instinctively for the weapon hanging
at his side. Alaquin, sensing more than seeing Carric's reaction,
gently covered his hand with hers to avoid any rash move by her
companion.

The elf girl's touch sent bolts of desire and warmth coursing
through Carric's entire body. His legs felt weak, and his stomach
churned uncontrollably. It felt like his heart would burst. He just
wanted to take her into his arms and caress her silken tresses, kiss
her warm plump lips and never let her go. He had never felt this
way about a woman before. He thought he never would. At that
moment, he knew he would never be happy again unless she became
his wife. Sensing Carric's turmoil Alaquin removed her hand. Carric
felt crushed when she withdrew her petal-soft hand.

The voices continued their bantering tones.

"I heard laughter, I swear on my mother's grave."

"Mother's grave?" chimed in a second voice. "You reprobate.
You don't even know who your mother is."

"Ah, forget it," replied the first voice. "But I know laughter
when I hear it."

The second voice responded, "I think this mist is playing havoc
with your mind and hearing. No one lives on this god-forsaken
tomb of an island, and the entire island is ringed by life form
sensors so no one could approach the island without the monitors
knowing, let alone land."

With a definable tremble, the first voice replied, "Then maybe
the place is haunted."

With a snort, the second man began to chortle uproariously.
"You and your superstitions kill me Rafe."

A smile crossed Alaquin's lips as a solution to their current
danger presented itself. Alaquin began to chant in a low murmur.

Then she began to make signs in the mist and strange characters began to glow tangibly in the air, hanging ominously.

Carric, crouching behind Alaquin, thought to himself, this is a strange and at times frightening woman. Carric watched as the colorful but strange runes danced in the mist and collated into some semblance of order and purpose. Rafe, hearing the low murmuring chant, motioned to his partner to follow. They approached Alaquin and Carric's hiding place, cautiously, weapons drawn. The whisper of Carric's weapon being unsheathed was muffled by the thick cloying mist.

"There!" shouted Rafe pointing directly at the two hidden co-conspirators. Carric stood ready to defend, to the death, Alaquin. Braced for the attack, Carric wasn't prepared for what happened next. Rafe and his companion stopped in mid-stride mouth's agape. They dropped their weapons and twirled in unison as if the move was choreographed meticulously. Screaming in utter horror, the two frightened men fled into the mist. A chill ran up and down Carric's backbone as he sensed rather than saw a disturbance in the mist which appeared to be in pursuit of the frightened men.

Alaquin twirled lightly on her toes to face Carric with a capricious smile framing her slightly angular face. "See violence isn't the only solution to resolving dangerous and difficult situations."

Carric, looking in puzzlement first at his sword then at the elf girl, asked' "What did you do?"

Still smiling, Alaquin answered, "I cast a spell of illusion. Those men saw their worst nightmare appear before them, whatever that fear may have been."

Alaquin and Carric could hear the men's screams fade into the distance.

The grin faded from Alaquin's face. "The spell should have worn off by now. They're well beyond the scope of the casting."

Then suddenly the screams of terror were replaced by equally terrible screams of pain and death. The screams ended abruptly, casting a pall of haunting silence that reinforced the palpable threat of danger suggested by the insipid clinging mist.

Carric and Alaquin glanced at each other in wonderment and curiosity then continued their trek towards the interior of the island. Alaquin, while crossing what appeared to be a meadow and unable to distinguish details through the thick mist, stumbled over something. She barely managed to keep her balance. She bent over to get a closer look at the impediment. Letting a out a strangled gasp, the elf girl took a step back, bumping into Carric nearly knocking him off his feet. She began to wretch uncontrollably, splattering her last meal on the rocks and thin shrubs.

Once Alaquin regained her composure, she looked more closely at what appeared to be the mangled remains of a man. She hadn't gotten a good look at the men that had spotted them, but since this was a fresh kill, she assumed this was one of them.

The corpse was decimated. Even if she had known the man intimately, she wouldn't have been able to recognize him.

His face was ripped from the skull and lay in a mangled pile beside it's owner. His legs and arms were twisted at impossible angles and broken bones protruded from the skin. He no longer resembled a man but looked more like a pile of discarded garbage. Carric began to search the surrounding area. He had one of the weapons at the ready that one of the frightened men had dropped earlier. Carric found the slaughtered body of the other sentry a few paces beyond the first.

"What kind of creature could have done this?" asked Carric, a quiver of nervousness perceptible in his voice.

"I don't have any idea," replied Alaquin. "I thought," Alaquin nodded her head in the direction of the dead sentries, "they said there were no living creatures on the island."

"There is at least one," quipped Carric as he tried to disguise the fear in his voice.

"We had better hurry on before whatever did this returns," said Carric, nervously.

Although the rocks were still numerous and treacherous, the vegetation was beginning to change in character from thick stemmed sea grasses to small shrubs and a smattering of broad leaf trees. Albeit, the trees were truncated and sickly looking. The raging sea was becoming a dull murmur in the distance as they continued into the interior of the island.

The fog had all but dissipated as the two began an upward journey into the island. The acclivity wasn't extreme, but it was a steady upward climb. Carric and the elf girl began to tire from the endless upward climb of the slope.

"I think we should take a break," said the outlander.

"No! I think, I see the crest ahead," said Alaquin, pointing up the hill.

Finally reaching their short term destination, the two plopped down on the grassy crown of the hill for a much needed rest. Carric, although sitting, kept a vigilant eye on their surroundings. He didn't want the two of them too become dismembered victims of that vicious monster lurking in the mists below.

Alaquin, less concerned, began to yawn. The sun was perched precariously on the rim of the world.

"It'll be dark soon," stated Alaquin, in a matter of fact manner. "I'll gather some wood for a fire," she continued.

"I wouldn't suggest it," replied Carric.

"Why not?" asked Alaquin, a little irritably.

"A fire will betray our presence," answered Carric amicably.

"Oh, I guess your right." Replied Alaquin, apologetically.

The elf girl stood up and peered over the ridge. What little warmth from the sun that had penetrated the island mist and mostly cloud laden sky was lost to the cold dampness of the night, which methodically and relentlessly began to seep into their bodies. Swinging her arms back and forth, Alaquin tried to keep warm while searching the crescent shaped valley below. She spotted a glow emanating from behind a grove of trees.

In a low whisper, she called Carric. Carric was sitting slightly behind and below where Alaquin was standing. He responded with alarm by retrieving the outlander weapon that he had set on the ground beside him. He created such a stir that the pollens and seeds topping the waist high grass dispersed in an irritating cloud. Carric and Alaquin both pinched their noses closed as they fought back sneezes but Alaquin lost the battle. She began to sneeze convulsively and without restraint.

When she finally stifled the urge to sneeze, she glared at Carric with disapproval and asked, "Need you react so spastically?"

Carric answered in a low and obsequious tone, "Sorry."

Alaquin began giggling once again. "You look like a poor scolded puppy . . . forgiven," she replied.

When Carric reached her side, she pointed out the bright light.

"What kind of magic could create so much light?" Before Carric could answer, she continued. "Is the light created by your magic called Science?"

"Yes. And I think we've reached our destination," answered Carric.

Grabbing Alaquin's arm, Carric pulled her roughly to the ground putting two fingers to her mouth to shush her. He moved closer to her, brushing his lips across her ear which sent waves of desire coursing throughout her body and whispered, "There are sentries below. I think they may have heard you sneezing. They're coming in this direction. Lie still. Maybe they won't spot us in the dark."

Her desire faded, quickly when she began to shiver. She wasn't sure whether it was from the cold dampness of the night air or fear. Silently, the elf girl cuddled against Carric's warm vibrant body which seemed to leach the chill away. Alaquin listened to the oddly silent night of the dead island.

Alaquin strained against the silence in an attempt to hear the sentries approach to no avail. The startled elf girl nearly cried out when a black boot settled in a thick cushion of tall grass inches from her face. The disturbed chaff from spent seed husks began to swirl and drift through the damp night air, finally settling on her face, flaunting flirtatiously with her allergies. Alaquin struggled heroically to defeat the reflex to sneeze, but she failed miserably.

A searing, burning, pain coursed violently through Alaquin's body. Her body convulsed. Alaquin tried to scream for the pain to cease, but she was unable to make a sound. Finally the pain ceased, but Alaquin was unable to move. Her muscles wouldn't or couldn't respond to her commands. Her muscles felt fatigued beyond description. Alaquin was exhausted even though she felt the worst fear of her life. She drifted off into a deep, coma-like sleep.

*   *   *

Simentoo's journey back to consciousness was slow and laborious. He flirted with consciousness coyly as if, courting a favorite lady. Finally, he sat up with great effort and groggily surveyed his surroundings, unable to focus his eyes with any consistency. Simentoo peered into the darkness that surrounded him. He felt as if the darkness was a living, writhing creature trying to envelope him and make him part of the greater whole.

"I see, you've returned to the land of the living, Troll Brother," said a familiar voice with a hint of joviality.

Startled, Simentoo reached reflexively for the sword usually hanging at his side, but found it was no longer there. He turned his head in the direction from which the voice had come, trying desperately to focus his vision and concentration so he could ascertain his situation accurately, but all he could see were two dim and flickering lights framing a darker area.

"Whoa!" exclaimed the voice. Tinged with concern, the voice continued, "It's me> Kanef."

Recognition and relief flowed through Simentoo like a river during spring floods. Finally Simentoo's eyes began to adjust to the sallow light cast by two flickering, smokey, and sputtering torches on the far wall. "Where am I?" asked Simentoo in a nearly inaudible and quivering voice.

"Deep within the bowels of the Caspar Mountains," replied Kanef. After a short pause Kanef continued, "We're in the Troll lairs."

"Troll lairs," repeated Simentoo incredulously.

"Where else would they take an injured Troll Brother?" questioned Kanef facetiously.

Disoriented and weak from his recent travails Simentoo missed the subtle jest.

The acrid smoke emitted by the sputtering torches and a small cook fire on which a pot stewed, assaulted Simentoo's eyes relentlessly, causing them to water profusely. Simentoo wiped his eyes, with his equally irritating hands, rubbing grime and dirt into them. Frustrated and in pain, Simentoo laid back down. Kanef, understanding Simentoo's frustration, approached the warrior, placing his hand on Simentoo's shoulder in a show of camaraderie and sympathy. Simentoo would normally shrug off such a gesture, but he accepted Kanef's sincere expression of concern and support, although others from his Warrior Caste would have considered this willingness to accept comfort as a sign of weakness and not worthy of a true warrior.

Kanef spoke. "I'll bring you something to eat."

Simentoo's vision was still blurred, but he could hear Kanef's footsteps retreating. Soon after, Kanef returned with a steaming bowl of stew. Simentoo sat up and took the proffered bowl. He wasn't aware how hungry he was until he took the first bite. He quickly emptied the bowl.

Kanef asked, "Want more?"

Simentoo shook his head in the negative. Exhaustion was beginning to take over again, so he lay back on the bed and fell into a deep slumber. Kanef gently covered the exhausted warrior with a bear skin blanket.

*   *   *

Crassius Longsleeve, from atop of his mount, surveyed the deployment of his troops. The enemy was massing at the foot of the nearby mountains. There were many strange creatures large and small. These creatures were hideous and quite frightening in appearance and obviously quite formidable in strength, endurance, and ferocity. Longsleeve expected little sympathy or mercy from such creatures, and he informed his troops of this fact.

The sun was high in the sky. Longsleeve calculated the time to be near midday. Longsleeve was returning to his Command Post when he heard the battle horns signal the troops to take up defensive positions. His troops on the left flank were under attack. The crash of metal on armor and weapons were deafening. The cries of men and creatures in pain and death were audible above the general din of battle.

Longsleeve shook his head in sadness. He was a veteran of many wars, but he still abhorred the useless destruction, maiming, and deaths that were the result of war. There were many veterans of past battles and first battle soldiers going to die today. Many more who would be maimed of limb and or mind would wish they had died today.

Battle horns down the line joined into an eerie and frightening cascading symphony of death as the entire front lines from left to right came under attack. Messengers from the front lines began to bring reports of the ensuing battle from up and down the line. Captain Longsleeve conducted the battle through these messengers, push forward here and fall back there. As dark neared, a disturbing report was received from the left flank. The defensive line was near collapse and the possibility of reserve troops reaching them before their collapse was unlikely. The left flank had been attacked from behind by burrowing creatures.

Longsleeve called forth a large contingent of reserves, more than what he would have preferred but. If the reinforcements couldn't reach the beleaguered troops in time to prevent a collapse of his left flank, he would need a strong enough force to reestablish a new defensive line. Otherwise, this battle was over, and Xlanta would be overrun.

Schwellen exited the forest at the head of a contingent of Clodtrip's kinsmen and demons. It was near dark, and a battle was fully engaged. A decimated contingent of the Xlantan army was in a dire predicament. They were surrounded and being chewed up by the enemy. It didn't appear that reinforcements from the main army would reach them in time. Schwellen stood there watching in horror as Clodtrip stepped up to her side.

He said, "If we're going to help them, we had better get to it."
Unsheathing her sword, the adrenalin began to course through
her veins. Spurred on by the excitement and fear of battle, chanting
the Halhoren battle song, Schwellen charged into the melee. The
demons, taken by surprise, were quickly routed. The few demons
that stood their ground were dispatched viciously and without
mercy. Schwellen, now silent, saving her energy for slashing, cutting
and stabbing, opened a wide swath in the demon forces.

The enemy, now in a full a fledged retreat, disappeared quickly
into the nearby mountains. Schwellen began to feel a burning
pain like someone plying a red hot sword against her skin. It was a
green corrosive goo that flowed for blood in the veins of those
horrible creatures burning her flesh.

Exhibiting great speed for a human, as Clodtrip would
comment at a later date, she ran to douse herself in a nearby river
with many others of like mind.

CHAPTER 33

Alaquin, lying on her back, awoke in a dimly lit room. She tried to move her arms, but they wouldn't respond to her commands. She began to fear that she may be paralyzed. Then she giggled, foolishly, and spoke out loud, mostly to reassure herself.

"Silly, you can feel the aching muscles in your arms."

That's when it occurred to her that she was being restrained. It seemed like her entire body was fastened to whatever she was lying on because she was unable to move any part of her body.

"Awake, I see."

Startled by the disembodied voice, Alaquin shivered in bewilderment and fear. She sensed the motion of disturbed air as someone approached her. A dark skinned man stood over her. A cruel smile blanketed his face, a face marred with countless angry scars but the eyes, they were depthless, cold, calculating and exuded pure evil.

"Sorry for the rude hospitality but I'm, quite aware of what magic an elf is capable of with her hands."

She sensed the sarcasm and disdain in his apology. Alaquin was surprised he hadn't just killed her.

"Wondering why you're still alive, I bet?"

Alaquin's surprise at his question must have flitted across her face.

"I thought so," he replied, answering his own question. "I have special plans for you." Then he turned, abruptly, and left Alaquin alone with her thoughts and fears about that ominous comment.

The man left the room and walked down a narrow corridor a few paces. He turned and faced a featureless wall. The man was tall and lanky. He moved effortlessly even though he had a slight limp.

The man pressed the palm of his hand against the sterile, white wall. The wall opened silently, revealing a small hatch-like doorway. The man had to duck as he passed through the portal.

"Ah, Carric, glad to see you're up and around," the man said.

Carric arose from a squatting position in a confrontational manner. "Where is she? Malto, you better not have hurt her."

"Or what, you'll kill me?" Malto laughed, tauntingly. "Sit! You're in no position to make threats."

"Oh, by the way, I have someone, whom wishes to, greet you. He's so pleased you're still alive. Come in, Bartley."

Malto stepped back from the doorway to allow the man entrance. Carric flabbergasted, by this unexpected turn of events, took a step backwards, nearly tripping over his own feet, lower jaw dropping.

"Bartley, why?" Was all Carric could say. Malto quipped, unable to conceal his amusement with Carric's abject feelings of despair and betrayal, "The age old reason for betrayal, greed!"

Then Malto began to laugh uproariously, bending over, slapping his knees. Bartley, not so amused, looked over at Malto with disapproval. Malto tried to control his laughter to please his partner.

Malto said, "Bartley, you always were a stick in the mud. No sense of the ironic or humor."

Malto, unable to contain himself, spoke up in Bartley's defense. "There is something you should know, Carric. If not for Bartley, you would have been dead rather than landing in the desert."

Carric shifted his penetrating gaze from Bartley to Malto.

"Clarify, please!" replied Carric in a forceful and demanding tone. Carric had finally regained his composure after the shock of betrayal had worn off.

"I wanted to kill you but Bartley here refused. Instead, he sabotaged your lander as opposed to destroying it like I wanted to do. Even in betrayal, he still has some loyalty left. Commendable, wouldn't you say." Then the roguish outlaw began to chuckle, pleased with his own witticism.

Alaquin, lying on her back helpless, began to concentrate and search within herself for a solution to her present situation. The question was, could she conjure magic without the use of her hands? Suddenly, it dawned on her. She didn't need the use of her hands any longer to use her magic. She was half human not just elf. She had inherited, from her father, spiritual magic. She was no longer restricted to the magic of the runes.

Concentrating deeper, Alaquin began to draw on the formidable power that lie dormant within her because of the unusual mix of Spiritual and Elf Magic. She was the most powerful wielder of magic ever to exist. Alaquin could feel a tingling and prickling sensation creeping up her spine. The magic was building. When it reached its apex, the energy escaped her physical body and began to emanate around her. A bright glow engulfed the elf girl.

Alaquin's ethereal-self separated from the physical body. Alaquin found herself floating over her body. She was astonished. What at one time she would have thought impossible was now possible.

Alaquin, now floating freely in her spiritual form, circled the room. Then she passed through the door of her cell. Floating through the narrow hall, she passed guards and others without being seen. When she passed close to someone, they would shiver as if caught in a cold draft.

She sensed Carric's presence when she passed the room where he was being held. Alaquin passed through the door to see how Carric fared. There were two other men talking with Carric. She could sense the feelings of betrayal and disappointment Carric harbored toward one of the men, but she knew that he was in no immediate danger.

Satisfied that Carric was safe, relatively speaking, she left the room. There was a power beckoning her. Alaquin suspected this was the force that was disturbing the equilibrium of the Space and Time. Alaquin's ethereal form passed through walls and doors, entering sleeping quarters, dining and living areas with ease, searching for this mysterious energy force.

Finally, she entered a small cubicle shaped room from which the energy force was emanating. Hovering near the ceiling, Alaquin glanced around the room but her attention was quickly drawn to a small pyramid shaped object in the center of the room. There was a bright, fluctuating, multicolored light emanating from the pointed top of the object. The light appeared to be entering a dark hole of nothingness.

Alaquin floated closer to the light. She was drawn to and mesmerized by the light. She felt that if she entered the light, all her struggles and problems would be cleansed from her mind and soul.

Alaquin was startled back to reality when she glanced upward into the dark hole of nothingness. She saw a demon leap from the hole into the light. Alaquin watched in horror as the gruesome creature was disassembled and absorbed by the light. Alaquin quickly backed away from the light awash in understanding. The light wasn't being projected into the hole but was the energy of Space and Time being siphoned.

She needed to do something to stop this insidious leaching and disassembling of the fabric of the Universe, but in this form, she could do nothing. She would need her corporeal form. Alaquin quickly returned to the room in which her body was confined. Her ethereal formed hovered above her corporeal form. Her spiritual-self examined the hard unyielding platform on which her body was trapped. The material appeared to be as hard as any metal on her world but the texture insinuated that it was something other than metal.

Alaquin noticed a box-like structure protruding from the side of the platform. There was a green, flashing light adorning the box. She passed her ethereal hand through the box. She sensed a flow of energy. This energy was feeding the energy field holding her corporeal form to the platform.

Realizing she was unable to effect the physical world in her present form, she reentered her body. Alaquin opened her eyes and stared at the ceiling. She began to focus her mind on one spot on the ceiling. She closed her eyes and began to guide the concentrated energy through her body to a point near the flashing box and with a concerted effort, she pushed the energy from her body into the box. The box blew apart, filling the room with a strange odor.

Alaquin free, arose slowly, stretched her stiff and sore muscles. Burning pain coursed throughout her body. Alaquin draped her legs over the table edge and sat there unmoving for a few moments. Moving her legs and arms slowly, she stretched the complaining and noncompliant muscles some more and with each new movement her muscles became more limber.

Alaquin slid off the table and when her feet hit the floor, her knees buckled but she avoided complete collapse by bracing herself against the table. Angry with her weakness, she began to mentally flagellate herself. She thought to herself, this won't do, Carric was in danger and the fabric of the Firmament wouldn't hold much longer. That strange talisman of the outworlders must be destroyed.

Alaquin began to draw from the spiritual side of her magic. She concentrated on drawing the energy from her surroundings into herself. The air around her began to crackle and pop. She could feel the hair on her body stand up and her skin began to tingle, and there was even a slight burning sensation as the energy began too migrate into her body.

A loud booming sound resonated off the walls of the small cubicle as her body finished re-energizing. Alaquin turned towards the door quickly in response to a shouts in the hall outside her room. Instantly and without hesitation, she raised her arms, hands open, as if reaching for the door. Then, slowly and meticulously, Alaquin closed her hands, as if crumpling a sheet of paper. The door cracked and moaned. Then suddenly it imploded releasing a burst of energy which exploded into the hallway. A few brief, agonizing wails emanated from the hallway followed by silence.

Alaquin chanted as she began to write runes in the air before her. The runes, a shimmering shade of blue, began to dance to the rhythm of the chant. The runes completely encircled the elf girl in a protective envelope. When she finished weaving the rune barrier, Alaquin entered the hallway.

She looked up and down the hallway. There were men coming from both directions but Alaquin felt no fear. She reveled in her power. She knew no one could harm her as long as she was cloaked in her rune constructed energy field. She would have never been aware of the possibility of constructing such a protective shield if not for the outworlders trapping her within one.

She moved in the direction where she knew Carric to be. The men both in front and back of her demanded her to stop or they would fire on her, but she ignored their commands and continued her advance on the men to the front. The men fired their weapons which spouted an energy wave. The energy wave strengthened her protective field and seemed to enhance her power as she approached the men. When the protective envelope that surrounded her touched the men, they evaporated. The men before her, fearful for their lives, retreated at her advance, but they continued, along with the men to her rear, firing their weapons.

Alaquin reached Carric's room. She turned and faced the seamless wall. Alaquin extended her arms, hands open, palms facing outward and began to concentrate. The wall began to crackle under the extreme duress created by the elf girl's magic. The outline of the once hidden door became evident as she slowly closed her hands, but Alaquin's concentration began to wander.

The intense bombardment from a multitude of weapons was strengthening the energy field that surrounded her. She was finding this increase in energy was making it harder to control the protective field. She knew that would be sure destruction for her and most likely would incinerate this entire complex. As much as she hated to. Alaquin turned her magic on her assailants while still facing the tortured door.

Alaquin, with open palms, thrust her hands outward to both sides, causing columns of energy to erupt from her protective envelope. There was a blinding flash of light and a loud crackling explosion, then absolute silence. The outworlders were vaporized. The only evidence that they had ever existed were their ashes wafting through the narrow passageway.

*   *   *

Darith unbound and attempted to rouse the trio in vain. Darith decided he would stay and help his new benefactors, if possible.

The wagon rattled and bounced down the road incessantly. Even at that, Darith, exhausted from the days events, managed to doze off but was immediately alert when the wagon rolled to a bumpy and unceremonious halt. Darith could hear the men adamantly discussing something, but he couldn't discern the conversation.

Darith, alarmed by the situation, accidently grasped the Crystals when he attempted to awaken Crysillnia. Darith tried to release them but was unable to open his clenched fist. A burning sensation began in the palm of his hand, coursing up his arm, then engulfing his entire body. Darith felt as if he was being drawn into the Crystals. A deluge of visions flashed through his mind, horrible visions, visions of destruction and death, and there was Crysillnia, the bearer of the Crystals, orchestrating the evil scenario.

"Darith! Darith! Awaken! Let loose the Crystals!" pleaded Crysillnia. The energy that the boy had ignited had awakened the sleeping trio. The boy's complexion was as pale as the light of a waning, moon and his eyes were glazed and fixed. Prodded by Crysillnia's plea, Darith pulled himself back to reality but fear clouded his eyes as he faced Crysillnia. Crysillnia gasped in shock as she sensed the boy's fear. The fear was directed at her.

In one fluid motion, the boy exited the wagon, turned, and fled. The trio heard one of the abductors shout in bewilderment, "Where did he come from!"

Another man replied, "I don't have any idea but go get him, and you, check the prisoners."

The three in the wagon heard the plop of two feet hitting the ground and the rapid footsteps of someone running, followed by another person dismounting and walking towards the back of the wagon.

Tanof nudged Talok, nodding his head towards the back of the wagon. Talok acknowledged the gesture by nodding his head in agreement. Tanof assumed their captors had hastily searched for his weapons because they had missed the small dagger he had strapped to his forearm. Talok had drawn his leg back like a gigantic spring, and when the man with the shuffling gate peered under the tarp, Talok, with great force, kicked the man in the face which was the signal for Tanof to act. Tanof sliced through the tarp and, as he rose from the wagon, he turned, flipped the dagger to a throwing position and with a quick snap of the wrist, skewered the man.

The man, with a surprised look on his face, grasped futilely at the small dagger protruding form the side of his neck. Then a grotesque dance of death began as the blood spurted from the man's severed jugular vein with each beat of his heart, spraying blood on everyone in the wagon. The man finally toppled over the side of the wagon with a anticlimactic thud.

Tanof, soaked in blood, turned to the back of the wagon. The man that Talok had booted so viciously, lie on the ground, his head twisted at an odd angle. Talok was no longer in the wagon. He was hefting a rock about the size of his fist, judging its weight. The third man was still following the fleeing boy, not yet aware of his companions inauspicious demise.

Talok threw the rock, and with uncanny accuracy, hit the third man in the back of the head. There was a audible thud, then the back of the man's head collapsed driving crushed bone into his brain, pulverizing it. The man was propelled a few feet more by the force of the blow and his own momentum, before he collapsed into a gelatinous heap.

Crysillnia watched the boy disappear into a copse of Thorn Oak. She understood what had spooked the boy and deep down in her soul, it thrilled and excited her. Talok and Tanof had also observed the boy in his wild flight, vanish into the thicket.

Talok, scratching the back of his head with his calloused hand, asked, "What got into the boy?"

Tanof nodded hid head in the negative and Crysillnia, with a sly grin crossing her lips fleetingly, answered, "He accidently grabbed the Crystals trying to wake me. They must have frightened him."

"Do you think we should go after him?" continued Talok, with an intonation of concern.

"I think not. We'll never be able to find him in those trees, and if he wishes, he'll catch up to us later," said Tanof. "Well, we better be moving on before their friends or someone else comes along, and we have to explain this mess," said Talok.

The others agreed.

They gathered up their belongings and Crysillnia said, "Follow me."

Talok fell in behind the woman while Tanof took the rear guard. Tanof wasn't pleased. He knew there was something not quite right, but he couldn't put his finger on his unease. He had seen Crysillnia's grin. If he didn't know better, he would have interpreted malicious intent behind it.

CHAPTER 34

Calert was consumed with foreboding. He had been able to follow Crysillnia's trace to Altonea but lost it in a dingy, little tavern. This should not have happened. He had raised her ever since he had rescued her from the tavern in Caspar City. He had taught her how to control and use her magic and should be able to follow her magical signature.

Each individual's magic had a distinct and unique marker or signature but was usually only detectable when the magic was in use. But even if their magic wasn't used, traces of their signature were left behind and could be tracked by anyone who possessed magic and was attuned to that person's signature. This confused Calert. Had her signature changed? He didn't think that was possible, but when the Crystals where involved, nothing was set in stone. Calert had cast a spell to see if he could detect the Crystals' magic but came up empty.

All this had occurred earlier in the day. Calert's thoughts were broken by the sting of sweat as it dripped off his brow, into his eyes. Reflexively, he desperately swathed the sleeve of his blouse across his forehead in an attempt to head off another painful incursion.

The desert heat prohibited Calert from wearing his typical attire, the robe and cowl, so he had purchased a light colored, long sleeve blouse and pants in Altonea along with a pair of leather boots that covered the legs above the calf muscles for protection. There were many unfriendly creatures that could deliver deadly bites in the desert, creatures that would feel obliged to make an unprepared traveler aware of their presence.

He was following the trace, skirting the desert that was used as the main trade route to the Distant Mountains, Calert's thoughts returned to the results of the Spell of Seeking he had invoked in the tavern. The invocation had revealed, unexpectedly, the treachery that the tavern owner had perpetrated on Crysillnia and her companions. Calert had had to use a rather painful truth spell on the tavern owner to discover what had become of Crysillnia, but the licentious fellow didn't know who was behind the abduction. All he could tell Calert was in what direction they had gone.

Calert's thoughts were interrupted once again by a rustling of the brushes near the road. There had been no traffic on the road today, and it was near mid afternoon, so ths rustling sound drew his attention immediately. Calert warily watched the side of the road without breaking stride. It was hard to say what or who might appear out of the dense copse of Sage Trees. There could be a variety of large and feral creatures living in the area or possibly thieves and murders awaiting unwary travelers.

Calert stopped, nearly in mid-stride, as a boy popped out of the copse. The boy was disheveled, exhausted, and covered with numerous cuts, abrasions, and bruises. The boy looked as if he had wrestled with a thorn bush. The boy paused when he spotted Calert. He glanced around furtively as if he was searching for an avenue of escape. There was a reflection of fear in the boy's eyes, but there was also a glimmer of hope that Calert would be his salvation.

Why, Calert never knew, but the boy ran to him and collapsed, sobbing and babbling, into his arms. Calert embraced the boy and soothed him for uncounted minutes. The boy finally relaxed and quit crying. Calert gently shook the boy's shoulder with his wizened old hand.

"Boy, boy, are you awake?" Calert asked in a soft and gentle voice.

The boy answered in a trembling but defiant voice, "I'm not a boy. I'm twelve seasons and my name is Darith."

Calert smiled at the boy's spunk and firmly gripping both of the boy's shoulders, he pushed him back so he could see the boy's tear streaked face.

"Ok, Darith. What is your dire consequence?"

"She's changing! She's becoming evil! She'll destroy all of creation! I saw it all!"

With each successive comment Darith became more and more hysterical, and his voice began to crack and break with emotion.

Calert, realizing the boy was about to lose coherency, commanded, "Settle! Speak like one with twelve seasons under his belt."

The assault on the boy's pride had the intended affect. Darith squared his shoulders, shaking loose of Calert's firm grip, and took control of his emotions.

"Boy, I didn't mean to insult you, but I need a more coherent accounting of what you're telling me," Calert apologized.

As he clasped the Crystals. Darith told Calert about his visions in more coherent detail. Calert moved off the road to allow two wagons passage that were heading toward the city. Calert, with his back to the wagons, still facing the boy, caught the look of astonishment as the boy's complexion waxed a shade paler.

Darith pointed at the second wagon, hand shaking uncontrollably. "That's their wagon."

Calert turned. Raising his hand, Calert tried to stop the wagoners, but they refused to stop, fearing a robbery. The first wagon was pulled by a team of four scrawny oxen, stacked to near over flowing with an assortment of sacks, casks, and crates. Calert was amazed that it didn't roll over, considering how it swayed as it trundled over the rough road. The second wagon was pulled by a pair of equally scrawny horses, covered by a tattered tarp and appeared to be empty.

The wagoners tried to urge their beasts of burden to move faster by enthusiastically applying the whip. Calert spoke a few words, and the beasts planted their hooves, refusing to budge no matter how cruelly they were beaten.

"Might as well quit abusing those poor animals. It won't do you any good. They're under my spell." Said Calert.

"Oh! Oh! Oh!" cried the wagoner on the second wagon as he tumbled from the wagon in a heap.

Calert rushed to aid the stricken man. "No need to have an apoplexy," Calert said as he helped the stricken man to his feet, brushing the dirt from the man's clothes, that is, the dirt, that wasn't there before the man had fallen.

"I just want to know where you acquired this wagon?" asked Calert as he walked towards the back of the second wagon.

The driver that had fallen off the wagon moved his lips but nothing managed to escape but a few whispered grunts, sort of like the sound a strong breeze creates, rattling the long, dead limbs of an ancient Oak Tree. When Calert reached the back of the wagon, he understood where some of the fear of the two men came from: there were three corpses.

The man in the first wagon spoke. "We found them, Wizard, Sir! We were just taking them back to the city, so we could claim salvage rights on the wagon and team."

Calert's frown deepened. The second man, seeing the expression on Calert's face and fearing for his life, quickly backed his partner's statement in a quivering voice.

"That's the truth. If you have any claim on the wagon and team, you can have them."

The man began to back away. The first driver began to protest. "But they . . ."

The second man raised his hand to silence his partner.

Calert noticed the fear in the two men's eyes. Shaking his head and waving his hand, he released the animals from his spell.

He said, "No, go ahead and take the rig. I believe you. I've no claim here."

The second man quickly mounted the wagon seat, and the two men in unison whipped their teams into a frenzy and hurriedly left Calert in the dust.

Calert turned to the boy. "You want to come with me or go back to the city?"

Darith stood there, a moment, undecided, staring at Calert, then he smiled. "I think, I'll go with you."

So as the afternoon faded into early evening, the two continued their trek in the direction of the Distant Mountains.

*   *   *

Simentoo, now alert, was sitting by the fire with Kanef. He was holding a bowl of stew with one hand while he shoveled the contents of the vessel into his mouth with the other. Both men were sitting facing the entrance to the room. Kanef was honing his knife. Neither were talking. The silence in the room was almost palpable. They could hear the distant din of battle.

The troll entered the room like the whisper of a gentle breeze, taking both men by surprise. Kanef clutched his knife in a defensive manner, and Simentoo dropped his bowl in the fire, reaching, searchingly, for his sword, as the smell of scorched stew wafted towards the cave's ceiling.

A rough, grating sound of laughter escaped the huge troll that had presented himself so unexpectedly.

"Sorry that I frightened you" said the troll, as he continued offending the two men's ears with the caustic sound.

The troll sat down by the fire, facing the two men.

The troll addressed Simentoo and asked, "How are you feeling, Troll Brother?"

Simentoo answered, "Feeling better."

"That is good. We were worried at first. We thought you would die and were sad, but the demons died for their trespass and are continuing to do so. We will soon rid our mountains of the vile creatures," continued the troll.

Simentoo, shaking his head in agreement, said, "That's good. Which brings up another point, I wish to discuss with you."

"Go ahead," said the troll.

"Would the trolls help the humans fight the demons?"

The troll's grating voice became even more so as he answered the question with a question. "Why should we help those that despise us?"

Simentoo shifted where he sat as if trying to get more comfortable. He sat, staring into the fire, mesmerized by the now waning flames. Simentoo watched the blue, yellow, and orange flames as they heated the glowing coals. The warmth that emanated from the fire was a welcome comfort against the damp chill in the dark cavern.

Simentoo was jolted back from the deep abyss of his thoughts when another troll entered the room and deposited more wood on the fire. The warmth of the fire was lessened as some of the energy was needed to kindle the newly added wood.

Looking across the fire at the troll, Simentoo continued.

"If the humans lose this war against the demons, then the trolls will be on their own. At the moment, you are winning, but the demons are fighting two wars and are unable to mount a full-scale attack against you."

The troll didn't answer immediately. Simentoo and Kanef watched the troll closely but trolls didn't show emotions outwardly, like humans, which made them impossible to read. Simentoo didn't think that trolls felt the emotions of joy and happiness the same as humans, but anger and aggressive patterns were definitely part of their emotional inventory. The troll was taking so long to answer that Simentoo began to doubt whether the troll was planning on continuing the conversation.

"You make a good point, Troll Brother. I will talk to the Troll Council and present your arguments," replied the troll.

"How soon will we know?" asked Simentoo.

"That I can not answer. It will probably be several days. We trolls do not make decisions quickly."

The three sat there watching the fire ravenously devour the newly added wood. The flames licked and danced as if trying to reach the cavern ceiling. Then the burning wood began to sizzle and crack as pockets of superheated vapors tried to escape, spraying dying embers and hot burning coals around the fire indiscriminately. Kanef and Simentoo both jumped up, brushing themselves off, voicing a few choice expletives when a few of the glowing, hot coals had landed in their laps. The troll was unaffected by the showering of hot coals and embers, even when they settled on his body, still in a state of conflagration.

Kanef, quiet up to this point, spoke. "We don't have a few days. I have urgent business in Caspar City and, if Simentoo is willing, I could use his help."

The troll replied, "That is all I can tell you. I do not have the power to commit the others."

Simentoo broke in. "We don't need to wait for an answer. If the trolls are willing, they can notify us."

"Well, if you're strong enough, I think we should leave." said Kanef.

"I'm able," replied Simentoo.

"Then I will guide you through the mountain," said the troll.

*   *   *

The battle was going poorly for Jarrett and his men. The day after Simentoo had entered the mountains, the demons attacked. The battle was entering its second evening. Jarret's forces were near collapse from exhaustion. Shasheek had used what magic he could to assist in the battle, but his magic had a limited effect on demons.

Jarrett had ordered a retreat to avoid a route. The consequences of a route would, most likely, end with the death of the majority of his soldiers. Jarrett couldn't understand why the Casparian army didn't offer any help, although many appeared eager to join the fray.

Jarrett stayed in the forefront of the battle to boost his men's moral, but discipline and order were beginning to unravel. Jarret had nowhere to retreat. There was no safe haven for his soldiers to hide. They were on the open rolling plain before the pass into Caspar Valley. There was a pine forest, that was an extension of the mountain forest, to the right, but to enter the forest would mean separating his forces, which would make them easy prey for the demons.

When the collapse began, it was sudden and unstoppable. The demons overran the right flank. Now Jarrett, at one time in the center, was now part of the troops considered the right flank. They were inexorably driven back. The demons surrounded the few soldiers left, but, inexplicably, broke off the assault and instead encircled Jarret and his men.

What was left of Jarret's meager forces were mostly Halhoren Horsemen now on foot. They had sent their horses away late in the afternoon of the day before. Jarret supposed they knew that they were doomed and wished to spare the lives of their noble mounts. Jarrett and his men were preparing to die. The Halhoren laughed and promised to meet on the other side of the Veil of Life.

The demons, with wild screams, whistles and roars, began the final assault. Jarret and his men were situated on a swell in the plains just below its crest. The doomed men were prepared to die, but their objective was to destroy as many of the demons as possible.

The adrenalin was pumping through Jarrett's veins, causing the hairs on the back of his neck to raise and cold chills to course up and down his back. He had never felt such excitement and fear or savageness. He was ready to die. It was intoxicating, like he was looking forward to death. A feral and primal rage enveloped him.

Jarrett, waving his sword in large circular motions above his head, shouted, "Lets make the devils pay dearly!"

Jarret's spirit and excitement spread like a contagion amongst his troops.

A small group of men began to chant, "Send the devils back to their Master in death."

The chant grew in volume as more and more of the men picked it up until everyone was singing, joyously, "Send the devils back to their Master in death."

Like a miracle, Kenchon, with a great host of Halhoren Horsemen, charged over the hill into the melee. The unexpected appearance of reinforcements created calamitous pandemonium, amongst the demons, which forced them into a chaotic retreat. The horsemen drove the demons into the forest, killing scores before the demons vanished into the deep dark dankness of the pine forest.

The adrenalin rush over, Jarret collapsed with fatigue. He was covered with grime and mixture of his, his comrades, and the demons blood. He sat and watched as Kenchon took command and instructed the troops to check for wounded men and to dispatch any wounded demons that they may find scattered across the field of battle.

Kenchon rode up to Jarrett, his horse delicately stepping over the corpses of demons and humans alike. When the horse could go no further without trampling on the dead, Kenchon dismounted and approached Jarrett on foot. He appeared not to be affected by the carnage that lie around him.

When he reached Jarrett, he hunched down in front of him. With a big grin and a sweeping gesture of his open hand, palm up, he said, "I'm impressed!"

Then they both sat there, looking out over the battlefield, without comment. It was so quiet, especially after the deafening clamor of clashing weapons and the screams of dying men and demons of the last two days.

Kenchon's horsemen were scouring the battlefield. They were searching for wounded soldiers and dispatching, with out mercy, demons that were still alive. Jarrett, fatigued beyond his comprehension and aching from head to foot, felt like his body would implode into a heap of gelatinous goo. Occasional an ear rending roar or a shriek would shred the eerie silence of the battlefield when a demon was destroyed.

Kenchon, spitting in the direction of the Casparian troops that had watched the battle, said vehemently, "Look at those dogs over there! We've come to help them, and they do nothing!"

Shasheek approached Jarrett and Kenchon. Kenchon gave the Dark Elf a suspicious and disapproving glance. He didn't think much of elves, dark or otherwise. Jarret seemed unaware of the elf standing above them.

Jarrett noticed Shasheek only when Kenchon stood and said, "I see one of my scouts returning. I must hear what he has to report."

Shasheek, standing over Jarrett, observed the future King closely. Jarrett, looking up at the elf, seemed dazed.

Shasheek, with concern in his voice, asked, "How are you?"

Jarrett, refocusing his concentration, answered, with a tinge of regret shading his voice, "Alive, which is more than I can say for many of my men."

Trying to assuage Jarret's remorse, Shasheek continued. "There was no more you could have done. The odds were against you."

Jarret didn't respond. He only shook his head to the negative.

"We need to move on before the demons regroup," said the elf.

"I agree," said Kenchon, as he approached Jarret and Shasheek from behind. "The demons aren't our only problem, according to my scout. The army of Zealots is reforming and heading in this direction."

"They must have demon leaders," said Shasheek.

Kenchon motioned for his scout to approach. The scout did so promptly.

"Were there any demons amongst the army?" Kenchon asked the scout.

"I didn't see any, sir," answered the scout tersely.

"Some demons are changelings and can disguise themselves as humans. These changelings are probably the ones that led the revolt," replied Shasheek.

Jarrett, with emotion welling up in his throat, said, "That means we won't be able to bury our dead." Shasheek answered, "Sadly, you are correct."

Kenchon spoke, "Not burying our dead will gain us valuable time. The demons will feast on the dead before they attempt to follow us."

Jarrett looked up at Kenchon, with incredulity.

Kenchon, seeing Jarrett's reaction, said, "Don't misunderstand. I regret having to allow such desecration of our dead, but we have no choice at this point and time. I'm a warrior and a leader. Sometimes, one has to make hard choices, and this is one of those times."

Jarrett stood. He had to check on his men. He had allowed his exhaustion to overcome his responsibilities for his men. Jarrett nearly collapsed when he stood so abruptly. Kenchon and Shasheek both reached out to steady him.

Jarrett said with concern in his voice, "I need to check on my men!"

"I'll take care of that," said Kenchon. "You're too weak. Wait here, I'll have a horse brought over for you."

"I won't ride while my men walk," said Jarrett.

"No worry. There are enough horses for everyone," said Kenchon.

It was nearly dark by the time they were ready to march, and the demons were starting to appear at the edge of the forest. They were peering lustfully out of the darkness provided by the forest's canopy.

"We need to move now," said Kenchon.

The Halhoren mounted when Kenchon waved his hand over his head in a circular motion. The soldiers that weren't Halhoren didn't respond immediately but got the idea quickly. Kenchon moved his hand forward, and the troops moved out.

They headed away from the forest with the mountains on their right. The gentle sway of his horse lulled Jarrett into a light slumber. Jarrett wasn't aware how long he slept, but he was awakened when he lost his balance as his horse came to an abrupt stop. Two strong hands on each side caught him before he fell from his mount.

With a smile on his face, Kenchon rode up to Jarrett and commended him. "There aren't many other than Halhoren that can sit a horse so well while sleeping."

Jarrett, still trying to shake the residual affects of his slumber, rubbed his face with his hands.

Jarrett took in his surroundings. It was a cloudless night and the moon shined brightly across the plains, giving them a surreal glow. He could make out the faces of those closest to him, but those further away were like ghostly shadows wafting on the night breeze.

They had stopped by a meandering stream. The stream bed was littered with an assortment of different sized stones, gravel, and sand. The flow of the stream nearly cut back on itself in places.

"When the horses drink their fill, we'll travel upstream and look for a spot to set up camp," said Kenchon.

"Why did you come back?" asked Jarrett.

"What do you mean?" asked Kenchon, as a shade of puzzlement crossed his rugged, sun weathered face.

"I thought you were chasing that rogue faction of your tribe. Did you find them?"

The horses had finished their watering and were fat and sleek once again. So with the standard hand signals for mounting and moving forward initiated, they continued their trek.

"No. We were planning to track the traitors when the horses of our comrades appeared."

Jarrett raised his eyebrows in confusion.

Kenchon continued. "Whenever Halhorens are confronted by overwhelming odds, and they are unable to escape, there mounts are released. Halhoren horses are able to sense other horses of their kind across great distances, and they seek them out. Also, Halhoren's have special bonds with their mounts, and the horse will lead reinforcements to those in peril. Therefore, when I saw the horses, I knew you were in distress."

"Oh!" Said Jarret.

Like a wraith, startling Jarrett, a scout appeared beside Kenchon. The two talked quietly, and Jarrett was unable to hear what was discussed. That didn't bother Jarret. What bothered him was the fact that he wasn't aware of the scout's presence until he appeared. Jarrett felt that the skills he had honed as a hunter were eroding.

When Kenchon turned to Jarrett once again, he saw Jarrett's look of disappointment and mistook it for anger.

"Sorry, I didn't mean to be rude," he apologized.

Jarrett, jarred out of his mood of self flagellation, returned his attention to Kenchon.

"What?" asked Jarret.

"I usually converse with my scouts in privacy," continued Kenchon.

Jarrett, realizing what Kenchon was eluding to, responded, "That's not what I'm worried about. I'm angry that I didn't sense your scout. My instincts must be failing me."

Kenchon chuckled and said, "Don't worry. My scouts are the best. If they don't wish to be detected, no one, not even I, can sense them."

Kenchon's answer didn't do much to assuage Jarret's concern. "According to my scouts, the demons didn't follow us far before they returned to the pass, and the Zealot's army haven't altered their course to pursue us. There are a lot of messengers traveling between the two armies which confirms the theory that demons are commanding the Zealots. They are more concerned with keeping the Casparian's bottled up than with us."

Shasheek, who had been riding slightly behind Jarrett and Kenchon, rode up beside Jarrett. "We need to stay within striking distance of the pass to aid the Caparian's," said Shasheek.

Kenchon, spitting at the ground, replied with ire dripping form his words, "Help those cowards! Why should we. They wouldn't help us!"

"I agree with Shasheek," said Jarrett.

"Alright," said Kenchon, throwing up his hands and shaking his head with disgust.

Silence prevailed as they continued following the stream. Although the moon was bright, Jarrett couldn't imagine how the horses maneuvered so adeptly without stumbling over the uneven ground of the plains, blanketed with runnels, rocks, and animal boroughs.

"There, up ahead," said Kenchon.

Jarrett startled by Kenchon's sudden breaking of the silence, reached for his weapon. He was looking for an impending attack.

"There's no reason to be alarmed. I meant that bit of high ground would be a good place to camp," explained Kenchon.

Kenchon rode ahead to examine the spot he had chosen. By the time the rest of them had arrived, Kenchon was unloading his horse. They ate a quick meal of dried meat. Little was said during their brief repast. Kenchon suggested to Jarrett that he rest. Jarrett didn't argue the point. He rolled up in his bedroll and fell into a deep slumber.

CHAPTER 35

Crysillnia, Tanof, and Talok had moved deeper into the desert. Tanof didn't like this sparse and barren land. Breezes of hot air capriciously and sporadically rolled across the desert. One could hear the wind crossing the desert landscape long before it arrived.

When the wind rustled the nearby vegetation, it made one think that there was a huge animal or creature of unimaginable terror ready to burst forth and devour them all, or the copse of bushes and shriveled trees had burst into flames.

The land was littered with wind eroded rocks and boulders. There was a wide variety of vegetation which consisted of thorny plants, some with hard wicked-looking thorns and others with small, petal-soft bristles. Bushes and trees grew in small copses, usually in or near wind and water eroded, sandy ravines which suggested that it must rain at some time in this dry and unforgiving land.

Crysillnia had taken the lead, Talok was second while Tanof was the rear guard as they wove their way between copses of bushes and trees and climbed in and out of ravines of varying acclivities. They had to be vigilant at all times, for the unexpected dangers hidden in this vicious and cruel land or suffer the consequences.

Tanof chose to bring up the rear because it gave him the ability to observe his companions without them being aware of his scrutiny. His observations were setting off alarms in his head, especially since the incident at the wagon when the boy had run off.

Crysillnia seemed to have changed. She had become colder and more matter-of-fact about the boy and the killings. She seemed to be more comfortable with the Crystals, which Tanof held with suspicion and disdain. He sensed that the Crystals were evil and may be more of a curse than savior.

Talok was harder too gauge. He was your typical mercenary, hard to read, with motives and loyalties always suspect. But Tanof felt that Talok seemed to hold Crysillnia in reverence.

Tanof's thirst was becoming unbearable, but he knew they had to conserve their supplies. They didn't get the chance to restock their packs in the city.

Tanof broke the ear-ringing silence of the desert. "We need to keep an eye out for any signs of water."

The only recognition he got that anyone had heard him was a surly grunt from Talok. Crysillnia appeared to be totally focused on her purpose, and nothing else seemed to matter.

Tanof returned to his thoughts which centered on the killing of the three men yesterday. Talok was unaffected which would be expected from a mercenary. In fact, Tanof had sent many men to the Guardian of Death, but he didn't do so lightly. The men he had killed were in self-defense. The taking of a life was something that couldn't be undone. A life is not something he could return once taken. But Crysillnia took the killings rather cavalierly. She wasn't the same person that he had met a few days back.

This worried Tanof. She was his half sister. The daughter of his mother, abandoned when their mother had taken her own life. This brought back painful memories. He had loved his mother, and she had loved him and his brother. He couldn't blame his mother for being swept off her feet by Prince Kanef of Caspar.

She was a beautiful and vibrant woman. Tanof's father was a poor farmer and when he wasn't in the fields, he would sit around their hovel drinking corn liquor of his own making. When things would go poorly on the farm, which was most of the time, his father would take his frustrations out on Tanof's mother by beating her senseless.

The last time his father had beat his mother, Tanof was twelve seasons and big for his age. Tanof had to take a club and knock his father unconscious or his father would have killed his mother. Tanof believed his father had begun to suspect his mother's infidelity. She left the next day. Tanof never saw his mother again.

Tanof walked into what felt like a stone wall. Talok grumbled an expletive, then turned around to face Tanof, remarking truculently, "Boy, your mind appears to somewhere else. Watch were you're going. I don't appreciate you climbing my back."

Tanof, chagrined by his lack of attentiveness, reluctantly apologized. Tanof didn't care much for the big dwarf and resented, due to his own carelessness, having to make an apology. Talok sensed that Tanof's apology was less than sincere, but he accepted it, begrudgingly.

They had halted on the edge of a depression in the shape of an irregular circle. There were crushed and shatter rocks littering the sides and bottom of the depression. Some of the rock had been turned to glass, evidence that this depression, at some time, had been forged by fire. The only vegetation that grew within this harsh environment was a purple petaled flower with splotches of crimson that resembled droplets of blood.

But the real attraction was the three people picking the flower's petals a man, woman, and little girl. They were wearing what appeared to be burlap bags with holes cut in them for their heads and arms, belted at the waist by thin strands of frayed rope. The three hadn't appeared to have bathed in years. They were putting the petals in bags made of the same material as their clothing.

Talok said, "Stay here. I'll go down and ask them if there is any water nearby."

When Talok started over the rim of the depression, he dislodged loose stone which rolled, skidded and hopped into the depression. This startled the three below. They looked up. Fear was mirrored in their faces. They fidgeted nervously and searched furtively for an avenue of escape.

Tanof watched as Talok approached the people below. He wasn't able to hear what was said, but the three appeared to be obsequious. Talok took a waterskin from the man who appeared to surrender it reluctantly. Talok tossed his empty waterskin at the feet of the man.

Talok returned and nothing was said as the three continued their journey. Tanof looked over his shoulder at the man below.

The man watched them leave with a look of dejection and hopelessness framing his face.

Tanof had an ebbing of empathy for the man's plight. This feeling was new for Tanof. His philosophy on life was to show no mercy under any circumstances, that pity was a weakness and people reaped what they deserved. They headed towards the fast approaching mountains. Tanof felt that this man and his family did not deserve their fate and that life had been unusually cruel and capricious in respect to them.

*   *   *

Calert, finished with his desert lizard stew, watched Darith as he gulped the last morsels of his evening repast. The boy had caught the fair sized lizard while Calert gathered bits and pieces of wood and sage brush to kindle a fire. Finished, Darith wiped his not so clean hands on his, equally filthy and tattered tunic.

Calert reached out and tousled the boy's disheveled and knotted hair. Calert liked Darith. For some reason, he felt close to the boy. When he had touched the boy's head, he sensed that Darith possessed magic, not only magic of his own but part of Crysillnia's magic. Magic matured later in boys than girls, and Darith was approaching the age when magic begins to manifest and develop.

Spiritual Magic consisted of two parts: Light and Dark. A person's personality usually dictated which magic would prevail, but the strength of Dark Magic could be enhanced by other's magic if the person being influenced had feelings of self-doubt or harbored great animosity within themselves.

Darith was now in possession of Crysillnia's Light Magic. The Crystals must have forced Crysillnia's Light Magic to migrate to the boy. Calert dropped his head as sorrow washed over him. Tears began to well and flow. She was lost, permanently turned to the Dark Side, without her Light Magic which now belonged to another.

Weariness washed over Calert. He was nearing the end of his existence in this world, and he had spent most of it keeping the dark minions from seizing the reigns of power. Now with Crysillnia turn to the Dark Side and in possession of the Crystals, his task had become extremely difficult, if not impossible.

He had been training her to take his place. Calert looked over at the boy. He wondered if he would have time to train another. Maybe the boy wouldn't even be interested in taking on such a grave, life consuming, and unrewarding responsibility, saving the world. How did he get here, Calert thought, as he sat by the fire shaking his head as his thoughts regressed to the beginning.

He didn't belong to this plane of existence. He was an entity of energy, not corporeal. His home was a place of nothingness but rife with magic. His home is what the humans refer to as the Void.

Out of boredom, those in his plane of existence had decided to use the magic of the Void and create the Universe but there were unexpected consequences. The Creation ran amok and began to siphon more magic than expected.

After eons of debate, it was decided that the only way to stop the negative effects that the Creation was having on the Void was to destroy it. But by this time, life had been created, so then it became a moral debate. Could the destruction of the life forms be justified?

It was decided that it couldn't, which meant there would have to be another solution to remedy the leaching away of the magic. But there were those who disagreed, and decided that their existence was more important. This began The War of Creation and he, Calert, was a soldier for Creation.

He, along with four others, were set on this world to preserve and protect it from the Anti-Creation faction's efforts to sabotage and destabilize this section of the Universe. There were many more of these anchor points throughout the Universe, and if enough of them were destroyed, the Universe would simply disperse like the leaves in an Autumn breeze and return to nothingness.

Their life forces were anchored and dependent on five crystal obelisks in the Valley of Blue Sands. Each one had a specific aspect of the world assigned to them, except for him. He had been the team leader and had power over all of the aspects.

The aspects were water and wind signified by the blue obelisk, red for land and fire, green for life, black for energy and raw power, and the fifth was clear which was the conduit to separate and combine the other four. The clear obelisk was his.

They couldn't wander far from the obelisks without risking their life force. This limited their powers and range of movement, so that there would be no contact with the sentient inhabitants of this world. Also, there was a force field and illusionary devices to hide the valley and keep intruders out. But the others discovered that, if they took the form of a living creature, they could travel beyond the valley. But there was a drawback. They didn't age in their energy form, but when they took the form of a living creature, they lost their immortality for the period they held the alien form, and aging occurred. They were also limited to the time that they could hold a corporeal form without risking their ability to return to their true form.

The others began to exploit the sentient creatures of this world for their own pleasure and enjoyment. They set themselves up as Gods and demanded worship. The human race took the brunt of the abuse. They would enslave some and would ferment wars between others.

Eventually, the humans revolted and abandoned them. By this time they were so addicted to the power that they tried to create sentient life forms themselves which resulted in the creation of the Rock Trolls. But they found that the Rock Trolls were less compliant than the humans.

So instead of creating another race, they decided to import one from another dimension. These creatures, the demons, were compliant, but they were stupid and violent.

Their failure to come up with a useful servant race led them back to the humans. They sent the demons out to capture a few humans, but they found that the human's were strong willed and refused to allow themselves to be subjugated. So these would be Gods decided to create a spell to subdue the human's defiance by stripping them of their will. I saw this as a opportunity to correct the injustice perpetrated on the humans and also a chance to instill in the humans magic, which would protect them from future enslavement by my morally bankrupt comrades.

I led my charges to believe that I was with them but had been covertly plotting ways of stopping them and regaining control of the mission. Their incantation was very complex and was easy to corrupt.

The casting was unsuccessful as far as achieving their purposes, but what they didn't realize, and it didn't become evident until much later, was that my goal had been accomplished. That same day, I, Natas, permanently took my present corporeal form and left their ranks, never to return.

A few days later, I helped the enslaved humans escape their captivity. When these humans began to have children, their children and their children's children sapped part of the Essence of their former captors, diminishing their power and giving the humans magic. This had been my contribution to the spell. By my taking of the corporeal form, I was unaffected by this draining of the Essence.

My former companions weren't aware of their peril until the second generation of children were born. It then became apparent that they were losing their Essence. They didn't know the cause until the fourth generation had come into the world.

When they understood how their Essence was being syphoned, the four declared war on the humans. They used the more intelligent demons to kill elves, dwarves, and trolls. Then they had the demons place false evidence implicating the humans. This began The War Between The Races. Humans were slaughtered in great numbers.

The Four thought that by killing the humans their Essence would return to them, but, instead, their Essence was attracted to humans of magic who had a strong aura of Essence which enhanced their magic even more. This strengthened the humans, making them more powerful and formidable. This strengthening in magic turned the tide on their attackers. They were able to defeat the elves, dwarves and trolls in one battle after another. The humans nearly exterminated the other three races.

The dragons, finally took interest in the war. They forced the warring factions into treaty negotiations, ending with the Belok Treaty which segregated the races. Their plans thwarted, the four became desperate, as their Essence was lost to the humans everyday. They instructed the demons to destroy the humans.

That's when I decided to intervene once again. While The Four were concentrating on their war with the humans, which consumed more of their time and energy because the demons didn't have the intelligence to fight the war on their own, I created the Crystals from pieces taken from the five obelisks. The Crystal that I created from my obelisk collected the escaping Essence when a human died.

Over time, when enough energy had been collected in the White Crystal, I returned to the Valley of Blue Sand and confronted The Four. A pitched battle ensued. I defeated them and sealed them each in a separate Crystal. Once I had them sealed away, their powers diminished to a fraction of what they used to be. With them out of the way, I was able to exile the demons into the void, where they could do no harm.

Calert was brought back to the present by a nuzzling pressure. He looked down to find Darith with his arms wrapped around himself for warmth, shivering, cuddling up against Calert, in an attempt to share the wizard's body warmth. Calert, compassionately and with gentleness, picked the boy up and lay him close to the fire. Since Darith didn't have a bedroll, Calert removed the robe from his gear and covered the boy. Calert conjured a spell of protection to cloak the two of them so that he could also sleep. If anything or anyone approached, he would be aware.

The fire was now a small bed of glowing coals in its death throes. Calert looked up at the many twinkling stars in the heavens. The last vestiges of the setting sun were fading over the horizon. What a beautiful sky, he thought.

Calert's attention was drawn toward the mountains that shielded the Valley of Blue Sands. A narrow beam of multicolored, light ascended into the evening sky. The light hovered over the mountains for a moment. Then streaked towards Xlanta passing directly overhead.

Shaking his head with disappointment, in a low tone he admonished himself. He knew tomorrow that he would have to backtrack. Then he bowed his head to begin his meditation. As he began his mental mantra, his thoughts touched on the regret he felt for his failure in protecting Crysillnia.

*   *   *

Schwellen was looking across the battlefield, wondering why the demons hadn't attacked since their last assault, which had ended rather abruptly, when a multicolored light had appeared over the battlefield in the early evening, a couple of days ago. The light had hovered over the battlefield for several moments. Then, with a flash, it disappeared.

The putrid stench of decay that wafted across the field of carnage and death, on the capricious winds of the Xlantan Plains, sickened Schwellen. Captain Longsleeves, last night, had dispatched a few of the demons, who had allied themselves with the humans, to infiltrate the enemy camp. None of the demon spies had returned as of yet.

Schwellen drew her sword to inspect it.

As Clodtrip approached her from behind, he asked, "How does it look?"

"The music is gone," she answered.

Perplexed, he asked, "What are you talking about?"

Schwellen sheathed her sword and drew it again. The sword made a dull, gravelly whisper as it cleared the sheath a second time. Schwellen presented the dull scarred, and pitted blade to Clodtrip.

"See what I mean? The sword should ring, slightly, as it clears the sheath, but that green goo and the unusually hard bones of the demons has taken the blade's life. Look at the blade here," Schwellen said, as she moved closer. "The edge is badly damaged. Look at all these nicks. I don't think that I can whet these out."

She crouched on one knee and began to draw the whetstone along the tortured blade.

"You think that's bad look at mine."

Clodtrip pulled his sword which didn't draw with ease. The sword snagged on the inside of it's sheath, and Clodtrip had to give it a violent jerk to pull the blade free. The blade of his sword was scarred and pitted worse than Schwellen's. He showed Schwellen his sword and he continued. "See here . . ." Schwellen quit honing her blade to look at what Clodtrip was emphasizing. There was a large chunk, near the tip of the blade, missing.

"I went to the blacksmith to see if he had an extra sword. He told me that he and his apprentices had been working day and night, and they were just beginning to get caught up. And the only reason they were catching up was because of the lull in hostil1ties of the last couple of days. He told me to come back in the morning. He should have a few extra swords by then."

Schwellen looked at her sword again. Then she sheathed it and put the whet stone away.

"This sword is a lost cause. I'm going to go with you tomorrow and pick up a new weapon, myself," Schwellen said. Schwellen looked back towards the mountains where the demons were holed up.

Then, motioning sideways with her head, she said, "Let's go get something to eat."

Clodtrip shook his head in agreement. They both turned and headed back to camp.

*   *   *

The night was clear and crisp with a few high clouds passing overhead, at times blocking the soft luminesces of the full moon. Jarrett, Kenchon, and Shasheek were sitting around a campfire, soaking in the radiated heat offered by the hungry blaze, finishing their evening repast. A scout approached.

The scout stopped beyond the light emitted by the fire, waiting for permission to come before Kenchon. Jarret could only make out a dark silhouette against the moonlit backdrop of the plains. Kenchon motioned for the scout to come forward.

Jarrett recognized the man. He didn't know his name but knew this was one of Kenchon's most reliable and respected scouts. The man looked at Jarrett and Shasheek. He was reluctant to speak in front of an audience. Usually his reports were given to Kenchon in private.

Kenchon, with agitation apparent in his voice, said, "Speak-up! These men are our allies. We don't need to hide, what you've observed from them."

"Yes Chief!" said the Scout. Then he began to brief the three men on what he had seen.

"Last night, a many colored light, traveling from Xlanta, appeared in the early night sky. The light hovered over the enemy camp and then disappeared into the Caspar Mountains. Not long after the light disappeared, the enemy broke camp and are now marching towards Xlanta. We followed them the entire night and most of today to make sure it wasn't a ruse. I instructed the others with me to continue following and report on any changes in their movement."

With a wave of his hand Kenchon dismissed the scout. The man faded into the darkness as quietly and quickly as he had appeared.

Kenchon spoke, "What do you think they're up to?"

Shasheek stared off into the darkness, as if he were trying to spot the enemy. Then he spoke. "I think they're going to reinforce the demons battling on the Xlantan Plains."

Kenchon responded, "if that is so, I suppose we should follow."

Jarrett asked, "What do we do about Simentoo? He's expecting us to wait for him."

Kenchon answered, "I'll leave a few men here, and if he shows up, they can inform him of the circumstances."

The next morning was clear and cold. A coating of white enveloped the heavy grasses of the plains. The frost added a prismatic brilliance as the rays of the freshly risen sun passed through the crystalline formations of the frozen droplets. The heat from the sun was rapidly breaking the frost's icy grip as Jarrett, Kenchon, and Shasheek led the horsemen in pursuit of the demon army. They were planning to flank the demon march and arrive at the Xlantan Plains first.

Not long into their forced march, another scout arrived. He informed Kenchon, Jarrett, and Shasheek that the enemy had been joined by the Mountain Tribesmen and Cave Dwellers.

Shasheek said, rhetorically, "That was where the light was going when it passed into the mountains."

Kenchon grunted in agreement while Jarrett shook his head to the affirmative.

CHAPTER 36

Simentoo was waiting for Kanef in the room they had rented which was located in one of the more seeder sections of Caspar City. They had been in the city for a few days but hadn't made their presence known. The city was in turmoil. There had been several murders of prominent citizens, including most of the nobility and the High Priest.

The trolls had informed Kanef and Simentoo before they left the mountains that they had observed changelings entering the city with impunity. Kanef had asked what a changeling was. The only definition the troll could give was that they were shadow demons, and they could take any form they wished. The changeling was a rare breed of demon, because they were highly intelligent. The troll said that they were thought to be the corrupted spirits of elves, but no one was absolutely sure.

Simentoo turned as the door swung inwards with a loud grating protest from the rusty hinges from which the battered, single planked, oak door was hung. Simentoo reached instinctively for his short sword. The sword leapt from its scabbard with a slight whisper and emitting a distinct chime, warning of death to anyone violated by this weapon.

Kanef secretively entered the room, glancing behind him furtively.

"I believe, I may have been followed," Kanef whispered.

A cacophony broke out in the tavern below, the sound of tables and chairs being turned over. Loud cursing by patrons and the tavern owner were quick to follow the violations of persons and personal property. Heavy footfalls and the clanking of weapons were heard, rushing up the stairs.

"Quickly, out the window!" urged Kanef.

Simentoo turned to the only window in the room. There was no glass in the window, just a vertical slat shutter. The shutter was designed to open to adjust the lighting in the room and for ventilation. There was no way to open the window wide enough to allow a man egress. Simentoo retrieved a badly battered wooden stool from the far corner of the room, and, with all the strength and speed he could generate, he slammed the stool into the shutter.

The shuttered splintered, showering the street below with debris, inundating a wagon load of fodder. The precipitation of splintered and shattered wood struck the horse harnessed to the wagon. The horse pawed the air in fear and pain. The driver tried in vain to calm the angry and frightened beast.

Simentoo leapt from the window into the wagon. The fodder cushioned his fall. There was a light coat of snow covering the fodder and the street. There was a light and misty pervasive snow falling. Simentoo quickly alighted from the wagon expecting Kanef to follow.

Kanef slammed the door shut, rattling the feeble door frame, and slapped the door bar in place just as a strong shoulder contacted the other side of the door. The door buckled slightly but held fast. Kanef grinned as he heard the man yelp in pain followed by a long line of curses that would curl one's hair. Kanef turned toward the window as more men began to batter the door. He knew the life of the door would be short. He ran to the window. As he passed the bed, he retrieved Simentoo's wool jacket that was hanging from the bedpost. Without a second, thought exited through the window.

The two men ran down the street dodging pedestrians, along with people on horseback, wagons, and carriages. Kanef was in the lead. The snow had changed from flurries to squalls. The wind nipped at their heels, driving the snow around them in eddies. This was to their advantage. It made it impossible for their enemies to spot or pursue them. Kanef turned into a narrow alley with Simentoo close on his heels.

Kanef stopped and began pounding on a door a short distance down the alley.

A harsh and truculent voice admonished Kanef. "Go away! I don't want any company!"

"Garnetch, let me in, please!" Kanef pleaded.

The sound of a chair scraping along a stone floor came from behind the door. The door was opened a crack, so that the occupant could peer out without allowing entry. Simentoo could see a truncated and gnarled old man through the slight opening. When the old man recognized Kanef, his face lit-up and he swung the door open. The gnarled old man stepped out of the way to allow them entrance. The two men quickly entered. Simentoo appraised the small room in to which they had been ushered.

A table, surrounded by four battered and rickety old chairs, on which a steaming bowl of stew sat, was the center piece of the room. A poorly made bed was against one wall. There was clothing and other personal affects strewn haphazardly around the room, giving the room a cluttered appearance. Shelves lined another wall and an open fireplace occupied the back wall.

"Come! Come! Remove those wet cloaks and let them dry by the fire," the old man said, pointing to the fireplace with a motion of his hand. "Kanef, my boy its been a long time. Where have you been? The last I heard, you were living on the Ice Fields."

"I was until a few weeks ago. But recently I've been on a quest of sorts . . ." answered Kanef.

"Where are my manners? Pull up a chair and sit," the old man collapsed into the chair in front of the bowl of stew. "There are some more bowls on those shelves over there, if you would like to eat with me. It's not much, but it is quite good, if I do say so myself."

Kanef and Simentoo didn't refuse the old man's hospitality. They retrieved the bowls and filled them to the brim with hot steaming stew from a pot hanging over the fire.

"I don't have any bread, or I'd offer you some," continued the old man.

Simentoo said, gratefully, "This is fine."

The three sat in silence while they ate. Finally, the old man finished his stew by tipping the bowl and drinking the last few dregs. He sat there and watched his unexpected guests eat, but his curiosity overwhelmed him.

"What brings the Prince, and future ruler of Caspar, to my door after so many years?" he asked.

Kanef stopped eating and looked directly at the old man. "For one thing, we were being chased by the Palace Guard," replied Kanef.

"Those pretenders, they're not the Palace Guard. The Palace Guard was imprisoned for treason or that's what your father claims. I don't know where your father got his new guards, but I've been hearing some unsettling rumors, one of which is that he has sold us out to the demons. There have been some strange goings on around here of late," said the old man.

Silence reigned while Kanef and Simentoo finished their stew. Kanef plopped his empty bowl down on the table. He first looked over at Simentoo. Then he returned his attention to the old man.

"Garnetch, is the army backing my father?"

"I don't believe they're even aware of what is happening. They have been assigned to the outer reaches of the valley in a ruse to protect the valley from enemy encroachments," answered Garnetch.

"The entire army?" repeated Kanef with incredulity.

"Yes." replied Garnetch.

"I need some help, and I need it now. I don't have time to go find the army and bring them back." Turning to Simentoo, Kanef said, "We'll have to free the Palace Guard."

"I'm willing, but how do we get into the palace?" asked Simentoo.

"Through the sewers. I used to play in them when I was a child. I discovered a tunnel that circumvents the palace security. I would use it to leave the palace when I didn't wish a contingent of guards following me around. Guards could be, such, a bore. They took all the excitement out of my excursions beyond the palace walls. Plus, I couldn't experience the real world when I went among the people. They would coddle and treat me special."

Kanef jerked his gaze back to the men in the small cluttered room. He had been staring at the floor while reminiscing. Kanef nearly leapt from the chair.

"We need to be going."

*　　*　　*

It was late afternoon when Crysillnia and her companions exited the mountain. They had entered a valley of the purest blue sand she had ever seen. The free flowing energy that emanated form the sand was pervasive. She could feel the energy flow around her body, caressing her gently and seductively, calling for her. Far across the valley, she could see five huge crystal obelisks reaching towards the heavens. The obelisks refracted the light of the late day sun, painting the surrounding mountains in a myriad colors.

Crysillnia was mesmerized by the beauty of the spectral fantasy. She was so enthralled by the beckoning siren call of the valley, that she was unaware of the searing pain that the Crystals were inflicting. She was roughly awakened from her reverie by Talok's huge calloused hand as he jerked her backwards.

Talok commented, as he nodded with his head and a look of consternation framing his face, towards the Crystals.

"I don't think they wish you to step out there."

Finally aware of the pain that the Crystals were trying to inflict on her, Crysillnia yelped and grabbed the pouch in which the Crystals were nestled. She pulled her unforgiving guardians away from her tortured skin.

"Thanks Talok. I wasn't even aware of their protest."

Talok, in acknowledgment of her gratitude, nodded his head. The pouch now bulged with five crystals. The Fifth Crystal had been retrieved from the heart of the mountains, looming with a foreboding presence, behind her. It hadn't taken long for them to locate the companion crystal to the other four of which she had possession. The four tyrannical crystals had guided them to it.

There was no danger from the dragon protecting the crystal because she was already dead. When they first approached the carcass of the deceased beast, they were unaware she was dead. In the diffuse and eerie light provided by the Crystals, the only illumination they had to maneuver within the anhydrous and stagnant bowels of the mountains, the desiccated body, of the dragon appeared to be napping, at first glance. The three closely observed the hulking, beast for an indeterminate time. Their eyes, adjusted to the darkness, could surprisingly detect fine details. Tanof had been the first to mention that the dragon didn't appear to be breathing.

He approached the dragon cautiously, sword extended. Using his sword, he poked at the hulking beast and was greeted with a noxious explosion that temporarily took away their breath. The gaseous and putrid stench of death quickly dissipated. All that was left of the dragon were the explosion ravished hide, a disheveled pile of bones, and the Fifth Crystal.

Talok brought Crysillnia back to the present when he asked, "Should we return the way we came?"

Crysillnia shook her head, emphatically, and answered, "We need to reach those obelisks," pointing in the direction of her desired destination.

Tanof asked, "Why?"

"I don't know. I sense a desperation from the Crystals," replied Crysillnia.

"How are we suppose to reach the obelisks?" countered Talok.

"I sense from the Crystals that there is a path. But to find it we need to follow the outskirts of this oasis of blue sand," answered Crysillnia.

After circumventing approximately a quarter of the valley, They reached a breathtaking sight, a path constructed of reflective pebbles. Each perfectly rounded pebble appeared to be a finely polished mirror. Crysillnia delicately placed her foot on the path in fear she might crush these exquisite jewels of workmanship. The finely polished pebbles rolled a little, but they were sturdy and safe to traverse.

Crysillnia couldn't help but watch the hundreds of mini-reflections of herself as she followed the path to the obelisks. She couldn't help but let a little giggle escape. She, almost, felt like a child again.

Crysillnia, curious about her companions reaction to the Trail of Mirrors, a name of her own creation which seemed appropriate, looked back and found that Talok and Tanof appeared equally mesmerized by the mini-mirrors. She even thought that she might have caught a brief glimmer of a smile on Talok's grim visage.

Their joy was overshadowed when they reached the massive obelisks which gave Crysillnia the impression of five hulking and brooding behemoths. The obelisks surrounded a courtyard of white stone, decorated with golden whorls, polished to create a dazzling sheen. The entrance to the courtyard was flanked by the red obelisk on the right, blue obelisk to the left. The distance between these two was approximately the height of one obelisk. The black and green obelisks were behind the first two, flared out at forty-five degree angles, the green on the left and the black on the right. Their distance from the first two was twice the height of an obelisk. The clear obelisk was further back and centered with the entrance and equal in distance from the previous two's distance from the entryway.

In the center of the courtyard was a obsidian pedestal with a bowl-shaped, concave top. The pedestal was also polished which caused the slightest glimmer of light to reflect from its surface in a greater magnification than normally possible.

Crysillnia stood over the pedestal which reached her to waist. Within the bowl shaped top, there were five insets. It was obvious to Crysillnia that these were placements for the Crystals. Without hesitation, as the sun made its final dissent, she pulled the Crystals from her neck, opened the bag, and dumped them into the bowl. The Crystals clattered and rattled around the inside of the bowl before seating themselves into the proper inset.

Tanof stood slightly behind and off to the side of Crysillnia. Talok stood to Tanof's right. Tanof watched with apprehension as Crysillnia unceremoniously dropped the Crystals into the bowl. His unease increased as he watched the Crystals' glow intensify after seating themselves.

Red, blue, and green colored lights infused with black entered the clear crystal, creating a tumultuous roiling of colors within the violated crystal. Then, the once cold surface on which they stood, began to heat up to the point of discomfort. Then, with an ear-piercing ringing chime, the clear obelisk lit up with the multiple colors of the impregnated crystal. Like an arrow released from an over taut bow, the light exited from the pointed top of the obelisk, the only one of the square monoliths with a top that tapered to a point.

The multicolored light streaked through the recently darkened sky in the direction from which they had come. And Crysillnia, without hesitation, retrieved the Crystals and placed them back in the pouch and hung it around her neck. She turned to face Talok and Tanof. She flicked her head, a habit she had never been able to break, as if trying to clear the hair from her face.

"We should rest. We have a long trek ahead of us," she said.

*   *   *

Alaquin and Carric had returned to the Elf Woods a couple of days ago. She had been searching for the Rune Plaque that had disappeared weeks before. Her original fear had been that the Chaos Demon had taken the plaque, but, to her surprise and relief, the Chaos Demon had returned to its rest.

Alaquin's thoughts were disrupted when she had spotted a Rune Board that would satisfy her needs. She pulled the spectacularly colored board from the bottom of a stack situated on a shelf slightly above her head.

She was in the storage hut nestled in the center of the elf village where the Rune Wood was stored. She placed the rune board on the work bench. She was going to create another plaque to replace the one that was missing. Once she started her work, her thoughts returned to her search for the missing Rune Plaque. Carric and she had gone to the place were the plaque should have been located. She had cast seeking spells in an attempt to find the missing plaque but had failed to turn up any clues.

The high pitched whistling sound had grown in volume and power. The whistling sound was caused by escaping Elf Magic captured within the four Rune Plaques located at each corner of the Elf Woods. This magic kept dangerous magical creatures within the confines of the Elf Woods. If the leak wasn't soon plugged, the magic in the woods would be so far out of balance that it would be impossible to maintain the forbidding that kept the magical creatures enthralled, and they would escape the woods. Even though she was unable to sense the plaque, she did sense a magical signature. The signature was familiar, but she was unable to place the owner. The magic signature, she suspected, harked from her childhood.

Alaquin's thoughts returned to the present as she put the finishing touches to the new plaque. She scrutinized the plaque on which she had engraved runes that would return balance to the woods. She would engrave the activating rune at the spot where the plaque would be anchored.

Alaquin and Carric followed the trail leading out of the woods. There had been a rain shower, earlier in the day, which enhanced the pungent aromas of the woods. The sun was playing hide and seek with the clouds and, every once and awhile, a light breeze would capriciously churn the leaves, dumping their miniature ponds of water on the travelers, soaking them to the skin.

When they reached the edge of the Elf Woods, they left the trail. Alaquin was looking closely for the proper spot to set the new Rune Plaque. She was still amazed at the beauty of Rune Wood. The wood was brilliantly colored and the whorls around the knots in the board offered a spectacular display in varieties and mixtures of color.

The Rune Tree was a rare species. It had special properties which allowed the enhancement and longevity of the Rune Magic. Rune Plagues were harvested only from dead Rune Trees because of their rarity. When a deceased Rune Tree was discovered. The elves would fall the tree and harvest the rune boards and store them for future use.

Alaquin's attention was drawn away from the plaque by the rustling of a nearby Callenberry bush. She sensed the same familiar magic signature that had permeated the site of the missing plaque. Alaquin turned towards the disturbance while pulling Carric closer to her. With a wave of her hand and chanting an incantation under her breath, she conjured a protection spell to envelope the two of them.

When the bushes finally parted, she sucked in a deep breath in surprise and disappointment. Her childhood memories resurfaced of the time when she and Chandok would use their magic to play practical jokes on one and other. Their childish pranks continued until caught by one of the Elders. The Elder had scolded them so harshly for making such frivolous use of their magic, that Chandok and she never used their magic in that manner again.

"Why, Chandok?" she asked, disappointment palpable in her voice.

"Simple, Alaquin. I wish to bring the Shadow Land here and the only thing hindering my endeavor is the magic of the Elf Woods," Chandok answered.

"I don't understand?" she continued to question.

"The answer to your question should be obvious. If the Shadow Land is brought into this world, we elves would have absolute control of the world's destiny. We could rule all races. We could stop all these foolish wars that the other races insist on conducting."

Alaquin was taken aback by the gleam of madness that shown in Chandok's eyes.

"Give me the plaque," demanded Chandok, as he reached out towards Alaquin.

Alaquin gripped the plaque defensively and said, "No!"

"Don't make me use my magic against you. You should remember from our childhood games that my magic is stronger than yours," threatened Chandok.

Alaquin replied calmly, "You don't scare me."

"You should be scared. My powers are stronger than ever."

Carric watched, as the verbal fencing continued, sword at the ready. Carric thought that Chandok's last statement and attitude were amusing. Chandok puffed his chest out like a big toad. This elf was quite proud of himself.

Alaquin noticed that Chandok was standing in front of the stone in which her plaque needed to be embedded.

"Out of my way Chandok! I don't have time to discuss this with you, any longer!" She demanded, a definite edge too her voice and a distant rumble of thunder seemed too punctuate her mood.

Carric prepared himself for action. He could since Alaquin's anger building and knew that things would start happening soon.

Chandok's confidence appeared to waver for a moment. He hadn't expected such defiance and lack of fear from his childhood friend, but the moment was fleeting. With a wave of his hand Chandok summoned forth allies hidden in the surrounding forest.

"Leave this alone, Chandok. I don't wish to harm you!" Alaquin warned.

Chandok's face flushed red with anger at the gall of this obstinate girl. He began, in unison with the other elves that had formed a circle around Carric and Alaquin, to chant a Rune Song and form the runes in the air. Carric sensed that Chandok's allies were adding their power to Chandok's Rune Magic. The runes began to dance through the air, advancing slowly and methodically towards Alaquin and Carric. The runes encircled them, but Alaquin did nothing to counter the encroaching magic. Carric began to fear that maybe Chandok was correct in his assumption, that his magic was more powerful than Alaquin's.

Carric was readying himself to strike their attackers when he noticed Chandok's wolfish and maniacal grin slowly fade into an unpleasant frown. The dancing runes were beginning to fade, at first slowly, but then in a cascade fashion, the runes faded to nothing quickly.

"I warn you one more time, Chandok! Leave now!" Alaquin said, her voice dripping with ire.

The approaching thunderstorm accentuated her mood and lightning began to paint the sky overhead with streaks of incandescent light. Chandok refused to heed the elf girl's warning. With a wave of his hand, he ordered his allies forward. Alaquin raised her hands above her head. Balancing on the ball of one foot and pushing off with the other foot she pivoted, completing a full circle, casting a spell on the attacking elves. Lightening struck a nearby tree, incinerating it, spraying the combatants with charred and smoldering splinters.

All the elves, except Chandok, began to screech loudly as excruciating pain wracked their bodies. Blisters formed on their faces, and their tongues swelled, protruded from their mouths grotesquely. Then their eyes bulged out of their sockets. As the thunderstorm reached its crescendo, the elves' heads popped open like overripe Snow Melons.

Carric became sick to his stomach at this macabre sight. He had seen a lot of death in his life, and in fact had been responsible for many of those deaths, but this was the most gruesome sight he had ever seen. The nearly decapitated corpses fell into big globs of gelatinous flesh and bone.

Chandok's mouth dropped open at the sight of what had happened to his companions. Fear now predominated his carriage and facial expression. He began to back away from what he now, perceived to be a monster, the elf girl.

"Not so quickly!" shouted Alaquin.

She pointed a finger at Chandok which appeared to freeze him on the spot. Alaquin approached the immobile elf.

"Your punishment shall be to have your worst nightmare come into existence for the remainder of your life."

Alaquin placed her outstretched finger on Chandok's forehead. She chanted an invocation. She then stepped back from Chandok. Alaquin watched him closely for a reaction which wasn't immediate. Chandok stood there for a short period. Then his body began to quake and quiver. Chandok began to babble and then cry, as he fell to his knees.

"What have you done to me?" he blubbered between sobs. "I feel so insignificant and powerless."

No mercy in her heart Alaquin flashed a cruel smile at Chandok, and then she shoved him aside. She answered, "What you most deserved. It appears that the deflation of your ego is your worst nightmare."

Ignoring the pleas for mercy from Chandok, Alaquin approached the plaque stone. As she placed the plaque on the stone, a torrential rainstorm was unleashed. She appeared oblivious to the rivulets of water that plastered her golden locks against her face. The rain stopped as suddenly as it had started when she began to weave the rune spell to anchor the new plaque.

The air, trees, and ground seemed too reverberate as Alaquin formed the rune letters. Her chant was beautiful and mesmerizing. Alaquin's lilting voice was enchanting and enthralling. As if in joyous response, the clouds parted and allowed the sun to applaud her performance.

There was a flash of energy as the runes entered the plaque and fused it to the stone. In fact, Alaquin had done more than attach the plaque to the stone. She had converted its basic elements and made it an integral part of the stone. She stepped back from the stone with a relaxed smile, pleased by her accomplishment. Carric sensed a change in the forest. It became peaceful and calm.

Still smiling, Alaquin turned towards Carric.

"See, darling, isn't it fantastic? The Calmness has returned. The magic no longer escapes." Then a stray thought crossed her mind. She said, "We must go. We are needed on the Xlantan Plains. A dangerous and powerful evil force is about to join the battle. My magic will be needed."

Without waiting for a response from Carric, Alaquin headed in the direction of the setting sun.

Looking up at the fading sun, Carric said, "It will be dark soon."

Alaquin shrugged her shoulder in response to Carric's concern and continued on. Carric raised his eyebrows in annoyance at Alaquin's gesture but fell in behind her as she led them down the trail that took them back into the Elf Woods.

CHAPTER 37

Kanef and Simentoo had returned to Garnetch's cramped quarters with the rescued palace guards. Garnetch's curiosity was insatiable. He was quizzing Kanef on how he had managed to accomplish the rescue.

Although Kanef didn't want to squander valuable time, he felt that he owed the old man something, so he decided to recount Simentoo's and his adventure, for Garnetch's sake, in an abbreviated form.

Garnetch clapped his hands with glee, like a small child, but the old man didn't sit while the story unfolded. He set about dishing food for the few guards who had survived the ordeal. There were a dozen or so hungry, emaciated men gulping down the savory stew and tearing chunks of bread from small loaves that Garnetch had baked earlier in the day.

Kanef began his story. "We entered from the sewers in the deepest recesses of the palace keep. It was as dark as the void. If not for the light stones that the trolls had given us, we wouldn't have been able to navigate the deep, dark regions of the palace."

Garnetch unable to control his enthusiasm and excitement interrupted. "I thought you knew every nook and cranny of the palace from your childhood excursions."

"That was long ago and when I was a boy most of the passageways were lit by torches. This is no longer the circumstance," answered Kanef.

Kanef returned to his story. "We had managed to escape notice, even though there were many demons roaming the deep recesses of the palace." Kanef's demeanor became more truculent. "The demon stench was abominable," I knew my father was a despicable person but this . . ." Kanef was so overwhelmed with

305

disappointment and an even deeper loathing for his father, he was unable to articulate his feelings completely.

Before Kanef could continue his narrative, a commotion outside drew the attention of all of those inside.

"What's all that noise about!" blurted Garnetch with excitement and a touch of fear.

The clamor increased in intensity.

Simentoo reaching for his weapon, said, "It sounds like soldiers."

"I agree," said Kanef.

He rose from his chair, hand on the hilt of his sword, and approached the door.

Kanef opened the door just enough to peek outside. Simentoo followed Kanef and stood behind him, sword in hand. The sun was setting. The air was nippy, but all signs of the recent snow had disappeared which wasn't unusual in Caspar this time of year. In fact, the weather could turn and become quite, warm.

"Whatever is happening, is happening on the street and not in the alley," said Kanef, truncating the anticipated barrage of questions from Garnetch. Kanef opened the door wide enough so that he could slip out. Simentoo followed on his heels, but before he exited, he turned to those in the small room and told them to stay put.

At the head of the alley, a crowd was gathering. Kanef and Simentoo approached the crowd, cautiously. There was movement in the street beyond the crowd. Kanef began to force his way through the unruly mob, angering many in the crowd, and some of them pushed back.

One burly and licentious appearing character turned on Kanef and Simentoo. He apparently had thoughts of striking out at the annoyance attempting to push him out of the way but changed his mind when he realized his tormentors weren't men to trifle with. The burly man turned away from Kanef and Simentoo, moving out of their way, cursing them under his breath.

Kanef and Simentoo watched troops marching through the streets of the city.

"What's going on?" Kanef asked a wizened old woman.

"Civil war, I hear," as her reply.

"Its about time," said a disembodied voice from somewhere in the crowd.

Another spoke up. "The Casparian Guard has declared King Falef a traitor to the Kingdom of Lenar and Province of Caspar. They are taking Caspar back for Prince Kanef of Caspar."

"Hail to Prince Kanef!" shouted another person in the crowd.

The crowd was becoming more vociferous and unruly. Kanef beckoned with his head to Simentoo, in the direction from which they had come. The two had to struggle even more desperately to reach the rear of the crowd.

They returned to Garnetch's. When they entered, Simentoo noticed a small group of shadowy figures that appeared to be following them. He kept his observation to himself. He wasn't absolutely sure and he didn't want to alarm anyone unnecessarily. Garnetch, for an old man, exhibited a lot of energy when he began to grill Kanef and Simentoo about the commotion in the streets. Kanef related what he had heard to all of those in the cramped and inauspicious room.

Garnetch asked Kanef, "What are you plans?"

Kanef, sitting on an unstable and rickety chair, looked at Garnetch with a far away expression, as if he hadn't heard the question.

He was reasoning out his next move. Garnetch began to repeat his question when Kanef answered. "I'm going to join the army and help them however I can. My father's greed and lust for power has to end. Now!"

Everyone in the room shook their heads in agreement.

Kanef continued, "We must not all leave at once. We should leave in groups of no more than three, or we may attract unwanted attention."

Kanef and Simentoo left first. Simentoo opened the door and peered up and down the alley.

Kanef, curious about Simentoo's extreme precaution, asked, "Is there a problem?"

Simentoo answered, "I thought we might have been followed earlier, but I see no signs of anyone lurking about."

The overcast sky only allowed a dim and unreliable light to filter into the chasm like alley, so Simentoo and Kanef stealthily crept through the alleyway, Kanef in the lead.

"I know ways we can leave the city undetected," said Kanef.

Kanef and Simentoo entered one of the less traveled streets from the alleyway. When they turned the corner, they encountered three rather surly and dangerous appearing men. Not wanting any trouble, the two turned to go the other direction but found their way blocked by three more men, quite as dangerous looking as the first three.

Simentoo realized immediately that the shadows he had been suspicious of had been these men. Simentoo recognized the burly man from the crowd. In the waning daylight, the distant rumble of wagons and horses moving along the main thoroughfare, shouts and curses from a nearby tavern, echoed off the surrounding buildings.

Simentoo reacted, years of training and instinct took over. In unison, unsheathing his broadsword, he pivoted. Allowing the momentum of his heavy broadsword to facilitate the power of his swing, Simentoo lopped off the heads of two of the men who had been behind him with. The sword's momentum spent, it sliced through the shoulder and buried itself in the chest of the third. Blood burst like molten rock from a fire mountain into the air, soaking the combatants from head to foot. This all occurred before Kanef could free his weapons. The other three men, slack jawed from shock, covered in the blood of their comrades, turned in unison, fleeing their own demise.

Kanef, holding his hands out to his side, blood dripping from his finger tips, half-jokingly said, "Could you have made a bigger mess?"

Simentoo looking at the pool of blood in which he stood, only grunted.

Simentoo despised unnecessary killing. He could never return a life once taken.

Gesturing with his head, Simentoo said, "Hadn't we better be moving on before we attract more attention."

Kanef, nodding his head in agreement, took the lead, and they faded away into the darkness.

*   *   *

Jarret sat on his mount, overlooking the Calowi River Gorge. This was the spot where his unanticipated adventure had begun. Jarret looked back the way he had just come. He had under his command approximately half the Halhoren Horsemen. They sat patiently, waiting for Jarrett to continue their journey. Smiling to himself, he thought, if nothing else, they were patient.

Jarrett and his contingent of horsemen were following a troop of demons that had broken from the main force and returned to the Caspar Mountains. This had occurred a couple of days after he and Kenchon, with their troops, had passed the demon horde and were setting ambushes and traps to ensnare and kill as many demons as possible before they reached the Xlantan battlefield.

The demons were definitely headed to Caspar. Their trail was easy to follow. They left piles of excrement and other nasty appearing leavings along the trail, some unidentifiable. And the trail was marred and scarred from the many foot, paw, and hoof prints left behind by the demon contingent.

Jarrett urged his mount to move on. Jarrett was amazed with the Halhoren horse. It was a magnificent animal. It wasn't the prettiest thing to look at, but it was a superb war horse. It was extremely surefooted, intelligent and able to anticipate its rider's moves. Albeit raised on the plains, the horse was as competent on the mountain trails as on the open plain.

The animal appeared to fear nothing. Most horses would shy away from the demon scent, but the Halhoren horse ignored the scent completely. In battle the Halhoren horse was like having another warrior. They will fight to the death to help, and if necessary, die protecting their rider.

Jarret was jostled from his thoughts when his mount side stepped a stone that had fallen from the hillside above the trail. They were on the downhill acclivity heading into the valley. They would soon be approaching the garrison that guarded the pass into the valley, but Jarret feared what he might find. His fears were confirmed when they rounded the last bend in the trail and faced the small, stone walled fort. All the occupants were dead. Many of them were mauled and mutilated beyond recognition while others were half eaten.

Jarrett became sick to his stomach and even the immutable horsemen appeared disturbed by the sight.

Latcin, Jarret's second in command on this excursion, commented, "We shall exact revenge for these atrocities."

Jarrett turned to the man and was confronted by a grim tight faced frown. Jarrett wouldn't want to be the one on the receiving side of this man's revenge.

Jarrett said, "We had better be moving on. They appear to be heading towards Caspar City."

Latcin nodded his head in agreement, then spoke. "We should travel through the night."

Jarret agreed with a nod. So with a forward motion of his arm, the troop continued their march.

*   *   *

Kenchon and his horsemen had been harassing the demon horde for days. He had received reinforcements a couple of days after Jarrett had left which had consisted of the horsemen that had been followers of Sub-Chieftain Kroll. When they realized that Kroll was allied with the demons, they rescinded their allegiance to him. They asked Kenchon if he would accept their vow of allegiance. Kenchon accepted them with an open heart.

They were now in the foothills of the Dragon's Mountains. Great stone ridges extended from the mountains like massive tree roots. Although they had assaulted the demon horde many times, Kenchon's troops had not managed to inflict much damage or even slow the horde significantly.

Kenchon and Shasheek were sitting their mounts looking into an immense chasm. The bottom of the chasm was littered with razor sharp, stone pillars.

Kenchon said, "We need to find a way to lure the horde into this chasm. We could destroy their entire army."

"If you can get them this far, I can assure you that I can lure them into the chasm with my magic," replied Shasheek.

"The question is how to get them to follow us. In our many attacks, they have not been inclined to chase us. The demons appear to have a single-minded determination to reach their destination," said Kenchon.

"The reason they haven't attempted to chase you is that you haven't piqued their blood lust," replied Shasheek.

Kenchon sat there for a few moments mentally digesting Shasheek's comment.

"How do you suggest we pique this blood lust?"

Shasheek, massaging his chin, didn't respond immediately. He was in deep thought, mulling over the problem.

Then, looking Kenchon in the eyes, he answered, "You've been using hit and run tactics. I believe to coax the demons into following, you need to hit them with a full on assault. Then retreat slowly, leading them in this direction. If they leave off the pursuit, you need to attack them again until they're so deep into their blood lust, they can't resist the urge to follow."

Kenchon, running his fingers idly through his horse's mane as if trying to unravel the tangles in the coarse hair, pondered Shasheek's advise.

Kenchon finally said. "That will cost a great many lives."

There was a long pause. Kenchon quit playing with his horse's mane and looked up at Shasheek with a melancholy expression and continued.

"But, I don't see any other solution."

It was the next day that Kenchon and his men waited for the demon horde. He had divided his horsemen into three separate but equal contingents. The plan was simple. When the demons reached the closest approach to the chasm, Kenchon would launch the assault. The first group would strike the demons in a straight on attack and continue the assault until either his men began to fatigue or the casualties became to great.

No matter which occurred first, Kenchon's men would begin an organized retreat in an effort to lure the demons to the chasm. If this first attack didn't succeed, the second group would attack. The three contingents would continue this rotation, over and over, until the demons were lured to their deaths.

The demon horde reached the specified point by midday. The demons were in the forefront while the human component of the horde lagged behind bringing up the rear. This created a problem for Kenchon's battle plan so he took a few men from each contingent and had them attack the rear guard. This halted the forward movement of the horde while they prepared to defend themselves. This enabled the Halhorens to herd the strugglers back into the main force.

His objective accomplished, Kenchon, sitting his mount on the ridge which was situated between and overlooked the road and chasm, signaled for the first attack. Kenchon was usually in the forefront of an attack but, due to the delicate and critical timing factors and the possibility of unexpected and chaotic variables, was left with no choice other than to direct the battle from the ridge.

Kenchon, agitated at his inactivity, watched the battle unfold below. His men fought well but they were badly outnumbered, and the demons were thick-skinned and hard to kill. When he thought his men had taken enough of a beating, he gave the signal to retreat.

The retreat went has planned. It was slow, methodical, and well executed. The horde began to follow the retreat, like ants following a trail of honey, but when the Halhorens increased the speed of the retreat, the horde quit the chase. They hadn't been driven into a frenzy yet.

When Kenchon spotted the horde's tendency to fall back, he sent the second contingent to engage the demons. This battle was more ferocious, and Kenchon didn't dare allow this assault to last as long as the first. This retreat was also well executed but picked up momentum a lot quicker than the first. The demons were definitely in a frenzy. The horsemen disappeared over the ridge with the horde hard on their tail.

Shasheek cast a spell to conceal the presence of the chasm and to make it appear that the horsemen were crossing the hidden chasm. The demons would be easier to trick than the human element of the horde, so Kenchon sent the third and first contingents to follow and finish off the stragglers. He also wanted to keep the human's attention away from what lie ahead and, if necessary, to drive them into the chasm.

The planned worked as anticipated. The demons were easily fooled, but the human's recognized the deception and attempted to halt their forward momentum. But, with the Halhoren's relentless attacks from the rear, the humans that were not aware of the danger forced their comrades over the edge.

The battle was over by sunset. The demon horde was destroyed. Kenchon and Shasheek were discussing their next move, when Kenchon's attention was drawn away from the elf by an approaching horsemen leading a tethered man.

Kenchon was elated by their victory and casualties had been lighter than expected. He became somber when he recognized the captive. The horseman presented his prisoner to Kenchon by putting his foot into the middle of the man's back and forcing him to his knees.

"Kroll, what do you have to say for yourself?" asked Kenchon.

Kroll, dirty and covered with many cuts and abrasions, exuded defiance. "There is a new world order coming and I wanted to be part of it. I want the power that is due me that you deny me. I have no regrets."

Kroll spat, vehemently, to express his defiance.

For several moments, the tension built. Nothing was said.

Kenchon commanded, "Stand!"

Kroll obeyed. Neither man took their eyes off the other. Kenchon moved his steed forward and sidled up to Kroll. Kroll took a step backwards to keep his balance. Kenchon, in one fluid motion, unsheathed the sword draped over his back and decapitated the traitor. The blow was so violent that the orb that hung around Kroll's neck flew high into the air. Kenchon snatched the orb out of the air as Kroll crumpled to the ground, spouting blood with each beat of the heart.

Kenchon pocketed the orb with out examining it. He gave the order to move on. The orb glowed in his pocket. The dry soil of the battlefield hungrily devoured Kroll's life fluids, and a light breeze ushered in the darkness. The weary warriors vacated the arena of their victory.

*   *   *

Calert stood outside the Xlantan soldiers camp. Darkness was easing into dominance and the sun slipped over the horizon.

He was holding the sister orb to the one he had given Kroll. He had felt the disturbance in the orb. It could mean only one thing. The renegade sub-chieftain was dead.

He had given the orb to Kroll for communication purposes or that is what he had led the sub-chieftain to believe, but in reality it was to keep track of Kroll. He suspected that Kroll was an agent for the demons. He couldn't obtain any more information about the circumstances of the renegade's death or where the orb was. The only thing he could be sure of was that the orb was in a dark place.

Calert was planning to enter the Xlantan camp under a concealment spell. He felt this was the best way to observe the army's viability as a force against the evil. The sun had disappeared, and the residual glow on the horizon was quickly, fading.

Calert approached the camp but had to do so cautiously. The Xlantan's had set many traps around the camp to snare any one attacking or trying to enter the camp undetected. The Xlantan Army was a professional organization which grew out of their aggressive nature.

Calert turned to talk with Darith.

"We'll wait here until the deep dark of night settles in."

"Why?" asked the boy.

"Because a concealment spell, especially the one I plan to use, is better in the dark."

"Oh," was Darith's response.

The two of them sat in silence for a few moments, listening to the din emanating from the busy camp. Calert broke the silence.

"Do you know the history of the Xlantan Confederation?"

"No," responded Darith.

"Well, since we have time, I'll give you a brief history lesson."

"Before the formation of the Xlantan Confederation, the country wasn't unified. It consisted of several warring tribes. The slightest provocation would set one tribe or group of tribes against another tribe or group of tribes, depending on the alliances at the time and these allegiances would shift routinely."

"This changed abruptly when they were invaded by an army from across The Great Sea. The tribes separately were being conquered by the invaders. A Chief from one of the tribes recognized their weakness and was able to convince the tribes to fight together. This Chief's name has been lost to history, but to this day they revere him and refer to him as the Great Chieftain Warrior."

"When the invading armies had been driven from their lands, the Great Chieftain Warrior, with persuasive speeches along with the timely demise of those who opposed the continuation of the alliance, was able to keep it from falling apart. They formed a Confederation which was administered by a council of men hand picked by the chieftain of each tribe."

"Over time the tribes ceased to exist as separate entities, and the general population was allowed to elect the Councilmen. From this pool of elected officials, the army chose the Head Councilman. All elected positions were held for life. If they performed poorly, took bribes, or did some other illegal act while in office, they were executed. It was a great honor to be a Councilman."

In the early days of the Confederation, there was still a problem with the aggressive nature of the tribes. So, to combat their bellicose nature, the Council would hire the army out to other countries which also helped fill the government coffers. All male children were taken into the army at a young age, and those that failed to perform adequately were forced to become laborers, which was a disgrace."

"I'll have to cut the lesson short. It's time to go. Stay close behind me. I don't want to lose you in the bustle of the camp."

Focusing on the encampment, Calert uttered a few words and waved his hand in front of him to cast the concealment spell. The soldiers were doing a variety of chores. Some were cleaning and sharping their weapons, weapons that were badly damaged and corroded by the demon blood. There were those repairing shields, tack, and clothing. Calert approached one of the many campfires and listened to their conversations.

One in particular caught his attention. One of the soldiers was picking at another.

"Rafe! Why are you bothering to sharpen your sword? You don't know how to use it anyway."

All the men sitting at the campfire broke into uproarious laughter. The man that was the butt of the joke turned and scowled at his tormentor.

Then, mirthfully, he said, "You ought to ask your wife who's the expert swordsman."

All fell silent waiting to see what would happen. The first man was silent for a few moments.

Then he began to chuckle. "That whore! You better check to make sure you still have your equipment."

Everyone began to laugh, and the tension melted away.

Calert was surprised by the men's high morale. He figured it was due to the usual Xlantan bravado. Calert and the boy continued to wander amongst the men. He decided he should find the commander and make his presence known. During his search, he passed many wounded and sick men, but even these men, in their dire circumstances, showed their Xlantan bravado.

Calert was surprised when he came across an encampment of elves amongst the Xlantan soldiers. Finally, Calert spotted what appeared to be the command post. He approached the tent cautiously. There were, several people setting around a campfire outside the tent. There were guards posted around the perimeter just beyond the light cast by the fire. So that they wouldn't be silhouetted against the backdrop of the fire. There were two

Xlantan's, a Halhoren woman, one of the hoof people, and an elf. Calert decided not to introduce himself immediately. He wanted to eavesdrop on their conversation. He stood in the dark listening. That's when he noticed the small, winged demon sitting with the humans.

The demon was saying, "My spies have returned and they said that the one the demons were waiting for has arrived." "The conversation was interrupted when a young soldier approached one of the men by the campfire. Calert guessed the age of the soldier at about sixteen seasons. The soldier saluted and waited, fidgeting nervously, to be given permission to speak.

The man that the soldier was standing by said with irritation coloring his voice, "Speak up, man!"

"There is someone here that wishes to speak with you," blurted out the guard anxiously.

"I'm busy! Tell him to come back tomorrow."

"No, I'll speak with you now!" came a sharp retort from the darkness.

Then an elf girl stepped from the shadows into the flickering light of the campfire with a male companion close behind.

"By the way," she continued, "I at least have the courtesy to announce myself, not like those that lurk in the dark, shrouded under a concealment spell."

The elf girl then looked right at the spot where Calert and Darith stood.

Those around the campfire stood, searching the darkness for the spy, weapons at the ready.

One of the men said, with deadly intent, "Show yourself or else."

Calert was surprised and impressed that this elf girl could detect his spell.

Resting his hand on Darith's shoulder, he said, "Wait here until I get this straightened out."

Calert stepped into the firelight revealing himself. All turned to face him. The surprised and embarrassed guards, with spears poised in a threatening manner, surrounded the infiltrator.

The man that the young soldier had addressed asked in a commanding manner, "Who are you, and why are you skulking around my encampment?"

Before Calert could speak, another soldier drug Darith into the firelight by the scruff of the neck.

"Are there anymore of you out there?" the man asked angrily.

"No," answered Calert.

"My name is Calert. I'm a Kelatan Monk."

The man interrupted Calert. "Just because, you're a monk doesn't give you the right to spy!" growled the irate man.

"You're right, I apologize for my transgression," apologized Calert. "The answer to your question," he continued, "I'm here to help defeat the demon army."

A little less anger in his voice, the man interrogating Calert asked, "How can a monk help us?"

"I'm not just a monk. I'm a wizard of considerable wherewithal." Then, looking at the elf girl, Calert said, "I'm obviously mot the only one here that possesses strong magic. Who, may I ask, are you young lady?"

The elf girl now found that she was the center of attention. "My name is Alaquin, and this is my friend Carric," She answered

Then she glanced back at her companion. Calert scrutinized Alaquin carefully. He suspected that the elf girl had strong feelings for the man, more then just friendship.

Calert didn't know how she was able to detect the subtle stress that his magic had put on the Firmament. He had used Spiritual Magic or Magic of the Essence. This magic shouldn't have fallen into her realm of knowledge. Elf Magic was dissimilar and was based on different precepts than Spiritual magic.

Calert, unable to resist the urge, began to probe her aura but found his efforts thwarted. Alaquin glared back at him.

She said in a low, nearly guttural voice, dripping with ire, "Don't try that again, monk!"

Even though his examination was truncated, he was able to detect the Essence of her magic. Calert's discovery was extraordinarily miraculous. It bordered on the realm of impossibility. This elf girl possessed both Spiritual and Elf Magic.

The man who had been questioning Calert, sensed the tension building between the newcomers, and knew he had to regain control of the situation before it spiraled beyond redemption.

"I'm Captain Longsleeve, commander of the Xlantan forces." Then he introduced the others around the campfire. He introduced the leader of the Elf forces last.

"This is, Supreme Commander, Trantwan."

Trantwan had the typical elf characteristics: slim, light skinned, and shockingly pale hair which gently brushed his shoulders. He also emanated an air of cruelty. Although elves were aloof, they weren't usually a cruel lot. Calert immediately disliked Trantwan. Introductions completed, Captain Longsleeve, with an open hand gesture, invited Alaquin and Calert to sit across the campfire from him. Once everyone was seated, Captain Longsleeve instructed the guards to return to their posts.

The Captain turned his attention to Alaquin and asked, "What is your purpose in coming here?"

"I've also come to offer help."

Then she turned to the demon and asked, "I heard you saying something about a new power figure."

Captain Longsleeve was a little vexed at Alaquin for preempting his question, but he decide not to interrupt because he was also interested in this new development.

Calert watched and listened. He feared that he knew who the this person was, but this also gave him an opportunity to study those gathered here. He sensed that Trantwan had a strong dislike for Alaquin. Captain Longsleeve was a strong and competent leader. Schwellen was an angry woman, and Clodtrip was truly concerned for those he defended. Demons were hard to read, so he couldn't draw any definite conclusions concerning it. Alaquin was the most mystifying. How could an elf have spiritual magic, a magic inherently human? The only possibility that would explain this anomaly is that she had some human lineage. It was probably the reason Trantwan didn't like her.

The demon turned to Alaquin to answer her question.

"I was informed by my spy that a woman with short and extremely black hair was the one that they were waiting for and this woman possesses the Crystals of Power. She is presently freeing more demons from the dimension that they have been imprisoned in for so many years."

The demon redirected his gaze towards the snapping, crackling, and whistling embers in the waning fire.

Alaquin said with a sadness in her voice, "That's what I was afraid of."

Captain Longsleeve, detecting the sadness, asked, "Do you know this woman?"

Alaquin shook her head in the affirmative. The firelight highlighting the golden glow of her hair.

Calert interjected, "Her name is Crysillnia."

The Captain turned to Calert and asked, "How do you know her?"

"She was my apprentice," Calert answered.

Alaquin flashed an accusative glance at Calert, then queried angrily, "Then why didn't you do a better job of protecting her?"

Calert shrugged and said, "I underestimated the influence the Crystals would have over her. Also the dark side of her magic was more powerful than the light. Crysillnia's light magic was driven from her and has taken harbor in this boy."

Calert, warmly, placed his arm around Darith's shoulder. The boy had nestled up to Calert's side and had fallen asleep.

"It's useless making recriminations. We need to focus on ways to defeat her," Interjected Captain Longsleeve.

"I agree," said Trantwan in support.

Schwellen spoke. "How do we defeat an army of creatures that are so hard to kill."

"We need to discover what their weaknesses are and exploit them. There isn't any creature alive that doesn't have a weakness of some sort," answered Clodtrip.

Everyone turned their attention to the demon.

"Do you have any suggestions?" Captain Longsleeve asked.

"Fire. We demons are highly combustible. Our hide is tough, but our blood will burn readily. Once you pierce the hide, if you can ignite the fluids oozing from the wound, the demon will light up like a torch."

Captain Longsleeve replied, "Good. During the lull, I've had my men constructing catapults. My intentions were to bombard the demons with boulders and fireballs. We'll just use the fireballs then, and I'll have some of my greener troops collecting and rolling pitch balls."

Calert suggested, "Maybe Alaquin can disperse the fireballs while they are above the horde giving them wider coverage and making them more effective."

Alaquin turned towards Calert and replied curtly. "No! I plan on confronting Crysillnia. She's my blood. I have hopes of talking her down. You stay and disperse the fireballs."

Calert opened his mouth to argue the point but, realizing it would be futile, acquiesced.

Trantwan said, "I'll have my archers tip their arrows with fire."

Captain Longsleeve acknowledged Trantwan's plan with a nod in the affirmative, then said, "We'll keep the elf archers behind the assault line on the left flank and the catapults will be on the right flank."

The group spent the remainder of the night discussing battle tactics and plans.

CHAPTER 38

Kanef and Simentoo waited until the sun had risen before approaching the encampment of soldiers laying siege to the city. The morning dawned bright and crisp, hinting at the possibility of a warm sunshiny day, not typical weather for this time of year. Usually Caspar was beset by low, dark clouds and cold, misting rains or snow.

When Kanef approached the sentry on duty, the man lowered his spear and ordered him to halt.

Kanef asked, "Who is in command here?"

"Nobleman Asmoth," was the sentry's curt reply.

"Take me to him," commanded Kanef.

"My orders are not to disturb him while he and his officers are in the strategy tent," replied the young sentry, insolently.

Not to be slighted, Kanef stood his ground. "Soldier do you not recognize me?"

The soldier, weapon at the ready, closely scrutinized Kanef and Simentoo. "No, sir. I don't know, either one of you."

Sargent Krylan was making his rounds of the sentry posts, and overheard the argument. He quickly arrived on the scene.

"Lower your spear, soldier, and address the Prince with respect."

The soldier lowered his weapon, knelt before Kanef, and stuttered an apology.

Simentoo felt pity for the boy. He couldn't be much past his sixteenth season. The boy was quite pallid.

Sargent Krylan kneeled before Kanef. "I apologize for the ignorance of this poorly educated soldier."

"Stand! The both of you!" commanded Kanef, a flicker of anger crossing his face.

The boy's pallor became even more pale, if that was possible, thought Simentoo.

Then Kanef changed his stark and angry expression to a light-hearted, smile. He clasped the Sargent's sword calloused, hand and pulled the gruff soldier towards him, embracing the Captain of The Guards warmly. Krylan returned the embrace, grinning from ear to ear.

"Its been a long time," said Kanef.

"You were the best student I ever had. Let me have a look at you, boy," said the Sargent as he took a step back. "You look a bit thin, but, other than that, you don't look any worse for the wear."

"I need to see Asmoth. I understand that he's in command of the troops," said Kanef.

"You hear correct. He's a bit pompous and flashy for my taste, but I believe he's a quite capable leader. Follow me, I'll take you to him."

Krylan shoulder his way through the gathering crowd of soldiers which quickly parted and dropped to their knees when they recognized Kanef.

The three entered the dimly lit tent. It took their eyes a few minutes to adjust. Asmoth was sitting at a table on which the plans of the city were laid out. There were several officers, including High General Charranif, heatedly discussing their options. When they recognized who had entered the tent, all stood at attention, except Asmoth.

Asmoth and Kanef made eye contact. The long-standing animosity between the two was tangible, but nothing was said.

Asmoth commanded, gruffly. "Everyone leave. I need to speak with Prince Kanef alone."

The tent emptied quickly. Kanef stood unmoving. Silence blanketed the tent.

Finally, Asmoth stood and said with sarcasm polluting his voice, "Have a seat, Prince."

Kanef approached the table stiffly and pulled up a stool across the table from Asmoth.

Kanef asked, "How did you become Commander of the Army and why?"

"Prince, you were right. Your father, King Falef, and I use the title King with some trepidation, is a despicable, evil, corrupt, and power hungry man."

Asmoth paused for a moment to allow Kanef's mind to digest what he had just said. Then he continued.

"In answer to your question, I'll tell you what has happened while you've been gallivanting around the provinces in search of those accursed Crystals. Your father has had all the prominent citizens, friend and foe alike, executed by his murderous new friends."

Asmoth paused again, glaring at Kanef, his animosity for the Prince quite apparent.

"I'm still alive because I was inspecting the borders with the High General the week the murders occurred. That is the only reason that the High General and I are still alive. When we returned to the city, it was in chaos. Fear was running rampant, and, before we entered the palace grounds, we were warned off."

"The High General insisted that I take command of the army and take vengeance for the atrocities that were committed on the citizens of Caspar. The High General said, the army would only follow someone of nobility. Since I was the only one left, I was given command of the army and nearly all the troops backed me."

"So I suspect you want to take command of the army now."

Kanef sat on the stool quietly elbows resting on the table as he caressed the several days growth on his chin. He was observing his long time rival and nemesis carefully. The decision he made now could hold long time repercussions for his future rule of Caspar.

Decision made Kanef responded.

"No. I leave the command of the army in your hands, but I will stand beside you, at all times, to advise you. If your decisions are detrimental, I'll take command. I see no reason, at this time, to confuse the troops any further. Their loyalties are most likely stretched to the brink of their understanding as it is. Plus the fact that I've been out of Caspar for far too long. My face isn't familiar to many of the men, and they need a leader they can recognize on sight in these uncertain times."

Asmoth's was taken aback. He hadn't expected to keep command of the army when Kanef had walked into the tent. Astonishment and shock framed his face. Asmoth's opinion of Kanef changed slightly.

The High General rushed into the tent.

"The King has moved his troops outside the city walls. They're forming an assault line. I've ordered our troops to arms and to take up a defensive formation."

Kanef looked across the table at Asmoth and said, "There's something not right about this. My father could hold up in the city for a long time. He's up to something."

"I agree, but what?" questioned Asmoth.

The High General turned to Kanef and asked, "What do you wish me to do, Prince?"

"Asmoth is in command," replied Kanef. Charranif was surprised but appeared pleased with this unexpected turn of events.

Asmoth answered the High General as Charranif turned towards him. "I leave that up to you. You're the High General."

"Permission to leave, sir," said Charranif, as he saluted by crossing his arms across his chest, fists clenched and standing at attention.

"Permission granted."

The High General turned and exited the tent.

Asmoth and Kanef left the tent to inspect the preparations being made for the impending battle. The din and clamor of the bustling camp were deafening. Soldiers were rushing around chaotically, gathering up their gear and weapons. Curses were being flung around copiously as men bumped into each other while they rushed through the camp, trying to find their squadrons.

Kanef's attention was drawn to a section of the camp where men were donning metal suits.

Pointing at them, he asked, "What is that? I've never seen anything like it."

"That is our heavy calvary. This is a concept that your father has been developing, in secrecy, for many years," answered Asmoth.

"I have been gone a long time. I wasn't aware he had anything like this," continued Kanef.

"Not many were aware, although most of the Noblemen suspected something was going on," said Asmoth.

"I happened across it, by accident, one day while hunting near the Ice Cap Mountains. I kept the discovery to myself."

"Why?" queried Kanef.

"I don't know. I figured the King would inform everyone when he was good and ready."

Simentoo was amazed at this new, Heavy Cavalry concept. Men completely covered in steel from head to toe. The armor was made from strips of Keltan Steel bound together by leather bindings. Simentoo could imagine what an enemy would think as these alien warriors bore down on them, the sun reflecting off the highly polished armor. They would probably think they were being assaulted by the Gods.

Simentoo happened across men donning suits of armor after he had left the tent. He was walking through the camp inspecting the men's preparations, a habit left over from when he was a captain in the Lenarian Guards. Instinctively, he caressed the remnants of the flaming sword adorning the front of his well-worn army tunic.

The Heavy Cavalry moved into their battle array, fifty men across three lines deep. The horses on which these men were mounted appeared to be ordinary work horses. The horses were also partially clad in armor with face, chest, and leg plates.

Each man was armed with a heavy spear, sword, knife, and a spiked ball attached to a wooden handle by a short chain. The men were sitting on a leather seat strapped onto the horse's back. This seat also had footholds which made it easier to mount the horses and gave the cavalryman a better purchase and stability on the horse so that he wouldn't slide off.

Simentoo's thoughts were disturbed by a blast from a horn. Looking out across the open field, he watched as the enemy went on the offensive. They were putting their infantry into motion. When the enemy had reached midfield, the High General ordered the first wave of his Heavy Cavalry to attack.

The first line moved forward at a walk. Then the horses were urged into a trot, and finally the animals were given free reign and whipped into a full gallop. As the first wave reached its full stride, the second wave was launched. The Caparian archers began to fire on the advancing enemy infantry, but the holes left by the fallen were quickly filled.

King Falef's first line of infantry carried spears with long iron shafts that came to a point and body length shields. When the Casparian cavalry came within range, the enemy infantry launched their spears and fell back behind the second line. This line had the same style of shield but they carried a heavy handled long spear.

The long, pointed, iron spears were able to pierce the Casparian armor of horse and man alike. A deafening din of crying and screaming men and horses filled the bright and quickly warming morning air. As they crashed to the ground, some of the horses were crippled and others were in their death throes. But Falef's infantry was unable to break the charge.

When a horn sounded, two blasts, the second line of King Falef's infantry stopped, kneeled, and planted their shields and spears in the ground. The spears protruded from the wall of shields. Then a third line of infantry placed themselves behind the kneeling men and placed their shields in a similar manner that protected them and the men in front from the Casparian archers.

The Casparian horses balked at this impediment. Some of the horses stopped in mid stride, unseating their riders. Others tried to turn causing them to collide with the horse beside it. Chaos reigned. A third horn blast sounded and, up to now well camouflaged and hidden demons erupted around the panicky horses causing even more terror and chaos. The demon scent created pandemonium amongst the Casparian Cavalry, as the wide-eyed and maddened horses attempted to flee from the hateful demons.

The unseated cavalrymen who weren't trampled to death by their horses were mauled by the demons. The demons even pulled some of the stricken cavalrymen from their horses. At times, the horses were pulled down with their riders. The infantry now joined with the demons in the carnage and slaughter.

The Casparian High General ordered a retreat. As the horn blast was initiated, the Casparian Armies flanks were assaulted by other well concealed demons in the field to their left, and demons poured out of the forest on their right.

Kanef turned to Asmoth and said, "I knew it."

The two of them went to help the men on the left flank fighting desperately to keep from being overrun. Simentoo was engaged with demons on the right flank.

The Casparian soldiers fought desperately but were slowly being pushed backwards. Simentoo knew unless there was some Devine Intervention that the Casparian Army was doomed to the same extinction as the Lenarian Army. The only difference would be his death this time which he preferred over being the only survivor.

$$* \quad * \quad *$$

It was midday and Jarret was listening to the dire report of the scout who had returned from Caspar City. Jarret was looking out across the plain to the distant forest while he listened. Jarret wiped the sweat from his brow. He thought, this is an unusually warm day for this time of year.

Something unusual, coming from the direction of the mountains, caught his attention. It must be a mirage, Jarret thought. It looked like the rocks were moving.

"What does that look like to you?" Jarret asked his second in command, nodding his head towards the point in question.

Latcin looked in the direction Jarret indicated. "It appears that the mountain has decided it no longer wishes to stay where it was. One of my scouts is returning. Maybe he can enlighten us on the straying mountain."

The scout pulled his horse up short in front of Jarret and Latcin pointing back the way he had come.

He said, "The trolls are on the move."

"Did you ask them where they were going and for what purpose?" "No, Commander," replied the scout with a sharp snap of respect in his voice.

Latcin addressed Jarret. "Supreme Commander, I think someone should go and talk with the trolls and discover their plans."

Jarret grinned. The title Supreme Commander was an interesting creation, so the Halhoren could pay deference to Jarret without calling him King. The Halhoren are ardently independent and recognized no sovereign non-Halhoren.

"I'm inclined to agree with you."

"Shall I go Supreme . . ."

"Just call me by name. No need for titles. As far as I'm concerned, we're equals," Jarret said, cutting Latcin off in mid title. "No. I'll go but, I wish you to accompany me."

Latcin bowed his head in acquiescence.

Jarret urged his mount forward. Latcin raised an open hand and five other Halhoren fell in behind. Jarret and Latcin galloped side-by-side across the plains in the direction of the trolls. Jarret couldn't estimate how many trolls there were, but they were a formidable force. They slowed their mounts to a trot as they approached the troll army. Jarret didn't want to alarm the trolls, if that was possible.

One of the trolls approached the intruders but said nothing. Finally, realizing that the troll wasn't going to initiate any dialog, Jarret spoke.

"May I speak with your Commander."

The troll, standing motionless, was still silent. After several minutes had past, he responded with a deep grating voice.

"Trolls have no commanders. We make our decisions as a collective, on all things. You may speak with me."

"It appears you are heading towards Caspar City." Jarret stated.

"You are correct."

"What are your intentions?"

"That is troll business and none of yours," responded the troll, irritably.

Jarret, realizing his mistake in his method of questioning, changed his tactics.

"We are going to Caspar City to reinforce the embattled Casparian Army."

The troll, showing no emotion, replied, "We are going to help Simentoo, a Troll Brother."

"Then, since we have a common goal, maybe we should travel and work together."

The troll responded, as he turned to join his companions who had continued on in their travels, "Do as you wish."

*   *   *

Simentoo, bruised, bloody, and near exhaustion had just dispatched a Cave Dweller. He was leaning on his sword, hoping for temporary respite. He glanced over the battlefield and became disheartened. The Casparian Army was in disarray. There was no definitive line of defense. The battle had turned into more of a brawl than a cohesively executed battle. In other words, it appeared to be every man for himself.

Simentoo was struck from behind. He fell to the ground dropping his sword. Simentoo rolled as a club arced through the air in an attempt to crush his skull. The club was being wielded by a, rather petite demon, as demons go. Simentoo had to roll over a dead soldier, to avoid the potentially devastating blow.

The soldier's helmet had a huge dent in it and coagulating blood was pooling under the corpse. Simentoo was surprised to discover that the corpse was none other than High General Charranif. Simentoo, still unable to regain his feet, had to continue rolling in an attempt to avoid the persistent assault by the demon. He rolled over another prone body, that of Asmoth. He was breathing, albeit shallowly.

Simentoo desperately grasped the broadsword lying at Asmoth's side. Still on his back, he positioned himself so that he was facing the demon as it continued its attack. Although the broad sword was constructed for slashing and not thrusting, he thrust the sword into the belly of the onrushing demon. The momentum of the grotesque creature added power to Simentoo's thrust.

The sword barely penetrated the creature's nearly impenetrable hide. Using the leverage of the sword and the creature's momentum,

Simentoo catapulted the demon over him. Rolling head over heels, Simentoo followed up his offensive, ending up on top of the creature. Using all of his weight and strength, he drove the sword all the way through the creature's mid section, pinning it to the ground. The creature, oozing bright green viscous fluids from the wound, let out a final ear splitting and anguished cry before it died.

Simentoo sprang up and away from the death throes of the writhing creature to avoid being splattered by the acidic, viscous fluid that was the life blood of the creature. His attention was quickly drawn away from the dying creature by loud screams of men and horses, emanating from the forest. Then, like a summer windstorm, Halhoren Horsemen burst from the confines of the forest, followed in short order by raging trolls.

These unexpected reinforcements raised the morale of the beleaguered Casparian troops which energized their efforts. The demons were equally bewildered. An apparent victory had been unexpectedly wrenched from their grasp. This welcome deliverance brought a welling of joy to Simentoo's heart and tears began to blur his vision.

Simentoo reached instinctively for his empty scabbard when he heard something or someone approaching him from behind.

A disembodied voice calmed him, saying, "It's just me. Great sight to see, isn't it?"

Simentoo turned, grinning from ear to ear, to answer a weary and disheveled Kanef.

"Yes, my Prince, quite a sight."

A look of pained disgust painted Kanef's face, and he waved his hand in a negative manner at the formality of address Simentoo had used, but he said nothing.

Within minutes the demoralized demon army and their allies were routed. The Halhoren's harassed demons, Mountains Tribesman, and Cave Dwellers, exacting retribution all the way back to the mountains. The trolls mopped up any stragglers unfortunate enough to be left behind.

Kanef took the reigns of command since the High General was dead and Asmoth was incapacitated. He order that the battlefield be scoured for Casparian and enemy wounded. The Casparian wounded were to be carefully tended to, but the enemy wounded were to be dispatched without prejudice, whether human or demon. His justification was anyone that served the Forces of Darkness was beyond redemption. This harsh, unyielding attitude would characterize Kanef for the remainder of his life.

The next morning Kanef called for a briefing with the remainder of the Caparian Army Officers which consisted of only a handful. He was discussing possible strategies for regaining control of the fortified city. The meeting was interrupted by an out of breath sentry.

Kanef, annoyed by the disruption, turned an acerbic eye on the soldier.

He said with an intensity that nearly unnerved the interloper, "This better be good or you'll find yourself on latrine duty."

"Si-Sir! The city gates are open and they're flying a flag of surrender," the sentry managed to stutter.

Expressions of disbelief mirrored the faces of all those present.

"What's dear old dad up to now?" said Kanef and then he motioned for his horse to be brought to him.

"Want to come with me?" he asked Simentoo.

"Sure." replied Simentoo.

After mounting, Kanef turned to the other Officers.

"Clanton, you've been promoted to Captain, and Krylan you are now a Lieutenant."

The two newly promoted soldiers, standing at attention, helmets tucked under their arms, bowed their heads in acceptance and respect.

"We'll need an escort," ordered Kanef.

Six soldiers were chosen by the newly promoted Captain Clanton.

"You're in command until I return," Kanef instructed the Captain.

Kanef urged his mount towards the city. The escort took up protective positions around Kanef and Simentoo, two in the lead, two as rear guard and one on each side.

"I have a favor to ask of you," said Kanef as they approached the city.

Simentoo replied, "If its within my power, I'll oblige you."

Kanef continued, "With the death of High General Charranif . . ." Simentoo glanced over at Kanef. He suspected where the conversation was heading. "I want you to take his position, if you would. With your experience, and you are Casparian by birth, you are the most qualified for the position."

They rode on for a few more paces before Simentoo answered. "I accept."

Kanef, smiling, turned to Simentoo and said, "Thank you."

Simentoo replied, "No. Thank you for the honor that you have bestowed."

The two fell silent as they neared the city. The only sound was the steady, rhythmic drumming of the horses hooves as they cantered across the open ground.

Kanef ordered his small contingent to halt when a rider exited the city gates. Kanef watched the riders approach while surveying the surrounding terrain for a possible ambush.

"I don't trust my father. Its not like him to just surrender."

Simentoo had been scrutinizing the approaching rider carefully. The man was wearing the colors of the Palace Guard.

"Doesn't he look familiar?"

Kanef now focused his full attention on the approaching horseman.

"Yes, Simentoo. I believe he does. In fact, I think he's one of the men we rescued from the dungeon."

"I wonder why he's speaking for your father?"

"Well, we shall know soon enough," replied Kanef.

The Palace Guard, with a somber expression, pulled his mount up before the lead escorts. Kanef and Simentoo's escorts had their weapons at the ready. The rider saluted Kanef.

Then he said, "I wish to address his Majesty, King Kanef of Caspar."

Kanef's guards turned to him in askance. Kanef, taken slightly aback by this formal request, said nothing but urged his mount forward. He stopped directly in front of the man and then acknowledged the salute. The Palace Guard pulled his sword from its resting place which precipitated a panicked response from Kanef's escort. Kanef even reached for his weapon.

But the man presented the sword, hilt first, to Kanef with the phrase for unconditional surrender.

"I abdicate by surrendering the Sword of the City."

The sword was the man's personal weapon. The offering of his sword was symbolic.

Kanef accepted the sword, then asked, "Why isn't my father surrendering the city?"

The man grinned and then answered Kanef. "Well, the problem is . . . He has disappeared. He slipped out on us during the night, as we besieged the palace."

"Besieged the palace?" Kanef queried.

"Yes. After you and Simentoo left us, we decided to stay behind and see what we could do from inside the city. We were surprised at the ease we were able to find allies and ferment discord. While you were fighting out here, we were overthrowing the former King within the city walls. He holed up inside the palace grounds and when we finally managed to breach his defenses, he was nowhere to be found."

"He must have used the escape passage that ends in the swamp," Kanef said, as he turned to one of the guards by his side. "Return to camp and tell Captain Clanton to send a search party to the swamp and see if we can pick up my father's trail. Maybe we'll get lucky."

The guard saluted Kanef and, quickly, in his excitement, reigned his mount around causing the animal to rear and paw at the air before the angry beast leapt forward eyes wide with pain and fear.

"Sorry, but I don't know your name," said Kanef.

"Palek Cralion, at your service, my liege."

"Lead on then, Palek. Take us into your city."

"Yes, my liege," Palek replied with a huge grin painting his face.

He turned his mount towards the city. Palek urged his horse forward by lightly digging his heels into the animals flanks.

CHAPTER 39

Alaquin and Carric were standing on an, insignificant knoll rising above the battlefield, watching the sunrise. The morning was cool and crisp. The thick saw grasses, prevalent on the Xlantan Plains, appeared to bow in reverence to the rising sun as a light breeze caressed their golden crowns. The clear, powder-blue skies were decorated with a collage of pure white, puffy clouds, wafting aimlessly along. The tingling created by the warming rays of the sun on their exposed skin, hinted at a hot and sultry day to come. But even the beauty of the morning couldn't mask the morbid stench of death that permeated their senses.

Carric turned to the elf girl and asked, "How do you plan on handling your niece?"

"I don't know, but first I have to find her."

Alaquin, still watching the sun drag itself slowly and methodically from its resting place, creating the illusion that the sun was rising out of the plains, stood in silence for a few moments, then continued, "I hope to talk some sense into her."

The two were standing behind the battle lines to the rear of the camp, slightly beyond its periphery. Alaquin, in deep concentration, turned towards the camp, not seeing or even hearing the clanging and clamor of men, preparing for battle and, most likely, their death.

Coming out of her trance like mood, she commented, "War is sad. All those in the camp are preparing themselves for death, humans, elves, demons and horsemen."

Tears welled up in her eyes and slowly rolled down her cheeks. Carric, towering over the Elf Girl, wrapped her in his arms in an attempt to soothe her. She pressed her face deep into his chest and began to sob. Carric gently caressed her long, pale-golden locks.

He felt heartsick for the woman he loved and at the same time helpless for his inability to heal her breaking heart.

Their moment of truth was broken by the calamitous sounds of battle. Carric and Alaquin turned towards the battlefield but could see no advancing enemy. The camouflaged, spike filled trenches that the Xlantan soldiers had dug as a first line of defense were erupting in flames which were created by elf magic. The magic could only be tripped by demons being impaled by the sharp wooden spikes placed at the bottom of the trenches.

"An invisibility spell, she must be using an invisibility spell!" Alaquin shouted as she began to run towards the front line.

Chaos had enveloped the encampment as frightened camp followers ran mindless around the camp not sure what to do or where to hide. Demons were frightening enough but an invisible enemy was horrifying.

Alaquin and Carric tried desperately to thread their way through the ensuing madness with little success. When a tall and rather large woman with braided hair flailing around her head and face ran into her, the large woman's progress wasn't hindered in the least by Alaquin's slight build.

The air whooshed out of Alaquin's lungs when she landed flat on her back. Disoriented and confused by the trauma, she fought desperately to keep her wits about her. She slowly regained her breath and composure. Her eyes refocused and awareness returned. She took Carric's proffered hand. He pulled her to her feet with ease and asked if she was alright.

Incensed by the woman's carelessness, she said, "Enough of this foolishness! Stay close behind me."

Alaquin then erected a protective envelope around her and Carric. One that wouldn't harm others, just ward them off or push them out of the way. The two of them had no further mishaps on their way to the front lines. Schwellen and Clodtrip were already there, standing behind a prickly wall of shields and spears formed by the Xlantan infantry. Alaquin approached them from behind.

She asked, "Have any of them managed to cross the trenches?"

Schwellen nearly jumped out of her skin. She instinctively freed her sword from its restraint as she pivoted.

Alaquin backed away with hands up and said, "It's just me. Alaquin!"

Schwellen, with an irascible inflection tinging her voice, said, "Don't do that to me," and stomped her foot in frustration. "I nearly skewered you." "I'm sorry," Alaquin apologized.

Schwellen waved her off, her scowl changing to a grimace when she tried to smile.

"Not that I'm aware of," Schwellen answered. "But how can one be sure, when you can't see the devilish monsters." In answer to her question, a scream reverberated from behind them as a young woman, one of the camp followers, was cut to ribbons with no apparent cause.

Alaquin's attention was drawn away from the horrible sight by a low thwacking sound. She turned her attention back to the battlefield in time to see a series of fire pots launched by the Xlantan catapults. Then a streak of light, a deep red color, struck the pitch filled fire pots, dispersing the burning contents over a wide area. The burning precipitation coated the demons with fire. The demons, so affected, were now visible to the defenders.

Alaquin realized that this was limited to a small number of the creatures. The fire pot assault couldn't possible reveal the entire attacking host, and the flying demons would never be exposed. Then it occurred to her that she was standing on the material that had been excavated from the trenches. It had been scattered so that the enemy would not be aware of the trap that had been set for them.

Alaquin acted quickly. She called on the Rune Magic. Once the runes were formed, she sent them up and down the line. Astonished warriors took a step backwards as the multicolored runes appeared to dance and pirouette as if they were living creatures performing a strange ritual of their very own.

When the runes were complete, Alaquin began to chant the Rune Song. When her voice reached its highest peak, the runes vanished, and a wind, starting out as a light breeze, blew across the battlefield, concentrating its energies behind the trenches. The wind's velocity began to swirl and increase in power, creating a vortex which sucked the dirt excavated from the trenches into the sky.

There was a loud crack, followed by a sizzling sound and then the suspended soil rained down on attackers and defenders alike, coating all with a thin coat of dirt. The ground shook and reverberated. Everyone, on both sides of the trenches were either staggered or knocked off their feet. The flying demons, before not visible, winked into view and then incinerated.

Alaquin was knocked to the ground by the violent confrontation of her and Crysillnia's magic. She lithely sprang to her feet. She spotted the demon that had killed the woman a few moments before. It was sprawled out on the ground. Shaking its huge head in confusion, the beast was futilely trying to take flight, but one of its huge webbed wings was severely twisted and broken.

The creature turned in Alaquin's direction. It balanced itself on two powerful rear legs. It was about the size of a horse. It had two shorter forelegs equipped with three very large and extremely sharp talons on each leg for rending and tearing. It had a raptor shaped mouth and three upward curving horns above its prominent eye brows. The demon's eyes were a piercing yellow, and the pupils contracted and expanded continuously. Its body was covered with large brown triangular shaped scales. The creature had a long, whip-like tail with three large bony spikes which it flicked nervously.

The nervous flick of the demon's tail reminded Alaquin of a cat tracking its prey. Even with a broken wing, the creature moved with an unexpected alacrity as it charged her. Alaquin, mesmerized by the demon's hypnotic gaze, was brought back to her senses by a shout from Carric.

Alaquin quickly erected her envelope of protection against the assault. The creature bounced off the shield with an ear piercing shriek of pain and frustration. Alaquin called on the spiritual side of her magic and formed a bright blue ball of fire in the palm of her hand. When the creature attacked again, she dropped her protective envelope so she could throw the ball of fire at the creature. The ball of fire hit the demon squarely, engulfing it completely. The creature gave one final shriek of pain before it was consumed by the intense fireball.

Alaquin turned to the battlefield. The demons cover of invisibility had dispersed, and the creatures were retreating. They were being decimated by the fire pots and the elves' flaming arrows. She sighed with relief and thought to herself, another catastrophe averted.

A dirt covered and scowling Schwellen approached Alaquin. "Couldn't you have come up with a cleaner solution?" Then she broke into a hardy laugh and gave Alaquin a slap on the back, nearly knocking the elf girl to the ground. "Good job." Calert startled Alaquin when he approached her from behind and said, "I found that interesting and unexpected."

Alaquin turned to face Calert and asked, "What, wizard?", a hint of distrust shading her voice.

"Crysillnia's and your magic clashed, nullifying the affects of both. That's was the reason for the loud crackling sound, the ground quaking, and the demons becoming visible."

Alaquin didn't care for the wizard. She felt that he was somehow responsible for Crysillnia's situation. She turned away from Calert rather abruptly.

"If you wish to continue our conversation, you'll have to follow me. I haven't had anything to eat, and it appears I've a chance to remedy that oversight."

Calert, not at all abashed by the elf girl's rudeness, followed her back to the campfire. There was stew simmering in a huge kettle, suspended from hook above a bed of hot but ebbing coals. The black cast iron kettle was hung from a cast iron tripod centered over the dying embers. There was a ladle hanging from an extension attached to the top of the tripod. It extended beyond the fire so that the handle wouldn't become too hot.

Usually one of the camp followers was tending the stew, to stir it and ladle the stew out, but there were none around. They were frightened away by the attack. The wooden bowls and spoons were scattered across the ground. Evidently, in the confusion, someone had stumbled over them in their frenzied flight.

Alaquin picked up a couple of the bowls and spoons. She inspected them for cleanliness and wiped off any dirt she found. She lifted the lid on the kettle, setting it aside, and ladled out a bowl of stew. She handed the bowl with a spoon to Carric and then filled her bowl. She stooped down on her haunches and began to eat.

Carric had sat down on a nearby boulder. He watched the wizard and Alaquin in silence as he ate his morning repast. Carric couldn't help it, but he thought it was sort of comical, as Alaquin tried to ignore the wizard, while he stood in silence watching her, hands crossed in front of him, waiting patiently for a signal from her to continue their conversation.

Alaquin sat down on the ground, legs crossed. She cradled the half-empty bowl in her lap.

She looked up at Calert and said with vexation, "Well! Are you going to continue, or am I to anticipate the conversation?" Waiting for Calert to respond, she absentmindedly stirred the contents in her bowl.

Calert grinned, enigmatically. "What I had intended to say was that your power and Crysillnia's are near equal. Crysillnia's power has matured more quickly than it should have. In fact, since Darith has a portion of her magic, she logically should be a lot weaker not stronger."

"Speaking of the boy, where is he and how did he come to be in possession of my niece's magic?" Alaquin asked, suspiciously.

"He's sleeping." Then Calert related the boy's adventure, as he understood it. "But our main concern is you and Crysillnia with the obviously formidable magic you both possess. A direct confrontation between the two of you could rip the fabric of the Firmament apart."

Alaquin shoveled the remainder of her stew down her throat. She put the empty bowl aside and stood, facing the wizard, she asked. "How did she gain this strong magic so quickly?"

"I'm not sure but suspect she is channeling the power of the Crystals."

Their conversation was interrupted by the thump-thump of the catapults being released.

"The demons must be attacking again," cried Carric, as he dropped his near empty bowl of stew splattering the ground with its remnants. The three rushed to the front line.

The demons were concentrating their attack on the right flank, behind which the catapults were situated. They were carrying various large objects with designs of using them to bridge the trenches.

The three of them rushed up the line with difficulty, dodging nervous soldiers and other obstacles. By the time they reached the point of contention, the demons had successfully crossed the trenches, and there was a general melee ensuing. The screaming of dying demons and men and the clash and clang of weapons was deafening.

The larger monsters had sacrificed themselves against the wall of spears and shields of the Xlantan troops. The weight of these creatures became too much for the soldiers to hold and the line collapsed. The demon horde poured over demon and man alike, crushing both and leaving broken men and demons in their wake.

Soldiers were fighting desperately, trying to protect the catapults.

Calert said to Alaquin, "Hurry we must protect the catapults."

Calert, Alaquin, and Carric went to the aid of the soldiers defending the catapults. One had been lost and was in flames. Calert and Alaquin began to throw flaming balls of fire at the enemy.

Their attack was so extreme and unexpected, the demons backed off. Alaquin quickly started an incantation to enfold the remaining catapult batteries in her envelope of protection.

"Hurry, Calert! Get reinforcements! I can't hold out for long!" she shouted.

The demons threw themselves against the magic shield. Her shield of protection, held but it was so weakened, it didn't kill the demons. Her power was overextended. Calert went in search of reinforcements and found that they were already on the way. The Xlantan's had thrown their own platforms over the trenches and were moving their center, in a pincher movement, to attack the demons from the rear. The elves, along with Clodtrip and his warriors, were moved up to plug the hole in case of an attack on the recently vacated center.

The demons responded immediately to the offensive move made by the Xlantan's. They launched a new wave of attacks against the entire Xlantan line. The Xlantan cavalry was sent to protect the soldiers of the pincher movement. Horses screamed in wild, frenzied, fear when the demons rolled into the cavalry. The cavalrymen finally had to dismount and fight on foot because their mounts were uncontrollable. When the horses were released, they fled in a state of near madness. The cavalrymen were at disadvantage on foot, but they fought valiantly and were able to hold their own for awhile.

Calert returned to the catapults to aid Alaquin in anyway he could. Alaquin's shield was beginning to falter. She was tiring. The sun had risen high in the sky and the heat of the day battered her unmercifully. The acrid black smoke from the nearby burning catapult and pitch pots was hampering her breathing and concentration.

A few of the demons were able to penetrate the shield, and they targeted her. They wanted to take her out so that the shield protecting the catapults would cease. Carric and a few of the soldiers who were inside the shield when it was erected protected her.

Up and down the entire line, the demons were breaking through. The cavalrymen who had been having some success were being decimated. They wouldn't be able to hold out much longer.

Tanof was standing beside his sister watching the battle's progression. Talok, Tanof and a few demons were all that were left to protect Crysillnia. She ordered the remainder of the horde to attack. She reveled in her new found power. Tanof didn't like what was happening to him. He couldn't believe that he was allied with demons. The thought repulsed him. This wasn't right.

He watched his sister closely. Her attention was focused on the distant struggle for the catapults. Her face contorted with anger when it became apparent that someone else's magic was creating problems for her army. She had become extremely irate when her concealment spell had been broken, and now she was becoming even more agitated, because her rival's magic was still confounding her efforts for total victory.

"Follow me. It's time I confront, face-to-face, my nemesis," Crysillnia said, as she began to walk towards the beleaguered catapults.

Talok hefted his hammers, squeezing the handles hard, causing his massive forearm muscles to bulge, conspicuously. "I agree! I'm bored with all this standing around."

Tanof followed, quietly, dreading every step.

Schwellen was fighting beside Clodtrip. The demons had overrun their line and the once organized battle had become a free-for-all. Schwellen spotted a horse running towards her. Its eyes were rolling in their sockets, its flanks heaving and coated with a frothy sweat. When the horse ran by her, she grabbed a fist full of the beasts mane and vaulted onto the horse back.

Schwellen fought with the horse, trying to gain control of the maddened animal. The horse continued to careen down the line. Schwellen pulled the horse's head around and tried to force it to back into battle. It pawed the air in protest, nearly unseating Schwellen. She finally came to the realization that the horse was useless. Its fear of the demons was in complete control. She thought, if only she had a Halhoren horse. She dismounted and allowed the animal to flee.

She was immediately assailed by four demons. Three had clubs and the fourth had a sword with an Xlantan emblem. Demons didn't use weapons, as such. They liked to kill with their teeth, talons, or hands. The weapons they carried were for defense only. They would use them to perry blows and strikes from their enemy.

She fought with great skill and determination but was overmatched. Schwellen was knocked off her feet a backhand from one of her attackers. She lost the grip on her weapon, and it flew from her hand, landing beyond her reach. She thought she was dead, and then her attackers were overwhelmed from behind by a group of goblins.

The demons were quickly dismembered. One of the goblins stood over Schwellen. She expected the grotesque creature would finish the job that the demons had started, but the creature offered her a twisted and gnarled hand. She reluctantly accepted the proffered hand. The goblin pulled her to her feet and another handed her a sword. Then they turned their attentions back to the battle.

Schwellen looked on with amazement. There were hundreds of goblins battling the demons. Schwellen joined the unexpected allies fighting side-by-side with them. But the demons still possessed superior numbers, although the odds were becoming more evenly matched.

*   *   *

The creak of leather, the jingle of chain mail and clank of weapons were overshadowed by the rhythmic click-clack of horseshoes resounding off of the well-worn, cobblestone streets of the city. Kanef loved Caspar City. It was as far as he was concerned, the most beautiful place to live in all of Lenar, Upper or Lower. The city, constructed of stone quarried from the mountains that embraced the valley lovingly, rose out of the valley like the petals of a Mountain Rose, embossed on the sublime backdrop of the Casparian Mountains.

The Open Market square was the first part of the city one entered once past the gate. This was where anyone was allowed to trade or sell their wares ranging from agricultural to artistic to weapons. You could buy most anything here. But to hock wares deeper in the city, permits and licenses were required. This was legislation requested by the Merchants Guild to protect the more prominent and permanent merchants of the city. But today there were no peddlers in the square. It was littered with wooden cages filled with prisoners. Kanef pulled his mount up before the first line of cages.

He turned to Cralion Palek and asked with an edge of danger shadowing his voice. "Are these the traitors?" "Well," he answered nervously, quite aware of Kanef's ire, "they're not really traitors."

Kanef's piercing gaze intensified. "What is that suppose to mean?" Kanef lashed out vehemently.

Cralion shifted in his saddle, nervously. "Your father hired these men. They're mercenaries. Evidently your father suspected he would have a difficult time convincing Casparian's to ally themselves with demons. What I have gleaned from these men is that they were hired months ago and had filtered into the city in small groups over a long period of time so that they wouldn't attract undue attention."

Kanef shifted his gaze from a nervous Cralion to the caged men. They were a bedraggled, unkempt, and licentious lot. Even under the grime of battle, he could tell that they didn't have a soldier's carriage or pride. The mercenaries cowered under Kanef's scorching gaze.

Kanef reigned his mount about heading towards the inner city. He urged his horse forward by slightly squeezing the animal's flanks with the heel of his boots.

His back to Cralion, he said, nonchalantly, "Execute them. Execute them all."

The doomed men began to lament and wail, begging for forgiveness and mercy. Cralion blanched at the unexpected order and looked at the hundred or so doomed men. The soldiers guarding the cages began to bang on the sides of the enclosures to quiet the protesting men.

"Your Majesty, your Majesty." Cralion called.

Kanef reigned his mount around, a quarter turn, to face Cralion. "Yes, Corporal."

"How would you want it done?"

"You mean the executions?"

"Yes, your Majesty."

"Hang them over the parapets as a warning to anyone who might consider in aiding evil."

"By the way, Corporal, are you the highest ranking Officer in the city?" Kanef queried.

"Yes, your Majesty. In fact, I believe, I'm the lone surviving Officer of the Palace Guards."

"And you orchestrated the retaking of the city," Kanef continued.

"That is correct."

Kanef sat on his mount scrutinizing the tall, thin, dark haired man. Cralion fidgeted, nervously, with the reigns of his mount under the dark gaze of his Sovereign.

Kanef broke the silence.

"Since we don't have a Captain of the Palace Guards, I"m now promoting you to that status. You've proved that you can be counted on and can take the bull by the horns when necessary. I expect you to whip the Palace Guard back into shape, and you have my permission to use what ever means necessary."

"Thank you, my King. You can rely on me," said Cralion Palek, as he saluted Kanef, beaming with pride and excitement.

Kanef ordered, as he turned his mount back towards the inner city, "Send someone out to inform Captain Clanton that he can bring his troops into the city.

"Yes, Your Majesty!" responded the newly appointed Captain.

Simentoo grinned at the exuberance of Cralion. He thought to himself that the new Captain may regret this day when the full burden of command reared its ugly head. Simentoo's mood changed when he turned to follow Kanef. The order to kill the prisoners didn't sit well with him.

*   *   *

Falef was riding across the plains. He was heading for Xlanta. He was approaching a smashed carriage. It brought back fond memories. A cruel grin painted his face.

One of the wheels on the carriage began to turn eerily. He was startled. There was no wind to excite the wheel. He approached the carriage, cautiously, sword in his hand. There was a flash of light followed by a loud scream.

CHAPTER 40

Kenchon and his men were watching the battle that unfolded before them. It was well past midday and the Xlantan Plains spread out before them sublimely. The grasses were thick and lush and basked in ample sunshine, waving as if in welcome to the Halhorens in response to a gentle but capricious breeze. Widely scattered groves of Quignut trees dotted the horizon. The Halhorens were mesmerized. They were used to the open plains but not one as lush and beautiful as the Xlantan Plains.

Kenchon could see flashes of magic and black, sooty, smoke swirling and capering in the fickle breeze. He wasn't particularly fond of magic, but he wished Shasheek was with them. Their mysterious ally had disappeared after the defeat of the demon horde a few days back. Shasheek's magic had been instrumental in their victory, and Kenchon thought it would most likely be useful in this situation.

The breeze's intensity changed suddenly. What was once a loving and gentle caress had become a cruel and harsh cold wind. Kenchon's mount shifted it's hooves nervously, and its mane fluttered chaotically. Kenchon realized there was something seriously wrong. Halhoren mounts were unflappable and steady beasts. They did not scare easily.

Bits and pieces of grass and other refuse swirled around the Halhoren's. Their shoulder length hair flailed about their faces as if trying to flagellate them for some wrong they may have committed. Kenchon looked toward the sky and spotted something approaching in the distance.

Kenchon focused his full attention on the mysterious object in the sky. It appeared to be a huge black and ominous cloud but a more meticulous inspection when it came closer revealed the blob in the sky to be hundreds of very large birds or what appeared to be birds.

One of his men queried, "Do you suppose they're demons?"

Kenchon replied, "It wouldn't surprise me, but I hope not. We had better be prepared for any possibility. Ready your bows!" commanded Kenchon.

One of the creatures broke away from the others, heading in their direction.

Kenchon ordered, "Hold your arrows and wait for my command to loose."

The other creatures hovered in place. When the single creature approached him, Kenchon was able to discern its shape. It appeared to be a hawk but it was the biggest hawk, he had ever seen.

The hawk circled the Halhorens once as if it were trying to size them up. Then it landed a short distance away. The creature approached the wary horsemen. Its form began to transition and take the shape of a tall man in a dark robe with his cowl pulled up around his face. It was Shasheek.

Kenchon reared back, mouth agape, in total shock and surprise. He was so taken aback that he was left speechless.

Shasheek said, mirthfully, "Aren't you going to greet an old acquaintance?"

Kenchon, composure regained, answered, "I knew there was something strange about you, but I never suspected that you were a shape-shifter."

Shasheek pointed to the skies. "I brought some reinforcements, but I imagine they are becoming quite fatigued, especially fighting the high winds up there. Is it all right for them to land?"

"Yes, sure. Do whatever you want. Men put your weapons down," commanded Kenchon.

When the Halhoren's put their bows down, Shasheek motioned to those hovering above.

While the shape-shifters descended on the plains like a dark and ethereal cloud, Shasheek asked, "Did you gather up the weapons from the human and demon armies we destroyed?"

"Yes." answered Kenchon.

"Good," replied Shasheek.

It was unsettling to watch the shape-shifters land. They didn't land and then change. They would change in the air and, sort of, transcend to the ground. If one didn't know who and what they were, one would think they were wraiths, ghostly apparitions.

They all wore dark colored robes with cowls that concealed their faces. The now raging winds wrapped the loose fitting robes tight around the shape-shifters, revealing their forms to be slender and slightly bent with truncated legs.

The winds ceased, as quickly, as they had started. The air was dead calm. Kenchon's mount stomped and shifted its weight from one hoof to the other, nervously. Kenchon knew their was something gravely wrong.

A queasy feeling came over him. He felt sick to his stomach. The air and ground around Kenchon quivered and quaked. The sky above the battle, where the magic was being used, appeared to be coming apart. A black hole was forming in the sky and slowly growing.

With a worried inflection, Shasheek stated the obvious. "They're using to strong and to much magic. They've ripped a hole in the Firmament. We must hurry and see what we can do to help."

Kenchon had the weapons quickly brought forward and distributed amongst the shape-shifters. The weapons, for the most part, were of poor quality. They consisted of badly pitted and rusty swords and daggers, whatever a poor peasant could glean from refuse piles or dig up from old battlefields.

Kenchon had his men line up on the right and the shape shifters on the left, two men deep. He ordered the charge but allowed the shape shifters to set the pace. Kenchon was surprised by speed of the shape shifters. In a short time, they slammed into the chaotic melee of battle.

*   *   *

Darith was hiding behind a bush watching the horrific conflict. He knew he wasn't suppose to be here, but he had to know what was happening to his friends. Alaquin had discontinued her ineffectual efforts to protect the catapults. Calert and Alaquin were in a life and death struggle with Crysillnia. One, it would appear, they were losing. Crysillnia had the Crystals arrayed across her bosom like a jeweled necklace.

The Crystals glowed as Crysillnia drew on the magic they possessed. She appeared to be lost in the thralls of power. Her stare was blank and her eyes were dark, deep pools of madness. Her smoke smudged face was cratered with an evil grin. Her hair was disheveled and matted with human blood, and, in spots, it had been seared away by demon blood but she apparently didn't notice or care. Seeing her this way left an empty feeling in Darith's heart and made him sick to his stomach.

The dark hole that had formed in the sky had now reached the ground behind Crysillnia. A multicolored shaft of light was arcing from the tear in the fabric of the Firmament directly to the White Crystal.

Crysillnia spread her arms wide to bask in the surge of power. Her mottled hair had begun to flail about her head as if each strand was an entity in its on right. Her aura flared with a multicolored brightness that nearly blinded those watching.

Darith couldn't believe what he was seeing. Someone behind Crysillnia stepped forward sword extended. The Crystals leapt from Crysillnia's chest. An anguished scream of fury and rage emanated from her and with a backward sweep of her hand, she sent the interloper flying through the air, legs and arms flailing about him uncontrollably, as she released her magic in retaliation.

*　*　*

Tanof found himself lying with his back propped against the mutilated corpse of a demon. He had managed to survive the powerful surge of magic that Crysillnia had directed at him. His sword had taken the brunt of the energy. All that was left of it was a shriveled sliver of metal in a scorched and warped hand grip.

He had decided to move against his sister when she began to siphon energy from the tear in the Firmament. Tanof had no love for the Xlantan's or anyone else as far as that goes, but he couldn't see living in a world ruled by demons. That is, if there was a world left.

She had become obsessed with the magic she commanded, and the Crystals seemed to be the focal point of this evil obsession, so he hooked his sword under the strange necklace from which the Crystals were hung and with a flick of his wrist, he sent the Crystals flying which had precipitated her attack on him.

Tanof, carefully and quietly so as not to attract any undue attention, rolled away from the vile creature. The demons corrosive life fluids were severely burning his skin. He became nauseous, dizzy and disoriented from the excruciating pains that lanced through his body. Tanof realized that he was extremely fortunate to still be in this world.

He dropped his useless weapon and retrieved a dead Xlantan soldier's sword. Tanof pulled the dagger from his belt and used it to cut a piece of cloth from the dead soldiers uniform. Using the piece of cloth as a swab be wiped the demons blood from his neck and back. Then he quietly crept away.

*　　*　　*

Darith was frightened by the rage displayed by Crysillnia. Even though her umbilical cord to the black hole' was severed, she still possessed great power. The Crystals had landed several paces in front of her, and she held her hand out, palm up, calling for the Crystals. She raised her arm. The Crystals responded by floating into the air. She then beckoned with her finger, and the Crystals began to move in her direction, but before the Crystals could reach her they were trapped by a magical net of runes. The runes danced energetically around the Crystals before the runes faded from sight, invisible but still effective.

The ground began to quake, the air to shimmer and reverberate as the two incompatible magic energies competed for dominance.

Calert rushed to Alaquin's side and cried frantically. "You must desist! I'll take over."

Alaquin's sweat streaked face glanced over at Calert and said, "Okay, wizard!"

She released her magic and Calert began the struggle for the Crystals.

Without the support of the Crystals, Crysillnia was no match for Calert. The Crystals were being drawn away from her slowly, inexorably. The strain of her excruciating effort was evident on her face by the furrows on her brow and the twist of her mouth. It appeared that she had lost the battle for possession of the Crystals. But the Crystals struck out at Calert, hitting him with a multicolored bolt of energy that pushed him backwards and broke his hold.

The Crystals were back in Crysillnia's hands before Alaquin could react. Crysillnia, with an iniquitous glint in her eyes, flashed Calert and Alaquin a wry smile. Clutching the Crystals tightly to her bosom, she began to draw on the Crystals' energy. Her aura began to glow brightly, pulsating and changing colors rapidly.

Alaquin and Calert covered their eyes so as not to be blinded. Crysillnia raised the Crystals over her head and marshaled the Crystal's magic. She combined her magic with that of the Crystals, using the White Crystal as the focal point. Searing white light began to expand and move outwards. The light arced around her, silhouetting her. The pulsating light moved away from her, destroying everything in its path.

Everyone, including the demons that were near the expanding conflagration, stopped battling and began to flee frantically. Alaquin and Calert backed away. The ground began to quake and undulate. The sky began to shimmer. The Firmament was unraveling, and there was nothing anyone could do about it.

Calert thought to himself, she had won but exactly what had she won. The world that would be left would not be one he would want to live in. Then he heard a wild, high pitched scream. Darith sprang from his hiding place behind the bush. He ran with hands raised over his head, flailing uncontrollably.

Calert ran after the maddened boy. "Stop!"

He screamed at the boy, but Darith either didn't hear him or ignored the command. Calert nearly caught the boy, narrowly missing the his trailing tunic tail.

Crysillnia either didn't see the wild eyed assailant or didn't fear him for she did nothing to stop his headlong rush. Darith ran into the pulsating and expanding light. Crysillnia's magic focused on the point where the boy came into contact with the brilliant, pulsating, energy field. There was a flash of light and a thunderous crash. Darith was tossed into the air, arms and legs windmilling uncontrollably, and Crysillnia was thrown backwards. She was staggered by the tremendous release of energy.

Calert heard the sickening snap of breaking bones when Darith landed a few feet away. He rushed over to see if he could aid the boy. Darith was lying, in the midst of several dead soldiers, broken spears, bloody shields and swords, unconscious. Darith's right arm was bent at an odd angle and pinned beneath his body. Calert gently rolled the boy onto his back. Darith moaned in agony and his eyes fluttered, like a leaf in the wind, but he didn't regain consciousness.

Crysillnia had been driven, by the clash of energies, to the edge of the dark abyss she had created, tottering on the edge of oblivion. She looked in the direction of Alaquin just in time to see the blast of magic that Alaquin had summoned to drive her into the dark abyss of oblivion. She hurled a blast of energy at Alaquin before she was consumed by the darkness. Alaquin dodged the parting shot easily. Alaquin then cast a rune spell to seal the tear in the fabric of the Firmament, locking Crysillnia away. Alaquin rushed over to Darith and Calert to see if there was anything she could do to help. Calert had gently straightened the boy's arm and set it. He secured pieces of broken spear haft with strips of cloth torn from the uniforms of the dead soldiers to the boys arm.

Alaquin knelt beside Darith. She placed her hand on the injury. In a low monotone voice she chanted a healing spell. The boy's arm under her hand glowed green.

She removed her hand and looked up at Calert and said, "He'll heal."

Calert, cradling the boy's head in his arms, didn't look up or reply. The boy's eyes fluttered open. He smiled weakly at Calert.

Calert noticed a strange twinkle in Darith's eyes. Calert realized that something had changed in the boy. He dared not speculate on whether it was for better or worse. Carric walked up behind Alaquin.

He placed his hand lovingly and protectively on her shoulder and asked, "How is the boy?"

*   *   *

Schwellen was tiring. This battle had been going on for far too long. It would be dark soon and her arms felt like two oak logs. She knew she soon would be too exhausted to swing the sword, and the demons didn't appear ready to quit anytime soon.

So when Kenchon rode up beside her, swinging his sword methodically, she was overjoyed.

"Hello, big brother. It's about time you showed up."

Kenchon, despite the cacophony of the ensuing battle, heard her reprimand, and smiled.

"I thought you didn't need any help, baby sister," he jibed. "You won't let me forget that comment, will . . . ." She started to say when a blinding flash of light, followed by a thunderous explosion, interrupted her.

"What was that?" she asked.

"Must have something to do with that accursed magic," replied Kenchon.

The demons, without ceremony, dropped their weapons and fled. Relieved, Schwellen drove her sword into the ground and used it as a leaning post.

She smiled up at her brother and said, "I sure need a rest."

EPILOGUE

When Crysillnia was locked away, the demons fled, to whatever dark place they could find to secret themselves away. The Crystals had disappeared. No one knew if Crysillnia still had them when she had fallen into the dark abyss or whether they were destroyed in the explosion.

Jarret was crowned King of Lenar. He was a good, kind, strong, and compassionate ruler. He had many difficulties to overcome after the War of the Crystals. He had to rebuild the army, the economy, and defend against an invasion by the Xlantan's.

He was greatly saddened by what happened to Crysillnia for he had loved her deeply, but he went on to marry a woman of Noble birth from Capitol City. He had many sons and daughters and a long life. He passed beyond the veil late one winter. The Kingdom mourned his death for many seasons.

Schwellen was accepted into the Warrior Class of the Halhoren and proved to be one of the most celebrated warriors of her time, but she still had complaints. She wanted to be a Sub-Chief but that was still too radical of a concept for the Halhoren. A woman Sub-Chief. She died in a border skirmish with the Desert Nomads in her fifty-first season.

Kenchon continued as Chief of the Halhoren's for many years after the War of the Crystals. He formed a strong alliance with High King Jarret to guard the borders against any incursion across the border by the Desert Nomads. He died a couple of seasons after Schwellen in a hunting accident.

The demons that had helped the humans were given some land near the Elf Woods. They trade agricultural goods with whomever will deal with them. They are excellent farmers and are prospered.

Tanof slipped away from the battle field undetected. He had some life altering experiences during his impromptu adventures. He left the lands he knew to discover himself and sort through his confusion which led to many new adventures.

Talok died in the calamitous release of the wild magic between Crysillnia and Darith. The disappearance of the dwarves is still a mystery. Rumor has it that Talok used black magic to dispose of them. His reason was revenge. He never forgave them for abandoning him. Without the dwarves' knowledge, the production of Kelatan steel ceased.

Darith survived his confrontation with Crysillnia and continued his training in magic. Darith went off to great adventures of his own which are scribed in The Chronicles of Darith.

Once Calert had completed his tutelage of Darith, he disappeared from the scene. Some say he died. Others think he went into the Caspar Mountains, where the trolls watch over him, to sleep until he's needed again.

Troll and human relations improved, slightly, but has a long way to go. The elves returned to their isolationist ways. There is still little communication between elves and humans. Clodtrip and his tribe returned to their homeland and continue sporadic relations with the humans.

Carric and Alaquin married. They moved to a farmstead on the edge of the Elf Woods. They raised many children. Carric died at the ripe old age of seventy seasons. Alaquin built a monument to him in the Elf Woods where she buried him. She would go every day to visit the grave sight for many seasons after his death.

One bright and sunshiny morning before she went to visit Carric's grave. She visited with all of her children and friends. Alaquin left with a light heart and smile. No one ever saw her again. Legend has it that her spirit lingers, around Carric's grave, in case she is needed again.

King Kanef's men followed the former King of Caspar's tracks to the remnants of a royal carriage on the plains. His trail ended there and no further traces of him were found. The speculation is that ghosts from the past had exacted their revenge.

Kanef ruled with a strong hand for many years. He built a strong alliance with the trolls. Before his death, he ended the Monarchy of Caspar and instituted a Council elected by the people.

The End

Printed in the United States
50325LVS00007B/97-102